DRAGON GODS

KIERSTEN MICHELE

We support human creatives. No generative AI was used in the creation of this story, any of its art assets, or marketing.

CONTENT WARNING

This book is a new adult/adult fantasy book with some darker elements, including physical and emotional child abuse (on page and off), non-explicit torture (on page and off), physical violence, government-sanctioned oppression, murder, and death.

This book also contains explicit language and sexual content, including on page sexual activity (all consensual). If you wish to skip the explicit scene, it happens at the end of Chapter 32.

Please take care of yourself and read what you want!

To anyone who's felt rage deep enough to wake a dragon.

And for my sister and sister-in-law, I finally wrote a book about dragons.
I apologize for the sex scene; please don't read it.

Wueco
N
THE RESISTANCE BASE
THE FARMS
THE WALL
THE DROWNED QUARTER
Suvi
THE SLUMS
THE MILITARY QUARTER
THE ROYAL QUARTER

CHAPTER ONE
SOFIA

The air in the rainforest used to be thick with humidity even in the dry season, but that was before the Dereyans massacred the dragons. Now, underneath the shadowy canopy of trees and ferns, the plants on the forest floor were dry and brittle, burned brown along the edges. They crunched softly beneath Sofia's feet as she moved, an insignificant shadow among the towering trunks.

It took all her energy to ignore the growing number of dead trees along her route. Those that hadn't dried out in the nearly nonexistent rainy season last cycle had suffered frostbite in the bone-chilling temperatures of the cold season. There had been a few weeks where the morning frost never melted, the sun unable to warm the frigid air. Her ancestors hadn't even had a cold season, but the weather was only growing worse with each passing cycle. The disappearance of the dragons had been the start of the world's end. Wueco was dying.

Sofia wasn't even supposed to be out in the rainforest, especially not alone and armed with illegal weapons. No one was allowed outside the city wall, except for the men of the king's army. And *her people* hadn't been allowed to carry weapons for over a hundred sun cycles, since the first rebellion had failed. But every Dragonborn knew that you didn't walk beyond the city walls without protection. Even the king's men who refused to believe in the so-called dragon-filth myths knew not to wander too far into the wilds. As if some innate instinct told them of the dangers that lurked in the shadows.

She heard the small rabbit before she saw it, rustling around against the dried leaves and trying to free itself. With the racket it was making, it didn't take long to find the creature, its back leg tangled in the snare she'd set a few days before, pulling tighter with every jerky move. It had been trapped just long enough to begin to panic.

It was a small thing, eyes wide and tawny ears pulled back tight against its head. She set her pack aside, pulling out the sharp dagger from her belt. A quick death was a kindness.

But when she reached forward to grab the rabbit by its neck, it twisted, back legs kicking as it bit down on her finger with more aggression than she expected from the little creature.

She hissed and pulled back her hand, giving a small laugh at the blood its sharp teeth had drawn. The rabbit was no longer struggling, but facing her, body taut and posed to attack again.

"You're a feisty one," she said, watching its nose twitching. It blinked and she almost thought it might have understood her. Not that magical rabbits existed, as far as she'd ever read.

Her hand twitched forward once more and it lunged, teeth bared. Another might have found the creature pathetic, struggling against its inevitable death, too weak to change its fate. But Sofia knew what it was to be small and hopeless and still keep fighting. Maybe that's why the third time she reached forward, she only held it down as it lashed about before gently unhooking the cord from its leg.

The moment she let go of the rabbit, it disappeared into the underbrush, its tawny fur the same color of the dead leaves. She'd find more food elsewhere; there were plenty more snares to check and it wasn't the purpose of her mission anyway.

She reset the snare and continued on, keeping her own footsteps as silent as she could on the dying land. Despite how often she dreamed of it, Sofia hadn't been alive when the dragons disappeared. Her great-great-great-grandmother hadn't even been born yet. But she had memorized every story she'd ever been told or read in secret. She absorbed the words like water in soil, storing them away to feed her hope in the darker moments.

A book she'd read once about the history of Wueco spoke of the forest as a place full of magic where the leaves always glittered with freshly fallen rain and the forest floor was nearly impossible to traverse with its thick undergrowth. Back then, humans could harness the magic of the world, challenging even the worst of the faeries that hunted in the rainforest. And the gods swept through the sky feeding the earth and watching over their people.

Now the green of the trees was wan and the undergrowth along the floor was dead except for in the shadiest regions of the woods. The only magic Sofia had ever felt was the occasional sprinkle across her skin at the peak of the rainy season. And if faeries still lived here, they didn't dare get too close to the city wall where any movement was met with an arrow through the head. Still, she was more comfortable here amongst the dying rainforest than between the tall stone buildings of the city that towered as high as trees and always reached out to suffocate her.

Sweat beaded along her brow, just beneath the leather mask she wore and she took a moment to wipe it away. Her tight curls were a tangled mess, but they were tied back and out of her face. Even still, a few flyaways had come free and were plastered against her skin. She hated the mask and thought it was ridiculous to wear in the middle of nowhere like this, but who was she to question Micael and his rules.

Just thinking of the older man with his perpetual frown made her roll her eyes.

She stopped every few minutes to search the other snares she'd lain and after an hour, she had a line of dead rats and a couple of rabbits hanging along her belt and back. After two hours, she'd taken another haphazard circle, giving up on the hunt altogether. She was seeking bigger prey than the rodents, anyway. Her belt was heavy and the sun was stretching higher in the sky, leaving her unsettled and restless.

Somewhere after the third hour, she gave up her circling. Her fingers burned from where she'd been picking at her skin and she had to clench her hands to stop the nervous twitch. She couldn't keep circling and waiting. She needed to *do* something. So she veered right, almost hearing the hissed words of annoyance from the others on the wind. If they were real or just in her head, she didn't know. She ignored them either way.

She was less familiar with this part of the forest, each step taking her away from her usual haunts. As she crossed over a fallen log, she noticed the small patch of bright blue and silver flowers blooming from the rotting wood, life fed from death.

The forest was never quiet, a constant whistle of birds, the hum of insects, and the scuffling of the creatures in the underbrush. It made it easier to sneak unseen through the trees, even with the brittle breaking of leaves. But it also made it easier for others to sneak up on her. Hunting was the constant balance of focusing on her own steps while staying constantly aware of the forest around her.

As she stepped carefully over another log, she heard the snuffling of something large and very much not human somewhere ahead. She stopped for just a moment, to get her bearings and note the current in the air. She'd need to remain downwind as she approached. Her steps turned more delicate as she moved. When she was a few feet away, close enough to hear the distinctive snort of the boar beyond a large fern, she paused again.

Even a small boar could injure her if she attacked outright and most the boars in this area were anything but small. She didn't have a bow, only a few poison darts that would do nothing against the creature's thick skin and her daggers that would require getting up close and personal with the boar's tusks. Javi would tell her to leave it. They all likely would. This was not the plan. But an average-sized boar could feed their base for two weeks. They might have enough to donate to the poorer families of the slums. Plenty were starving.

Making the decision, she set her bag down and all but one of her kills. She slipped onto the lowest branch of a nearby tree. It moved beneath her weight, but she was quiet as she climbed. It took a few minutes to make her way onto a large branch, hovering just above where the boar was snuffling through an old and rotten log.

It was wide and squat, its tusks long and curved, and she swore she could smell the fetid stench of it from where she perched.

She pulled the small rat left on her belt, slicing it through the chest with her dagger. Even though it was already dead, the blood sluggishly welled at the incision. She rubbed the tips of her poison darts along the edge of her dagger until it shined in the dappled sunlight from above. Even with her missing ring finger, the movement was steady and well-practiced. Sending a quick prayer to the dragons, she dropped the rat onto the ground below.

The boar's head immediately perked up, ears turning to where the rat had fallen. It took a second for the beast to make the decision, but then it was moving, nose pressed lightly to the ground as it searched out its prize. It seemed so excited for this new development.

"Sorry," she whispered, more to herself than anything, before she jumped down from her branch, landing directly on top of the now squealing animal. She didn't let it get out a second wail, jamming her dagger into the soft skin of its neck. She straddled it, holding it against the ground, even as it continued to buck and thrash underneath her. It took a few seconds for the poison she had wiped along the blade to take effect, but eventually the boar slumped forward, body heavy in death.

She stumbled up triumphant, ignoring the sharp sting of her breaths in her throat from the exertion. She didn't love taking the life of an animal, but there was something thrilling in the fight and the win.

As she took another breath, the small wheeze in her chest told her she'd pushed herself too far, and she began to prep the beast. She was so focused on her new job, she almost missed the rustle of leaves and the smell of soap and sweat on the wind.

A human. A Dereyan.

She froze, hands covered in blood, and smiled. She'd finally been found and the true hunt had begun.

CHAPTER TWO

FOX

Fox was on the hunt. When he'd set out that morning with the others, after arguing with Ian for ten minutes about how he was most definitely coming with them, he'd had high hopes. He imagined himself strolling back into the city with the head of the Dragonborn resistance's leader dangling from his fist. The scene was beginning to feel less tangible as he swatted away another buzzing insect, surrounded by the stench of dying trees.

Ian had sent them all on a wild rabbit chase. He'd probably only seen an old marking from before Suvi even existed and mistaken it for something meaningful. They'd been out in the forest well before sunrise and it was already nearly noon and so far the most dangerous thing Fox had seen was some poison vines. As he nearly tripped over a root, dodging another said vine, he thought about turning around, marching back to Ian and telling him as much. Ian was a rank above him, but they'd known each other long enough that Fox never felt guilty pushing the high sergeant's buttons.

The fact was, he wasn't even supposed to be out here. He'd taken High Specialist Luna's place in the search party when he'd heard what they were after—the resistance's base. After nearly an entire sun cycle of raiding pathetic excuses for bases within the city that usually comprised a single family whispering about forbidden myths across the dinner table, Fox was ready to make an actual dent in the king-damned rebellion.

So despite wanting to turn around and tell Ian exactly what he thought of his ridiculous plan, he kept moving. And when he finally heard a rustling in the trees ahead of him, too big to be a rabbit or fox, he pulled his bow and prowled forward.

It was impossible to be truly silent in the forest, the dead leaves and plants always happy to make his life more difficult, but with the slight breeze and constant buzz of animals and insects, he could blend in with the cacophony of sounds fine. He kept his distance at first, careful not to startle whatever it was, but as he approached, seeing the flashes of movement between the trees, he bit back his shout of triumph. *It* was a *she*, a *Dragonborn* caught outside the city walls.

Being out here was already grounds for arrest and imprisonment, but if she was here on resistance business, she could lead him back to their elusive base.

Ian might have given them the initial intel, but Fox would lead them to the nest and he'd be the one to cut off the viper's head. He imagined the homecoming, the chief commander welcoming him with open arms, his own father at his side beaming with pride. He'd prove to the man once and for all that he could be a true king's man and military leader. That he could fill his brother's shoes.

Why anyone would risk their lives to be out in this treacherous place, he had no idea. The rainforest smelled of rotten wood and moss, and with the worsening droughts, the greenery couldn't be considered pleasing. It was simply brown dirt, brown mud, and brown death. Even the animals didn't seem particularly excited to be out here. But Fox had given up cycles ago trying to understand the minds of dragon-filth who insisted his people with their polished stone houses and paved streets were the ignorant ones.

He almost tripped over a root as he circled toward where he'd seen the woman through the trees. His heart beat heavily in his chest as he crouched and brushed his hair from his face, sticky with sweat. A wild boar sniffed around a small clearing a few yards away, but there wasn't a woman in sight. His chest tightened, but before he could think to run, the woman dropped from the tree above the boar, landing on it with a short cry and pulling a dagger across its throat. It was a feral display of blood and violence and though he'd never admit it, he was almost impressed.

He had a clear view of the woman when she stood, looking down at her kill. Her olive skin was smeared with dirt and blood, and her hair was a distinct nest of umber curls that appeared nearly black until they caught the light. For a moment, he questioned if she was even from Suvi. He had heard rumors of unregistered Dragonborn roaming beyond the wall. But despite the grime, her clothes were too well-tailored to be from anywhere but the city.

More importantly, she'd just proven she was not only outside the walls, but possessed a set of illegal weapons, hunting the king's animals. Although not proof of resistance ties, hope swelled inside him. He could arrest her then and there, take her back to the city, and interrogate her. But if he could follow her without being seen—

Before the thought had even finished, she froze in what she was doing, body going rigid. She looked up. He had barely moved, taking a single silent step backward and yet she was staring directly at him through the branches and vines.

A small leather strap was wrapped across her face, obscuring the top half, but her eyes were still visible and her gaze sharp. Her high cheekbones gave her an air of haughtiness that almost had him stepping back again.

The decision had been made for him.

He moved forward, an arrow already aimed and ready to fire if she ran, but she didn't. She had turned back to her kill, eyes focused on her hands as they made quick work of the giant pig's innards. Fox's stomach turned at the sight.

"Don't move," he said, voice clear despite them being the first words he'd spoken since morning. "You're under arrest, in the name of the king, for illegal hunting, possession of banned weapons, trespassing on royal land, and suspected rebel activity."

She ignored his command, standing up slowly and turning to look at him.

"You. Of course, it's you," she said, a muscle twitching in her jaw. He wasn't sure what to make of the comment and her face was carefully neutral. He sneered at the blood splattered across her cheeks and mask like freckles. Her eyes, nearly too large for her face stood out starkly against her dirt and blood-streaked face, bright and round and the color of moss. She blinked.

"Drop your dagger and get on your knees," he said, unnerved by the lack of expression. Perhaps she was dull-witted.

She twisted the dagger in her hand around, but didn't drop it.

"I don't want to fight," he said, teeth clenched in frustration.

"Maybe I do," she said, smiling.

"You'll only lose."

"But it might be fun." She took a step forward and he moved his arrow in threat. "We could dirty up those pretty clothes of yours."

"Or I could just shoot you and carry you back to the city over my shoulder."

"Is that supposed to convince me to cooperate?"

His arms twitched and he let the arrow fly, the head embedding itself in the soil next to her feet. He may not be a hunter, but he knew how to aim.

"Drop your weapon and kneel," he said again.

She complied, the smirk on her face not even flickering as she stabbed her dagger into the soil and kneeled, ignoring the blood of the boar that soaked into her pants.

"Throw the dagger here."

"Do you want to be clearer with that order?" she asked, raising an eyebrow.

He kept his face blank, raising his own in turn. She relented at last, gently tossing the dagger a few feet in front of her.

"And your belt."

She opened her mouth, as if to argue, but then closed it before unbuckling the belt and tossing it forward. He moved around her, checking her back for any other obvious weapons as he picked up the discarded belt and dagger and added them to his own weapon harness. He noted the supply of darts and another small dagger on the belt.

"If I search you, am I going to find any more weapons?"

"I don't know. Will you?" she said, face blank.

"I already have you on enough charges to send you to the working farms. Why make it worse for yourself?"

"What, are you going to charge me with sass?"

"Harassment of a king's soldier."

She rolled her eyes but slowly brought her hand to her boot and pulled out a tiny dagger that was tucked there, throwing it across to him.

"That's it," she said, flashing him a bright smile that looked all the more horrific with the blood drying across her face. It cracked with the movement. "I promise."

He didn't take her word for it, switching out his bow for his dagger as he pulled her to her feet and swiped a hand across her body, brusk in his movements. He refused to acknowledge the curves and softness beneath her clothes, but he found no other weapons.

He turned her roughly, pulling down the strip of leather that served as her mask. The splatter of blood meant the clean skin left the impression of a mask behind, but with her face fully revealed he still didn't recognize her. Not that he expected to, but her comment had unnerved him. *You.*

She did appear to be about his own age, now that he could see her full face, but her plain looks with her barely visible freckles against skin the color of clay was anything but remarkable. Her eyes though—he imagined he'd remember those eyes.

Shaking off his thoughts, he turned her around roughly, pulling her hands behind her back to tie them. He silently noted the missing finger on her hand and the faded brand on the inside of her wrist, a sign that this wasn't the first time she'd flouted the king's laws. He brushed his thumb across the brand before he covered it with ropes and grinned.

"If you wanted to touch me, you could have asked nicely."

"If I wanted to touch someone, it wouldn't be you. You smell worse than the dead pig."

He pushed her away, wiping his hands on his pants to get rid of the feel of her skin.

A red blush crept up her neck and he took a moment to appreciate he'd finally wiped the smirk off her face. He pushed her forward with a jab of his bow, sending her staggering in front of him, back the way he'd come. He was happy the afternoon sun was visible through the thick foliage above, pointing his way back south to the city.

THE GRACE she'd exhibited in her fight with the boar was gone as they walked. She stumbled along, tripping over roots and branches with nearly every step.

"Stop falling," he snapped after the fifth time having to catch her and pull her back upright.

"If you wanted me to touch you, you could have asked nicely," he said, mockingly. She ignored the jab.

"Have you tried walking like this? It's hard to stay balanced with my hands tied."

"I suppose I could just untie you and trust you don't try to stab me."

"You have my weapons," she replied as she looked at him with those unnervingly bright eyes, wide in feigned innocence. "Or are you scared of a defenseless Dragonborn?"

"I doubt you're defenseless even without your illegal weapons." He gave her a small shove and she nearly tripped again, letting out a string of curses.

"Be careful which gods you send to curse me or I'll have you on heresy laws, as well." She glared over her shoulder, but he only smiled.

"My gods wouldn't leave any of you left to charge me."

Her grin reminded him of the feral cat that lived in the alley behind his father's home as if she might bite him if he got too close.

He kept them moving forward, never letting her get too far ahead. There was very little likelihood of her being able to run away while tied up, but he still didn't trust her. Her people worshipped the rainforest and he wouldn't be surprised if she thought being trapped alone out here was somehow better than being in Suvi. He sometimes wondered why they didn't just throw all the Dragonborn over the city's walls to live in the rainforest like they all so dearly wanted.

Although, that was one of the main issues with the rebel faction. Some of them did live out here, somewhere among the trees. Despite cycles of trying to smoke them out and crush their ridiculous movement, the military still hadn't managed to do more than keep them running and hiding. They'd raided the occasional safe house within the city and arrested plenty of instigators over the cycles, but nothing had quelled the unrest the resistance stirred. Nothing had stopped the bloodshed and terror they spread through the city.

At least not yet.

He found his eyes going back to the faded, but still evident scar along her wrist—the twisted "T" branded there probably cycles ago. She'd been found guilty of treason once before, at a young enough age to escape execution or the farms or perhaps her crimes hadn't been easy enough to prove back then. But now he had her on half a dozen charges, illegally hunting just a few miles from where Ian had found evidence of a resistance base. This could be the shift in the war they needed, an insider with a very good reason to turn on her comrades if she valued her own life. And he was going to be the one to deliver her to Chief Commander Harlow.

CHAPTER THREE

SOFIA

Sofia despised the ropes rubbing against the skin of her tied wrists. She was breathing through her nose, trying to quell the anxiety that churned in her stomach. She had felt his thumb, callused and warm, brush against her inner wrist, tracing her brand before he'd tied her up. The thought of him seeing it made her teeth clench until her jaw ached.

Fox Ocon. Of course it was him. Of all the people Vato could send their way, it had to be *his* son. She wondered if he knew just how many scars his father had left on her—nothing compared to the silly little brand.

He was taller than she remembered—not that she had seen him since they were both children and only then at a distance. She didn't consider herself a short person, particularly for a woman, but he still towered over her more than a few inches. The scrawny mess she remembered had been replaced with muscles that showed the cycles of training he'd likely had as a part of the king's army. And the ease at which he held his weapons along with her own made it clear the muscles weren't just for show. His hair had grown out, neatly tied back into a bun, still the bright, nearly white-blond she remembered, unique even among the Dereyans.

She hated that she found him imposing. She wanted to see him on his knees, bleeding and begging for her to spare him. As she pictured it, his face shifted, nose narrowing into a sharper peak and eyes going from silver to an icy blue. She blinked away the vision as her throat went dry. As much as she hated being captured by Ocon, she needed to remember that he wasn't his father and she'd make sure they never made it back to Suvi.

She let her toe catch on another root, wincing only slightly as her knees came down onto the hard dirt of the forest floor. Ocon stood above her, looking smug. He hadn't caught her and his eyes were dancing with enjoyment as she struggled to right herself. She had to bite back a smile of her own. He was only playing into her own game by allowing her to slow them down.

The feel of the rough ropes against her wrists and the bite of stones in her knees didn't quite permit her a true moment of contentment or humor. There was a niggling in the back of her mind reminding her how far off course she'd wandered in her little adventure and hunt. They'd already been walking for longer than they should have, him pushing her along beside him toward the city and a sure death sentence.

If they didn't catch up to her and Ocon in time, it would be her own fault. But the chance to kill that boar may have been worth it. The droughts had been at their worst this past rainy season, leaving much of the city hungry and tired. The rations had hit the Dragonborn the hardest, of course, and the resistance could only do so much to spread food under the nose of the king. If she and the others didn't hunt, then people would die. Either from starvation or from stealing and being sentenced to a long and arduous death on the farms.

Of course, at this rate, the boar and small pile of animals she'd amassed over the course of the morning would be stolen by a passing jaguar before anyone found them. The thought made her empty stomach turn.

She wobbled for the umpteenth time on a loose root, slowing their gait and letting out a dramatic *oof* as she caught herself. Ocon didn't bother with gentleness as he pushed her forward, nearly sending her tumbling.

"Do you enjoy pushing women around?" she bit out, partly to make noise and partly because she was rankled by the manhandling. "Or just dragon-filth?"

"You call yourself that?" he said, almost sounding offended by her use of the slur. It wasn't like Dereyans didn't throw it around under their breaths constantly, but then again they always loved pretending virtue when pressed. She snorted, looking back to ensure he saw the look of derision on her face. "I have nothing against Dragonborn." He said the words as if he thought she should be impressed.

"These ropes say otherwise," she said, wondering if her eyes could get stuck if she rolled them too hard.

"You're under arrest because of your treason not your blood."

"Yet it's my very blood that makes anything I do treasonous. Do your people get arrested for holding weapons? For feeding themselves?" She hated that true fury was rising in her voice. He didn't deserve her energy.

"You can thank your ancestors for the thousands they massacred. They are the reason you lost your rights. And what do your people do? Continue to murder innocents."

"Is that what they teach you in those towering buildings in the inner city? That we're the murderers?"

"The blood I've felt on my hands after your attacks has taught me plenty."

The words were muttered, but still clear and Sofia had to bite her tongue to not respond. She hated the self-righteousness in his tone and the set of his shoulders. He was so sure of his own beliefs. Any blood on the hands of the resistance had been a necessary evil in their fight for freedom, not that anyone ever listened or cared.

"And you think the Dereyans haven't shed innocent blood?"

"You've broken how many laws? Don't try to argue with me about innocence."

She spit on the ground in front of him as she slowed her steps and came to a stop.

"I don't claim to be innocent; I know you saw my brand. I don't fight for my own sake, though. I fight for every single Dragonborn who's died for the crime of being hungry or scared or simply wanting to hold on to their history."

She saw his silver eyes go wide and his face stretched into a smile that looked almost maniacal.

"You've all but admitted to resistance ties and actions against the king. Such a sharp tongue for someone with such dull wits."

He stepped toward her. They were only a few inches apart now, and she could feel the heat of his body. She had to bend her neck back to look him in the eyes, regarding the triumph that danced there. Her tongue darted out, practically tasting his satisfaction as she wet her lips, and his eyes flickered down to trace the movement.

"With that brand and you admitting to resistance ties, I can have you executed on the next new moons. But," he paused, eyes tracing across her face. Her smile faltered at the hunger she saw there. Not for her, but for something *more*. "If you give me information on the resistance base, just a location or a few names, I'll make sure you get sent to the farms."

She sneered, refusing to back away from him. "So you offer me a clean, fast death or a slow one enslaved to your king?"

"I'll make your death as comfortable as you please if you give me the resistance base's location."

She smiled.

She heard the quiet twang of a bowstring somewhere to the left of them, and she watched the look of triumph melt from his face.

He flushed so pretty when he was scared.

"Better yet," she said, "I'll take you there personally."

She leaned closer until her lips barely brushed against his ear, sending a shiver through him that made her feel all the more powerful. "You should have let me go."

SOFIA

AGE 7

When the outer wall was first built by the King Jorgan, it was an act of protection. The kingdom had been plagued by violence from the outside, the remnants of the feral tribes that refused to bow to true ruler of Wueco. It wasn't until nearly two centuries later that the wall would come to serve a new function: to protect the loyal civilians of Suvi from the violent Dragonborn both outside and inside the wall. This separation from their more primitive ancestors is what allows for the taming and education of the Dragonborn. This author would argue that this firm segregation is not just helpful, but necessary if we wish to continue the assimilation of the Dragonborn into natural society.

-Lird W. Viona, Assimilation or Elimination: A Philosophical Debate

In less than a sun cycle, Sofia would be too big for this work. Another smaller girl would be sent through the narrow tunnel of the latrine to ensure it was cleared out properly and Sofia would be happily standing on the outside, yelling at her to hurry up, as if the task were the same burden to them both.

As it was, Liza's raspy voice echoed through the stone tunnel, her drawl of annoyance clear. "Are you done yet?"

The sound of it made Sofia's entire body tense, but she bit her tongue. Yelling back only ever made things worse. She kept scrubbing as fast as she could, focusing on the movement of the task instead of the fetid smell in the small space. When she had first been given this duty, she had thought to breathe through her mouth and avoid the smell altogether. But she quickly learned that she could taste the air, and vomiting up her meager breakfast only ended in more work for herself.

"I have other jobs to do and the smell is starting to get to me," Liza said, voice sounding distant. "I'm going to leave you soon if you don't say something."

Sofia gave a last scrub, scooping the last of the feces and waste into the small bucket before tugging at the rope around her waist. She maneuvered backward as best she could before Liza started pulling at the rope, helping her slip through the tight space with only a small scrape against her elbow. Last cycle she had barely needed the help to crawl out, but now she could barely make it out without the consistent tugging of the rope. She hadn't gotten any rounder over the cycle, but as her mother always pointed out when she was trying to dress her in the morning, she was all elbows and knees now.

Perhaps if she managed to steal enough food over the next few blinks, she'd ensure getting pulled off latrine duty a bit earlier.

"Gods, you smell foul." They were the first words Liza said as Sofia slipped from the tunnel, the sun blinding her for a moment. When Sofia had first started working with the girl she'd talked back, at one point noting that Liza's nose always looked like she'd smelled something foul. But the girl had gone running back to the head housekeeper and Sofia had been the one whipped with a switch five times. She'd quickly learned there was no use in arguing with Liza. Ms. Garcia might claim not to play favorites, but it was clear she had a soft spot for the girl with her pale skin. Nothing like Sofia's own dark complexion that Liza constantly pointed out blended perfectly with the feces she cleaned out daily.

It was clear that, while Liza had been born a Dragonborn the same as Sofia, she had ancestors from the northern lands beyond the sea. It was a mark of privilege in its own right, as if the Falais or Terdun being willing to have relations with a Dragonborn made them inherently better than their peers. And Liza could have even passed as a Dereyan if her token wasn't requested.

Not even bothering to help untie Sofia or dump out the bucket, Liza gave a wave of her hand before turning and stomping away.

"Thanks," Sofia said under her breath.

"She's nice," the boy waiting by the cart said with a twist of his lips. He was only a cycle or two older than Sofia, perhaps ten at most. She'd only seen him a few times and she was unsure if he was a temporary replacement for Simon or a new trainee. Either way, she didn't care to make friends in the manor. She only shrugged as she finished untying herself and cleaned away the last of the latrine's waste.

As she walked back to the servants' entrance, she could do nothing for the shivers racking her body beneath her sodden clothes. She had cleaned herself off in the canal behind the house, knowing she wouldn't be let in to pick up her wages or shawl if she was still dirty. Yet now, she was dirty and wet, and the setting sun was blind to her suffering. It was still the rainy season, but the air held the promise of the cold season to come.

"You're late," Ms. Garcia said as she came into the kitchens, nearly gasping at the change in temperature. The cooking fires were roaring heartily and the air was thick with beans and stew.

"I'm sorry," she said, voice soft and words automatic. Pointing out that Liza hadn't helped with her duties and she'd been left to finish and clean up alone wouldn't do any good.

"That's the third time this week. Plus the broken vase, yesterday." Ms. Garcia loved listing her crimes. It was best to keep her mouth shut and look properly ashamed. There was always a list, no matter how fast she moved or how much her fingers bled from scrubbing.

"Well go on then, take your coins and go before you miss curfew!" she snapped, as if Sofia had been the one slowing down the exchange. But she dutifully jumped forward, letting the rounded woman place the pitiful pile of coins in her hand.

"You're two short," she said, before she could berate herself for even daring.

The slap barely echoed in the din of the kitchens, not a single worker even flinching or turning their head in acknowledgment of the act. Her cheek stung and she couldn't quite bite back the wetness along her eyes.

"That's for the broken vase. Now get out before I deduct another for your insolence. The master doesn't allow for sloth in his house. If you don't like the job, you can go beg on the streets like the rest of your kind."

Sofia bowed low, hiding her face as the tears threatened to spill over. Her face was hot and her stomach churned with ineffectual rage, but the words she wanted to say stay locked behind her tongue.

"Thank you, Ms. Garcia. I don't know what got into me." She kept her back bent as she backed away, not looking up from the ground until she saw the woman's shoes turn. Ms. Garcia was paying attention to someone else now and Sofia was invisible once more. Nothing and no one. She scuttled out of the kitchens before anyone could notice the small bread roll she'd slipped into her hand during her pleading.

She ate it in two bites once she was out the door, coins already tucked into her pockets, along with a rag. It was never safe to walk home through the slums with her pockets clanging with coins. The icy air cooled the heat of her anger, but the shame still quaked just beneath the surface. She pressed her fists into her eyes until the burning stopped.

She barely made it out of the royal quarter before dark. The guards at the gates gave her a heavy scowl as she ran the last block, bowing low as they locked the doors behind her. Only a few minutes later and she would have been locked in on the other side. It had happened once before to her, and she'd spent the night shivering in the shadows, trying to stay silent as her stomach growled and her teeth clicked together. It was worth an arrest and whipping to be caught in the military or royal quarters after curfew without a pass and she was never given a pass, even on the days her shifts went long.

Once she was into the outer quarter, she slowed down, no longer desperate to get home. Her parents would notice the missing coins and she'd need to explain how she'd managed to break a vase. The fact that Liza had told her to clean it despite the delicate piece sitting two feet above her head wouldn't stop the disappointment from filling her mother's eyes as she tucked the coins away in their box. They'd be hungry again this week, and whether or not her mother said it out loud, it was Sofia's fault. So instead of turning right at the first corner, she went straight, ignoring the numbness in her fingers as the cold of night set in. She found the grimy alley with the barely standing building and its crumbled staircase just inside the cracked wall. Her footsteps were careful, each weakness in the steps memorized.

But the view was worth the delay. As she came out onto the roof of the old building, she could see the small and evenly spaced fires that marked the outer wall. And beyond that, the rainforest. It glowed, green and purple and blue. Above it, the two moons of the dragon mother rose, large and unblinking. From where she stood on the edge of the roof, it felt like she might reach out and brush her fingers across the tops of the trees. Would they be soft like grass or rough like the spiky weeds that grew along the canal's shore?

But of course she couldn't touch the trees and she never would. The forest might as well have been a million miles away. As much myth as the dragons that once watched over their land.

She closed her eyes and said a prayer—not to the old kings, but to the dragons—unsure if anyone was left listening. She prayed that tomorrow nothing would go wrong and she might walk home with her chin held high. She prayed that she'd make her parents proud and she might be the best worker the master had ever seen. Because that's all she could hope for.

CHAPTER FOUR
FOX

Fox saw the victory in her eyes in the same moment he heard the bow string. He didn't even have time to register what direction the sound had come from as two figures dropped from the trees above, one on either side. He shoved his captive hard in the chest, satisfied as she fell back on her ass with an indignant yelp, and he pulled his sword.

But before he could do more than step forward, cold metal pressed against the back of his neck, just beneath his hairline.

"Drop it."

He froze, calculating his chances against three armed Dragonborn and the tied woman at his feet.

"If you prefer to keep your blood inside your body, I'd listen to her," another voice said. An older man stepped out from behind a thick bush and moved toward where the woman was lying, bruised from her fall but smiling. He was an imposing figure, with broad shoulders and an air about him that told Fox he was used to having his commands followed. His hair was gray and curled around his covered face.

They all had matching masks to the one the woman had been wearing, blocking their faces. Not that it mattered to him. They were treasonous scum and he'd kill them whether or not he knew what they looked like.

The tip of the weapon at his neck pricked his skin once more as its wielder brought it around the side of his neck and against his throat. It was a dagger by the feel of it, sharp enough a drop of blood leaked from where it had nicked his skin.

He dropped his sword, hand spasming with reluctance.

The blade on his neck didn't waver as unseen hands made quick work of his belt and harness, his weapons falling to the forest floor along with what he'd gotten off the Dragonborn—the apparent bait for the trap he'd fallen into.

At last, the cold bite of the dagger left his neck and he was pressed to his knees. He took the chance to examine the people who had surrounded him.

There was the older man, who had untied the young woman and was whispering sharply in her ear. There were also two younger men holding arrows on him, both with unremarkable brown locks. The person behind him finally came around once his hands were tied and he saw the long dark hair that was braided down her back. She was taller than even the woman he'd first captured, nearly his own height. Maybe they were on to something when they said these people were born from dragons.

"You two," the older man snapped, drawing Fox's attention. "Follow their tracks back to where he captured her. She says she left behind a boar and some more game."

"I can lead them back," the woman said. His captive—or now his captor, he thought bitterly—looked petulant.

"You'll be coming with us. We need to talk."

Fox almost smiled at the clear slight against the woman, but before he could truly appreciate it, a sack was slipped over his head. It was thin enough to see the light through it, but not much of anything else. His heart rate spiked, his predicament just beginning to set in. Ian and the others were likely a mile or more away and they had no idea what was happening.

And Fox was about to find the resistance base—his goal since joining the king's men—trussed up as their prisoner.

As he was half-dragged through the forest, Fox was all too glad for the sack covering his face. It caused the sweat to drip down his face and sting his eyes, and his toes were starting to bruise from the number of times he'd tripped over the unseen ground. But at least his captors couldn't see the expression on his face, shifting rapidly between anger and fear with every beat of his heart.

He still hadn't come up with a plan beyond *escape*, which wasn't so much a plan as a need at the moment. As much as he wanted to find the resistance base, he knew his chances of escape would get harder once he was there.

The sack smelled of his own sweat and stale corn flour, particles tickling his nose with every breath in and out, and he focused his mind on the sensation. He needed to think. He could tell they were walking in a relatively straight path—the small snippets of the sunlight never shifting in direction as they wove through trees. He could almost assume they were walking west, based on the flashes of sun through the coarse fabric, but it was possible he was simply disoriented. Either way, he needed to keep his head on straight for if—*when*—he escaped.

Three hundred and forty-two steps later, and Fox was at a loss. He tried running once, a stupid move, but a chance to see their reaction time and organization. His arm had been caught in an iron grip before he'd taken two steps. He'd also attempted screaming, but whoever was holding him had only cracked the dull end of a weapon against his skull and tied something across his mouth, tightening the sack there and making it nearly impossible to do more than grunt.

And then the group's energy shifted. He knew, even before he was pulled to a stop, they'd reached their destination. He listened carefully, the sounds of the forest hadn't changed. The birds were still cawing and chirping at random intervals, the leaves rustling, and insects buzzing incessantly. His captors didn't talk, seemingly using some type of hand signal language to communicate. But then Fox noticed a new sound. An echoing hollowness in the air and he felt a cool wind through the bag on his face. It brought the smell of salt and moss.

He was so focused on trying to understand the shift in the smells around him, he nearly jumped when he heard the woman beside him, her voice almost familiar now.

"I'm just going to make a decision," she said. He didn't think she was talking to him. "We're sending him down the easy way."

With that, her hand shoved him hard between the shoulder blades and he stumbled forward, muscles straining as he tried to throw his hands out to catch himself. But he didn't hit the ground. His foot shot forward and caught on to *nothing*. There was no ground beneath him.

In the same instant that he realized he was falling through the air, his body hit the icy waves below and he sank. The slap of the water wasn't as hard as the ground might have been, but even as he gasped at the pressure in his chest, he was sucking in water as it rushed up around him, soaking through his clothes and the sack over his head.

He thrashed and choked, the rope around his wrists only tightening as he struggled. He was blind and helpless and drowning. He would die out here and Chief Commander Harlow would never even know what happened to him. His mother—

A large hand wrapped around his upper arm, pulling him until his head broke the surface. He choked, coughing out the water he had swallowed before he managed a breath. His lungs burned at the intrusion, but he could only cough and breathe again. He was happy the strip tightening the sack to his head was at least gone.

"Get him to shore before he drowns himself," an unfamiliar voice said. It was difficult to judge distance with the echoes that bounded around, nearly drowned out by his ongoing struggle to swim with his hands tied.

"Stop squirming," the feminine voice said beside him. A moment later, the hood was pulled away and he blinked up at the woman who was holding him. Her hair flashed a brilliant red in the light coming down from above, her face in shadows. He might have almost smiled, but before his lips could do more than twitch, the woman dropped him and he sank back into the water.

"Stop being dramatic and stand up," she said at the same moment he felt the sandy bottom beneath his boots. It took him a few seconds to regain his balance, arms still tied and useless, but eventually he was standing.

The fiery angel that had pulled him from the water was walking away, not even looking back at him and he saw another three people standing along the shore, watching him with wary eyes. He collapsed onto the ground the moment he hit dry land, knees shaking from his fall and too tired to stand and breathe at the same time.

No longer in fear of drowning, he was able to take in his surroundings. It wasn't the sea he'd been tossed into, but an underground lake.

The walls of the cavern arched overhead; a small hole in the ground above showed the sky and the canopy of trees where he had just been. The bright light contrasted with the shadowy cavern and made it difficult to make out details. But it was easy enough to hear the dripping of water as it cascaded down the walls and the vines that hung over the lip of the opening.

Fox was lying at the bottom of a cenote. This might have been helpful information if this land wasn't scattered with thousands of the natural sinkholes, which were constantly changing shape and some impossible to find. But it did explain why their people had had so much trouble locating the hub of the resistance movement.

As he watched, a rope ladder unfurled from above, two of his captors making their slow descent. He didn't see the woman and a moment later, a zip of motion out of the corner of his eye caught his attention and he looked in time to see her plunge into the water where he'd just nearly drowned. She made the jump look graceful as she easily pulled herself through the water and toward him. Of course, she actually had her hands free and hadn't been pushed into the lake without warning.

He didn't think. His hands were still tied behind his back, but he stumbled to his feet as best he could and ran at the woman as she pulled herself from the lake. Using his shoulder, he threw his weight against her, sending her slipping backward against the stony bottom of the lake's edge.

"What in the gods?" she said, using her hands to push him back away from her. He stumbled, unable to balance himself with his hands tied.

"If you wanted me dead, you could have just slit my throat earlier!" He could feel the heat of his face turning red, his pale complexion always ready to show the barest trace of a flush. But he didn't care, he wanted to strangle the woman. Screaming was the best he could do. "I almost drowned."

"Calm down," she said, walking past him, carefully wringing the water from her hair with barely a glance his way. "You're clearly fine."

"And if I couldn't swim?"

"You're a rich kid from the military quarter, of course you can swim."

"How did you know—" he snapped his mouth shut. She didn't just know him, she knew *who* he was.

"We caught General Ocon's son," she said, looking up as his other two captors made their way over to where he was lying. The older man's eyes flashed with something that Fox did not like one bit.

"A lucky catch indeed," he said, smiling coldly. "Go grab him dry clothes and bring them by the cell. He won't be any use to us if he freezes to death."

Fox watched with the smallest hint of amusement to see the woman's eyes narrow at the command. But she didn't argue, only marched away with a silent look of disdain. The younger man grabbed him and pulled him up and the older led them across the shore of the lake toward a crevice in the cavern's side.

The moment they turned the corner, Fox realized that the cenote was larger than he'd first assumed. A large sitting area stretched out in a second cavern and dark tunnels led away in various directions. He was pulled down the rightmost path, a line of lanterns lighting their way. He tried to keep track of their route, but with each turn and twist he felt more disoriented than when he'd had the sack over his head. Every tunnel looked the same, dimly lit with half a dozen crudely cut wood doors lining each side.

His stomach twisted in unease wondering how many rebels were tucked away behind those doors. They'd always known they were dealing with a festering problems when it came to the resistance, but even the chief commander likely didn't know how many there were.

After six turns that Fox was only seventy percent sure he could replicate, they finally stopped in front of a heavy wooden door. On the other side were the accommodations Fox was expecting. A chair sat in the middle of the room, a blanket draped across the back. A bucket tucked in the corner was the only other piece of *furniture* in the space, which was very obviously lacking even a lantern.

"Untie him and check him for weapons again," the older man commanded.

Fox only flinched a bit as the cold blade of a dagger brushed across his wrists and a moment later his arms dropped free. He was polite enough to not punch the man who proceeded to carefully pat him down, as if his sodden clothes could have hidden anything.

"So what are you going to do with me?" he said, sneering around at the room.

"We're just going to have a chat or two," the older man said, blithely shrugging.

"I don't have any important information."

"We'll be the judge of that. You never know what might be important to us."

"So you think I'll help you murder more innocent lives?" He spit on the ground between them. "I'd rather die."

"That can be arranged." The woman's voice was cold as she came around the corner, holding a pile of clothes in her hands.

"Don't," the older man admonished and Fox smirked. He could see the muscle in her jaw tense as her mouth snapped shut. She looked at him, eyes narrowing at his expression, and her face twisted into something he recognized well. Hate and disgust.

He didn't imagine his face looked much different.

Not breaking eye contact, she stepped forward, dropping the clothes on the ground and kicking them toward him. They dragged against the dirt floor, picking up the traces of mud scattered about from his dripping frame.

"Do you expect me to change while you watch?" He didn't lean down to pick up the clothes. As much as he was excited to feel dry again, he didn't want to break eye contact with the three rebels staring at him.

"No," the old man said at the same moment the woman said. "Yes."

The older man, clearly the boss, gave her an annoyed wave and ushered her and the other man out.

"Don't try anything funny," the woman said as she pulled the door closed behind them. "If you try to escape, I'll personally cut off your ears and send one to your father and the other to Chief Commander Harlow."

With that, the door shut and the hint of light from the lantern outside was extinguished.

He took a deep breath, keeping an image of the room in his mind as the blackness wrapped around him, constricting his chest. The room was wide, long enough to lay down twice over. It was plenty large.

Breathe.

He'd been through training on how to withstand torture and how to escape from situations such as this. This wouldn't be how he died, not at the hands of Dragonborn and not when he'd finally found their base. He would do what no other king's man had ever managed. He would get out of this and he'd march his brothers-in-arms right back here to kill them all.

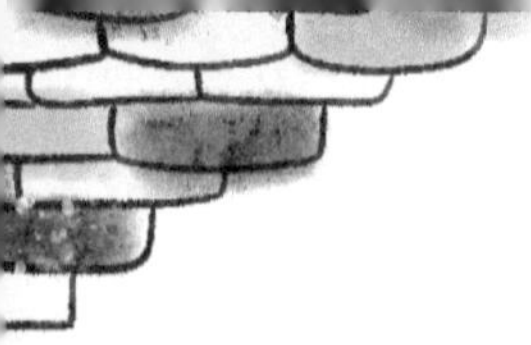

FOX

AGE 18

While the Dragonborn were given the chance for assimilation with the creation of Suvi and placed under the protection of the crown and god-kings, no further movement was made toward conversion. The so-called Dragonborn continue to practice their heretical ways in secret, indicating either a blatant ignorance of truth or a purposeful scheme to undermine the rule of law.

-Elna F. Bello, Assimilation or Elimination: A Philosophical Debate

The front door burst open under the second kick of his boot, wood splitting beneath his heel with a crack. The other specialists moved forward through the new opening with quick precision. They were anything but quiet, but the rebels inside wouldn't have time to run now. The hovel they called a house was two rooms, pressed against another building on the back with only two windows to escape, both guarded by their men already.

This wasn't the first raid that Fox had participated in. He'd been sent on a half-dozen or more since he'd gotten his promotion to junior specialist. So far they'd resulted in the arrest of about ten rebels and two false alarms. For the last one, when they'd burst in on a family sitting down to dinner only to not find a scrap of evidence toward rebel activity, he'd wondered if their tip had come from a jealous neighbor. But then again, he and Ian had talked afterward and the high specialist had pointed out that not every rebel was so easily caught out. Some were stupid enough to wear their prayer belts beneath their clothing while inside their house, but others knew not to break the king's rules in obvious ways.

He knew the moment he stepped into the house that this family wasn't going to be the smart type. Hanging just off the side of the entry was a colorfully woven tapestry showing the three types of dragons hovering over the landscape of Wueco, sans Suvi of course. Having artwork referencing the dragons wasn't illegal in itself, but the small altar underneath most definitely was.

"Don't hurt him!" The woman's voice cracked with fear and he almost rolled his eyes. He wasn't sure what the Dragonborn expected when they went around flouting the king's laws. Fox turned away from the altar display and saw the woman shaking and pale in the hands of another specialist. Her husband, or so Fox assumed, was crumpled on the ground, nose bleeding. He saw one of the soldiers picking up the knife that had fallen to the ground with the man and he had no doubt the punch had been warranted.

High Sergeant Guil stepped through the door a moment later, assessing the room.

"Report," he said to no one in particular.

"I have a dragon altar here, sir," Fox said, nodding to the display.

Specialist Toma, who was holding on to the wife, lifted the woman's blouse with a satisfied smirk. "At least one prayer belt, High Sergeant, and the husband tried to attack us when we came in."

The wife blanched at this last comment. Fox imagined anyone might react poorly when their door was burst through in the evening hours without warning, but attacking a king's man was still an act of treason.

"Specialists Toma and Franco, take the prisoners to the cart. Specialists Ocon, Julian, and Nicolas, continue the search and document any other contraband found. Inform me immediately if you find evidence of resistance connections. Our tip indicated that they may have received packages from the rebels, so keep an eye out for any explosives and weapons."

With that, he turned on his heel. The two men holding the husband and wife followed, leaving Fox and the other two junior specialists behind.

"Ocon, you take the bedroom, and we'll take the main room," Julian said as he started opening up the cabinets in the kitchen and dumping out the contents. Fox almost wanted to argue simply for the sake of argument. He hated when the other junior specialists acted like they were above him simply because they'd been in the position for a few blinks longer.

But he only shrugged and moved past the other two and into the small adjoining room. It was the bedroom, equipped with a single bed that sagged in the middle, a crooked shelf weighed down with clothes, and a single trunk.

Not bothering to be careful, he swiped a hand across the top shelf, pushing the clothes to the ground before moving on to the next. On the third shelf, two prayer belts fell out of a folded skirt and he moved to grab them and toss them onto the bed. But as he picked up the first, he saw the delicately woven strip was only a little over a foot in length, half the size of the prayer belts he'd seen before.

It was a child's belt. He grabbed the second one, noting the same thing and looked back at the bed behind him. The report hadn't mentioned children and the house didn't seem nearly big enough for them, but it wouldn't be the first time the Dragonborn had chosen to hide their offspring instead of reporting them to the registry.

Glancing at the door to make sure the other two couldn't see him from where he was in the room, he crouched down slowly and lifted the skirt that wrapped around the bed, hiding the narrow gap beneath.

Wide, brown eyes met his as he peered under the bed. It was a young girl, thick curls tangled in the ropes of the bed above her, face ashen. She didn't make a sound as their eyes met, but he heard a faint whimper all the same. He looked to where her arms were wrapped around something and saw the even smaller form of a boy tightly held to her side. His eyes were nearly black, already shining with tears as his lip quivered.

Fox was afraid if he looked at the boy much longer his whimpers would turn into a full sob. He let the skirt of the bed drop back down.

He made quick work of the rest of the room, pulling out a small book tucked away in the trunk, along with a few other trinkets that looked like they might belong to the altar. There were no weapons in here, though.

"Did either of you find anything?" he asked, stepping back into the main room, casually shutting the door behind him.

"Just some unregistered meat and a worthless-looking dagger. If this is what the resistance is peddling, I expect they'll crumble soon."

Nicolas had made a small pile of the contraband on the kitchen table and Fox added his own to it without comment.

"What the afterworld is this?" Specialist Julian picked up the smaller of the prayer belts, holding it up to the lantern he was holding.

"It's a child's prayer belt. It was in their trunk with some ancient-looking baby clothes, so I can only imagine it's a relic from one of their childhoods."

Julian sneered at it before throwing it back in the pile.

"It's ridiculous enough they feel the need to make and wear this superstitious garbage, but then they keep it as if the shit isn't treasonous."

"Dragon-filth aren't exactly known for their intelligence," Nicolas said, laughing as he tore the tapestry down from the wall and added it to the pile. "There was nothing else in the room?"

"A dead rat under the bed, but nothing of any value." He pulled out the sack from his belt and began throwing the things from the table inside. "We should head back to the barracks so we can write up the report for the high sergeant."

"Did you check the mattress?" The man moved to go into the room and Fox gave his best sneer.

"I'm not an idiot and I don't need you to double-check my work," he said, picking up the contraband from the table that he could carry.

The other two gave in, neither wanting to do more than required, and picked up the remaining items off the table, leaving out the front door.

Fox left the door hanging open behind them, not looking back. The children would make it out or they wouldn't. He wasn't their hero or savior. They weren't his problem.

CHAPTER FIVE
SOFIA

Sofia watched Ocon's sneering face disappear into darkness as the door shut. His eyes glinted with an impotent rage that made her gleeful and she saw the moment Micael noticed it, his own eyes going hard.

"Need I remind you, you're not in charge here?" Micael said, voice low and icy.

"I didn't say I was."

He didn't acknowledge her statement, waving the others off with a sharp look. When Sofia attempted to follow Javi, Micael's large hand landed hard on her shoulder, stopping her from moving. Her cheeks burned hot.

"I want you out of here by tonight. Go back to the city and clear your head."

Sofia's mouth dropped open, not bothering to hide her anger. "I have another day before I'm expected back."

"Then you'll have time to let off steam and relax before you go back to work."

"I'm staying. I'm not a child to be sent to her room."

Micael turned on her, eyes black and hard. "No, but you are under my command. I don't trust you. I saw you with him and that was after

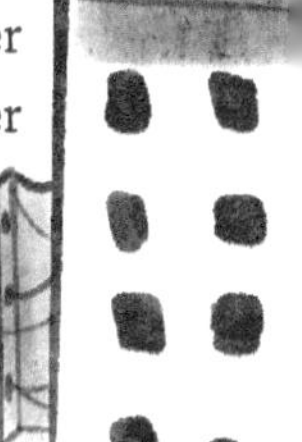

you failed to follow directions and almost ruined the plan we'd been putting in place for over two dragon blinks. Your part in the plan is done and the resistance thanks you."

The words were hardly grateful, each one a sharp shard of glass, slicing at her.

"You realize who that is, right?" she said, voice going thin in the way she hated. She took a breath. "He'll have insider knowledge on the castle, the prison, and half the royal and military quarters."

He'll be able to get her back into the chief commander's house. Into his study where he kept his books.

"He's not who we expected, but he's going to play the same role either way. We're getting Dia and Sari back unharmed. And that means delivering that man in there *unharmed*."

"We can still interrogate him. Get information while we have him." She wasn't going to let up. Micael knew how she felt about this plan from the start. The crown didn't negotiate with the resistance and the chances of this trade working were thinner than a dragon's wing. But he was desperate and desperation lead to stupid decisions, even for him. "Just in case this plan doesn't work."

She hated the way he blanched at the words but they had to be said. There was a chance the king and chief commander wouldn't negotiate the lives of their prisoners, even for the life of General Ocon's own son.

"We'll cross that bridge *if* we come to it. Until then, you're needed back at the inn keeping an ear out for any news about the kidnapping and the crown's reaction."

He turned away, the dismissal clear, and she was left standing alone in the darkened hall trying not to think of the man that sat just out of reach.

"I know the stakes just as well as anyone," Sofia said, throwing her sparse possessions in her bag without much care. She usually only carried a few trinkets from her time before the resistance and a single outfit when she came in and out of the city. It was best to pack light while committing treason.

Flor was standing across the room, already packed. Her eyes were focused on the door, as if she were waiting for Javi to come bursting through the door at just the wrong time.

"It's his granddaughter," she said, as if it explained everything.

"I know that," she snapped. "Javi's sister is in that prison, too. But he and his moms aren't acting like idiots."

Flor's eyebrows pinched together in the way that reminded Sofia of her mother with a small pang of grief.

"How would you know? Have you even spoken to Javi since Dia was arrested?"

Sofia opened her mouth to respond, but Flor cut her off, reading her mind. "And talking to him about how you're going to kill the chief commander and king in revenge is *not* what I mean. They're already grieving. He doesn't show it because it's Javi, but I've heard him crying into his pillow at night, and his mothers have already completed the ritual to send Dia to the Depths if she dies."

"She's not going to die," Sofia said with as much conviction as she could muster. "If Ocon can get us into the prison, we can break her and Sari out."

"You assume any information he gives us under duress can be trusted."

Sofia wanted to argue more, but Javi did walk in then, dark curls hanging limply in his face. Perhaps Flor was right. She looked at her friend, truly looked at him, for the first time in weeks and she saw the deep purple bruises beneath his eyes that his tight smile couldn't hide.

"I shouldn't have been worried about you leaving without me, Sofia. You manage to take forever to pack even when it's just a single dress. As if Micael's going to change his mind."

"We can only hope one day he grows a brain." She matched his smile, throwing an arm around his shoulders and placing a kiss on his cheek. "And I would never leave without dramatically complaining to you about it, anyway."

Flor rolled her eyes, but joined the hug, wrapping her own arms around them.

Javi seemed to suddenly notice the bag slung across Flor's shoulder. "You're leaving, too?"

"Micael said that I'm due back the day after Sofia anyway and I could help with—"

"Babysitting me and making sure I don't get into trouble," Sofia interjected.

Flor elbowed Sofia, hard enough to hurt. "With gathering information now that the plan is in effect. Micael wants to know if the king or chief commander makes any proclamations or moves."

Javi's face went pale, but his smile didn't falter. Sofia had to give him credit for never showing his hand. Even after cycles, she never knew exactly what he was thinking or feeling. But she understood he had to be hurting. Dia was six cycles his junior and barely associated with the resistance thanks to his own work in keeping her out of it. But five weeks ago, when she'd been arrested for being on the wrong side of the gates past curfew, she'd had a small dagger on her. It had been barely the size of a thumb, just large enough for self-protection when Javi wasn't home to watch her. It was enough to have her sent to the prison on illegal possession and suspected resistance ties. And he had been the one to gift it to her.

Micael's own granddaughter was arrested two days later trying to get a message to Dia and found guilty of conspiracy. The only reason they weren't dead yet was because the chief commander suspected, rightfully so, that they had information regarding the resistance. Sofia could only imagine what the two girls had been put through in the five weeks they'd been imprisoned. She was extremely familiar with General Ocon's methods of interrogation. Neither of the girls knew exactly where their base was, but they had enough information about the resistance's activities in the city that if the girls had broken, the entire resistance would have been arrested or killed by now. Sofia didn't know how long two girls, barely sixteen cycles old, could survive the torture.

"We'll get them back," Sofia said, the words slipping out before she reminded herself she couldn't make such a promise.

Javi squeezed her shoulder, but didn't say anything. Perhaps he knew how empty a promise it was.

"We should head out," Flor said. "I want to make it to the mangroves before dark."

They said their goodbyes, Sofia purposefully ignoring Micael. But she gave Viola and Carmen an extra tight hug, pressing a kiss to each of their cheeks as if it might bring their daughter home sooner. Javi stood beside his mothers, his blood-mother, Viola, holding his hand tightly in her own.

"We'll be back in less than a week," Flor said as Sofia stopped at the lip of the cenote, not ready to take the first step back toward Suvi.

"They're wasting an opportunity by not questioning him," she said, looking back at the cenote as if she might will Micael to change his mind and call them back.

"I'm sure they'll do so, but you're assuming he'll give us anything."

"He would if we put a blade to his throat."

Flor gave her a flat stare, rolling her eyes once she was sure Sofia was looking at her.

"Do you truly think their plan will work?" Sofia's voice was quiet, too afraid of her words echoing down into the cenote where Javi and the others might hear.

"It's the best one we have, and the sooner we get to Suvi, the sooner we'll know what's happening."

Flor pulled Sofia toward her, linking their arms before turning south.

THEY WALKED IN SILENCE, their soft footsteps and breaths the only sounds to challenge the general hum of the forest. Even though they were still a few hours' travel from the wall, neither of them wanted to speak. The sun was starting to set and it was all too easy to slip from one shadow to the next. But, as much as they'd built a system for coming in and out of the city unseen, there was always the chance that a scout's habits would change or they'd run into the military out here. And even though plenty of king's men might arrest them, it was always easier to simply shoot the rebels and leave them to rot out here in the forest. It was less paperwork. Micael always enjoyed reminding them that he'd lost a few members of the resistance that way over the decades.

They made it to the mangroves shortly after dark, when the sun had tucked itself away behind the horizon, leaving the stars and moons to rule the sky. The dragon's eyes were opening, the two moons wide crescents already high in the sky. It made it easier to move, but easier to get caught, as well.

The mangroves twisted their way along the western coast of the peninsula, their branches and roots a dense wall between the land and sea. It wasn't the easiest path back into the city, but it was the one that guaranteed stealth. Even at low tide, the scouts didn't venture too far into the area, fearful of the crocodiles, the blood monkeys, and the other fanged creatures that made their home here. But the Dragonborn had never forgotten the knowledge of their ancestors and it was easy enough to avoid angering the creatures. Just don't splash around or make eye contact with the monkeys and you'd rarely be bothered.

It was just coming on low tide and the ocean that normally flooded the area had receded just enough to reveal the bridge of tree roots that stretched and twisted across the low waterline. They both removed their shoes, more sure on the wet roots of the trees in their bare feet. They made their way across the twisted trees, never even touching the water. It was a long and arduous journey, taking another hour to cross the small span of shore, but they bypassed the wall completely—the Dereyans never managing to build the stone structure through the thick mangrove trees.

They'd made the mistake of tearing down the eastern mangroves when they'd first settled down and decided to claim the entire southern tip of Wueco as their own. Now the entire sector of the city flooded twice a day with the flow of the tides. Not that the Dereyans cared when they simply ensured their people never had to live in the drowned quarter.

Sofia and Flor made it back to Suvi before the first moon had even set and they were back at the Wall's Inn less than an hour later. Luckily, despite how strict the Dereyans were in tracking the Dragonborn by day, even they didn't like traveling through the edge of the slums at night. The only soldiers this side of the inner gates were either in their barracks along the wall or tucked safely away in a room at the inn with a Dragonborn or two for company.

The only people they passed were huddled in shadowy corners of alleys or swaying as they made their way down the street. Flor walked with one hand on her club, staring down anyone who dared make eye contact with her. The small blunt weapon was the only one Dragonborn were allowed legally by the crown. Sofia, branded for treason, wasn't even allowed that. She'd simply taken to wearing enough iron rings on her right hand that any passerby might second guess trying to rob her. The smell of the city felt suffocating, even at night when the worst of the filth was hidden by the dark, but she could still smell the human feces that lined the alleys and the constantly thick stench of sweat and vomit and grime that coated her throat when she breathed. She hated it here, even though the inn had been their home for five cycles and every night in the small and dirty-floored room was better than a night on the streets.

The back rooms at the Wall's Inn where she and Flor rented a space were relatively quiet when they arrived, the other employees who lived there having gone to sleep hours before. But even back here, the sounds of the inn seeped through the walls, moans and slurred curses, the sounds of passion that constantly vacillated between pain and pleasure, anger and lust. Alcohol and sex: the chorus of the city as Sofia had come to know it. She'd gotten used to falling asleep to the sounds of grunting men and yelling women after a sun cycle living here, but it was always a bit of a shock returning from the forest.

Sofia didn't even bother changing out of her dirty travel clothes. She simply slipped her muddy sandals off, haphazardly wiped her feet on the meager rug in the center of their small room, and flopped onto her cot. Her eyes were already closed and she didn't even hear Flor finish changing before she was asleep, the sounds of a woman's long, over-drawn moan through the wall the last thing she heard.

CHAPTER SIX
SOFIA

The next few days went by in the same steady and slow monotony as always, Sofia's mind barely registering a difference between each morning and evening. Frankie hadn't blinked when they had shown up to work a day early and she was all too happy to assign them work. Sofia cleaned the rooms she was assigned and scrubbed the pots and pans after each meal, Flor working beside her. They listened carefully through the walls and to the gossip, waiting for some mention of the soldier that had gone missing or the king's current mood, but nothing of consequence was said. Even the women who serviced the soldiers at night, at least those Flor and Sofia were friends with, hadn't heard anything of use during the past week. Sofia was beginning to wonder if the chief commander was simply planning on hiding the kidnapping of his general's son.

The morning she woke up for her last day of work something felt different. The clouds that had blown in over the last few days were gone, and the small hole cut high on the wall of their room that acted as a window was letting in a breeze bordering on pleasant. Flor was already awake, washing her face in the small basin in the corner.

She turned and looked at where Sofia was stretching, sleep still heavy in her eyes. "Can you braid my hair?"

Sofia gave a small smile and motioned for Flor to sit back on her cot. The shorter woman gave a soft hum as Sofia combed her fingers through her hair, slowly taking out the knots that had accumulated through the past few days. This small ritual of theirs had started when they were still living on the streets together. Sofia's mother had taught her how to braid when she'd been younger but Flor barely even remembered her mother. From what she knew, her father had been a Dereyan man who'd knocked her mother up and then left her without a backward glance. By the time Flor was four, her mother had died of pneumonia, leaving Flor to fend for herself. She had been on the streets for cycles before she found Sofia.

"You know I could teach you how to braid your own hair?" Sofia said as she twisted the strands of red hair between her hands. She'd had to relearn the technique after she'd lost her finger, but the moves were second nature once more.

"But then I wouldn't have an excuse for you to do this," she said simply. Sofia laughed and tugged lightly at the hair.

Breakfast was nearly done by the time they made it into the kitchens, Flor snagging two burned rolls from on top of the garbage, handing one to Sofia. She ate it in two bites, happy it was still warm even if the burned crust of the dough left a bitter taste on her tongue. She'd eaten worse.

Frankie didn't even look up from where she was scribbling symbols into a notebook.

"Flor, start on the pans and Sofia, *he* was asking for you this morning. I don't know if he's still there, but clean the tables off while you're out there. Charo's late again. We're closing at midday for a mandatory meeting in the square, so be quick about it."

Sofia's stomach dropped and she met Flor's eyes. A mandatory meeting likely meant no good, but Sofia knew exactly what *him* was asking for her and it gave her some measure of hope. Perhaps he had good news. Flor's face was grim, but neither of them could say anything in front of Frankie. While she was one of the few women willing to hire someone marked for treason, Sofia doubted her patience with rebels stretched so far as to tolerate outward resistance.

So instead, she turned away from Flor and swallowed back her emotions. Her nails dug into the skin on her hand until she could breathe again. She gave a sharp nod that Frankie didn't acknowledge and then grabbed a tray from the counter and made her way out into the dining hall through the narrow doorway.

Despite the late hour, the hall itself was teeming with people. The majority of the patrons at the inn were off duty soldiers. It was situated near the edge of the barracks and few Dragonborn who lived in the slums had the money to afford even a warm ale. Sofia usually tried to avoid being out and about in front of the soldiers, who were often drunk before lunch, taking advantage of every moment of their leave. Some of the soldiers were eating their breakfasts quietly, but another handful were already throwing back ales and talking loudly next to the fire. A few of the inn's workers were sitting on the men's laps, happily taking their own sips from the ale and nibbling from their plates. She didn't envy the women, knowing too well how they felt about the men they bedded for coin each night.

Frankie had spent the last few cycles trying to convince Sofia and Flor to join the ranks of working women. It paid well and would have been a more efficient way of gaining access to information and gossip, but Flor couldn't stand the sight of a man's penis and Sofia was just as likely to stab one of the soldiers out of pure bitterness as she was to bring him to orgasm.

She didn't see Vato among the crowd, but the lone soldiers had their heads down and were minding their business. She avoided the tables near the fire, picking up the dishes around the rest of the dining hall first, trying her best not to draw attention. When a hand fell over her own as she reached to grab an empty glass, she nearly jumped out of her skin.

"Fuck," she cursed under her breath when she saw the bright green eyes of Vato looking back at her. She took stock of the table and room, but the man was alone and no one in the room had heard her exclamation.

"I can't stay, but there is a meeting today," he said, pulling her closer until she was straddling his lap. She hated this part, but it was the only way for them to talk without drawing attention.

She let out a huff of frustration, but moved forward, pressing herself closer to him. "I know. Is it—?"

"I think. The general's been tight lipped. You captured him? Alive?" He whispered the words in her ear, brushing her hair back. She let out an involuntary shudder at the feather-light touch. He wasn't unattractive, but Sofia never mixed business with pleasure, and she hated that her body couldn't always tell the difference.

"Yes. We have him and he's alive for now. But gods, it was his damn son! It wasn't supposed—"

"I just came to make sure everything went to plan. I have to go."

He pushed her back with a splayed hand. It was gentle enough, but she let herself stumble as she stepped back giving him a snarl.

"Prude, I didn't want nothing anyway," he slurred the words, loud enough for the table next to them to hear. He stood, giving her one last look before he walked out. She was left with shaky knees and no more information than she started with.

SOFIA SPENT another twenty minutes clearing the tables as Frankie had ordered. There were half-eaten portions on plates left at tables from breakfast that still hadn't been cleaned and Sofia wondered again where Charo was. This wasn't the first time the woman had shown up late to work, but Frankie had never even threatened to fire her. Of course, Sofia also knew Charo had two kids at home and her husband was all but dead working on the labor farms. Frankie might have acted like a hard ass most days, but Sofia was pretty sure there was a soft heart under her biting exterior.

Once the rest of the tables were cleared, Sofia made her way over to the rowdy bunch of soldiers. They'd already gone through another round of drinks and the way the large man at the end of the table was gripping the woman on his lap made her lip curl. She recognized the woman's bronze hair and freckled skin—Belen. She kept her head down as she grabbed the empty cups from their table—enough that she knew they were on their fifth or sixth round already. Four of the five men were still wearing their uniforms, the insignias ranging from high scout to the one holding Belen showing the rank of junior sergeant. They weren't required to wear their uniforms off duty, but she knew they did so to ensure they could throw their weight around. No Dragonborn, no matter how highborn or wealthy would mess with the king's soldiers.

"Get us another round, Sweetie," one of the men—a high scout—said as he pushed his empty cups toward her. She didn't make eye contact, simply giving a nod. Serving the guests wasn't her job, but she'd tell Lidi of his request when she was back in the kitchens. She just needed to keep her head down and mouth shut.

Which would have been a perfectly doable plan, were it not for the large hand that fell against the small of her back and then moved lower until it squeezed her ass. She jolted upright, the cups on her tray quaking with her body, a few tumbling sideways. The junior sergeant was leering at her when she turned, her eyes no longer lowered.

"How much for a lay?"

"I'm on cleaning duty," she said. He was only a foot from her and she could smell the stale ale on his breath and see the fine sheen of sweat along his pronounced brow. He might have been handsome at some point, before the drink had turned his skin sallow and his eyes red. She shouldn't have stared. She should have averted her eyes like a good little Dragonborn.

"What are you looking at dragon-filth?" he asked with a scowl, showing off his yellowed teeth.

She opened her mouth, knuckles white as she clenched the tray she was holding, rage barely contained. But before she could say anything and dig herself into a deeper pile of trouble, Belen had turned back to the man and placed a fine-boned hand against the stubble on his cheek.

"Ignore the thing," she said, voice smoky. She traced a finger down his chin, drawing his eyes into her own before moving her hand down his chest and lower still. "She's just a kitchen maid, a waste of your time."

Sofia thought it had worked. His eyes were focused solely on Belen now and she was able to take a step back, putting more space between her and the drunk man she so badly wanted to punch. But before she could take another step, Belen went flying across the floor, landing in a small heap a few feet away.

"Don't tell me what my time's worth," he said, spit flying from his mouth. As Belen turned back to look up at the man, Sofia saw the blood dripping down her chin from a split lip.

"I didn't mean—" she started, voice no longer husky but quavering.

He stood, body moving in a way all too familiar, from the turn of his hips and shifting of his weight. He pulled his leg back to kick Belen. And Sofia acted, without thought or plan. She lunged forward, grabbing his wrist and twisting it sharply, forcing him to turn back toward her. He was nearly half a foot taller than her, but his face was plenty near enough for her to send the heel of her hand up sharp and fast against the soft cartilage of his nose. She felt the snap in the same moment she rammed her knee into his groin.

Only a second after her knee had connected with soft flesh, she was being pulled back, a rough arm around her shoulders, pinning her arms to her sides. She kicked out automatically, hating the feeling of being restrained, but another soldier cuffed her across the face and her head snapped to the side. The shock of the hit brought her out of her rage and she took in the scene before her. Belen was no longer on the ground, having taken the distraction to duck from the dining hall. The other two women who had been acting as company were gone too and the five men were all standing, circled around her. The junior sergeant stood slightly hunched, blood dripping freely down his face from his broken nose.

"You'll pay for that, Whore," he sneered, moving forward to grip her chin in his hand. The calluses scraped against her skin and her nose flared at his sour stench. "I could send you to the whipping post for hitting an officer."

Perhaps the thought should have sent more of a shock through her, but the fear of a consequence could only hold someone for so long before the inevitability of it turns to a numbed acceptance. She was just lucky they hadn't noticed the brand on her wrist yet that marked her as a traitor. There were no third chances for those who committed treason and they could send her to the labor farms or the execution block for less than a broken nose.

She could almost feel the axe blade against her neck as the man reached forward to grab her right arm.

"What's going on in here?" Frankie had burst through the back door, her hair frizzing in every direction from the humidity in the kitchens and golden eyes wide as she took in the scene. "What did that idiot do now?"

"Your whore attacked an officer," the sergeant said. He turned on the owner of the inn.

Frankie gave a bow, an act of respect a junior sergeant hardly warranted, as she shuffled forward. "My deepest apologies. The girl is an imbecile. I only hired her to do the most basic work. She's not even supposed to be out here with guests around."

Sofia wasn't surprised by the slap Frankie sent across her face as the woman dragged her away from the soldiers. "Get back to the kitchens and don't leave again!" She said the words slowly and loudly.

"It's my right to punish the girl!" The junior sergeant was still flushed with anger, and Sofia wondered which angered him the most, being bested by a woman or by dragon-filth.

"Of course, it's up to you what her punishment is," Frankie quickly amended. "No matter what, I have a switch in the back for matters such as this. And I'll see her fired and out on the streets once the whipping is done.

"Your tab is on me, of course."

The junior sergeant seemed appeased by Frankie's groveling even as Sofia's stomach plummeted. She looked past the owner and saw a sliver of Flor's red hair at the edge of the kitchen door, watching the exchange without drawing attention.

Before she could move toward the kitchens, a hand roughly gripped her chin, forcing her to meet the junior sergeant's eyes. He sneered and spit out his words.

"Tonight, when you're bleeding and cold, I hope you remember my face and my mercy." His words were slow and annunciated, but she bit her tongue and nodded her head quickly, even as her eyes burned with hate.

He slapped her hard once more across the face, as if for good measure, and she tasted blood. But the moment he let go, she scurried away, ducking into the kitchens without looking back at Frankie who was still cooing apologies to the men.

"Another round for everyone. I just got in a shipment of a new ale from northern Falais."

The door shut and the sounds of the dining hall disappeared under the general hum of the kitchens. Flor was gripping her face a moment later, soft fingers inspecting the red skin and the cut across her cheek and lip.

"What in the dragons were you thinking?" she demanded, words practically whispered under her breath.

"Thinking wasn't a part of the equation. He was going to kick Belen while she was on the ground and I—"

She didn't need to finish the sentence. The flat glare of understanding Flor gave her told her that her friend knew exactly why Sofia had acted and that Flor thought her crazy and stupid for it. She was still being inspected by Flor when Frankie walked in a few minutes later, face pale. She didn't say anything for a moment, simply looking at the two women before her, lips in a flat line. The weight of what she was about to say was visible in the set of her shoulders and Sofia pulled away from Flor, chin held high.

"I'll have my things packed by the end of the hour."

She thought she might have glimpsed the softness beneath Frankie's stiff lip and narrowed eyes. For only a second, Sofia could have sworn the woman looked guilty. But then she nodded and turned away.

"Good. Flor, I'll expect the entire rent from you until you find another roommate."

Flor cursed behind Sofia and she felt the guilt on her actions settling over her.

"I'm sorry."

"Don't," Flor said, holding up her hand. "I'll worry about it in two weeks when rent's due."

Her words didn't ease the ache of guilt that twisted in Sofia's gut.

SOFIA

AGE 8

No one outside of sworn men of the king can step beyond the wall for their own protection and protection of all of Suvi.

Dragon-tongue shall hereby not be taught in any formal education.

Dragonborn are prohibited from writing and reading beyond basic symbols for record keeping. Any writing will be subject to search and seizure.

Dragonborn shall not be allowed to own or use any form of weapon, including swords, daggers, spears, bows, black powder, and any other item deemed as an asset of war.

The worship of the dragons is hereby forbidden in any form. Any paraphernalia found in the possession of the Dragonborn will be deemed as proof of worship.

The Laws of Suvi - Royal Decree, 613th sun cycle of the kings

Sofia had never been so excited to grow up as she was the day her shoulders got stuck in the latrine tunnel and it took Liza ten minutes to pull her out. That evening, even Ms. Garcia couldn't deny that it was time for Sofia to be switched out for someone new. The next day when she arrived at the back door in her uniform, freshly patched where the dress had torn from getting stuck, she was introduced to her replacement. The girl was tiny and Sofia had to wonder if she'd been that size when she'd first been assigned the job.

Her face was heart-shaped, kinky curls framing her face in a short crop. Wide brown eyes stared up at Sofia as Ms. Garcia explained the job, as if Sofia held power, which she supposed she did now. At least over this one small child.

It was this sense of responsibility that did her in. When she watched the girl—Mina—crawl into the latrines, the same rope Sofia had worn just a few days before tied around her waist, she felt a sense of responsibility that she doubted Liza ever felt for her. She'd never had a little sister, her parents barely making ends meet with a single child.

They rarely exchanged words beyond the basic pleasantries each morning, but Sofia always stayed to help load the cart even after Mina was done. And she showed her the best place in the nearby canal to rinse herself without getting in the way of passing boats. It was a few blinks into working with Mina that Sofia showed up at their usual meeting spot only to see the patch of unmarked field empty. Not known for her patience, she waited, kicking pebbles along the grasses and wildflowers—greenery that only thrived here because of the workers like her who carted water from the canal to feed the soil. After a minute or two, she grew bored, the vicious morning sun beating down on her head, turning her dark hair hot against her scalp.

The canal was within eyesight and she'd be able to see when Mina showed up. So instead of going back into the kitchens to tell Ms. Garcia of the girl's tardiness, she made her way toward the glistening waters. She only made it a hundred yards, when she heard the high-pitched yell that had her stopping in her tracks. Mina may not have been a gregarious child, but Sofia recognized the scream well. She ran toward the sound, around the back of the house where the stables and live-in servants resided. In the middle of the bare patch of land that acted as a small courtyard for the servants' quarters, Mina lay on the ground surrounded by four boys who would have towered over the girl even if she had she been standing.

Sofia's heart thumped heavy in her chest as five pairs of eyes swiveled to meet hers. She didn't recognize the boys, but she could tell from the clean cut of their clothes they were likely Dereyan. And Mina—dragons bless her—was looking up at her as if Sofia had any chance of saving her.

"I—" she swallowed back the quiver in her voice, "I came to get Mina. She's late for work."

One of the boys snickered, nudging Mina where she lay on the dirt. "I don't know why we keep dragon-filth around. More trouble than you're worth."

Sofia bit her tongue and kept her face neutral. She just wanted to take Mina and leave.

But even as she moved forward to help the smaller girl up, one of the boys stepped toward her, shoving her hard in the chest. She landed in the dirt, a small squeak of pain escaping her lips.

"We didn't say we were done with her."

Sofia's hands clenched, nails digging into the dry dirt as she pushed herself up.

"Just let me take her. We need to go to work." She tasted metal on her tongue, her breaths sharp.

The boy stepped forward, leaning over her. "Beg for it."

"Please," she said, voice soft and eyes low. She hated herself for the deference.

"Get on your knees and beg properly like a good little dragon-filth."

Sofia moved jerkily, her body fighting against her even as she slowly went to her knees. She looked back up at the boy, eyes burning with tears, and bit out the word. "Please."

"I don't listen to filthy, disgusting, dragon-filth," he said, shoving her where she kneeled.

She tried to remind herself that there were four of them and one of her, but her vision went red and the blood rushed in her ears, singing loudly. She came back to her feet, body trembling.

"Don't push me."

The ringleader gave a laugh, launching forward. He pulled back his arm, ready to punch her. Sofia ducked to the side, easily avoiding his fist, but a moment later a set of small hands grabbed her from behind. The other three boys had joined the fight. The next punch landed, and even with his thin arms it made her head ring. She hissed and kicked like a wild animal, her foot making contact with the soft flesh of one boy's stomach and her head hitting against something hard. She heard their grunts of pain, but still she ended up facedown, a small boot in her side.

But she never stopped fighting. She didn't even notice when the hand that picked her up and dragged her to standing was that of an adult. She lashed out, smacking them across the face, only stopping when she heard Ms. Garcia's gravelly voice cursing in a way she'd only heard in the dirtiest alleys of the slums.

Her body went slack and she looked around. The boys were all gone and Mina stood nearby, the slightest hint of a bruise forming across her cheek.

"I swear to the old kings, you're more trouble than you're worth, Girl. What were you thinking starting a fight with those boys?"

She didn't have an answer, and Ms. Garcia didn't wait for one. There was nothing she could have said to defend herself.

Even the next day, when the boys came back with one of their fathers and she was given five lashes from each of them in punishment, she didn't defend herself. It didn't matter that they had started the fight. It didn't matter that the most she'd managed was to give one boy a split lip. They only cared that she dared to fight back.

Still she didn't cry. She didn't show them her weakness, and she never regretted her choice. At least she walked away with more bruises and cuts than Mina.

CHAPTER SEVEN
SOFIA

Sofia was packed before they had to leave for the midday gathering. It didn't take long. She only owned three outfits and lived out of her small pack most days anyway. Anything of true value was back at the cenote, tucked away for safe keeping. When she walked out of the inn, following the wave of others moving toward the main square, she didn't look back, refusing to feel the loss of the place. No matter how many nights she'd slept in the inn, it wasn't her home. The cenote was. The resistance was.

Flor walked beside her, at one point reaching over to stop Sofia from picking at her fingers.

"Breathe," Flor said, voice low.

"I know," Sofia said, probably more aggressively than necessary. The meeting could be anything. Last cycle, they'd called a meeting so that the king could announce a new initiative in providing gas lamps to line the outer wall. Something Sofia was sure that the entire city did not need to know about.

As they turned the corner to the main square, it became clear this wasn't a meeting about gas lamps. The square was pressed against the inner wall that divided the outer city from the inner city where the wealthiest Dereyans lived. A tall platform stood at the far end, overlooking the outer city, judging each and every Dragonborn as they went about their lives. The blood from the executed permanently stained the wood and stones, always the reminder of what stepping a toe out of line might mean.

Today, four figures stood on the platform, their hands tied behind their backs, lined up in front of the execution block. Chief Commander Harlow oversaw the crowd from the front of the platform while the king and prince sat on the wall behind him, their golden thrones gleaming in the sunlight of midday, shined to perfection for the occasion.

They were too far from the platform to make out faces, but Sofia still tried, needing to know who stood for execution—needing to know if Dia or Sari were among them. Flor seemed to be thinking the same thing because as the crowd around them began to come to a stop, content to stand back and watch the proceedings, she pushed forward, shouldering her way between others. She grabbed on to Sofia's hand and pulled her through the crowd. A few grunted in annoyance, but no one stopped them as they snaked closer.

And then they were in the center of the square, close enough to see Sari's gaunt face and wide eyes as she looked out over the crowd from her place between two other Dragonborn.

"No," Flor whispered, just loud enough for Sofia to hear.

Sofia's head spun as the chief commander stepped forward, his voice rising above the cacophony of the crowd. His voice thundered through the large bronze funnel that adorned the stage.

"The resistance claims to fight for freedom and peace. Yet at every turn they prove themselves to be nothing more than bloodthirsty brutes out for revenge. They plant bombs around the city and kill the innocent without regret. They ignore the calls from their own pleading for them to stop. And now, they kidnap and threaten one of the king's men. A man who has devoted his life to protecting this city and all who reside here."

Murmurs rippled through the crowd and Sofia clenched her fists, digging her nails deep into her palms. She focused on the pain and kept her face blank.

"The resistance, once more, proves themselves untrustworthy and weak. They do not want peace. They do not fight for the Dragonborn. If they did, they would not continue to force our hand. We enforce our laws out of necessity, not hatred. But we must continue to enforce them, as long as chaos thrives in the outskirts.

"I know that even as I speak to the loyal of Suvi, there are rebels among you, hiding in the shadows, too afraid to show your faces and admit your crimes. I speak to you now, the snakes and the rats that feed off the system even as you try to destroy it. You cannot win. We will not bow to your demands."

Flor's hand found Sofia's where it was still tucked in her pockets, prying it open before clenching it in her own.

The chief commander moved, waving to the hooded soldier that stood at attention next to him, an axe hanging in one hand. The soldiers pushed the first prisoner forward, forcing him to his knees. He was a scrawny man, his face speaking of cycles of near starvation and pain. But even as he kneeled, he kept his head high, looking out at the crowd with accusing eyes.

"Antonio Medina, you have been found guilty of treason, having known associations with the resistance and refusing to give up the names of your associates. As such, you have been sentenced to death."

Flor's hand clenched around Sofia's in a painful spasm as the axe fell and the man's head dropped from the platform and into the crowd below. There was a rush as those closest moved to destroy the head, stomping it into the ground as if he deserved punishment even in death. Sofia had made the mistake of going up to the platform after one of the executions, forcing herself to look at the scattered remains of blood, brain, and bone left behind by the people when they were done with their cruel ritual.

A sharp gasp from Flor brought her attention back to the platform and her knees went weak. Sari was kneeling now, her head tucked in the small divot, and the chief commander opened his mouth to speak. But Sofia didn't hear him. She couldn't hear anything over the roaring in her ears. And for a moment, it wasn't straight brown hair hanging over the block, but a set of familiar tight black curls.

The sound of the axe coming down and the roar of the crowd broke her from her trance and she felt herself jerk back into her body. Sari's brown hair was gone from the platform and the crowd at the front undulated in their dance of glee. Acid burned up her throat, but she swallowed it back down, Flor's hand her only anchor.

Sofia stood, watching but not truly seeing, as the last two Dragonborn were beheaded and the king stood to congratulate the chief commander on his defense of Suvi. The moment the king's hand raised in its dismissal wave, Sofia moved, no longer able to hold herself still.

She kept their hands linked as she pushed through the crowd, but she could feel Flor pulling at her, trying to slow her down. But she didn't care. *Couldn't* care.

Not when she could still hear the slice of the axe through bone and wood. The crowd roared, a cheer of glee as the blood of the Dragonborn rained down on them from above.

Her mind was screaming and her throat burned as if the sound were stuck there, unable to come out. She was choking on her own rage.

Blood. Screams. Pain. Death.

The king wasn't going to give up his power. He thought himself a god. He would kill every Dragonborn before he sacrificed a single thing to the resistance. Why not, when he saw them all as vermin to be exterminated?

Blood. Screams. Pain. Death.

And Chief Commander Harlow wasn't going to give up anything, even to save Fox Ocon. That much was clear. He'd killed one Dragonborn for every day that Ocon had been captured. He'd continued to kill them until something changed.

Blood. Screams. Pain. Death.

Only a god could challenge another god's power.

She heard the muffled voice of someone in her ear and she turned, eyes focusing on the person standing in front of her. Flor.

"Where are you going?"

Sofia tried to shake her head, tried to understand the words to form a response, but her mind spun and her breaths were coming too fast. Instead of answering with words, she tugged once more and started to move again.

She couldn't think, but she could still walk, and she knew the steps to the mangroves like the back of her hand. It was stupid to leave when the sun was still up and the tide was moving in. Another Sofia with a functioning mind would have known that. She *knew* it even now, but she didn't care.

The soldiers were feasting and drinking in celebration. The city was satiated in its bloodthirst and laying quiet now in the afternoon heat.

"What are you going to do?"

They were already in the mangroves, hands no longer linked, but Flor followed obediently behind her. Sofia looked back at Flor with her pale face and wide eyes. It clearly hadn't been the first time Flor had spoken the words and she seemed surprised to finally be acknowledged.

"I'm going to get that Dereyan bastard to give me a way into the prison and the chief commander's house. And then I'm going to kill him."

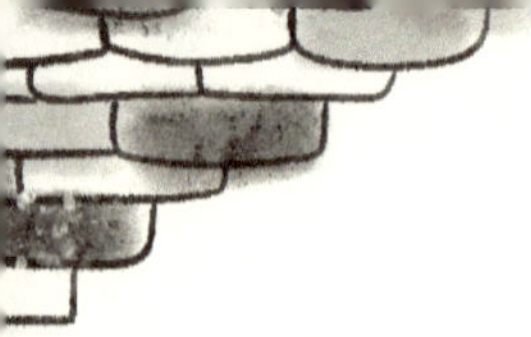

FOX

AGE 16

When the first king was only fifteen sun cycles old, the truth of the world was revealed to him. The dragons that his tribe and the others of Wueco worshipped were not gods, but demons spreading terror over the land. His revelation did not come from his holiness, but rather he transcended his human birth through the actions he took to free the land from the demons.

-The Legacy of the Kings: A History of Wueco's Creation by Francis Knoll

Being handed the axe was one of the greatest honors of Fox's life. Chief Commander Harlow's face was serious, mouth set in a grim line, but he could see the pride lighting up his eyes behind the mask of indifference. They were in front of the entire kingdom and it wouldn't be decent to show favoritism toward the general's son.

It wasn't common practice to allow a high scout to conduct the executions, but he'd been the one to catch the rebel less than a mile

from the outer wall. The Dragonborn had been carrying black powder along with a rough schematic for two houses in the royal quarter. The arrest was more than enough to ensure Fox's promotion to high scout, but the chief commander had decided he deserved an additional reward for the thwarted plan.

When Chief Commander Harlow had come to dinner with Fox's family to announce the plan to his father and him, Fox was thrilled. He'd even seen a flicker of pride that flashed for the briefest moment in his father's eyes before he turned the conversation back to the ongoing campaign to find out where the schematics had come from and who was working with the man.

And now he was standing on the platform with the cold wood of the axe in his hands and the eyes of the entire city on him.

"For the crimes of treason, weapon smuggling, conspiracy to commit mass murder, Pedro Luz, you have been sentenced to execution. We thank the king and his men for stopping you before you could kill those you'd planned, but their grace does not offer you absolution. Do you have any last words?"

The man on the platform in front of Fox didn't even move to acknowledge the question. He was already kneeling, head hovering just above the block. He knew the man couldn't have spoken his last words if he had wanted. They had taken his tongue as his last punishment after weeks of refusing to give up information on the resistance and his co-conspirators. Fox had been invited to three of the interrogations and he even made it through one of them without vomiting.

He wasn't feeling sick now, though, as he saw the man, laid low and pathetic before him.

The chief commander continued, having given the crowd enough time to be frustrated by the other man's silence. "You should thank the crown for your merciful sentence, but I know how ungrateful you *Dragonborn* can be. May your make-believe gods take you."

"High Scout Ocon, if you will."

Fox gave a nod of his head before stepping forward, eyes focused on the man's back. He could just see a quiver of fear in the man's muscles beneath his tattered tunic. It made him sneer in disgust. The man's death would be quick and easy, unlike the dozens of people the resistance planned to kill. Or the thirty men, women, and children that died in a bombing near the work farms just two blinks before. Most of them had suffered—the initial blast only killing a handful—but the horrific injuries took the rest over the next few days. This man might not have been one of those who set the fuse, but the weapons he had had were the same type used in the attack.

The chief commander spoke true that this sentence was merciful in comparison to the crimes. And yet the man cowered from his death.

This is for you, Leon. The words were a whisper in his mind—a prayer sent to the old kings in hopes that Leon might hear them.

Fox lifted the axe, the muscles in his arms tensed under the weight, eyes focused only on the neck stretched out before him.

He didn't hear the whistle of the axe or the thud of the metal into wood that followed. All he heard was the roar of the crowd gathered before him as the head fell forward, rolling off the platform.

He was glad to see it disappear. He didn't want to witness the judgment in those dead eyes staring up at him. There was nothing for him to regret. The man had planned to commit mass murder. Yet his stomach roiled all the same and acid burned up his throat. He clenched his jaw and breathed slowly through his nose, pushing away the nausea. There wasn't room for fear or regret in his world.

He didn't realize he was staring down at the man's body, laid still before him, until the large hand landed on his shoulder. The chief commander's grip was firm and warm.

"Well done, Fox," he whispered.

Fox's eyes flickered toward the stands set back behind the platform to where his father stood, looking prouder than he'd ever seen. The tightness that had been constricting his chest for the past week leading up to this execution suddenly released, snapped like a bowstring.

And Fox smiled.

CHAPTER EIGHT
FOX

Fox had lost track of time in the never-ending darkness. His captors fed him, gave him water and took out his bucket every couple of days. It was the politest captivity he could have expected, but it made him wonder all the more what their plan was. There had been a steady stream of rebels, and they were always masked, which he kept reminding himself was a good sign for his odds of survival. Still, it made him uneasy every time he was forced to look into the cold eyes of someone he couldn't see, save for the barest hint of their mouth and chin. That and those icy, hateful eyes.

What was their plan?

Why was he here?

How long would they leave him in the dark alone?

His hands had been retied shortly after they'd allowed him to change into dry clothes, but they were at least in front of his body now. It still made it difficult to do much more than eat and feel around the small cell, hoping to come across something useful. Other than the cold stone walls and the bucket he didn't like thinking about, there was nothing. He'd even spent a good few hours scratching at the corner of the room, wondering how long it would take to dig himself out, only to find the dirt gave way to stone a few inches down.

He hadn't seen the woman who initially lured him in since she'd thrown the clothes at him. Those he had seen were a mix of women and men, their ages varied from what he could decipher.

He mulled over the information he'd be able to bring back to the chief commander upon his escape, trying to ignore the coldness of the ground beneath him and the rock wall behind him. Numbers? Maybe. Locations? Possibly. Plans? Not yet. He was still counting up the different rebels he'd seen when the door gave a squeal. He hadn't even heard the key in the lock.

The shadow that stalked through the doorway wasn't holding a lantern. They were a silhouette against the light behind them, tall like many of his male captors. But the curve of their hips and the sway of their walk was plenty familiar. When the small hand wrapped around his throat and thew his head hard against the stone wall, he knew exactly who was crouched over him, face in shadows.

"Fox Ocon," she spit out, the words wet against his face.

"Nice to see you again," he said, the pressure on his throat painful, but not overwhelming. Her eyes looked nearly feral in the shadows and her hair stuck up in every direction, curls haphazard in their shape. She looked even more wild than when he'd first captured her. "And your name?"

"You don't have the power here," she said, letting go of him and stepping back. He resisted the urge to massage his throat. It would only show weakness. He noticed then that they weren't alone. The fiery red angel that had saved him from drowning was standing a few feet behind the other woman, a lantern swinging in her outstretched hand.

"Hello, gorgeous lady." He flashed her a crooked smile over the glaring woman's shoulder. His red-haloed angel only sneered back at him.

"So tell me, Little Fox," the woman still crouched over him snarled, "how many Dragonborn lives do you think yours is worth?"

"I'd say at least ten. Why do you ask?" The snarky words had left his mouth before he could stop himself, so the hard slap that followed wasn't exactly a surprise.

"You are worth less than nothing, yet four people died for you today."

Was he supposed to feel guilty?

"Sorry, I've been locked in a cell for the past week, so I'm a little out of the loop of current events."

"The chief commander just executed four innocent Dragonborn in your name."

"I doubt they were innocent."

Her hand came down, clenching around his throat once more as she leaned forward, their noses nearly touching.

"Sari's crime was trying to get a message to her friend. She was sixteen."

"If her friend was a treasonous rebel, she deserved what she got. Just like the rest of you dragon-filth."

He knew he had probably taken it too far, but he enjoyed seeing her face flush. And it did so with such a crazed passion he wondered if she might explode. Still, he wasn't expecting the punch that followed. His head snapped back, hitting the wall behind him with a crack. He let out a curse and bent forward, hands reaching for his face. There had been no snap of cartilage, but even touching his nose sent a shock of pain through him.

He cursed, looking up at her through watery eyes. "Impressive right cross."

"Sofia," the other woman hissed from behind her. It was under her breath and perhaps she didn't think he'd hear her, but he smiled widely.

"Sofia, huh? Nice to finally meet you, oh captor of mine."

"Get out of here, *Flor*," Sofia hissed back.

"Why? So you can kill our best chance at—" this time she had the forethought to not finish. Fox was only a bit disappointed. He was too focused watching the emotions flying across *Sofia's* face.

With only a flash second of movement, there was a dagger pressed against his throat, her hand steady where she gripped it.

"You had that and you punched me?"

"It was satisfying."

"So why bring knives into it?" He gave a pointed look down at the cold metal against his skin. "Scared of me?"

"I just want to see you bleed."

"Sof, the others are going to hear something. We're going to get caught."

Fox tilted his head, careful to not press the blade any deeper into his skin. "You're not supposed to be here, oh captor of mine? I'm honored you wanted so badly to talk to me."

The tip of the dagger pressed in, drawing blood, and he bit back the hiss that crawled up his throat.

"Let's start from the beginning," she said. "You're going to help me get into the chief commander's house unseen. Then we're getting the rest of the innocent Dragonborn out of that prison."

"That is a fascinating assumption. Especially for someone who just punched me while I was tied up."

"You're going to help me. Whether it's now or after I cut off each one of your fingers and toes is up to you."

"Sofia," Flor said again, this time moving as if to stop her. But she didn't grab for her, didn't physically restrain her, and Sofia didn't move.

"Leave unless you're going to help." The words came out in a hiss between her teeth.

Fox felt the first trickles of fear when Flor listened, setting down the lantern, eyes wide as she backed out of the room.

Sofia looked at him with cold eyes, the dagger held delicately in her hand. She moved slowly, stepping on either side of his legs where he was seated against the stone wall before lowering down to straddle him. If she'd been any other woman, the position would have boded well for some entertainment, but she didn't look interested in that. Even still, the warmth of her body was a shock after days in his icy cell and his breath caught in his throat.

She leaned forward, brushing the blade across his cheek in a gentle caress.

"Where should I start? Pinky? Middle finger?" She glanced between his legs. "Or perhaps I should start lower—take something more precious?"

"I don't know what your plan is, captor of mine, but even with that dagger between us, you won't get a chance to take my finger. It's not my fault you handed yours over."

He looked pointedly down at the missing ring finger, obvious in its absence around the knife hilt.

"Screw you."

"Not a chance." He smiled, shifting his hips slightly, if only to remind her that she was the one straddling him.

She didn't bother dropping the knife as she pulled her fist back and punched him again. He turned his head in time to send the hit wide, her knuckles skimming across his cheekbone, but the blade of the knife glinted inches from his eye. When she moved to take another swing, he ducked under her arm and bucked up his hips. She was already off-balance from her attempted punch and she fell sideways with a grunt as he stumbled to his feet. Hands still tied, he reached down for the knife clutched in her hand.

He just managed to grab the dagger, feeling her fingers begin to loosen on the hilt when her other hand jabbed forward, directly between his legs. He fell back with a groan, the knife dropping from both their hands as she lunged forward, tackling him.

"You feral b—"

She shoved an elbow into his gut and the air left his lungs in a gasp. He hooked his leg around her ankle as she moved to get up and rolled to the side. She let out a squeak as she went flying, followed immediately by a crack and a curse.

For a moment, he thought she might have fallen onto the lantern, but the light remained, dim but steady. He pulled himself up, using the wall behind him for support and saw what had caused the crack. Perhaps he should have felt ashamed, but his smile was stretched wide as Sofia let out a string of curses and pushed herself away from the bent bucket and the pile of excrement that she'd fallen into.

"You look cleaner than when I first saw you," he said, not hiding the glee in his voice.

She let out a growl and lunged at him, but before she could get her hands around his throat, two pairs of arms were on either side of her, pulling her back from him. It was Flor and the young man they'd been with. His mask wasn't even in place and he looked like Flor had pulled him directly from sleep.

"Be careful with her," Fox said, "she's gone wild."

"What in the gods' scales is going on in here," a voice said from behind them all. Even Fox froze with the others, smile dropping from his face. Sofia had gone rigid, Flor and the young man's faces gray in the lantern light.

The older rebel Fox recognized by his voice alone, stepped forward, his own lantern held in his hand. He wore his mask, making it all the more obvious the others were standing with their faces uncovered. The extra light only highlighted the brown streaks across Sofia's tunic and pants. He even thought he might have spied some in her wild curls.

"You three, out," he said with the same authority Fox often heard from the chief commander. No longer needing to hold her back, Flor and the man scurried out of the room, followed by a slower and more reluctant Sofia. "You and I will being having a very long talk after this."

The man closed the door in her face before she could retort and then turned back to Fox, examining the room slowly. Fox's heart gave a small jerk when the man's eyes fell on the dagger lying between them, but the man moved quickly to pick it up, frowning when he saw what it was covered in—what the ground was covered in.

"I'll be right back," he said, his scowl likely more a reflection of Sofia and her friends than Fox. He left the lantern and for a brief moment, Fox thought of breaking it and using the glass as a weapon. But before he could act on the plan, the man was back, holding a small pile of rags. He tossed them on the ground, and gave Fox a long look before moving forward. He had to resist flinching as the man took his dagger and sliced through the ropes binding his wrists.

"I'm sorry about that," the man said, already turned toward the door. He picked up the second lantern without looking back. "She'll be disciplined and won't be a problem again. She doesn't reflect our movement."

"Your movement? Is that what you call mass murder?"

"It's what we call our only chance at freedom," he said, the door snapping closed a second later and leaving Fox in darkness, untied and smelling of his own shit.

CHAPTER NINE
SOFIA

Sofia had heard others talk about their body taking over when they were angry and she'd even experienced that herself before, but what had happened in the cell was different. She hadn't felt a part of her body as she'd clawed at the Dereyan with his cocky smirk.

So when Javi and Flor finally dragged her away, fingers nearly bruising around her arms, she was almost happy. It was Flor who finally brought Sofia back to herself, pressing a kiss to her forehead before pushing her into the icy waters of the lake at the entrance to the cenote.

The water was a shock to her system and she slowly came back to herself, feeling Javi and Flor as they splashed her, cleaning away the shit and mud that was smeared across her body. They were standing in the water with her, both shivering with cold.

"Breathe, breathe," Flor said. The words were murmured into her hair even as she realized she was hyperventilating. She wiped away the tears on her face and pulled back from Flor, looking over her shoulder to the pale Javi.

"I'm sorry." The words came out in a rasp, barely intelligible, but Javi looked relieved to even hear that. Flor squeezed her into a tight hug before pulling back, hands cupping Sofia's face as she studied it.

"You're okay?"

Sofia nodded and Flor led Javi and her to the large bonfire that was burning on the shore. If there had been others sitting there before, they were gone now, leaving the three of them alone. The heat of the flames burned against her numbed skin, but she savored the pain.

"Then what in the gods' scales were you thinking?" Flor growled out, her teeth chattering with cold. "I can't believe you made me witness that! You made me an accomplice."

"Micael won't—"

"That's not the point! You can't lose yourself like that. My gods, we could have been caught just trying to leave the city with you in that shape." Flor's voice was louder and more strained than Sofia had ever heard it before. For all the trouble the two of them had gotten into over the cycles, it had never been the two of them facing off against each other.

"What happened in there?" Javi said, pushing in between them. "Someone explain to me what I just came into."

Flor spoke first. "Sari is dead. The chief commander practically announced he couldn't be open to a trade and killed four Dragonborn in the process."

Javi's face went pale and Flor seemed to notice her mistake immediately.

"Dia wasn't there."

"But she will be if we don't act," Sofia said, grinding the words out between clenched teeth. She hated the blanched fear on Javi's face, but she couldn't soften the blow. The chief commander would kill every single Dragonborn in the prison whether or not they gave Ocon back.

"We need to tell Micael," Javi said, voice strained. "We need to release Junior Sergeant Ocon back to them before they execute anyone else."

"Didn't you hear me?" Sofia said, her eyes burning in firelight. The flames only made the shadows stretch longer, painting their faces in shades of black and gray. She preferred it that way, the darkness softened the pain in Javi's eyes. "He'll kill them no matter what. That Dereyan bastard in there is only an excuse."

Javi's body crumpled at her words and Flor moved to hold him up before he fell.

"If we can get into the prison—"

She didn't finish the sentence as the click of boots moved around the corner from the area beyond.

"Sofia Maria Suarez," Micael's voice was more bark than order. "Unless you have information to prove that man was conceiving a plan to kill us all in our sleep, then you better start begging my forgiveness."

It wasn't the voice of a fatherly figure or even a mentor. It was the order of the commander of the resistance movement and Sofia's superior.

"I—"

"Sir, there were extenuating circumstances. You can't blame her," Flor said, moving to stand next to her.

Sofia stepped forward to block her attempt.

"No one else is to blame for my actions in there, sir. I—we—" she couldn't quite get the words out.

"Sofia, I have no doubt that you are fully responsible for what just happened in there."

Micael's voice was never particularly warm. His care was often given with cold consideration and distant approval. But the ice that threaded through his words now was something Sofia hadn't heard before. There wasn't even the heat of anger. Just icy cold resolve as he stood, glowering down at her.

"I'm sorry," she said, taking a second to collect herself when her voice cracked. "Whatever I can do to apologize and fix my mistakes. You know how I feel about—I shouldn't have acted without permission."

"Sir, we have news from the city," Flor said, this time managing to shoulder Sofia out of her way.

"Flor—" Sofia had no idea what she planned to say. She just didn't want to be here for this.

"Micael," Flor continued, voice softening. It was that gentleness that had Micael's eyes snapping from Sofia and meeting Flor's. He knew what she was about to say before she said it, yet they all held their breaths as if the words might come out differently than they knew they would.

"The king ordered an execution today. Sari was—Sari and three others…"

Micael gave a careful nod, saving Flor from finishing the sentence.

"And Dia?" he said, looking at Javi.

"Still in the prison from what we gathered," Sofia said.

Micael didn't speak again for another minute and they stood, carved in stone. None of them wanted to break the moment—wanted to accidentally break the man who had always seemed so steady in the face of all the horrors they'd witnessed. But even in the flickering light, Sofia saw the sheen of emotion in his eyes. He shook his head, and Sofia flinched at the sudden movement.

"You're done," he said, eyes boring into her own. Sofia's world dropped out from under her. "You're off active duty. You're citybound until we have some space to fix your mistakes and decide on our next steps."

"Sir, if we can get into the prison. If he can get us in there—"

"No," Micael said, no longer looking at her. "We continue with the plan."

"They're going to kill everyone!"

"Then that will be on my shoulders, not yours. Pack your things. I want you gone tomorrow."

"But…"

But what could she say? How she'd already screwed up? How she had nowhere in the city to go back to? How she thought she might die if she was forced to be trapped in the city once more?

She settled on saying, "You can't keep me from the rainforest."

"No," he said, eyes narrowing, "I suppose I can't. But you're no longer welcome in the cenote until I decide otherwise."

"Micael," Flor started, but he raised his hand before she could say more, a clear indication that he was done listening to them. Sofia might have accused anyone else of being dramatic as he turned on his heels and left, but he was grieving and she knew that anguish well. He left them standing silently and looking at each other.

It was Sofia who moved first, taking the turns back to their rooms with her head down. She thought she saw some of the others watching them from the dining area, but she didn't dare acknowledge them. Her shame was burning bright and hot in her chest, even as her still damp clothes clung to her body.

Back at their rooms, she fell against the wall where her bedroll was wrapped up, waiting for her since she'd left the cenote last week. Would it still be here in two weeks or two blinks from now when Micael let her back? *If* he let her back. If she survived being trapped in the city again, homeless, jobless.

And if she did survive? Nothing would change. The king would still think himself a god and the Dragonborn the mud to be scraped from his boot.

"He's not just the general's son. He *knows* the chief commander. He could get us into Harlow's home."

Flor shook her head. "No. No. You are not going down this road again. Killing the chief commander is a suicide mission."

"It's not just that," Sofia said, looking between Javi and Flor. She took a breath. It had been a few cycles since they'd truly argued, but she knew exactly what their last argument had been. "If the chief commander still has the books on the dragons..."

Javi's eyes went dark and his lips pressed together, but it was Flor who spoke, face going pink.

"Gods, Sofia, we've been through this. The dragons are gone. They're dead and they aren't coming back no matter how many books you read."

She shook her head. "You both know the stories same as me. Plenty of legends speak of the dragons disappearing before they were killed off."

"Key word: disappeared," Flor said. She grasped Sofia by the shoulders, forcing her friend to look at her. "This is not going to convince Micael to welcome you back with open arms. Do you hear me? You don't say this shit out loud. You don't let the others hear that you're even still thinking of the dragons. You know what Micael said last time."

Sofia bit her lip, tearing her eyes away from Flor's own pleading ones. Javi was looking at her with the same desperation, though, and she could only stare down at her feet. The last time Micael had heard her talking of dragons he'd sent her back into the city for two blinks and hadn't let her back in until she promised not to spread rumors about dead gods.

"He already hates me," she muttered.

"I'm sure he'll cool down soon and everything will be fine." Javi, ever the optimist, wrapped an arm around Sofia as he sat. "You'll be back at the inn for a few weeks at most."

Flor was still looking down at him, her lips sharply tilted down. "It's not that easy."

"What does that mean?" Javi asked, looking at Sofia when Flor raised an eyebrow at her.

"I was fired from the inn today—" *yesterday?* She had no idea what time it was. "I don't have anywhere to go back to in the city."

"I'm sure we can find something else," he said. "I'm not letting you end up on the streets again."

"I was lucky enough Frankie took a chance on hiring me, but no one wants a smart-mouthed Dragonborn with a traitor's mark on her wrist."

"I can see about getting you a job with me on the docks. It's not easy work, but it's good pay. I can speak on your behalf."

Sofia wished she could feel hope in the idea, but Javi's boss was just as likely to fire him for associating with a marked traitor as to hire her. Still, she wasn't the small child who first ended up on the streets without a family or home. She could do better this time. She would survive no matter what.

"You're not alone this time," Flor said, as if reading her thoughts. "Just don't talk about dragons."

Sofia could only nod. She knew if she opened her mouth, she'd crack and she'd cry more and they didn't need to see her break down again. They needed her to smile and tell them she'd be okay. They'd be okay.

So that's what she did. And whether or not they believed her didn't matter as they sat together in the dim room, holding to each other until it became clear they'd fall asleep this way if they let themselves. So they rolled out their bedrolls, blew out the lantern, and curled up together. Flor and Sofia had slept like this when they'd been on the streets together, pressed against each other for warmth and protection. It had become habit by the time Javi joined them, simply slipping into the warmth without question. Even as they aged and came to the age that others might frown and think it inappropriate, they often slept like this. But it was never anything beyond the simple protection of having their family as close as possible and ready to chase away the ghosts of the night.

Yet, as the rhythms of their breathing lulled Sofia into sleep and the darkness swept over her, she dreamed of the dragons and death, and a loneliness so deep she felt she might drown in it.

CHAPTER TEN
FOX

The room reeked even after he'd cleaned up the mess, the wet pile of rags sitting in the corner, letting the smell fester. They hadn't come back for the rags or to retie his hands. His body ached from the fight and he could feel the subtle sting on his neck where her blade had broken skin, but he had more important things to think about.

He worked carefully in the dark, fingers aching as he twisted and pried. But his mind was elsewhere, haunted by the look in Sofia's eyes. He'd never seen someone so wild with anger and hate, and *toward* him, as if he'd personally murdered her loved ones. It made his own stomach turn with acid and heat. How dare she hate him when *they* were the ones responsible for the death of *his* loved ones? *His* family.

And if his gut could be trusted, there was more death coming and soon. The resistance was planning something. She'd asked about the prison and about the chief commander. For all the bombings they'd managed, the resistance had never gotten near the military quarter and Fox wasn't going to let that happen now.

He let out a curse as a spike of pain went through his finger, the edge of the metal bucket cutting into skin. He sucked on his thumb for a second, letting the salty taste of his own blood coat his tongue before he went back to work.

Sofia may have been mad, but her antics only aided in his escape. The man had thrown some rags at him to clean up the mess, but he hadn't bothered to look at the bucket. He hadn't noticed where the side had bent in, snapping the wire handle and leaving the thin bit of wire free to maneuver. It was difficult to bend, the metal cold and hard, but he was making progress, slowly straightening it into a small pick.

At least the pain in his fingers allowed him to direct his focus away from the aches across the rest of his body and thoughts of what the resistance was planning on the other side of the door.

HIS FINGERS WERE tingling and numb by the time he'd shaped the wire into a pick straight enough to fit into the keyhole. The worst part of the whole experience was that the moment he slipped the metal into the door, the small trace of light from the other side disappeared, leaving him fumbling in the dark trying to feel the inside mechanics. He'd never picked a lock before—it was something they discussed in basic training, but Fox had skipped the advanced courses when he'd been promoted early. He almost laughed at the idea that he might remain trapped here in enemy territory because he was so determined to rise up in the ranks as fast as possible. He didn't see the point of sitting in classrooms talking about defending their city when he could be out there *actually* doing it.

Every few minutes he had to take a break to wipe away the blood from his fingers and the wire to stop it from slipping in his grip. It was slow and frustrating work, but if there was one thing Fox was good at, it was sitting with frustration. He was used to feeling useless and helpless. He'd spent the last few cycles trying to run as far from that child version of himself as he could, but that persistent little boy would always be there.

And then it happened. He heard the click of something within the contraption, and the handle moved beneath his hand. For a moment, the air left his lungs and he held himself there, too afraid to move or make a sound. Even the flame on the other side of the door seemed to hold its position, waiting.

When he couldn't hold his breath any longer, he cracked the door wider, slowly as to not let the hinges give him away. But he needn't have worried. Only silence greeted him. The hallway beyond was empty.

Reluctant to lose the light from the single lantern hanging on the wall, he nonetheless stepped out of his cell and extinguished the flame. It would be easier to sneak around, but he hated the feel of the shadows settling onto his shoulders again. The air was colder than when he'd first arrived and the hallway remained still as he stood, muscles tense. It seemed that night had fallen. He just needed to make it out of here before anyone saw him.

He walked with a shuffling gait, the toes of his boots moving carefully across the ground with every step, not skimming hard enough to make a sound, but enough to avoid tripping over any imperfections. The tips of his fingers ran along the wall to his right, keeping him centered in the hall. Every turn he took required him to stop and listen for movement before rushing forward and blowing out the next lantern. Perhaps it was stupid to make a trail of darkness for someone to follow, but he felt safer wrapped in shadows. It was also the only reason he knew he wasn't walking in circles as he took each turn, waiting to see something familiar.

Yet, he nearly stumbled into the main cavern before he realized he'd made it to the entrance. The echoing whispers nearby were the only thing to warn him where he was before he could take the next turn. He stopped, heart thundering in his chest loud enough he feared he might be heard. But the clip of the voices didn't waver and no one screamed out to grab him. He peeked around the corner, staying low to the ground, only to see a small gathering of people speaking quietly around a fire. They were at the entrance of the cenote, the night sky with its star just visible through the trees and vines above.

It was only once he was crouched there, looking up at the ground so far above that Fox asked himself what he had been thinking. He could almost hear his father's voice in his mind, berating his stupidity. Of course the entrance would be guarded. He wasn't climbing out this way without being spotted.

The voices drifted over to him on the wind, and he shivered from more than the cold.

"She might be acting rashly at times, but she may have a point. If they keep executing the prisoners—"

"I know the risk, better than anyone, but I'm trying to protect as many as I can. If we go running into the city declaring war, too many of us will die."

"If we sneak in—"

"That soldier in there is just as likely to get us caught as help us sneak in."

"That's what knives are for."

"Torture won't earn loyalty."

"But information—"

"Perhaps."

"I vote we kill him and give the kingdom a taste of its own medicine."

He bit his tongue until it bled. He swallowed, ignoring the tang in his throat and backed away from the turn before he did something stupid like rush out with a bent wire as his only weapon. They were still talking, but he didn't need to hear more.

With a tight chest, he retraced his steps back to the tunnel from where he'd come, trying to plan as he moved. There had to be another way out of the base. They wouldn't have a single escape option in case of attack which meant one of these back tunnels exited out somewhere else. He just needed to find which one—in the dark—without being caught.

He didn't miss the light suddenly growing ahead, a lantern swinging in the dark, but without any other place to go, he was left standing there as it grew brighter, a deer waiting for the hunter's arrow.

"What in the depths?" the man let out a soft gasp as he turned the corner. His mouth opened, readying to let out a cry as Fox moved. Fox's hand found the man's throat before he could finish his intake of air, fingers wrapping tight to choke the scream off. The man's hands scrambled at his wrist, nails biting into skin, but Fox only pushed hard, the other man's head smacking against the wall with a thud. The lantern fell to the ground in a crash that had Fox's blood running cold and the tunnel was thrown into darkness. He used the moment of confusion to twist the man around and press his entire arm into his throat. He barely put up a fight as his body grew heavy.

The man couldn't even let out a final breathy curse as he slumped, dead against the ground. Not wanting to wait around and be caught with the body, Fox picked up the man, wincing a little at the weight as he moved the last two turns to the room he'd first escaped from. He pulled at the man's cloak and belt, fumbling in the dark until he had the belt strapped around his own waist, the weight of a dagger comforting at his side. The cloak was a few inches short, but it was heavy and warm as he hooked it around his neck.

He felt no guilt as he shoved the body into the cell and pushed the door closed again as best he could. Without the key to lock it, it didn't stay shut, but in the pitch black it was impossible to see the door was just slightly ajar. He didn't have time for perfection. He needed to find the tunnel that led out of here and get back to the city. The last thing he wanted was to still be here when the rebels out in the main cavern decided to kill him.

If he was fast enough, he might be able to bring back a team of guards to raid the cenote before they disappeared. Either way, he knew some faces and names now. He knew the edges of their plans. And he knew that they were going to regret capturing him.

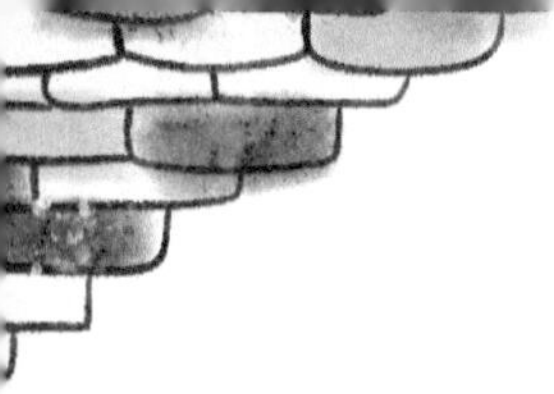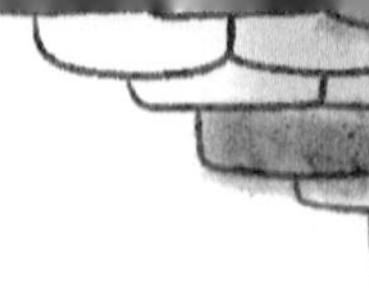

FOX

AGE 15

It was the fourteenth king who put into place laws against Drag-onborn possessing and reading books after it was discovered that written communication was used in the great uprising. While the utilization of crude symbols and numbers are now allowed for book-keeping, any form of written dragon-tongue is considered treason. All written communications between Dragonborn are immediately deemed suspect and cannot be withheld from inspection.

-The Laws and Rights of Suvi by Hurnica June

Fox couldn't help the startled jump as the young maid entered the library, footsteps so soft he only heard the squeak of the door on its hinges. He was holding his afternoon tea as he leaned over the book he was reading, warming his fingers against the chill of the cold season coming through the cracks between windowpanes.

He wasn't supposed to be reading in the library. He especially wasn't supposed to be reading the small fictional romance book he was leaning over, its pages so crisp it was clear he was one of the first to read it. Why it was even in their family library, he had no idea. Perhaps his mother had bought it before she'd married his father, who'd taught her quickly that reading for fun was a pointless endeavor and a waste of a woman's brain. Fox wasn't completely clear on whether he agreed with his father on that account, but he also couldn't help but enjoy *wasting* his brain occasionally when the weather was cold and the manor too empty and quiet. His father had been locked in his study with Chief Commander Harlow for the last two hours, so he thought it was as good a time as any to escape.

The squeak of the hinge, short and only loud because of the silence of the library, sent a wave of nausea through him and he jerked, eyes flying to the door. He expected to see the reddening face of his father, not the round face of a girl not much younger than him. Her eyes were wide and brown, skin tawny and cheeks freckled.

His eyes flickered away with disinterest, only to see the splatter of tea, drying along the edge of the book and onto the loose pages on the desk below.

"Shit!" He yelled the curse louder than he meant to as he stumbled back, placing the rest of his tea somewhere safe. Without much thought, he pressed his shirt into the pages, hoping to soak up the moisture. But his attempts were futile and the stain only seemed to grow and darken the longer he looked at it.

He could probably put the book back and his father would never notice the stains on the pages, but the stack of papers that he'd so carefully not touched on the desk had their own splatter of tea, the drops forming a beautiful pattern of his future pain. They were his father's documents, so there was no hiding the damage.

"Why did you sneak up on me like that?" he said, snapping at the girl. "What do you even want?"

"I'm supposed to clean—"

"Well, you've made a mess now."

She moved forward with a look of contrition, holding her rag like it might fix the problem better than his shirt. He couldn't stop the wave of anger that coursed through him and he grabbed her by the front of her dress.

"Are you stupid?"

"I'm s-sorry." She gave two bows, one after the other, as if they might help and erase the damage already done.

"What's going on in here?"

The sound of his father's voice sent an icy chill down his spine.

"Nothing," Fox said, taking a step away from the maid and trying to wipe his face of emotion.

His father's cold eyes took in the scene, glancing between him and the girl before moving on to the desk behind Fox. A hand on his shoulder pushed him to the side.

"I thought you were with the chief commander," Fox said, fumbling over the words. His father's eyes didn't leave the desk.

"I was. We had a very interesting conversation about you and a potential opening in the junior scouts. I am to find you to tell you about it."

Fox straightened his shoulders, trying to catch his father's eyes. "I would be glad to talk—"

"Tell me who is responsible for this mess."

Fox bit back the immediate response that the three drops of tea across the desk were hardly a mess, but he knew it would do no good. His father was a meticulous man who expected others to hold the same standards. The pens on the desk always perfectly arranged, his papers never out of order or crooked.

His father, with a look of distaste, picked up the book he had been reading, turning it to look at the cover.

"Is this what you were yelling at the maid about?"

"Yes."

"She was reading?"

Fox looked at the girl whose face had gone gray at the accusation. It was illegal for Dragonborn to read. She likely didn't know how to. Still, she didn't even open her mouth to argue, eyes pleading with Fox's own without words.

"Yes," he said, the words bitter on his tongue. "Though she was just flipping through the pages. I doubt she truly understood the words. She spilled the tea when I came in and found her.”

It was a ridiculous story, but his father didn’t question it. Perhaps they both wanted to convince themselves the lie was true.

“Well then,” his father said, carefully taking the book and papers and dropping them into the trash, “I expect you to punish her.”

Fox kept his eyes focused on his father, not wishing to see those of the maid. “I was going to fire her, sir.”

“You catch her engaged in treasonous activities, but you think firing her is the correct punishment?”

He thought he might have heard the sharp intake of breath from the maid, or perhaps it was his own. The room felt too hot and he had to fist his hand in his tunic to stop himself from pulling at his collar.

“As I said, I could tell she was only looking through the pages. I believe firing her and informing future employers of her laziness and clumsiness in her duties will be a fitting punishment. She’ll likely struggle to find employment in this quarter again.”

The silence stretched before his father finally nodded, a small smile stretching across his face. “I expect her to be marked for treason before you release her. Have her taken to the prison and then meet me in my office so we can discuss your promotion.”

Fox didn’t breathe again until the snap of his father’s footsteps faded into the distance. The maid was still standing, the only evidence that she understood what had happened in the shake of her hand as she held her rag with white knuckles. He focused on her hands, the red, dry skin along her knuckles and small enflamed cuts across her hands from cleaning. He did not look her in the eyes.

“Go downstairs and collect your last wages from Maria. If I see you again, I’ll send you to the prison for that brand.”

She turned, her hands no longer visible to him and rushed from the room before he could say more. He was relieved. He had nothing else he could say.

CHAPTER ELEVEN

FOX

He moved the opposite direction this time, away from the entry and the light, one hand dragging silently along the rough wall, keeping his direction in the dark. With every step, he was amazed at how far the tunnel went on. He was excited when the feel of the darkness changed and the wall on his left gave way to air. There was another tunnel here.

He stepped forward only to immediately regret the decision. The floor slanted downward and icy water closed over his boot. His toes went numb almost instantly even protected as they were, and he let out a curse that echoed in the darkness.

He didn't bother with a second step, stumbling back quickly to resume his journey down a different path. He turned down three more tunnels, all with the same problem before he finally found a dry one. It didn't solve the problem of his numb and aching toes, but he was all too glad for a change in his luck. He was still slow as he moved, all too aware the ground could slope at any moment, but he gained confidence with each dry step.

If anything, this path was slanting ever so slightly upward. After what felt like hours stumbling around in the blackness, he'd finally found what had to be a tunnel out. There were no doors along the wall that he could feel and the silence here was even more oppressive than the other halls, as if nothing but the worms had breathed this air in cycles. It had to lead somewhere and it was far from the rebels who wanted him dead.

He just needed to find the end before they noticed he was gone and came after him. His feet sped up automatically at the thought, the adrenaline of the last day pushing him through his exhaustion and hunger. His shoes had dried, but his toes still ached from the cold and his throat burned from lack of water. The thirst had only worsened when he'd tried some of the water back at the sunken tunnels. He'd spit it out, but not before the salty taste had dried his mouth out further. They had to have fresh water somewhere in the base, but he hadn't had time to search it out. It would be his first task once he came out of the tunnels.

He knew there had to be fresh water in the rainforest, even if it was rare. The land here didn't allow for rivers above ground, the greedy soil soaking up every rare drop of rain that fell from the sky. But the fresh water gathered into underground rivers and lakes. It was how the Dragonborn had survived before the king had created the filtration systems a couple centuries back. One of the bits of technology they'd brought to the Dragonborn who spit on them and called them evil in response for not cowing down to monsters.

Fox lost all track of time as he walked through the darkness, only aware of the ground beneath his feet and the cold air in his lungs. His eyes never adjusted to the pitch black, and even with the cloak, he started to shiver as the temperature dropped with each hour. He wondered if it was possible the tunnel led all the way to the northern mountains.

The icy peaks were near mythical despite being just over a week's journey from the city. When the Dereyans had supposedly defeated the dragons and won the tribal war, the king had wanted to expand Suvi's control farther into the Wueco forest and the mountains. Most of the Dragonborn tribes, too superstitious for their own good, had never ventured past the foothills. King Regold sent a handful of units to the mountains over the cycles, but no one ever came back. After a while, he gave up and focused back on protecting his city against the closer threat: rebel factions and tribes vying for power. As far as Fox knew, no one had been to the mountains in at least four generations. He didn't believe the Dragonborn stories that the mountains were haunted and humans couldn't cross into the snowy domain, but he still didn't want to be the first Dereyan to stumble into them unprepared.

Then again, if he was still stuck in this tunnel in a few days, he'd have bigger problems to worry about than mythical mountains—like water. His thirst gnawed at him. He could almost hear the sound of water rushing, like the ocean on a windy day. The fresh smell of icy air made his breath deepen and he almost smiled.

It took Fox several seconds to realize he wasn't going crazy or daydreaming. The air in the cramped tunnel had changed and he could almost smell the foliage of the rainforest. His footsteps picked up pace. He kept walking just long enough that he began to question his own instinct.

Then his hand hit something solid and cold in front of him. The tunnel had come to an end.

The stone felt as solid as the walls, but he refused to give up. He could smell fresh air, and no one digs a tunnel to nowhere, no matter how ignorant and blasphemous they were. Using all the strength he had left in him he pressed his weight against the stone and pushed.

Something shifted and scraped in the darkness. Giving himself only a short moment to breathe, he pushed again and the massive boulder that was set across the tunnel opening moved. A sliver of light scattered the darkness around him. He never thought he'd be so happy to see the wild rainforest. It took another dozen shoves before the opening was wide enough to allow him to squeeze through, stone cold against his shoulders as he finally fell from the underground tunnel.

The dirt was hard where he landed, without underbrush to break his fall. He couldn't stop himself from groaning as every bone in his body shuddered with the impact. He didn't move for a moment. He lay on his back, looking up at the swaying canopy of trees above him. They were taller than he'd ever seen before, and he had the same feeling of vertigo looking up as he'd had staring down from the eastern city wall for the first time as a boy. Looking back, he could barely see the tunnel he'd just come from, only a sliver of shadow in an outcrop of rocks from this side. If he hadn't just slipped through the crack, he'd assume it was simply a shadow, not an entrance.

After a few more breaths, he shifted carefully, taking in the aches across his body as he pushed himself up. He was bruised and weak and exhausted, but nothing was broken, and the cuts he'd received sometime last night were already clotted over and beginning to tighten into scabs. It was this thought that had his eyes searching the canopy, trying to read the sky beyond. It was daylight out, but as he took in the shadows around him, he realized it was likely almost sunset. He'd walked through the night and most of the next day. His absence would have been noticed by now.

And he had no idea where he was.

He definitely hadn't walked into the mountains, although the trees around him were unfamiliar and the ground here wilder than that around the city.

The shadows were lengthening with every second he spent standing still and he didn't know how far of a head start he had on any pursuers. But before he left, he had one more thing to do.

It took him a few minutes of searching before he found what he needed. One of the nearby trees had a single vine of black flowers twisting around it. The petals of each were furled tightly closed, only those closest to the forest floor beginning to loosen and open as night approached. He plucked one of these and peeled back the petals as he returned to the cave entrance. He smeared the flower's pistil across the gray stone in the symbol any king's man would recognize, happy to see the faintest glow as a shadow passed over it. The flower's job done, he discarded it before doing his best to push the boulder back over the entrance. He wasn't going to make it easy for anyone coming after him.

He also took a mental picture of the forest around him, trying to memorize the shape of the trees and the position of the stones. The flower's pollen would do the job of marking the opening, but he'd still need to find his way back to the spot if he intended to show his superiors. Something good would come of all of this. Perhaps his father would overlook his being captured if he brought them to the resistance's base.

Then again, his mind was getting away from him and his thoughts weren't focusing on the important pieces right now. Like the fact that he had no idea where he was, the sun had just about set, and he was still likely being chased. He needed to leave and find somewhere safe to get through the night. At least it would be harder for the others to find him in the dark.

He was grateful for the dry and hard-packed dirt on the forest floor, leaving behind little evidence of his footsteps as he moved. He didn't pay attention to what direction he was walking, not that he could have told without a view of the sun to lead him. Instead, he moved away from the tunnel, looking for a tree to climb. He doubted he'd be able to sleep perched on a branch, but he'd feel safer away from the ground and with the advantage over anything coming toward him.

But so far, the tall, towering trees with their wide trunks looked nearly impossible to climb. He kept an eye out for other rocky outcrops or low-lying plants that could hide him, desperate for anywhere he could find to stop moving. The forest was coming alive rapidly with the dusk, the black flowers glowing a dark purple as they bloomed and luminous green and red mushrooms peeking out from under dead underbrush.

It gave him light to walk by, but it also did nothing to help him feel hidden or safe. If anything, the subtle glow of the rainforest around him only made it possible to see all the slinking animals skittering around the ground. So far they'd kept their distance, but he didn't know how long that would last.

He was trying to push this thought from his mind when he heard a branch snap from the shadows to his left. His muscles froze, as if he might melt into the shadows himself if he were still enough. But then there was another snap, closer this time. He knew there was no hope in being invisible.

Someone—or something—had found him.

SOFIA

AGES 8 TO 10

The three types of dragons, while all born of the great mother Quelia, varied based on the areas in the realm they lived. The dragons of the sea were known for their bright white scales and pale blue feathers, which blended in with the ocean surf. The cenote dragons were a pale silver along their scales with deep blue feathers lining their spines and necks. Lastly, the mountain dragons, needing to navigate the rocky peaks were a dark silver and black in their scales with pale silver feathers. While every dragon was unique in their exact powers and strengths, the great mother blessed the dragons with the ability to manipulate the waters of Wueco, from the sea and rivers to the water in the very air. There were even accounts of dragons able to pull the energy from the moon and stars themselves, creating fire in the sky and bringing it crashing down onto the earth.

-In Praise of Dragons and Monsters by Maria Nunes

The day after Sofia was whipped for her fight defending Mina, Ms. Garcia pulled her off latrine duty completely. She was shown around the second floor of the manor and handed a bucket of caustic liquid and strips of fabric made of a nicer material than the dress she wore. Ms. Garcia decided that hiding her away alone in empty rooms was a safer option than trying to get her to cooperate with the other staff members. Sofia learned to scrub, shine, and polish, and new muscles were left aching at night as her shoulders and forearms continued to grow and strengthen.

Her duties left her with an independence that she savored and a silence she thrived in. There was no partner to watch her, no Liza to tell her she was doing it wrong, and no Mina to worry over. As long as her rooms along the second floor were scrubbed clean by the end of the day, Sofia was given her coins and left to run home. And it was this independence that led Sofia to a new type of freedom within her small world.

The library was on the second floor, a large room tucked behind two heavy mahogany doors with intricate carvings of beasts that were only whispered about at night. *Dragons.* But it was the wonders behind these doors that truly stole Sofia's attention. She'd seen a few books scattered throughout the house or glimpsed in the doors of Dereyan homes, but behind those heavy doors was a world worth of books.

They lined every wall. Shelves stretched across the room holding even more books, creating secret nooks and shadowy corners. The shelves seemed to tower over her, mythical creatures in and of themselves that might swoop down and eat her. The first few days of cleaning in the room, she tiptoed cautiously around, ready to flee if need be, but over time she became more comfortable with the feel of the rag sliding across the wood shelves, and she'd take a moment to run her fingers along the leather and paper of the books. Some spines were drawn with gold and others worn down to nothing but a bit of torn parchment. Some had symbols that she only vaguely recognized from the few times she'd seen the king's tongue written down. Others were written in symbols she recognized with a thrill from a single time when she was five cycles old.

She'd found an old children's book tucked at the bottom of her mother's trunk, nearly falling apart with age. She had begged her mother to read it to her, but her mother had only gone pale and given her an hour lecture about privacy and responsibility. She'd burned the book in their hearth in front of Sofia that night, face pale and eyes watery, but lips pressed in a firm line.

It had been written in dragon-tongue. The king had never been able to eradicate the language completely, too many Dragonborn unable to pick up the smooth consonants of the king's tongue. He'd ordered all writings in the original language turned over to the crown and destroyed. Perhaps it hadn't been purposeful; it made it all the more easy to ban Dragonborn's reading and writing a few cycles later. And over the cycles, generation by generation, even the spoken language was dying—fewer and fewer Dragonborn parents teaching it to their children, preferring they learn the king's tongue to better blend into society.

But Sofia craved knowledge. She craved to know what secrets the books whispered in their pages, tucked between the covers. Her mother's book hadn't just been the small scratched symbols. There had been beautifully painted landscapes and colorful animals Sofia couldn't have dreamed up. Would these books look the same?

It took her two weeks to gain the courage to slip the first book off the shelf and open its pages. It was thick and heavy and had the king's tongue written across the spine. She was disappointed to see the black and white pages with not even a single picture amongst the small symbols. But then she found another book, thinner and covered in colorful art and only the occasional letter. The pictures were of various trees, and after a while she understood what symbols went together to say *tree*. And then leaf. And bark. Her world expanded, blooming like the midnight flowers that glowed at sundown.

Each day, as she wiped the dust from the library shelves and shined the windows until the sun filtered through gleaming and bright, she looked at the spines of the books and learned. She found the small stack of children's books in the corner, seemingly forgotten, and she looked until she understood. She read. She devoured.

When she was done with the children's books, memorizing the tales of the Dereyans—with their trolls and goblins that only the king and his men could defeat—she moved on to the other books. She found those without pictures and those written by *her* people, translated into the tongue of the king. Stories of Dragonborn men and women who fought the creatures of the rainforest, men who protected their families and their tribes, women who could defeat the darkest of faeries. And for the first time, she saw all of the things her parents only ever whispered about behind closed doors.

ONCE SHE'D MEMORIZED every faerytale story she could get her hands on, Sofia moved to books on medicine and hunting and geography. The Dereyans, despite their distaste for the nature of Wueco, had cataloged much of the land, including the plants and animals that resided just outside the wall. It was in these books she learned about shifters, *ciervados*, and weeping willows. They were the things out of her faerytales, but they were written down and measured out on these pages like a scientific study. They were written on the same pages as drawings of mushrooms labeling which were poisonous and which tasted best cooked in oil.

She might have gone to her parents and asked the questions that spun through her mind had this been a normal world where reading was encouraged instead of punished. Instead, she could only absorb the words on the pages, trying to understand everything.

Perhaps it was why she didn't notice when the library lock clicked and the door opened with the soft woosh of air. The moment the heel of a well-polished boot hit the wood floor in front of her, though, her head snapped up, eyes wide and stomach dropping with dread.

The chief commander—head of the king's army and master of the house—towered above, looking down at the book in her hands and the words scrawled across the pages. She was on a chapter detailing the specific trees that made up the mangroves southwest of the city.

Maybe if the pages she was looking at had had some drawings across their faces, she could have gotten away with punishment for her sloth. But when her eyes met his above the pages, staring into their black depths, she knew that he knew. She had been reading—a charge worthy of losing her job and her freedom.

Her entire body tensed up, waiting for the blow that was sure to come. She swore she saw the twitch of his fingers against his thigh loosening and clenching as the two of them stared at each other in silence.

But he didn't lash out. Instead, his hand reached forward, palm up and she followed his silent instructions, placing the book in his grip before she stood, head bowed.

"Come with me," he said, voice as cold as his eyes. She followed, eyes tracking his feet as she walked. She expected him to bring her to the kitchens where Ms. Garcia would dole out her punishment. Or he'd just throw her into the prison himself. But they went down the hall a few paces. He waved her in when she hesitated outside his office door. She looked up again, meeting his eyes but unable to understand what he was asking of her. His face was blank and he only pushed her, a hand on her shoulder until she was forced to step into the room.

"Sit," he said, moving around his desk and easing himself into his large chair. She took the only chair on the other side of the desk, an ornately carved thing that left her feet dangling several inches from the ground. The cushion was soft and she sank into it before she made her muscles go rigid. "What's your name?"

She knew from faerytales that giving one's name was a risky thing—an act of trust and an exchange of power. But she didn't have a choice.

"Sofia, sir." Her eyes were tracing the wood grain of the desk. She wondered if someone could tell what type of tree the wood came from by the pattern.

"Who taught you how to read?"

Her eyes flew up and met his. She knew the question behind that one and quickly shook her head.

"No one, sir. I taught myself. My parents don't know."

"You taught yourself how to read?"

"Yes, sir. I swear it."

"How old are you?" He was examining her like a specimen.

"Ten, sir."

"And do you know the punishment for being caught reading?"

Despite the shake in her hands, she held his eyes as she spoke the words. "The labor farms."

He nodded, giving her a look somewhere between approval and pride. It made her stomach twist.

"How would you like to continue working here? To not go to the farms?"

Her eyes widened and her jaw dropped before she could control her face.

"I won't even punish your parents for allowing your crimes." He said the words warmly, as if they weren't part threat. She dug her nails into the skin of her wrist, picking at the skin there as she tried to pull her face into something neutral. "I need an assistant. Someone to help me with copying letters, tracking my schedule, and cataloging my books."

She stared blankly, not understanding how his statement applied to her but he was staring expectantly, a pale eyebrow raised in question.

"Me?"

"If you're stupid, tell me now."

"No, sir. Yes, I can do that."

He leaned back, nodding and still inspecting her more than looking at her. "Good, then all we need to do is talk about punishment."

Her stomach dropped. "Punishment?"

"I can't let you get away with your crimes without any form of punishment."

"Sir?" She hated how small her voice sounded.

"A finger, I think," he said, nodding to himself. "A finger seems a fair price to pay."

And perhaps it was.

But as Sofia walked home that night, her hand throbbing beneath the bandage, she wondered if it would be the last punishment she faced for daring to think.

CHAPTER TWELVE

SOFIA

The stub of Sofia's finger was aching when she woke, heart thumping. She had opened her eyes the moment before the axe that had taken her finger hit the wood table, but she still heard the crash shuddering through her body. It was so visceral that as she laid there in the dark, her ears strained to hear it. But the only sound was the soft hum of Flor's and Javi's breathing on her right. The room was cold, the blankets they had been sharing wrapped mostly around Flor at this point.

Sofia rolled over in the dark, burrowing her back closer to Javi and trying to steal back some of the blankets. The darkness was near complete, even the lantern outside not leaking its light beneath the door. Some days she might have found the shadows comforting. It never got dark in Suvi, the streets always lit with gas lamps or torches and the hall at the inn always lined with lanterns even at midnight. Darkness was something unknown in the city, but in the rainforest it was at home.

Yet, tonight, even the soft shadows of night couldn't calm her thudding heart. Thoughts fluttered through her mind like birds flittering and never settling. It wasn't until she felt the wet trickle of blood on her finger that she realized she'd been picking at her skin. She clenched her hands into fists, trying to distract herself from the urge to pick more.

She wasn't sure how long she laid in the dark, trying to even out her breathing as if she might summon sleep. Eventually, when she caught herself picking at the skin along her nails again, she moved. The ground was cold beneath her as she carefully rolled over, disentangling herself from the blanket and sleeping pads. Javi was a light sleeper and the last thing she wanted was to talk to either him or Flor right now. She grabbed her sandals and a shawl, wrapping it around her shoulders before she silently left the room and crept into the hall. She was wearing thin knit leggings and the chill in the air slipped through the fabric with ease. It was only after she had closed the door that she recognized the hall was as dark as the room had been, the lantern along the wall blown out.

She shivered in the cold hallway, trying to decide her next steps. There were matches inside the room she could go grab, but the chances of waking the other two wasn't worth it. The darkness was familiar to her and there were lanterns elsewhere. So after a few moments, she only shrugged and turned left, hoping to find a lit lantern and somewhere to sit with the warmth of a fire.

Yet at the next turn, she was still faced with darkness. There were usually two lanterns in this hall. One going out was common, three at the same time was unusual. Her stomach churned and her muscles tensed as she stood frozen, staring into the darkness. Something was wrong and she knew it like she knew the cadence of Javi's and Flor's breaths and the smell of the rainforest after the first season's rain.

Her mother used to say she was dragon-touched. She used it as an insult when she thought Sofia was daydreaming too much or dwelling on faerytales. But even when she was younger, she understood her mother just said it when she couldn't explain something Sofia *knew*.

She moved swiftly in the darkness, no hesitation in her steps, mentally checking through the roster of the other rebels staying in the cenote until she was relatively sure which room was empty. She still opened the door slowly, listening for the sound of breathing. When only silence met her, she ducked in quickly and grabbed the matches that sat on the shelf in every bedroom.

She pulled down the first lantern she found, relighting it before moving decisively toward Ocon's cell. Her hand reached for her belt automatically only to find her waist empty. She was still wearing her sleeping clothes, a shawl her only armor. The lantern only made the shadows around her darker as she moved forward, weaponless but determined. If something had happened, she needed to know now before she went running for help.

Her hand trembled as she pushed open the door. It had been closed but not latched, only deepening her dread as she strained to peer into the dark room. As her eyes adjusted and she saw the body lying on the floor, recognizing immediately the tight curls of Emilio. He had only been recruited a few blinks before after his mother had been killed, caught up in the witch hunt for the resistance. And now he was lying dead, discarded in Ocon's cell like the garbage the crown saw their people as.

Beside him, she saw the crushed bucket, the wire handle gone and she knew—this had been her fault. She'd broken the bucket. She'd let Ocon escape and now Emilio was lying dead. Jaw clenched tightly, she checked Emilio for weapons and found only a small blade tucked in the ankle of his boot. His weapons belt was gone. Ocon was running around with a dagger now, too.

As she stepped into the hall and looked around, she could hear Micael's voice in her mind.

Tell someone so we can put together a search party.

And Sofia was all too aware that search party wouldn't include her. This was just a further example of how she'd failed the resistance. She would be sent back to Suvi and maybe in a blink or two they'd remember she existed. Or perhaps they'd leave her there forever, rotting away in the gutters where she belonged.

Even with that image in her mind, she did almost turn down the hall to call out to Micael and the others. She wanted to play the perfect, loyal rebel. But before she could move more than a few yards down the hall, she saw the smeared footsteps in the dirt floor headed into the shadowed darkness behind her. He'd wandered deeper into the cenote toward the back exits. How long ago had he left? How much of a head start would he have by the time they put together a search party?

If she went after him now—if she caught him and brought him back for Micael alive and well, would that be enough to show her loyalty? If she could fix her mistake...

And then she was moving, down the hall toward the small storage room where they kept the weapons and supplies. She grabbed a small bag, packing away a flint, some rope, and a borrowed bow and quiver, not wanting to risk waking Javi by going back to the room to get her own. She switched out her lantern for a torch, easier to carry through the tunnels, and followed the smudges across the floor. Hunting a human wasn't any different than hunting an animal.

Her eyes stayed focused on the ground as she walked, as fast as she could without losing his trail. At times the tunnel floor became too compact to track the marks, but eventually they'd appear a little farther down. Each branch of the tunnel held another set of steps, moving forward until they hit the water and then retracting. Sofia couldn't stop the chuckle that slipped out as she noticed the third tunnel he had attempted to move down before turning back. He was trying to find a dry exit, which meant he was headed to the north-most tunnel that wound for miles and miles into the rainforest. All three of the other tunnels he had passed led almost immediately out of the cenote, though they took a bit of swimming. Anyone who knew the rainforest would have known this, but the king-worshippers had never bothered to hold on to such knowledge. They simply bent what they could to their will and built a wall to hide from the rest.

It was a few hours into her journey when she again questioned if she should have stopped to get help. She knew that even if Ocon only had an hour head start, it would be a while before she was able to catch up with him. The fact that she hadn't yet spoke to either an escape early in the night or the fact that he was being smart and running fast. But she'd catch up eventually. Once he was out of the tunnel, he'd have to figure out what direction to go and he'd be moving slowly again. She had seen him in the rainforest before and it didn't speak of stealth or even comfort. But she also knew that it would be half a day or more before she came back to the base with Ocon. Micael would notice them both gone, but what would he think? Would he assume she'd broken with the resistance and kidnapped him for her own gains? She didn't want to dwell on the rumors that might spread in her absence.

It would be worth it, though, to see the look on Ocon's face when she caught up to him, and the look on Micael's face when she walked back in with him alive and mostly uninjured—depending on her mood when she found him.

She was only a little surprised to find the boulder at the end of the tunnel closed over. But the fresh scuff marks all around the area made it clear that someone had been here and recently. She smirked to see the wedge untouched and still hanging along the wall to the right. He had apparently chosen to push the entire boulder over himself. Although, she also begrudgingly admitted to herself it was an impressive feat for a single man. His muscles weren't just for show.

Even with her height and strength, she knew there was no way she was moving the boulder alone. She grabbed the wedge off the wall and rammed it into the crevice between boulder and wall as hard as she could. The stone gave a groan as she flung her weight against the length of the wedge. Ever so slowly, the stone moved, a small opening appearing along the edge.

The moment it was large enough to squeeze through, she dropped the wedge, not bothering to rehang it. It was dark beyond the cave— already night again—but she put the torch out and tucked it away in her bag, not wanting to draw more attention than necessary once she was out in the rainforest.

She'd never been down the tunnel, nor had she been to this part of the rainforest before. She knew she was on the edge of what was considered Dragonborn territory back before the tribes war had destroyed everything. But the tunnel itself had been created only for the utmost emergencies and no one in her generation had ever had need to use it. Although she couldn't see the sky, the night-blooming flowers were only just unfurling. Sunset couldn't have been too long ago.

She was already breathing heavily from her trek and her stomach was reminding her that she hadn't grabbed any food to pack in her meager supplies and her last meal had been dinner the night before. But she still had to move. She had a fox to hunt.

Before she started her tracking, she found a luzia mushroom beneath the dead leaves surrounding a ceiba tree and plucked it from the ground. The cap was the size of her hand and let out a bright, nearly white glow even after it was disconnected from its root system.

It didn't take long to find Ocon's footsteps in the dirt, heading out into the rainforest. They were faint, but the markings were distinct compared to any other animal. She probably shouldn't have been surprised to see the haphazard path they took north of the tunnel. He wasn't even trying to walk in the right direction. If it was anyone else, she might have thought he knew something she didn't, but she wouldn't give him that benefit. She could only assume he was as unfamiliar with this part of the forest as she was and with none of the instincts.

She followed the trail. The light of the mushroom in her hands was just starting to fade when she heard the distinct sound of life nearby. It might have been an animal hunting in the dark, but a moment later she heard the sound of a human cursing and knew she had found who she was looking for. She slipped the bow from over her head and balanced a single arrow in her hand before moving forward at a clip. She wasn't going to let Ocon get away this time. She was going to prove Micael was wrong about her usefulness to the resistance.

CHAPTER THIRTEEN

FOX

Fox pulled the dagger from his belt, testing the weight of it in his hand. It was smaller than he preferred and he recognized with a small sneer it wasn't even steel, but iron, but it would have to do. He could only hope is was only a harmless monkey or frightened deer lurking in the shadows.

He squinted into the darkness, trying to make out the shadow slinking toward him. He was so focused on the subtle movement, that it wasn't until someone gripped his arm from the side that he realized the shadow in front of him wasn't alone. He pulled back, wrenching his arm free as he swung around to look. It was man, at least a foot taller than him with shoulders broad enough to threaten a jaguar. White teeth flashed in the dark, a smile like a wolf's.

Fox stumbled back, not caring if his terror was evident in his face, but he only made it two steps before he hit the solid barrier of a muscled body behind him. The second man was bare-chested and he could feel the heat of his skin through his stolen cloak. Fox pushed himself upright, trying to keep his chin high. Three towering figures formed a circle around where he stood. And they weren't just shirtless, but naked. Their bodies were chiseled from marble and shone in the night, as if their very blood glowed beneath their skin. There was something about their bare bodies, painted with scars, that made them all the more intimidating. He'd never considered himself a short person until this moment as he tried his best not to quake under their glares. The small dagger in his hand felt all the more ineffectual.

A nervous laugh bubbled up and he gave a tight smile, letting his arm fall loose, even as he tightened his grip on the weapon.

"Sorry about that, gentlemen. I thought you were a wild animal."

The man directly in front of him let out a gravelly laugh that made Fox's stomach twist tighter. They were standing preternaturally still, their chests not even showing signs of breathing. He tried to keep his eyes focused on their faces, not wanting to be caught looking lower.

"Anyway, I'll just be on my way," Fox said, voice creeping higher.

He stepped to the right, trying to move through the gap between them. The men closed in immediately and he froze, feeling his mouth go dry.

"What's a little boy like you doing out here all alone?" The man's breath tickled across the back of his neck as he spoke, and Fox shivered. He was starting to regret that the sound hadn't been a jaguar or even the Dragonborn bitch that had initially captured him. These men were looking at him like they wanted to eat him and they were big enough to have a chance.

"I just was heading back to the city," he said, not making the mistake of taking a step this time. They were closing in on him, somehow nearing without moving. The blade was still tight in his hand and their nakedness was only one less layer between him and their most important arteries.

"The city, he says," the tallest said, sneering. "We've caught a king's man did we?"

Fox didn't like the way that word rolled off his tongue, like the dirtiest insult he could speak. Were these men with the resistance? He hadn't remembered any of his captors towering nearly so high, but who else could hold such disgust for Suvi and its people? He was beginning to think he wouldn't be able to talk his way out of this. His grip tightened on the dagger, cold iron biting into his hand, as he brought forth his father's lessons in war. *Hit first.*

So he did.

He brought the dagger up hard and fast, striking toward the largest man's groin. It was an underhanded move that his father would have scorned, but it did the job. The curse and groan the man let out told Fox everything he needed to know as the blade made contact with skin and he quickly turned, moving to strike the next man. Before he had a chance, a large arm came around his neck, pressing him back into the body of the man behind him. He gasped uselessly against the grip, the pressure against his throat making it impossible to breathe. He swung the dagger back trying to strike the man somewhere it might hurt. But the third man was already on him, wrenching the blade from his grasp with little effort and tossing it aside.

Hands now empty, he scrabbled to loosen the arm across his neck, nails biting into the man's skin. The giant man let out a grunt behind Fox, but didn't loosen his hold. It was like fighting a stone wall. Fox's vision was beginning to blacken around the edges. In a last desperate attempt to dislodge the man from his back, he bent his neck forward with all his strength, opened his mouth and bit down hard. He didn't let up until he tasted blood and the man shoved him away with a cry of anger.

"The human bites!" he said. It might have been more comforting if the words hadn't been tinged with laughter.

Fox scrambled forward, grabbing a stick from the ground, barely wider than his wrist. It broke on the first swing as he hit one man across the leg and the beast only laughed as the wood splintered against his flesh, drawing blood.

Fox stepped back, taking a breath as the two men in front of him only stood, smirking. They didn't bother to attack—their confidence sending icy dread down his spine. He turned, but the third man had disappeared into the shadows.

"I don't want trouble," he said. "Leave me be and the king's men won't bother you. I didn't end up out here willingly."

"Sorry, pretty boy," the man on the right said, his dark hair falling into his eyes as he tilted his head in thought, "but you're just too good a trophy to leave behind." His smile was all teeth, glinting too sharp to be natural.

Fox didn't think this time, lunging forward fists first toward the closer of the men—the one that had just called him pretty boy. He might not have a weapon, but he knew how to throw a punch. His father had ensured that early on.

Then again, the moment his fist connected with the side of the man, he was beginning to question if he was even fighting humans. A groan of pain slipped from his lips as he brought his fist back into his own chest. The man's side was carved of stone.

"Who the hell are you people?" he asked, not quite expecting an answer.

"Oh, I think it'll be more fun for you to find out," the other said, stepping forward with a grin. His arm moved faster than should have been possible for a man his size.

A fist crashed down across Fox's face and the shadows went black.

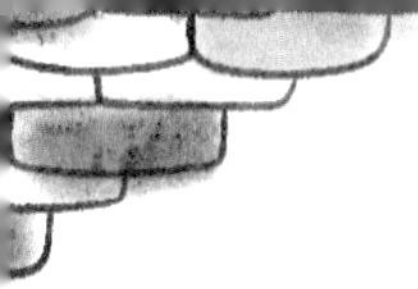
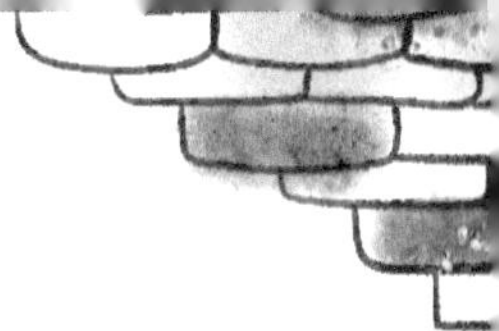

FOX

AGE 14

The first recorded attack from the dragons was in the 296th sun cycle of the kings. Without provocation, a sea dragon caused an enormous swell that towered over the king's fleet, sinking seven boats before it was killed by Major Jun Nicolas. While this was the first attack to be placed on record by the king's scribes, the incident led to a wave of reports from around Wueco of dragons being found responsible for human deaths.

-The Legacy of the Kings: A History of Wueco's Creation by Francis Knoll

"Get your ass up and keep going!" Arik's voice was a loud bark above where Fox lay in the mud, knees sharp with pain and ankle throbbing to the beat of his heart. He didn't move immediately, trying to swallow back the nausea in his stomach, and before he managed, Arik sent a swift kick to his side. Not hard enough to break anything, but enough to knock the wind from his lungs.

Miserable at the idea of another kick, he forced himself up from the

ground, ignoring the mud squelching through his fingers and the sharp stab that radiated thorough his ankle the moment he put his weight on it.

"Go, Boy! You have two more laps before you're done."

He didn't look back at Arik as he moved, more a wobbly limp than a run. He bounced on his left foot, taking the weight of his body hard on his right instead. The jarring motion did nothing to soothe the ache in his knees, but it was easier to ignore than what was becoming abundantly clear was a sprained or broken ankle. He could only breathe out sharply through his nose, focusing on each painful step toward the goal. He would get stronger. He would be better. He would be the soldier his brother had wanted to be.

It was a slow and arduous process, with the trainer continuing to yell and berate him for being too slow despite running through the pain. But at last, he crossed the line and let himself fall back onto the ground, rolling to look up at the sky. He was only somewhat annoyed to see Arik leaning over him a moment later. His wrinkled face was twisted in a scowl, his yellow teeth visible between cracked lips. Fox wondered if his face was naturally such a vibrant shade of red or if the man was so perpetually irate his skin had assumed the hue permanently.

"That was pathetic, even for you. You father will hear about this, so be prepared to do better tomorrow."

Fox clenched his jaw, biting back any response that would only bring down Arik or his father's wrath harder.

But he also needed to say something. "My ankle is sprained."

"You twisted it because you weren't paying attention to where you were going. Get used to pain if you plan on making it in the king's army."

With that, the trainer turned on his heels and stalked away, clearly annoyed with how much energy he'd already expended on Fox's behalf that morning. The sun was higher in the sky than normal and he knew he'd gone over in his training, likely in part because of the fall. He'd been working with Arik for blinks now and he didn't feel like he was getting any better. His arms were still scrawny and weak compared to what his brother's had been, and his sword fighting skills were beyond pathetic, as Arik was always happy to point out.

When his brother was his age, he'd already been fighting in the betting circles, winning the majority of his melees and making their father proud. His father had barely taken the time to stop by Fox's training to see how he was doing.

He kept his head down, not wanting to see the look of the servants as he passed by them. It was usually a combination of disgust and pity, both of which made his stomach twist in rage and shame. It wasn't until he heard the sound of heels clicking on the stone floor behind him that his head whipped up and his eyes darted around in search of the person he knew was there.

Mother was coming down the hall, a few doors away, long strides catching up to him quickly.

"My Little Fox," she said, kneeling down before him. Her face was full of concern and her eyes searched his face and body, registering all of his wounds. "What happened?"

He bit his lip, pushing back the burning behind his eyes. "Nothing, Mother."

"Your ankle is swollen and your face looks like you got into a fight with a pile of rocks. If this was Arik's version of training, I'm going to have a talk with him."

Her fingers smoothed back a strand of the pale hair that brushed against his forehead and he saw the mud on the tips of her fingers when they pulled away.

"Mother—" he started, but a second sound of footsteps stopped the words cold in his mouth. Over his mother's shoulder, he could see his father approaching down the hallway, the cane more an accessory in his hands today than an aid. He'd never let his knee pain stop him from fighting and working hard, as he often reminded Fox. Right now, his eyes were burning with something akin to pride.

Fox stood up straighter, pushing his mother away with a pinched frown.

"I'm fine, Mother. I don't need to be coddled."

He saw the flutter of her hands as she stopped herself from moving to grab him once more and he was glad for it. His father was upon him, a large hand landing across Mother's shoulder. He ignored the smallest of flinches from his mother, choosing instead to focus on his father's face and the rare hint of a smile he saw there.

"I heard from Arik you were complaining about a sprained ankle. I expected to find you pouting in the kitchens."

Fox's shoulders pulled back automatically. "I just needed to walk it off." He ignored the throb that shuddered from his ankle as if reacting to the comment.

His father's hand fell heavy on his shoulder. His fingers squeezed in something like comfort, but it only forced Fox to bite his tongue as the pressure sent another wave of pain and nausea crashing through him.

"Perhaps there's hope for you yet."

And with those parting words he left, not even looking back at his wife whose lips were pinched in a frown, the wrinkles at the corners of her eyes deeply set as she studied Fox.

Fox moved before she could breathe out a word, biting his tongue through the pain in his ankle to stop himself from limping. Ocons didn't limp.

CHAPTER FOURTEEN

SOFIA

Sofia crouched low to the ground as she moved, sliding between the shadows on silent feet. She was the hunter once more, tracking her prey. If she was lucky, she'd have Ocon back by the end of the day and she might convince Micael to forget these last few days.

She peeked around a small knoll overlooking a small ravine beyond. She'd expected Ocon and there he was. What she hadn't expected were the two large men towering over him, the king's man quaking beneath their glare. She didn't bother biting back the smirk that stretched across her face. There was no one there to judge her.

She was tempted to leave Ocon behind. The men looked like they were ready to eat him right then and there, and she doubted they'd be any friendlier to her. They weren't king's men or from Suvi, which meant they were from the tribes, likely shapeshifters if the power they were radiating said anything. The few tribes she knew that lived in these woods might have never attacked the resistance outright, but they'd made it clear anytime they crossed paths that they didn't want any part of the trouble those from Suvi brought.

But Ocon was no use to her or the others dead. Without him, Dia and every other Dragonborn left in the king's prison would be killed.

Sofia had the high ground, but night had fully settled over the forest and the shadows were deep and long. Her eyes were nothing compared to a shifter's even in their human form. She wouldn't be able to sneak up on them.

The air was cold as she crouched, motionless and watching. Ocon had moved on from talking to punching and his attempts only seemed to humor the men. But it gave Sofia a chance to see how they fought. They moved like large predators from the ripple of their shoulder muscles to the bend in their knees. They fought with brute strength and speed, but their moves weren't graceful or practiced. These shapeshifters hadn't trained for strategy. Muscular men never did.

She slunk slowly, skimming a circle around the ravine. They wouldn't want to leave their prisoner alone. So if she could lure one of them away and separate them, she might have a fighting chance. She wasn't going to go crawling back to the resistance to explain how she'd let Ocon escape and then watched him get himself killed out here.

One of the trees she passed by had branches low enough to the ground to give her a foothold. She could just make out the two shapeshifters grappling with Ocon, toying with him. She placed her foot on the lowest branch before she became aware that she wasn't alone. The sound of low breathing was coming from behind her, even as she watched the two shapeshifters below. With her own breath stuck in her chest, she turned slowly. A wolf stood a few feet away, mouth open and panting as saliva dripped from gleaming white teeth. Had he been standing only a few feet closer, his head would have nudged her chest. His paws were the size of her own hands.

There were three of them, and they weren't just shapeshifters, they were *wolf*shifters.

The wolf let out a low snarl as her hand twitched toward her dagger and she pulled it back, palms wide.

"I didn't come to cause trouble," she said, hoping the creature understood dragon-tongue. She repeated the words in the king's tongue just in case, hoping one of them would register with the shifter. The wolf blinked, yellow eyes not moving from her face, but his head tilt told her he had understood her words, at least in part. She noticed the matted tangle of his fur and wondered if the wet spots were dew or blood.

She counted in her head and sent a prayer to the dragons. And then she moved. One hand reached for her bow at the same moment her other pulled an arrow from her quiver. She had the arrow pulled and aimed in less than two seconds. But even that didn't matter because one moment the wolf was springing forward, and the next a naked man towered over her, smile pulled back in the same feral grin.

"Humans always cause trouble."

"Please—"

She started, but before she had the words out, he lunged. She let the arrow fly, but it only grazed his arm as he dodged sideways and bowled straight into her. The bow nearly snapped in her grasp as she was thrown to the ground. The air left her lungs, and she could only gag in silent pain as the shifter brought her head down again onto the hard forest floor. She didn't know if it was the ground or her skull that cracked through the black night, but the world split in two and then there was nothing.

SOFIA

AGE 11

What my colleague Dr. Viona continues to ignore in his argument toward assimilation is the Dragonborn's genetic weaknesses which make it nearly impossible to truly learn the king's ways. Research across the sea in Glosshire has shown that certain individuals are inherently unable to learn at the same capacity as others. The Dragonborn's inability to learn the king's tongue and their lack of interest in reading are simply a few examples of this inadequacy.

-Elna F. Bello, Assimilation or Elimination: A Philosophical Debate

The first week he taught her writing.

He forced her to spend hours at the small table set in the corner of his office, copying the same words over and over again until he approved of the slant of her letters. It was easier than learning to read had been, but by noon every day her hand was aching and she'd gained new calluses along her fingers and palm. But the chief commander didn't care how much her hand was cramping or if her eyes hurt from focusing. Once he'd eaten his lunch, they'd move on to her reading letters out to him while he took notes and tracked numbers she didn't understand.

She was lucky the days he didn't eat as much of his lunch. By the late afternoon, when he'd leave to go meet with his second-in-command, she'd take a break from copying the letters he'd assigned her and sneak the cold food off his plate. It had become clear after the first few days that he didn't realize Sofia actually needed to eat. The days he finished his food or the maid came early to cart it away, Sofia would be left hungry until she made it home for the night.

She savored the hours he was gone, when she didn't need to keep her expression neutral and tongue bit. She quite enjoyed telling the small statues he had lining his personal bookshelves how little she liked him and what she'd say to him if it wouldn't get her killed.

He had a number of books on the shelf of his office, though the spines indicated they'd be of little interest to Sofia. The volumes were dry histories of trade, descriptions of wars and battles in countries she'd never heard of, and the occasional guide on wildlife in the area that Sofia had already memorized during her time in the library. She hadn't been allowed near the library since she'd been caught, and she doubted the chief commander would leave any books of interest lying around for her, so she plucked out some of the most interesting-looking books, reading and rereading them any chance she could.

Even the war records had their fascinating moments, as she learned of a creature in countries across the sea that humans sat on and rode into battle. She found the idea of working with an animal both intriguing and horrifying when she thought of them being killed. It didn't seem the creatures had any voice in the matter. At least there were no records of their negotiations with the humans.

Her parents didn't know of her new position and they wouldn't find out from her. The chief commander hadn't outright told her that what she was doing was a secret, but it was clear every time he swiped the papers off her table before allowing the maid in that he was hiding their activities. She guessed that even for someone of his station, teaching a Dragonborn to read and write would be frowned upon.

So she remained his secret and she was left wondering what the rest of the staff thought about the young girl locked in the chief commander's office every day.

A HARD SLAP fell across her face and she flinched back, the letter she'd been drawing ending in a long scratch across the page.

"Stop daydreaming and go faster. I could have copied the entire page by now."

She refocused her thoughts on the parchment, ignoring the burning of her cheek as she attempted to make the best of the smeared ink. Despite it being his fault, she knew he would only blame her for it. His favorite form of motivation was either slapping her and pointing out how stupid Dragonborn were, as if she weren't *helping him.*

She worked, biting the inside of her cheek, focusing her mind on the pain, allowing her face to remain neutral. He hated when she showed her emotions, perhaps reminding him too much of her humanity. When he finally left for his afternoon meetings, the pages were completed and the inside of her cheek was bleeding freely. She swallowed the iron tang down, expressionless.

He left her with a small stack of charts to transcribe and organize, which she left sitting untouched on the desk as she grabbed the small leather-bound book she'd been reading the day before. It was her third reread, but she loved the chapters the author spent describing the terrain of Falais. The book itself was meant as a straightforward account of the strategies used to fight battles in the country, but Sofia savored the descriptions, picturing the foreign land in her mind as she read. The author described craggy cliffs of red stone, towering trees as wide as houses, and hundreds of waterfalls that traversed the land. Sofia could barely imagine a place with so much water and greenery.

It wasn't until she'd read the chapters over twice before she finally acknowledged she needed to complete the paperwork the chief commander had left her. She shut the book reluctantly, her reality of stone walls crashing down around her.

A knock sounded on the door as Sofia was slipping the book back on the shelf and she gave a small jump. The chief commander wasn't due back for at least an hour and she wasn't used to being disturbed in the afternoons.

"Come in," she said, hesitant to act as if the office were hers, but more scared to ignore the knock.

A small round face peaked around the corner and it took Sofia a second to recognize the bright brown eyes.

"Mina!"

She smiled before slipping into the room, shutting the door behind her.

"What are you doing?" Sofia asked, voice turning sharp with anxiety.

"One of the other cleaning maids said you were probably in the master's office."

"You shouldn't be here."

"I just wanted to say hi," she said, voice soft. Her smile had faded with Sofia's sharp words. "I'm off latrine duty. I've been assigned to this floor."

Sofia gave a tight smile despite her anxiety, hating to be the one to make the girl tremble even slightly. "I'm glad you've been reassigned. Did those boys ever bother you again?"

Mina gave a smile that showed off her crooked teeth. "Not after that day. I'd just call your name if they came toward me and they'd go running. I think Ms. Garcia gave them a piece of her mind for what happened."

Sofia gave a nod, happy the fight hadn't been for nothing. The fight was the reason she was locked up here now, constantly dodging the chief commander's anger.

"What do you do in here?" Mina said, looking around the room as if it were made of crystal and gold.

"I clean," she said, matter of factly before giving a wide grin, "and sneak around looking into the kingdom's darkest secrets."

Mina giggled and Sofia felt a lightness in her chest for the first time since she'd been caught reading in the library. As much as she always told herself that making friends with the other staff was a pointless endeavor, she hadn't realized how much she missed those brief moments of simply being with another child.

"You should leave," she said after another moment, checking the large clock above the door. "The chief commander can return at any time."

"Can I visit again?"

She bit her lip for a moment, a hundred reasons for saying no moving through her brain.

"Only between two and four o'clock though, and always knock first. If the chief commander is here and he calls you in, pretend you got lost." She made her words sharp, eyes focusing on Mina's to make sure she understood the seriousness of them. The little girl gave a short nod before turning and running out the door.

Sofia spent the rest of her alone time trying to finish her copying, but she kept looking down to notice flecks of blood on the paper from where she'd been picking at her nail beds. She had to start over from scratch again.

CHAPTER FIFTEEN

FOX

Fox's head was throbbing and he was trying his best to stay cognizant as one of the men held him by his neck, keeping him standing even as nausea roiled through him. He saw the third man return, something slung over his shoulder.

"Look what I found," he said, throwing whatever it was on the ground in front of them. Only after the others were laughing and tittering over the man's find, did Fox's eyes adjust enough to make out the dark curls against the shadowed ground—the Dragonborn woman who had started this. Her eyes were open, but unfocused, and he could just make out the dark smear of something dripping from her hairline.

The sight made his heart rate spike. Being recaptured by the resistance hadn't been the perfect plan, but it felt like a better option that being dragged away by these *things*. Now his only hope was lying crumpled on the ground looking just about as useless as him.

The man holding him by the throat dropped him. His legs crumbled beneath him before he had a chance to catch himself, and he tasted soil as his hands were yanked behind him. The rope was rough against his wrists, biting into the skin there. He was starting to get tired of being tied up and a small voice in the back of his mind wondered where three naked men had been storing the rope.

They didn't bother with his comfort, pulling the ropes tight enough to nearly pop his shoulder out of place. But it was least of his problems as he was picked up like a sack and thrown over one of the men's shoulders. The Dragonborn woman—*Sofia*—was flung on the back of another, her own arms also tied.

For the smallest fraction of a second, Fox regretted ever escaping from the tunnels. His body wouldn't ever be found out here in the rainforest. His name would simply be added to the list of those who disappeared in their duties to the crown, another forgotten soldier who didn't make it. Would his father be disappointed? He was proving him right, after all. He always had known Fox wouldn't make it. That didn't even hurt anymore. It was Leon's face that burned through his chest and made his body ache. If he didn't escape this, he'd fail every promise he'd ever made to his brother.

THE NEXT FEW hours crept by punctuated by pain and cold and fear. The men moved through the forest like animals, bounding more than walking, and not bothering to be gentle with their cargo. Fox felt his muscles aching and his head churning as he bounced across the large man's shoulders, unable to do more than brace himself. If he'd had any food left in his stomach, it would have been lost quickly. As it was, his head was swimming somewhere between nausea, exhaustion, and thirst. The man holding Sofia ran beside him and he caught occasional glimpses of her curls. He tried to make eye contact, but it was nearly impossible with the jarring bounce of his captor's gait.

When they were both unceremoniously dropped onto the ground as the men came to a stop, Fox was almost glad to feel his limbs tangling with hers. The three men spoke in low tones and then the smallest of them bolted away.

Too afraid to draw attention, Fox tried his best to turn slowly. He could feel the soft movements of Sofia behind him, but he couldn't tell what she was doing. He didn't particularly like her being behind him, even if she was the least of his enemies at the moment. In fact, she was probably the closest thing he was going to get to an ally out here. If they could get freed, they might have a better chance with two against three.

He had just managed to flip himself over, searching out the woman's eyes in the dark, when the third man returned. Fox looked on in utter horror to see the man dragging an entire elk behind him, casually holding it by the back hoof. He hadn't even processed the insanity of seeing a naked man dragging his kill—without a single weapon in sight—before all three men were on the elk, ripping and tearing into it with a frenzy.

If he thought he had felt nausea before, this was something new. Fox turned away, not hiding the gag that rose in his throat. He made eye contact with Sofia who stared back, wild-eyed at him. His stomach dropped to see the fear there. It wasn't until that moment that he realized he'd never actually seen her afraid, even when he'd first captured her. He should have known at that point it had been a trap. But now, there was a true flash of terror in her eyes.

They stayed like that for a few moments, Fox's own fear reflected back at him. He moved his lips silently, emphasizing each syllable as if it might help her read his words in the dark.

We need to get untied.

She nodded and he could only hope she understood him. They needed to get away from these men. They needed to work together. The tremor in her shoulders told him that she didn't disagree with his assessment.

He watched her as she squirmed, contorting her body as if she might just slip from her binds. A part of him wanted to laugh at the idea, but he'd underestimated her before. So he watched in silence as she twisted and moved before suddenly going still and letting a smile stretch across her face. Her moss eyes practically danced. Her movements were smaller now, as she continued to stare at him, concentrating on something. He bit the inside of his cheek, trying to stay patient.

But the silence and the waiting only gave him time to focus back on the sound of ripping from behind him. The men were still eating their kill—blood, skin, hair, and all. These weren't just Dragonborn or feral forest dwellers that had captured them. These were something else. And that, more than anything, terrified Fox. He knew the legends of Wueco, but that's what they were—*legends*. Myths to scare little children into never sneaking past the wall. Myths that had kept Dragonborn as slaves to the forest instead of progressing.

Before he had time to dig himself into such thoughts, he noticed Sofia looking at him again, mouthing something. He refocused and saw her motioning for him to turn over. With a startled realization, he saw that her right arm was in front of her now, a small dagger the size of his thumb tucked in her palm.

Biting back the urge to flip himself over, he shuffled with care, keeping his movements small and quiet. It took an extra few moments, but the men didn't even look up from their meal as he rolled to face them. The iron scent of blood hit him as he turned, a perfect view of the massacre happening just a few yards away.

The felled elk was torn apart, a gaping wound in its belly. They continued to reach into the pit, pulling out pieces of meat and flesh, raw as they devoured it. The glow of the forest around them only acted to highlight the gore and horror of the scene, casting their faces in a green hue and making the men look inhuman—witches brought to life from some ancient storybook, casting their spell through some macabre ritual.

The cold blade touched the delicate skin of his inner wrist and he feared she might dig it in deeper, cutting into him. But she didn't, the blade maneuvering carefully as she sawed at his binds. Even still, he felt the occasional nick and sting of the blade missing the rope.

"Not sorry," she whispered, nearly all breath from behind him. He scowled, but was careful not to move and give her more of an excuse to cut him.

It felt like hours before the ropes around his wrists fell away, the blood rushing back to his fingers. His shoulders loosened forward and he almost groaned in relief. The men were finishing up their meal, eyes flicking up to them as if remembering they had prisoners thrown off to the side. Before he could move another inch, he felt Sofia pulling his hands back together and tightening the cut rope around his wrists, stuffing the ends in his hands.

"Hold," she said.

He stiffened as one of the men stood and slinked toward them. Blood dripped down his chin and onto his bare chest, outlining the muscles there and Fox recoiled to see it dripping across the man's groin.

"I wonder what they taste like," he said over his shoulder.

"Don't," the largest man said from somewhere over the other's shoulder. "Not until Rom gets a look at them. He'll decide what they're most worth."

"Just a nibble won't hurt," he said, running a bloody finger across Fox's cheek. He smelled metal and felt the wet trail left behind on his skin as the man was jerked back by his friend.

"No."

The largest man seized the other one by his arm, throwing him a few feet away before he picked up Fox and threw him over his shoulder.

"Grab that one," he said to this companion who was still standing to the side. "I want to get back before the sun rises."

He heard Sofia grunt as she was picked up behind him. And then they were running again.

He kept the rope firmly grasped in his hand as they moved and he had to wonder if he was any better off than he'd been before.

He was untied, but he was still in the arms of a man too large and strong to be normal and days away from any part of the rainforest he might know. He twisted around, ignoring the pain as he moved, fighting against the rhythm of the man's steps. But it was worth it when he managed to catch a glimpse of Sofia a few feet from him, her own head hitting the back of her captor with every step. He saw the concentration in her face and the clench of her teeth.

He gave a groan, relieved when it worked to get her attention. Her own head spun, eyes meeting his. There was no guarantee their respective captors would stay beside each other much longer and he needed to know what the plan was. Her mouth was moving, but he struggled to focus on her enough to understand. His confusion was clear on his face because she continued to mouth, eyes burning with frustration.

Fox was proud the moment he did recognize what she was saying, although she looked like she was ready to kill him for how long it took.

I need a distraction.

He let out a loud groan, and then another when the first did nothing.

"I'm going to puke," he said, loud and throaty. It wasn't hard to fake, considering the feeling of nausea crawling up his throat as he spoke. "Please, stop."

"Shut up!" the man growled.

He gagged, the muscles rippling in his stomach and he felt a little bile coming up.

"Shit!" the man said as some of the liquid dripped from Fox's mouth and onto his back.

The man threw him off his shoulder and Fox hit the ground, the air knocked from his lungs.

"In the gods' names, Xanderi, pick him back up," one of the men said from above him.

"He threw up on me!"

Fox caught his breath from his fall and gave another dramatic groan, barely having to fake the retching.

"Maybe we should just eat him," one of them said. "He ain't worth the trouble."

Fox was quickly regretting his role as a distraction as the man leaned over him, dried blood smeared across his body. But before he could make a move, chaos erupted.

CHAPTER SIXTEEN

SOFIA

The moment she hit the ground, Sofia dropped the ropes around her wrists and moved into a crouch. The man who had been carrying her wasn't even looking at her, too busy laughing at his companion. They had stolen her bag and bow, but she still had the tiny dagger she'd taken from Emilio. It couldn't cut through much, but even a shifter's skin was only so thick.

She sprung forward, using her legs to propel herself up, wrapping her body around the shifter's. She didn't have much time if she wanted the element of surprise. So the moment she was on him, she aimed and sliced, pulling the dagger across his throat in one motion, cutting off his laugh with a gurgle.

His body was heavy as it fell, drawing the other two shifters' attention to where she was standing above his body, blood sprayed across her. They only blinked for a moment, their brains slow to process. They hadn't expected the sudden shift in the power dynamic. Using their surprise to her advantage, she lunged forward and grabbed her bag where the other man had dropped it in the mud when they'd stopped. She reached into it blindly, ignoring the sharp sting as one of the daggers caught her across the back of her forearm. At least it was sharp.

She snatched it out and turned just in time to see the two men diving toward her. The ground was soft as she fell back, the dagger held between her and the men. The first one that reached her grabbed for the weapon and she pulled back her arm slashing at his hand. She missed, but with her second attempt, the dagger sank into the palm of his hand. He automatically moved to grip his hand and she stabbed again, slicing his other hand. She brought her blade back, ready to strike, but he knocked her arm away with a feral growl, slamming his head into hers. The hit reverberated through her bones and she dropped the dagger with a groan.

He grabbed her, hissing in pain even as he used his ruined hands to pull her up and throw her across the ground. Her spine hit a root and her lungs ached for lack of air. She couldn't move. The shifter moved toward her, a look of pure malice on his face. He didn't even have a weapon, but there was an intensity in his eyes as he lifted his hands and the claws extended from the tips of his fingers. Sofia tasted metal on her tongue and she wondered what it would feel like to be torn in two by this creature. She didn't close her eyes, though, ready to face her death.

He pitched sideways before he reached her, falling on his knees before he faceplanted into the soil, unmoving. Ocon stood over him, a bloody rock gripped in his hand. She glanced behind him to see the other shifter crumpled on the ground, scrambling to push himself up but uncoordinated in a daze as blood dripped heavily from his face.

Sofia jumped to her feet and grabbed the dagger she'd dropped as the shifter stood, stumbling like a drunk. She tried to jump forward, hoping to catch him before he gained his senses, yet even in the second it took her to move, the shifter's body contorted and twisted.

And a second later a large gray wolf bolted into the forest.

SOFIA

AGE 12

While the many of the shifters of Wueco were integrated into the various tribes, the wolfshifters were a volatile and isolated group, rebuffing all attempts at unity or collaboration. They were known for their territorial nature and refusal to assimilate into human society.

- Tales of the So-Called Dragonborn by Jules Vond

Sofia and Mina fell into a comfortable routine. Friendship was something she had always avoided, but it was too hard to shut away the small ray of light that Mina brought to her monotony and loneliness.

More and more as she became proficient in her writing and reading, the chief commander left her alone, some measure of trust developing between them in the cycle since she'd started working for him directly. Some days he didn't even come into the office, leaving instructions for her to follow sitting on the small table. On those days, he was kind enough to have the maid deliver her a small tray of tea and bread for lunch, a kindness that she hated herself for appreciating.

Despite these occasional days of freedom, she and Mina kept their routine, with Mina only coming to the office after two and slipping out before four. Sometimes they had an entire hour to themselves swapping stories. Mina always heard the gossip during her time around the manor, including who was caught stealing a vase from the chief commander's late wife's room or the new stableboy that everyone thought was cute. In exchange, Sofia would whisper the stories she'd memorized in the books from the library, Mina listening with rapt attention.

She hadn't been looking for trouble the day she found it. She was bored after finishing her to-do list from the chief commander. He'd been out of the office for the past week, the only evidence that he hadn't died were the handwritten notes that were delivered every morning by one of the other staff members, a list of tasks for her to complete. Each morning the list got shorter and shorter, with no indication of what she was supposed to do otherwise. So she cleaned and organized and read through the books on his shelf she hadn't gotten to yet. They were as dull as she'd suspected when she'd first perused the spines the cycle before.

She had gotten to the highest shelf that day, a series of trade records that were half in code and nearly impossible to parse. But she refused to leave a single page unturned, so she started with the book on the far left, attempting to pull it from the shelf. It stuck on something.

She was tempted to ignore it for the next volume, but the silence in the office allowed her to hear the softest of the clicks from behind. Pulling over a chair that allowed her to reach the shelf better, she lifted the book out. It slipped free easily this time, and she examined the clean wood of the shelf behind it, no indication of what it had been stuck on. She ran her fingers along the grain of the wood until one of her nails caught on the vaguest hint of a crease. She pressed and a small piece of wood clicked toward her. Hooking a finger around it, she pulled. She barely caught herself as the entire shelf moved, nearly knocking her off the chair.

Her eyes went wide as she took in the small crack now visible behind the bookshelf. It took a minute to move the chair and wedge her hands behind the shelf, pulling with most of her weight until it swung forward revealing the room beyond.

"Gods' scales," she said, unable to hold back the words as she took in the shelves and shelves of books. The room beyond was the size of a large closet, but it was packed with more books than she'd think possible in the small space. Every wall was lined with books and a few more were stacked on the ground, haphazardly thrown there when the shelves ran out of space.

The closest stack of books by the door was familiar and she leaned down to run a finger over the cover of the top book: *Tales and Myths of the So-Called Dragonborn*. It was a book she had read the previous cycle, one that had been in the main library up until the day she'd been caught. There was a thin layer of dust across the cover and she was careful to grip it from the side as she picked it up. Below it was another she'd read, a historical account of Wueco in the first generation after the civil war. The chief commander had moved all the books she'd been reading into this secret room. She examined the space, careful to disturb as little dust as possible. Some shelves were cleaner than others and she could see the fingerprints from where the chief commander had more recently perused the shelves.

While the stacks on the floor held some familiar volumes, most of the shelves were filled with books she'd never seen before—books the chief commander had deemed too precious or too dangerous to have displayed in his library. That thought, more than anything, had her reaching for the first book she saw already cleaned of dust. *Assimilation or Elimination: A Philosophical Debate*. It took approximately two pages for her to put the book down, a mixture of anger and disgust churning through her stomach. She left that shelf and looked at another one, lips quirking into a smile at what she saw. There was an entire section dedicated to prayers and spiritual practices of the Dragonborn, another full of faerytales and histories written in the dragon-tongue. Even more shelves held what looked like historical records of Wueco before the tribal war—before the great king had even claimed dominion over creation and religion.

These weren't just children's books, like the ones she'd found before, but records of her people and the gods from before the king. Things that she was sure were *extremely* illegal to have and *impossibly* dangerous for her to know.

She needed to leave the room, lock the shelf back in place, and forget what she had seen, but Sofia had never been known for letting rules or common sense get in the way of knowledge. Instead, she took a moment to close her eyes, breathing in the smell of parchment, leather, and dust. And then she began to read.

CHAPTER SEVENTEEN

FOX

Sofia didn't even bother chasing after the man as he ran in the forest. At least Fox thought he had run away. One moment, Fox was looking at him and the next the man had crouched, folding into the shadow and then...

Fox shook his head, trying to clear his thoughts. He was exhausted beyond reason and his head was ringing with pain. He could only watch as Sofia turned on her heels, lunging at the other man who was struggling to stand after Fox had managed to bash his head with a rock three times. She drew the blade across his throat and he fell, unmoving. Perhaps he should have been relieved to see the man dead, but the coldness of the act made him shudder.

"Should we go after—" he started when she finally turned to look at him. Unable to finish the sentence, he gave a vague wave in the direction the man had run.

She raised an eyebrow. "He'll be miles away by now, unless you can run at the speed of a wolfshifter."

The sentence didn't make sense and he stared at her blankly. "He was injured, he won't make it that far. No man could."

"Shifters can do a lot of things humans can't," she said, matter-of-factly.

He clenched his jaw. "You keep saying that word like it means something."

"Shifters?" she said, not bothering to hide the sneer at his confusion. "Do you want me to explain it to you like you're a child? Those—" she pointed a finger into the dark "—were not just men. We're lucky to be alive. I don't know a human who's seen a wolfshifter and lived to tell about it."

"Shifters are mythical beings from Dragonborn stories."

"Well, you should tell them that," she said, kicking the man at her feet. "Or better yet, chase down the wolf that just shifted directly in front of you and tell him."

"I didn't see anyone *shift*," he said and he meant it. It had been dark—all he'd seen was the man crouch over and disappear.

"You're an idiot," she said bluntly.

His face burned.

"And this idiot just saved your life."

"I'm pretty sure, I saved yours first."

"I wouldn't have needed saving had you not kidnapped me."

"It was running away that got you into trouble!"

He threw his hands up in frustration. "Sorry, oh captor of mine. Next time, I'll stay tied up and quietly wait for you to chop me into small pieces."

"I was hardly going to chop you up," she said and he thought he could almost sense amusement in her voice. "It would have been a finger or two at most."

He didn't see the joke.

"Feral bitch," he muttered, plenty loud for her to hear.

She only rolled her eyes and turned away from him to pick up her bag.

"That's mine!" He moved to grab the dagger she was sliding into her belt, but she sidestepped before he could.

"I don't think so." She turned, pointing it at him, more in annoyance than as a threat. "A, this is Emilio's blade, not yours. B, I definitely don't trust you with a weapon. And C, you're still my captive."

Fox laughed, full-throated. He waved his arms around them, as if she might not have taken in their situation until now. "What do you plan on doing? Tying me up and dragging me the however many miles back?"

"I won't tie you up if you promise not to run or attack me," she said.

He couldn't hide the smirk that curled his lips. "You'll tie me up if I don't behave?"

She narrowed her eyes and he stepped forward again, attempting to swipe the blade from her waist. Before his fingers even brushed the hilt, she sidestepped and brought her smaller dagger across his forearm in a shallow, but decisive warning. He hissed at the flash of pain and pulled back.

She smiled. "Behave."

"I'm not going to follow you like an obedient animal to my own slaughter."

"Stay out here, then. The wolfshifters seem all too happy to make friends."

He looked around the forest and took in their surroundings. The trees had already been unfamiliar and towering when he'd first exited the tunnel, but now they were enormous, the roots twisting up from the ground nearly the size of him around. At some point over the past few minutes, the sun had crested the horizon and the shadows of the forest were starting to recede. The night blooms had closed and the morning birds were waking from their sleep, the trills beginning to replace the hum of the night insects. But none of that told Fox anything.

They were farther from Suvi than he'd ever been before—farther he'd guess than Sofia had ever been. With the pace the men had taken, he wasn't even sure how far they were from the tunnel he'd originally come through. They'd been running all night. He looked back at Sofia, unsure if it was more relieving or frightening to see his own uncertainty reflected back. For all her talk, she had no more control over their situation than he did—except perhaps a few more daggers. She couldn't drag him back to the resistance base without his cooperation, and there was no way he was going to be the one to follow her.

"I'm going to head south now," he said. "You can follow me if you want." He didn't wait for her to answer, and started moving. He was weaponless, hungry, and had no idea where he was going, but he knew she'd have to head in the same direction as he did. At some point over the next day or two, she'd slip up and he'd have a weapon. He'd decide then what his next steps were—running back to Suvi without her or bringing her back as a prisoner.

Sure enough, he heard the soft sound of her steps a few moments later. He glanced over his shoulder and saw her walking a few yards away, bag in hand and the bow and quiver tucked back in their place on her back. He wondered what supplies she had in there and if he could convince her to share. She was watching him with the same careful stare he was giving her, neither quite willing to turn their back on the other. Now that she was moving, Fox didn't want to have her behind him, and he fell back so they were walking relatively even, albeit still keeping a few yards apart.

They continued like this for hours, each watching the other more than the ground before them. Fox tripped three times walking like this, which only made him more bitter because Sofia had managed to jump over every root in her way without taking her eyes off of him. But she couldn't hide the exhaustion and hunger that was plaguing her just the same as him. They had been able to find enough morning dew on the lower leaves to slake their thirst, but Fox hadn't gone this long without food in cycles and he was beginning to feel the exhaustion of the last few days, the adrenaline having been left behind with the dead bodies.

It was midday before Fox stopped, eyes zoning in on the stack of mushrooms painted across the trunk of a large tree. He recognized the blue-capped fungi with their small yellow freckles. They were the same mushrooms his mother had cooked on special occasions and his mouth watered with the memory of their buttery taste. He moved automatically, steps suddenly lighter as he leaned over the trunk and plucked the mushrooms from the wood. He didn't care that they were raw and flecked with dirt, placing the first cap on his tongue—

"Stop!" Sofia was there suddenly, slapping him across the face and forcing him to spit out the blue cap.

"What the—?" he said, turning on her with fiery eyes.

"Are you trying to kill yourself?"

"I'm trying not to starve."

"Those are dragon scale mushrooms, not nobles, you idiot. One bite of those is enough to kill a jaguar."

He looked back at the mushrooms where they'd fallen, trying to understand what she was saying. "They...I know what nobles look like."

She leaned over plucking one of the mushrooms off the ground and turning it. "Orange gills, not yellow. And nobles grow on the ground, not on trees."

He was looking at it now, noticing the slight difference in the color and the size of the yellow freckles. His stomach turned.

"If your people spent as much time getting to know this land as they did tearing it down to build things, maybe you'd know that."

He rolled his eyes at the insult, wanting to point out that he wasn't to blame for the decisions of his forefathers. Instead, he turned to her smirking. "You saved me."

She scowled at this, giving him the satisfaction of showing her annoyance. "You're still my prisoner and I'm not going to let you die after all the trouble you put me through."

"I'm your prisoner?" he asked, looking around them. "So if I run off, you're going to stop me?"

"I don't need to. You'd die out there without me and you know it. Once we get back to our side of the rainforest, we're marching right back to the base."

"Once we get back to familiar territory, I'm arresting you for treason and kidnapping."

She stepped forward, drawing the small dagger she'd used to slit the throats of the men just that morning. It was cleaned of blood, but he could still see the shadow of where it had been. She pointed it at his chest, poking him just hard enough for him to feel the sharp tip through his tunic and cloak.

"I'd love to see you try."

He stepped closer to her, forcing the dagger a bit deeper into his skin. It stung, but he ignored it, wrapping his hand around her throat, just hard enough he could feel her swallow beneath his grip. He was taller than her and loved the way she had to crane her neck to look up at him when they were this close. The uncertainty that flickered through her eyes told him he had made his point. The only reason she'd caught him the first time was that he'd been unaware and she'd had a handful of allies. But out here, even if she had the weapons in the end, he was plenty taller and stronger than her. He still had the advantage.

He stepped back and dropped his hand, satisfied that he'd shut her up.

"We should find food," he said as he continued to walk back in the direction they had been going.

"You mean I should find us food," she said, coming up beside him, knife still in her hand as if she might stab him just for fun.

"Well, you apparently don't appreciate my contribution."

"If I want to die, I'll let you know. Keep an eye out for blue and yellow mushrooms on the ground. They'll be under the dead leaves. I'll keep an eye on the trees for some fruit or nuts. I know you probably think those only come in sacks at the market, but they actually grow naturally out here."

"I know where food comes from," he said, ignoring the fact that he'd never even gotten food from the market on his own. Food came on plates from the kitchens or the barracks' cafeteria, and he realized how ridiculous that was in this moment. So he bit his tongue when she let out a derisive laugh and did what she said, reluctant but too hungry to ignore her instructions.

The next mushroom he found, she let him eat. It gave him a stomachache, but he was still breathing at least. And that's all he needed for now—to stay alive long enough to get back to familiar territory, overpower Sofia, and take her to Chief Commander Harlow. He knew where their base was, knew what at least a few of their faces looked like. He knew more about her resistance than any soldier had in cycles and he was going to hand-deliver all that information to the chief commander. His father would no longer be able to deny his usefulness as a king's man, and the chief commander would have all the energy and support he'd put into Fox's training proven right.

He smiled even as his stomach cramped, imagining the woman beside him in chains.

CHAPTER EIGHTEEN
SOFIA

By the time the shadows started to lengthen once more, Sofia still didn't recognize the rainforest around them. At least she had found some fruit and nuts to eat throughout their hike, but they hadn't run into a cenote or water source beyond the leaves of trees. She was thirsty and hungry and her muscles felt like lead from a lack of sleep. Ocon wasn't doing much better.

In part, it was her fault for letting him eat the second mushrooms he'd found. They weren't poisonous, but they needed to be cooked to be truly edible and she knew they'd give him a stomachache. She didn't want him to die, but she didn't promise she'd make this trek comfortable. If it wasn't for him, she'd be back at the base right now, warm and fed.

Her stomach turned. Or perhaps she wouldn't. She'd be back in the city, homeless, jobless. She shook the thoughts away, nails biting into her palms.

No matter what, she needed to get back to the base with a breathing Ocon. She needed to prove to Micael that she could follow orders and toe the line. Perhaps she'd even be allowed to stay after all the trouble.

"We should stop for the night," she said, noting the small clearing up ahead.

"Tired, oh captor of mine?"

"You've tripped over the last three roots, so don't pretend you're not." She barely looked at him as she inspected the area with a satisfied nod. It wasn't much of a clearing, but it was wide enough to accommodate them and a fire, the trees arching overhead to protect them from the elements. They'd be safer in a cave or a cenote, but she hadn't seen a hint of either since they'd started out that morning. "I'm going to go hunt for some food before it gets darker. Try to find us some water or fruit if you can manage."

Without another word, she left, taking her bag of supplies with her. It would be harder to hunt with the daggers and bag weighing her down, but she wasn't going to leave them with Ocon. She almost wondered, as she walked away, if he'd be in the clearing when she returned. Perhaps he'd take this moment to run. Not that he'd have any idea where he was going. Not that she did either, though he didn't know that.

The trees in this part of the rainforest were larger and farther apart, but the underbrush was thick with bushes, brambles, and vines. There wasn't enough time to lay snares. She'd just need to find somewhere to wait the animals out. With night approaching, the crepuscular creatures would be waking and venturing from their homes to hunt their own meals.

She found a promising-looking bush with some holes dug in the ground beneath it and set herself on a low branch as far away as she could get without losing her line of sight. And she waited with the patience she only ever had when she was hunting. For the first time in cycles, she felt her focus going fuzzy as she crouched, eyes burning and heavy, neck barely strong enough to hold up her head. She pinched her wrist to keep herself awake, over and over again as the sun set and the world went gray. There were a line of small red marks across her arm by the time she saw the first signs of movement from the bush. Careful to keep the daggers on her waist from making a sound, she raised her bow, fingers pulling back the string and eyes focused on the small brown rabbit as it snuffled out of its hole.

She continued to wait until the next rabbit came—slightly bigger than the first—and then she let her arrow fly. It was a smaller target than she was used to, but the arrow still sliced across its side, drawing a large slash of blood. The other rabbit ran, its partner attempting to follow, but it stumbled, body half-limp with impending death. She didn't let herself feel the guilt as she caught up to it and broke its neck, ending its fear.

She traced her way back to the clearing, following the marks she'd made in the dirt on her way to hunt. When she broke through the last few bushes and Ocon sat in the clearing, she was almost surprised to see him. As she stepped on a pile of dead leaves, he jumped, swiveling around with a small log clasped in his hands. She only raised an eyebrow as he grimaced and turned away, going back to his attempt at lighting a fire.

He'd gathered an assortment of twigs and branches in front of him and had even created a small pile of wood shavings, but without a flint, he'd taken to a method that Sofia had only read about in books. He rolled a twig between his hands, attempting to create enough heat to spark a flame.

"Is that all you caught?" he asked, eyeing the rabbit hanging from her hand, not pausing his task.

"Do you want to try and do better?" she asked, throwing the dead animal beside him and watching his attempts at lighting the fire. If she wasn't so cold and hungry, she might have just let him continue to flail. But at this rate, they'd be there all night waiting for the wood to heat and spark.

"Do you know how to skin and prep the meat?" she asked after another minute of watching him struggle with the fire.

The wince told her everything, but she still dropped the small knife next to him.

"Drain it, slice across its back to take off the fur, and then gut it through the belly."

He sneered, looking at the dead creature as though it might jump up and attack him. "I'm making the fire."

"Not fast enough," she said, snatching the branch from his hands and throwing it into the pile with the rest. "I know you're not squeamish around death, Ocon. So go ahead."

She shoved him sideways and began to carefully rearrange the wood for the fire, clearing a larger area on the ground and digging into the dirt with a branch to make a small pit. With the lack of rain, the last thing they needed was to start a wildfire out here. She stacked the twigs neatly before pulling out the flint from her bag and piling the leaves beneath the wood. Ocon stared at her, unmoving, but she did her best to ignore him.

"You could have told me you had a flint," he said, voice flat.

She didn't hide her smirk. "Unless you want to eat that with the hair on, I'd get started."

He moved at last, rolling up his sleeves with practiced fingers. His forearm muscles flexed and the black dagger inked into his inner arm rippled subtly with every twitch of his fingers. Her eyes flickered up to his face, though he was seemingly unaware of her examination.

Her jaw clenched. She watched long enough to see him flip the rabbit and shove the tip of the knife into its neck before she turned back to the fire. She hated preparing animals just as much as he seemed to, but if she was going to share the meat, he was putting in some work, and she was all too glad to pass on the bloody task.

By the time he had done a passable job of preparing her kill, the fire was hot. She showed him how to use rocks to lay out the meat on the edge of the fire to cook it.

"You live in the city," he said. The words weren't a question, but he looked at her as if trying to understand something.

"Yes," she said, jaw clenched and eyes narrowed. If he was trying to make small talk, she was going to slap him.

"And you know how to do all this."

"Yes."

"How often can you possibly find yourself out here needing to hunt to eat?"

She looked at him, this time the one analyzing him. There was such a genuineness and openness in his face that she blinked. "I've been hunting to feed my family since I was young. The moment there's a food shortage, we're the first to lose rations."

"Only those who don't do hard labor," he said, shaking his head.

She looked at him, trying to understand. "And what exactly would you describe as hard labor? From the age of six, I was working ten hour days cleaning out literal shit, walking the hour to and from the slums to get there."

She might have suspected guilt passing over his face had he not immediately sneered. "Well, you look like you've been plenty fed."

"I'd like to remind you who caught the rabbit," she snapped, picking at her cuticles as she watched the meat cooking. "I might change my mind about sharing."

She wouldn't, though. As much as it pained her, she knew they had a few days' travel at least until they made it back to the base, and she wasn't going to listen to him whine and complain. Additionally, it was clear he was nearly helpless without her when it came to forest survival skills. She didn't understand what the army was even teaching its soldiers.

But at least the comment shut him up.

They ate their rabbit and the anemic mangoes Ocon had found in silence. Even Sofia was unsure if their reticence to talk was because of their dislike of each other or their first warm meal in days. She wasn't anywhere near full when she finished off the last bite, sucking on the mango's pit until there was nothing left of the sour pulp, but her stomach wasn't aching as it had been before, and her tongue didn't feel like sandpaper anymore.

Ocon appeared to be savoring the gamey meat and sour fruit just as much as she was, licking the last bit of juices from his fingers in a way she doubted polite society would approve of.

"We should take turns sleeping," he said when he saw her looking, quickly wiping his hands on his pants, as if she might be judging.

"Sure. I'll go first."

"I'm not tired," he said. "I can take the first shift."

"You look like you're barely keeping your head up straight."

"You don't look any better than me."

She knew he had a point, but the idea of lying down and closing her eyes with him so close made her stomach turn.

"Fine," she finally said, not bothering to move farther from the fire. She made sure the weapons were all in her bag and tucked it into her chest before winding her arms around it. "Wake me up when you get tired."

"Of course," he said in a tone that clearly read: *not going to happen because I don't trust you either.* She just shrugged him off, lying down wrapped around her bag, eyes focused on him.

He stared back at her, lips turned down in a scowl.

She wasn't sure how long they stayed that way, long enough that Ocon had to add a log to the fire a few times. After the third log, he laid down, facing her from across the flickering flames. She felt the tremor in her own body as he wrapped the cloak around himself. Her shawl just covered her shoulders and the thin leggings she wore weren't keeping her warm, even next to the fire. She wasn't cold enough to ask for help, though.

Time drifted like fog as they both struggled to stay awake, each second dragging heavier as the night went on. Until at some point, between one blink and another, the fire had gone out and the clearing had turned dark. Her body shuddered with the cold, skin icy beneath her clothes. Split between the choice of getting up to restart the fire or stealing his cloak and hoping he was a deep sleeper, there wasn't much choice. So she moved quietly in the darkness, barely able to see in front of her. The night blooming flowers that had lit their way previously were closed and Sofia had to wonder if they, too, were hiding from the frigid wind blowing down from the mountains.

It wasn't until she returned with a small pile of twigs that felt dry enough to burn that Sofia noticed the emptiness of the clearing. The remnants of the evening fire were dark shadows against the night, but nothing—no one—was nearby. Ocon was gone.

As if her sudden awareness of her solitude had summoned it, a sound echoed in the woods behind her—the snapping of twigs under foot.

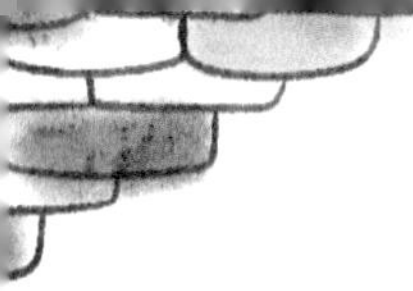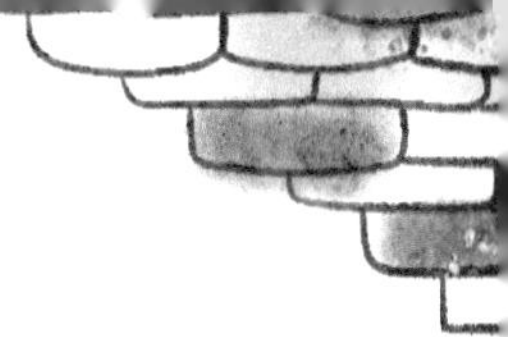

FOX

AGE 14

There are numerous accounts of mythological beings wandering the rainforest of Wueco, from the strange or creepy to the outright absurd. The Dragonborn wrote of beings that could shapeshift, creatures that fed off the energy of others, and ones that fed only on the blood of humans. It is unclear where the roots of these legends came from, but they likely represent a general fear and lack of understanding of the various dangers hidden within the forest.

- Tales of the So-Called Dragonborn by Jules Vond

"I want to go into the army."

Fox was standing in the doorway of his father's office, back straight even as his father barely acknowledged his presence. He'd knocked and been invited in, but his father hadn't even looked up from his desk.

"I want to go into the army." He repeated the words, as if it were possible that his father hadn't heard him. The sound of his pen scratching on the papers dominated the room.

"I heard you." He still didn't look up, dipping his pen in the ink bottle once more before finishing off whatever he was writing with a flourish. "I was just hoping you'd think better of the statement if given the chance."

"Leon was—"

"Leon was an expert with the sword, bow, and dagger by your age. The only thing you put any energy into is sneaking around the manor reading when I'm not looking and playing with that boy."

"Ian and I have been training."

"Playing. If I'm going to be left with a useless son, the least you could do is stay out of my hair."

"I know I'm not the best fighter, but I can learn. And I know I have what it takes to be a strategist."

His father looked up, eyes narrowing, inspecting him like a commander.

Fox had to stop himself from wilting under the glare.

"Every soldier needs to go through basic training and lower ranks before they start using their brain to avoid fighting. So what are you going to do until then?"

"I'll learn to fight."

"You'll be killed in basic training before you learn how to hold a sword properly."

"Which is why I need training now." Fox knew his father wasn't completely wrong. In the brief time Fox had trained with his brother, he'd done his best to go down as fast as possible to end the torment, rather than learning any skills. "I want you to hire Arik again."

DESPITE HIS PROTESTS and insistence that he didn't believe in what Fox was doing, his father still walked by his training sessions nearly every day. Perhaps he enjoyed having himself proven correct. The first six days of training, Fox didn't make it to the end, collapsing onto the ground in a useless heap.

On the seventh day, he finished the training just in time for his breakfast to race its way up his throat and onto the field. By the time he was done retching, Arik had disappeared. His father stood in the manor window, sneering down at where he was hunched. The heat rose in Fox's neck and he turned away, unable to stop the dry heave that rippled through his abdomen.

Once he was able to stand, he half-walked, half-dragged himself around the back of the weapons shed and sat heavily against the rough wooden planks that made up the wall. The training yard was on the north end of the manor, walled in with the same rough stones that made up the house itself, so he was hidden between the high wall and the shed. His father wouldn't be looking for him. His father hadn't even spoken to him since he'd asked for Arik's help.

Fox sat like that for longer than he should have, long enough for the bruise on his cheek from the wooden practice blade Arik had smacked him with to start swelling. When he couldn't take the cramps in his empty stomach any longer, he stood, every muscle in his body protesting. Lunch wouldn't be served for an hour or more yet, but he could beg some food off the cook with a smile and a wink before hiding in his room. The idea of eating lunch in the dining room while his mother looked at him with concern wasn't appealing anyway.

"What do we have here?"

Fox, too busy focusing on his feet, looked up in time to see three boys around his age staring at him. Their clothes were dirty and ripped, their skin the dark shade of the Dragonborn who spent their days working outside. He didn't recognize them, but it wasn't surprising. The manor had a good number of servants, and most of those that worked on the outside of the house rarely interacted with Fox or his family. Even if they had, they all looked the same to him with their haphazardly chopped hair and mud-covered faces.

He rolled his eyes and sneered in response, too tired to do more. He just wanted some bread and water. But as he attempted to push past them, they converged, blocking his path.

"Get out of my way, dragon-filth," he said. He injected as much venom into the words as possible given his exhaustion.

"What are you going to do, vomit on us?" The boys on either side of the leader snickered at the comment.

"You'd probably smell better." He didn't bother stepping forward this time. He needed them to move aside on their own.

The leader—a boy standing two inches taller than Fox and built like a wild dog—stepped forward and shoved him. Barely keeping his balance, Fox caught himself on his left leg with a wince and a bit back groan.

"Move out of my way," he said through clenched teeth.

"Make us," the boy said.

Fox wanted to snap back that his father could have them whipped and fired, but before he could open his mouth, he looked up to see his father striding across the yard with the chief commander by his side. They were deep in conversation, but the chief commander looked up, meeting his eyes with a small smile and a nod. He'd told the chief commander of his plans to join the king's army the same day he told his father and he'd promised him a place in Leon's old dorms if he passed the entry test. His father's eyes flickered only briefly to Fox when he saw his companion's distraction.

Straightening his shoulders as he looked back at the Dragonborn before him, Fox pulled his arm back and swung a punch at the ringleader of the group. A sharp pain reverberated through the bones of his knuckles as he made contact, but the other boy stumbled back. Fox smiled at the blood leaking from the boy's lip.

A snarled curse was his only warning as the other boys descended on him. Fox lashed out blindly, hands smacking uselessly against the other two as he lost track of the punches and kicks against his face, his side, his back. He curled his body, trying to block the blows.

Eventually, they stopped and silence fell. He didn't move immediately, hands still cupped over his face and legs tucked into his stomach, but when no one threw another punch, he looked up. The boys had run away, apparently bored with his non-response.

The rest of the courtyard was empty, his father and the chief commander having left through the open back gate.

That night, his mother knocked on his door with a package sent from the chief commander. He waited until she was gone to unwrap it, hand running across the small leather-bound book with its gold-embossed title: *Hand-to-hand Combat: Strategies and Skills.*

He began to read.

CHAPTER NINETEEN

FOX

Fox probably should have known that lying down wasn't a good idea. But as he stared into the fire, mesmerized by the dancing flames, his body felt too heavy to hold up. His muscles were giving up, slowly at first, and then altogether. He told himself when he laid down, that it would be easier to stay awake, taking away the pressure for his body to stay upright would leave energy for keeping his eyes open.

Sofia wasn't sleeping either and he couldn't help but wonder if she was waiting for his eyes to close before she jumped him and slit his throat. Or maybe she'd just tie him up and drag him back to their base. He wouldn't give her the satisfaction. So when his body gave up and the fire went from an undulating heat to a burned-out shadow in the clearing, his first instinct was to jump up in fear.

Another second of blinking and he realized he could still see Sofia's shadowed form on the other side of the fire. She was shaking, but clearly asleep, completely unperturbed by his movement.

He wanted to close his eyes. Sofia was dead to the world and no longer a threat. He'd promised to watch for the night, but they both knew their argument had only been a thinly veiled refusal for either of them to be the first to fall asleep. But even with the cloak wrapped around his shoulders, watching Sofia's body trembling in the cold made his own skin prickle with discomfort. The temperature had only dropped as the night progressed and the wind was cutting through the thick trees with icy knives.

He would light the fire and then he'd sleep, comfortable in his knowledge that she couldn't kill him while she slept, too.

As he slipped through the night, it baffled him how the forest could feel so dark and yet so familiar. He felt a sense of knowing as he walked, stepping over roots and finding branches. The tunnel had been inky black devoid of all senses, but the forest felt like a living thing, a breathing world.

Maybe that was why it didn't surprise him when he heard the soft feminine cry somewhere beyond the darkness. He assumed Sofia had woken from a nightmare to the dark clearing, but the cries were coming from a different direction—farther into the trees.

Half-asleep and numb with cold, he moved. Stepping deeper into the shadows, he chased after the cries, driven to help whoever it was. After what may have been two seconds or two hours, he caught a glimpse of white between the trees; a white so clean and bright it almost glowed. He moved with more confidence as he chased after the crying and the white and the woman.

And then she was there, sitting on a fallen tree, only a few feet from where he stood. She wore a thin slip of a dress, the fabric as pale as moonlight against umber skin. Her hair was as black as the night. It hung long and limp, almost covering her face, but he could still see the fine bone structure beneath. She was beautiful. Not in a way the women around town that his father introduced him to were. It wasn't in the shape of her body or the tilt of her lips. It was something else, as if whatever had shaped her had done so without the imperfection of humanity.

"Are you okay?" he asked, a dozen other questions moving through his mind at the same time: what was she doing out here, was she cold, what had happened to her, did she need his cloak?

She looked up, meeting his eyes from across the small clearing, as if she hadn't noticed him there. As if she hadn't known he'd been following her though the trees. For a moment, he thought her eyes flashed red, but then he saw they were silver, nearly glowing with their own internal light.

She didn't say anything. She simply stared, lips pulled down in a tight frown.

"Are you hurt?" He took a step closer, hands raised to show her he was no threat. She looked like a frightened rabbit, eyes wide as he approached.

He thought as he moved closer her features would come into view, and the imperfections would become more obvious. *How could she be so clean?*

Just as the thought passed through his mind, he saw the mud streaks, almost as if they'd materialized on her dress. Her face was smeared with mud and tears.

It did nothing to take away from her beauty though, only emphasizing the fine structure of her chin and curve of her nose.

Another step and he was almost within touching distance. She had stopped crying now and was just staring at him as he approached. She didn't look afraid, but neither did she look relieved to see him. Her head tilted and there was a hunger in her gaze.

But no—that was just the glint of another tear cradled in the waterline of her eyes.

"Take a step back, Ocon," a voice said, coming to him as if through water. "Don't get any closer to it."

He turned slowly, as if his body weren't responding to him alone. The air was thick around him, and a white mist swirled, encircling him. It nearly enveloped him from the waist down, and he could see Sofia only a few yards from him.

"Sofia?" he said, voice as slow as his body. As slow as the swirl of mist. What was she doing here?

"Get away from it," she said again, her arms raising, the bow held firmly in her grip.

"What are you doing?" he asked, mind catching up to what he was seeing. "Don't shoot her!"

"Whatever you think you see, I promise it's not real," she said again, looking past him, staring at the woman as if she were an evil and ugly thing.

"What do you think you're doing?" he stepped to the side, trying to block her view of the woman.

For her part, the woman in white hadn't moved. She still sat on the log, staring at Sofia with something between disinterest and annoyance.

"You can't just go around killing people."

"Ocon," Sofia said, in the tone his mother often used on him. "That is not *people.*"

He laughed. He couldn't help it at hearing the absurdity of the words even as her face remained serious and her stance firm. He took a step back as her fingers twitched on the bow, worried she'd shoot him out of frustration for not getting the joke.

"I don't know what you're thinking—"

Before he could finish the statement, a rough hand wrapped around his neck and he was pulled back against the body of something hard and cold. He choked on the smell of iron and decay, and he couldn't stop the tremor that worked its way through his body.

"Don't let her hurt me," a soft voice said. But when he turned, it wasn't the woman he saw holding him, but a monster whose face mocked humanity. Small red eyes sat high on its head and its mouth was opened wide, red lips stretched across sharp black teeth. Mist poured from its mouth and wrapped around him tighter, making his body go heavy even as he struggled against its grasp.

The woman—the thing—let out a high-pitched laugh as he shoved his elbow back, trying to break its hold on him.

Shit shit shit shit.

"Just shoot it!" he screamed, moving to the side as best he could with the arms braced around his waist and neck.

Sofia let her arrow fly. There was a whistle and a soft thud and he looked down at a thin wood rod protruding from the thing's chest a mere inch from Fox's arm. But its grip didn't weaken and it let out a throaty growl, letting go of Fox with one hand to pull the arrow out and toss it to the side. All Fox could do was watch in abject horror as mist poured from the wound and the skin folded itself back together, the hole gone a moment later.

He turned to see Sofia looking just as horrified as he did, the bow hung limply by her side.

"Shoot it again!"

"I don't think that's going to work," she snapped.

"Kill it!"

"Why didn't I think of that?" she yelled back.

Before he could retort, the touch of something icy and wet on his neck froze him. His eyes moved sideways of their own accord and he saw the creature's black mouth opened wide. Its teeth scraped across his neck again, hard enough to draw blood and a thin black tongue licked out across his skin. His vision went white for a second, not from pain, but fear.

"Iron," he said, the word trembling from his lips, eyes seeking out Sofia.

She was pale, eyes wide. "I don't have—"

"The blade I stole," he said, lips barely moving as he spoke. "The larger one."

He saw the recognition in her face in the same moment that the creature moved to sink its teeth into his neck. He moved fast, lurching forward and biting down hard into the arm that gripped him. The creature screamed as he tasted decay, black sludge coating his tongue. It pulled its arm away, knocking Fox to his knees with its other arm, clawed fingers biting into his shoulder.

"Ocon, catch!"

He looked up just in time to see the iron dagger spinning toward him, catching it by the hilt a second before it stabbed through his chest. He braced himself and turned, arching his arm toward the creature behind him and hitting his target. The blade slid through skin and sinew more easily than he expected and mist poured from the slash. The creature barely seemed to notice the wound.

"Aim for its heart!"

"I was trying."

"You missed," she said, blunt as always.

"I was a little distracted by the fangs," he snapped, seeing where the blade had gone in a few inches higher than where its heart probably sat. Although he was also basing this off human anatomy and hoping for the best.

He still gripped the dagger, a black *something* staining the blade. He moved again, trying not to see the black hole that was the creature's mouth as it leaned toward him. The dagger sunk into its flesh with a squelch and the smell of rot enveloped him. An instant later, the cold *thing* beneath his hands melted away into nothing but mist. The dagger fell to the ground with nothing left to hold it.

CHAPTER TWENTY

SOFIA

Sofia let out a string of curses as she watched the faery dissipate into mist, leaving behind the dagger and nothing else. Despite her cycles of reading about the magical creatures of the rainforest and their land, she would have been happy to have never met one face-to-face.

Ocon was frozen, staring at the ground where the monster had been standing a moment before. She moved first, sensation slowly returning to her fingers and toes. She bent over and grabbed the dagger where it had fallen, wiping the black stain off on a large leaf before handing it back to Ocon.

"You're lucky that was iron."

He shrugged, still looking at the piece of earth where the faery had been. "I know the difference between iron and steel."

He grabbed the dagger from her automatically, and then his eyes snapped up to hers as if registering what she was offering him.

"If you promise not to slit my throat in the middle of the night, you can keep it. It might be helpful to have a weapon against the other creatures lurking out here."

His voice was raspy as he replied, "You think there are more...*things* out here?"

"Didn't you ever wonder why your ancestors built the wall and refused to go out into the rainforest more than a few miles from the town?"

"Jaguars? Feral Dragonborn bent on killing us all?"

She winced at his phrasing, but chose to ignore it. Now that the adrenaline of fighting off the creature was draining from her, she remembered how exhausted she was and that it was still the middle of the night.

"Perhaps," she said, instead, "but they also fear the monsters and faeries that lived here that they couldn't control or understand."

"You talk of faeries and shifters and monsters as if they're fact."

She turned to start back toward the clearing. It was only a few minutes' walk, but her body grew heavier with every step. Ocon followed, his own steps stumbling.

"It's because they *are* facts," she said. "You can't pretend you just dreamed that creature up."

He gave a soft snort of laughter. "The women in my dreams usually have fewer fangs."

"Fewer, but not zero?" She saw the whites of his eyes as he rolled them.

"Exactly."

They fell into silence as they came back into the clearing, their small haven still hard and cold. Neither spoke, but Ocon followed her lead, gathering up whatever twigs and dry kindling he could find as she worked to relight the fire. Only after the wood was crackling did Sofia feel the tension in her shoulders loosening as she allowed the heat to suffuse her.

"Thank you," he said.

Her head snapped up at his voice. Ocon watched her from across the fire, eyes serious.

"I need you alive," she said, looking away from him, uncomfortable with the gaze.

"And it seems, if I want to make it out of here, I need you alive, too."

"Look at that, we have something in common," she said, voice dripping with sarcasm.

"I know you don't like it, and I don't like it much either," he said. "But I think we can admit that we need each other, at least until we're in familiar territory."

"Where you'll tie me up and march me back to your people?"

"Don't pretend you don't have the same plan."

"I know my plan. I just need you to know, you won't get a chance to implement yours."

He wrapped his cloak around him as he laid down on the ground next to the fire, but she could still hear his muffled words. "You talk big for someone who tried to shoot a faery with an arrow."

Too tired to come up with a comeback, she chose to follow his example, lying down on the ground as close to the fire as she could without fear of being burned.

For a few minutes, the only sound in the clearing was the crackling of the fire.

"How did you know about the iron?" She watched him shuffle slightly at the sound of her question.

"Iron is darker and heavier than steel."

"No, how did you know iron kills faeries?"

She saw the shrug of his shoulders from across the fire. "I just did. I don't know. I probably read it somewhere in some faerytale."

She wanted to ask what books he'd been reading that talked about Wuecan faeries. Yes, reading was banned solely for Dragonborn, but the king didn't look kindly on any of his people reading the true histories of Wueco. Another part of her didn't want to know the answer. Perhaps he'd read the histories from the same bookshelves she had.

Silence fell again and she let it, sinking into the sounds of the fire and the night. This time when she closed her eyes, it was to sleep with the knowledge that at least Ocon didn't plan on killing her tonight.

THEY WOKE EARLIER than she wanted, but the fire went out again and the forest was lit with dawn. They could only get so much sleep huddled on the hard earth. Sofia managed to find some non-poisonous berries a few minutes from the clearing and gave Ocon a brief overview of how *not* to kill himself finding food, but she didn't have the energy to hunt that morning and both of them were anxious to get moving. She didn't know how fast shifters could run in their human forms, but if all went well, they'd be back in familiar territory by tonight. Or at least back to the tunnel.

They were lucky enough that the cool night had left behind plenty of dew and for the first time in a couple of days, Sofia didn't feel too thirsty to think.

Still, as they walked, Ocon kept an eye out for water sources, constantly pointing to small puddles with a hopeful glint. But it hadn't rained recently and any water was stagnant and had grown a fur coat of scum and algae. After a while he got the hint, but he continued to stare at every puddle as if it might pour forth a stream of fresh water and Sofia had to actively ignore his pouting. Her own mouth felt like sandpaper by midday, but she wasn't going to spend energy whining about it.

"How far from the tunnel opening do you think we are?" Ocon asked. She watched as he split the bright pitahaya he was holding with his dagger and took a large bite from the flesh. His tongue flicked out to stop the juices from dripping down his chin and Sofia looked away, blinking hard. She focused back on her own fruit, which she was eating in small bites, carefully slicing one piece at a time.

She didn't want to admit that she didn't know, but she also didn't want to give him more information than he already had. She'd rather it take him by surprise when they made it back to rebel territory and hit him over the head with the biggest rock she could find.

So instead of answering, she shrugged, not meeting his eyes.

"You don't know," he sneered.

"I'm just not telling you. I need you alive by the end of all of this, but that doesn't require you knowing anything."

"Why do you need me alive? Other than you asking those few questions during your little breakdown, your people didn't ask me shit the entire time I was locked up."

She stayed silent.

"You clearly need me for something. You wanted to know about the prison. The prisoners..."

She could feel his eyes staring at her, cold and calculating.

"You're hoping for a prisoner exchange."

He said it as a statement and she dug her nails into her hands, focusing on the sting and trying to keep her face blank.

"A specific prisoner perhaps? It's clearly someone you all care about, considering you've never tried to save any of the Dragonborn prisoners before."

"Don't talk about shit you don't know."

Ocon continued, ignoring her simmering rage. "Did we catch your boyfriend? Girlfriend? I can't imagine anyone caring about *you*."

She threw the remnants of her pitahaya down and sprang toward him, the small dagger pressed against the soft skin of his neck a second later. His breath smelled sweet from the fruit as he looked at her, a gleam of triumph in his eyes despite the blade against his throat.

"Can't trade a dead body, now can you?"

"Your precious chief commander already started killing the prisoners before I'd even left the city, so what do you want to bet there is no one left to save? Maybe I should take that bet and simply slit your throat here and now. I'll leave your body at the foot of the wall and hope your people find you before the jaguars and blood monkeys do."

The muscle in his jaw jumped and she watched his throat bob up and down with a swallow. The cocky grin was gone, replaced by a rawness.

"You just found out you're expendable?" she said, almost wanting to laugh. "Your father couldn't even convince Chief Commander Harlow to make the trade to save your life."

Ocon kicked out, his boot making sharp contact with her shin. The hit reverberated through her body, and he stood as she stumbled back, his own dagger pulled and aimed at her chest.

A twig snapping echoed through the air, loud and clear above the cacophony of the forest and Sofia's blood went cold. Ocon read the look in her eyes and his eyes narrowed.

"It could be a rabbit."

"Too big," she said, voice barely above a whisper. They were standing chest to chest and she felt the sharp intake of breath from him at her words.

"Run?" he asked, voice just as soft.

"Too late," she said, eyes focusing on the movement behind him. Ocon turned and they both watched as a large gray wolf stepped out from under a large fern. Its face was bisected by a long, bloody gash across its left eye—milky white as it blinked. It gave a snarl and its body contorted, bones snapping sharply for an instant before the man stood up with a nasty grin.

"Fuck," Ocon whispered.

"Yes," Sofia agreed.

It was the wolfshifter that had gotten away from them before.

She whipped around at the sound of footsteps behind her and two women, just as naked as the man, prowled out of the woods, their mouths open in a mocking a smile, showing off sharp teeth. They were taller than Ocon, shoulders as broad as their male counterpart and Sofia's stomach dropped. The shifter had returned with friends.

Ocon's back pressed against hers and she pulled her bow, thankful she'd left the larger dagger with him.

"Any tips on killing these things?"

"Throat or heart," she muttered, not taking her eyes off the two women. "Anything else will heal before it kills them."

"Got it," he said, and before the words were even out of his mouth, she felt him launch himself forward. She didn't have time to see his attack though because the moment he moved, the two women reacted. Sofia shot the closer of the women, long black hair matted with leaves. The arrow embedded itself in her shoulder, inches from where her heart was. But Sofia's second arrow hit true, slicing into the flesh of the shifter's neck in a spray of blood. Sofia didn't have time to see if the hit was enough. The other shifter was on her.

Sofia pulled the small dagger from her belt, dropping beneath the woman's attack. The shifter was weaponless, just as the men had been, but her claws tore through Sofia's shirt, drawing blood.

She hissed in pain as she twisted and slashed the small dagger across the woman's heel.

The russet-haired woman growled in pain. But a moment later, Sofia went flying as the woman picked her up by her neck and threw her across the clearing. She landed, groaning, and the woman was already flying at her again, still fast despite her prominent limp.

Sofia rolled, the small dagger still clenched in her fist. As the woman moved to grab her once more, Sofia twisted again, trying to aim for her throat, but the shifter blocked each attempt. On her fifth attempt, the woman blocked her neck once more, but Sofia bent this time, her knife dragged across the shifter's intact heel. She slashed at her calves a few times for good measure as the woman screamed, rolling away from Sofia. She crouched for a moment, bloody dagger still raised, but the woman only stumbled in her attempt to stand.

Her bow was lying on the ground, beside the body of the black-haired shifter. She reached out, grabbing it quickly and sending an arrow into the woman's chest, hoping she hit the shifter's heart.

She searched for Ocon and saw him a few yards away, breathing heavily. He looked feral standing there, splattered with blood, hair fallen out of the knot at the top of his head. The shifter was on the ground, bleeding out from his side and neck, though it was difficult to see how deep the wounds were.

"*Now* we run!" she said, grabbing him as she started to sprint.

He didn't argue, perhaps for the first time in his life. He didn't even pulled his hand from hers until they were already a few minutes away.

"I think we're good," he said between breaths.

"They can track and we don't know if there are more of them," she said, trying to ignore the burning in her own chest. "We don't stop until we're out of their territory."

"How far is that?" he asked, dodging around a tree with impressive grace.

"No idea," she said, hating to admit it even to herself. Her lungs were starting to burn and she felt her throat closing up ever so slowly. She'd be lucky if she made it another half-mile at this pace, but slowing down wasn't an option.

The echo of a branch breaking in the distance made her stomach skip a beat. Looking at Ocon, she saw in the pale set of his features that he'd heard the same thing and knew what it meant.

"They'll catch up to us. We can't outrun them."

"So what do you suggest?" The words growled out, but she heard the fear beneath the tone. The terror in her own chest tightened even more, each breath taking in less and less air.

She needed to think before she ran out of air completely. She studied the landscape as they ran, and when she made out a small outcrop of rocks ahead, she thought she might be imagining them out of pure desperation.

With a sharp turn to her right, she headed straight toward the rocks. Ocon followed, reading her intentions.

"I don't know if I'm going to fit," he said slowing down as he saw the small crevice she was eyeing.

"Yes, you are," she said with a confidence she did not possess. The words wheezed out, but she didn't slow her pace.

"You first." She didn't wait for him to reply, pushing him sideways into the small gap between the two rocks. He gave a yelp, face going pale as she pressed him harder until she felt the give and he slipped through. She followed a second later, the sound of running growing louder behind her.

The rocks opened up almost immediately into a cave. Ocon was pressed against the side wall, watching out the crack with wide eyes.

Sofia turned, raising her bow in time to see a large russet wolf jump at the opening they had just slipped through. With practiced movements she shot two arrows directly into its neck. It gave a yelp and a small whimper before it collapsed back, still.

"Shit, shit, shit," Ocon chanted behind her, looking out over her shoulder. "Is it dead? Are there others? Should we keep running?"

Sofia turned, opening her mouth in an attempt to answer, but all that came out was a wheeze and a gasp. The band around her chest tightened and her knees gave out. She fell forward, Ocon's arms coming out to catch her before she hit the stone floor of the cave.

SOFIA

AGE 13

*The day the prince saw the village girl for the first time, he didn't fall
in love with her. Because although her eyes were the color of the sky
and her hair shone like honey, she was covered in mud and dressed in
rags. He barely glanced at her even as she brought him water to slake
his thirst from his walk and offered him bread. And when he left the
village an hour later, he didn't think of her again. At least not until
much later.*

-The Raven Prince by Emilio Laurn

Sofia ran into Gabriel the first time quite literally. She'd been running late for work, having taken the long way from the slums to the chief commander's manor. There had been a raid going on at one of the houses a block from her own. It seemed that someone had been using forbidden magic to heal the locals under the king's nose. Sofia paused at the end of the street long enough to see a woman she vaguely recognized being dragged from her home, already in cuffs, blood leaking from a wound on her head. The soldiers carried out the boy she'd been trying to heal next. They wrapped him in a blanket to avoid touching him, but the blue tint of his skin made it clear he had scalepox and he wouldn't last for much longer.

The king in all his wisdom had proclaimed there was no cure for the horrendous disease because it was a punishment to those disloyal to the crown. While Dragonborn healers claimed they could cure the disease, such *magic* was forbidden as treason against the crown.

The moment they dragged out a second woman, Sofia turned away. Her face had been streaked with tears, and she was screaming into the street that they would kill her son. Sofia didn't want to see the rest. The two women would be sent to the farms and the boy left to rot in the prison until the scalepox took him.

Even still, she had to walk three blocks out of her way before turning back to avoid passing by the prison wagon. When she came running into the chief commander's courtyard, she was focused on her toes, sore in her too-small shoes, and the sharp pain in her chest from running too fast. Her mother had said she had weak lungs. All she knew is that if she ran too fast, it felt like she was breathing in a shard of ice.

So she was distracted and breathing heavily and she smacked directly into the boy, falling on her behind with a growl of annoyance.

"Watch where you're going!" she snapped, looking up at him. She coughed, ruining any attempt to look intimidating.

His hair was a shade of black that challenged the night sky and his eyes were a warm honey brown. They were opened wide as he looked down at her before he finally blinked.

"I was just standing here."

She gave a short huff of annoyance, but couldn't argue the fact. Ignoring his proffered hand, she pushed herself up and brushed off her clothes as best she could.

He was smiling at her, the corner of his cheek dimpling in a way that made her stomach flutter uncomfortably.

"I'm Gabriel," he said, smoothly moving his arm back to his side as if he'd expected her to snub him. "I don't think we've met."

Sofia narrowed her eyes, but gave him her name. Before she could make her way around him, he gave a small bow.

"I can't wait to see you again, Sofia."

He sauntered away, leaving her to stare after him, wondering why the way he'd said her name had made her stomach flutter.

"Sofia Suarez," Gabriel spoke her name in the same honeyed tone the next week. She'd just come out of the manor after a ten hour shift in the chief commander's office and she didn't quite register the words until he was standing in front of her.

"How do you know my name?"

"I've been asking about you."

"Why?"

"I wanted to know about the beautiful girl that barreled me over last week."

Her face tinged pink without her permission and she tried to push past him before he noticed.

"I'll see you tomorrow!" he called out as she walked away. She tried to ignore him, but she couldn't resist one glimpse back.

The next morning, as she waved her token at the inner gate guard and stepped into the gaslit streets of the royal quarter, Gabriel came loping out of the last dawn shadows, falling into step beside her.

She refused to look at him, eyes focused on his shoes as she tried to understand how he knew when and where to wait for her. Only one idea came to mind.

I'm going to kill Mina.

"I hear you work for the chief commander directly."

Sofia's head snapped up and he flinched from her glare.

"Whoa!" he said, as if soothing an angry donkey.

"What's it to you?"

"I was trying to make conversation."

"Oh," she said, chastened by what may have been hurt in his eyes.

But he quickly wiped it away with that stupid smile and dimple. Her stomach did the fluttery thing again. Sofia had asked Mina about him after they'd first met and, sure enough, he was the stableboy that the entire younger generation in the manor was swooning over. And she could see why. Even when he wasn't smiling, his lips were soft and pink and difficult not to stare at.

He made a sound in the back of his throat and Sofia realized she'd been caught doing just that. She looked away, but not before she saw that damned dimple flash.

"Where were you working before the manor?" she asked, wanting to steer the conversation before he had the chance.

"I was down in the drowned quarter with the fishermen. I handled the donkeys used for shipments, but my boss was arrested last blink on treason. Turns out he was sneaking some of his supply off to the rebels this entire time." He gave a shrug that made it clear he didn't want to seem taken aback by all this, but she could also see a twinge of something like fear or anger in his eyes. "No one wanted to hire me after that, but the chief commander gave me a chance. He saw how I handled the animals during the raid and thought I'd do well with his horses."

She nodded. The king's men were never subtle in their raids and it often led to innocent bystanders being killed or arrested in the chaos. She could only imagine how the wild animals would react.

She asked him about handling the horses. Except for the few times she'd seen the chief commander's in passing, she had never been up close to a horse. There were only a few dozen in the entire city of Suvi, gifted from their neighbors on the other side of the sea a couple cycles ago. Apparently, they rode them everywhere there, but here they were only used as transportation by the king's employees between the different parts of Suvi. She couldn't imagine they'd be of much use in the thick rainforests of Wueco beyond the wall.

He explained the similarities between them and donkeys and why one would use one over the other. Which only made Sofia wonder why anyone would use a horse in the city.

By the time they made it to the manor and Gabriel waved goodbye at the kitchen door, Sofia had forgotten she was supposed to hate him. Three weeks after that, he kissed her for the first time. Not at the kitchen door, but pressed up against the stables in the evening shadows where the rest of the household couldn't see them.

She'd walked home that night, tasting him on her lips and smiling.

CHAPTER TWENTY-ONE

FOX

For a second, Fox thought she'd fainted, though from what, he wasn't sure. As he twisted her around to look at her face, he saw the glazed look in her eyes and heard the shallow wheeze of her breaths. She gave a weak cough closer to a gasp and sucked in air even as her faced turned gray.

"What?" He helped her to sit against the cave wall as she grabbed at her chest. He was happy the stone was at least dry, despite the cave smelling of damp moss and stone. "Is it poison? Are you choking?"

"My lungs. Can't—"

The words were a whisper—a wheeze—and he pressed a hand against her chest, feeling the struggle beneath his palm. For a moment, pure panic flared through him. He couldn't afford for her to die. Not yet. He pressed her hand against his own chest, taking an exaggerated breath. He was moving off pure instinct.

"Follow my breaths."

Her hands were still stained with blood, the not quite dry flakes leaving an imprint on his chest as she did what he asked. He watched her chest attempting to fall into time with his own, the breaths still shallow, but the wheezing seemed to lessen with each passing minute.

He watched her lips, the blue tint receding, their usual rose hue slowly returning, visible even in the shadowy cave.

They sat like that, hands against chests until he was sure her breaths, while pained, were full. It was only when her lips were a deep rose and her cheeks flushed with blood that he recognized he was still holding his hand against her chest. And he could feel more than just her lungs expanding beneath his palm. He could feel the heat of her skin and the soft give of her chest. Their faces were mere inches apart as he watched her own eyes flicker down to their hands pressed against each other.

He pulled his hand back and she did the same without comment, neither meeting the other's eyes.

"Do you need anything?"

She shook her head, the movements slow and pained. "Nothing you could do."

It felt like a pointed jab, but she wasn't looking at him and he didn't have the energy to argue. Happy to know she wasn't going to die in the next five minutes, he finally let himself collapse on the cavern floor. It was cold against his aching muscles and he pressed his hand against his side feeling a wetness that told him the man—the shifter—hadn't missed his mark when he'd clawed Fox. It was difficult to see in the shadows, but he lifted his hand and saw a dark smudge coating his fingers.

"You're hurt," Sofia said.

"Don't sound so gleeful."

"We should find somewhere to wash it and dress it before the sun sets. I have a few of my own."

He grunted in agreement. He didn't want to think about how dirty that man's claws were. Reluctant to see the damage, he lifted his tunic slowly and twisted so he could see his side in the thin strip of light bleeding in through the crevice.

The cuts weren't as deep as he feared. They would likely scar, but they wouldn't need stitches, which he was all too happy for. He didn't want to know what Dragonborn considered first aid out here in the middle of the forest.

"We should head out," Sofia said.

Fox was surprised to see her pushing herself up. Her skin still had a gray tint to it, but perhaps that was the lighting. He didn't argue, letting his tunic drop and standing despite his body's protests.

Squeezing back out through the rocks was easier, but Fox was careful to avoid the body of the wolf—the shapeshifter. This time, there was no pretending he hadn't seen what he'd seen. But just because a few of the myths from the old Dragonborn tales were real didn't mean anything. It didn't mean that the dragons were alive or had ever been gods.

Though his father had refused to suffer faerytales in his house, he'd read them the histories of Wueco. The great king had seen the creatures of the forest for what they were—a plague on the humans that needed to be cured. The wall had been built to protect them from those things that had refused to be tamed. The truth of the creatures may have faded into myth over time, but the great king had truly protected the humans from the dark that could have killed them all. Nothing good came from this place.

"You're going the wrong way."

Sofia's voice broke him from his thoughts and he saw she was walking left, between two particularly thick trees choked with vines. He muttered a curse, but followed her, unhappy as the sharp thorns on the vine pricked at his tunic and scraped against his side, aggravating his wound.

"What else lives out here?"

She didn't answer immediately and he looked up from where he was focused on not tripping to see her staring at him with something akin to hatred.

"Making a list so you can bring your fellow murderers out here to destroy more of the land?"

"You can't possibly have empathy for these blood-sucking faeries and murderous man-wolves? Why is everything in this rainforest so fixated on killing humans?"

"Because *certain humans* spent centuries hunting them and murdering them for daring to exist in the land that created them."

"It's normal to kill the things that threaten us. As normal as hunting to eat."

"They're threatening us because we're in their territory. Because for the past five centuries, we've been locked behind a wall and allowed the chaos to thrive. Because not even the dragons are here anymore to create the balance they were made for."

"Then I'm all too glad to be behind the wall. If you and your people are so desperate to leave Suvi, we should let you. You can die out here trying to find balance and be one with this evil shithole."

"Do you ever wonder why your king doesn't do just that? Let us go free into the rainforest?"

"He's your king, too," he muttered, but she ignored the comment.

"Because he knows that if we were allowed back in our native land, we would thrive. Because our existence threatens his claim as the true god. If we thrive without him, then what claim does he have to rule over any of us?"

Fox felt his face flushed red with anger. He wasn't as devoted as some to the belief that the king was a god, but to speak such things out loud was blasphemy—the kind that he usually arrested and executed people for.

"You forget who I am," he said.

She whirled on him, stepping in close even as it forced her to tilt her chin up at him. "And who are you? The spoiled brat son of the general? The chief commander's favorite little killer? The soldier not even important enough to give up a few Dragonborn prisoners to save? Tell me, *Ocon*, who am I supposed to think you are?"

"They didn't trade me because they knew they wouldn't need to," he said, spitting the words even as the band around his chest tightened. "And they were right. I escaped and your traitor friends were still executed. I call it a win-win."

He didn't see her move until her fist was already flying toward his face. He had only a second to dodge to the side, grabbing her wrist. Before he could further subdue her, she twisted, kneeing him hard in the groin. He bent in half with a groan. In all the fights he'd been in, it was the first someone had been dirty enough to aim there.

"Bitch!"

She pulled back her fist, but he grabbed her by the waist and toppled them both over before she had the chance. He straddled her, pressing her wrists into the hard ground as she continued to flail, hips bucking as if to throw him off. Fox gave a grunt as he held her down.

Her face was flushed red and her eyes burned with such intensity he thought they might catch fire.

"Afraid to fight me like a man?" she seethed.

"You're the one fighting dirty," he said, pressing her harder into the soil.

"Dirty wins."

She bucked beneath him and the friction of her body against his sent a thrill of electricity through him. He froze, suddenly aware of their positions. The last time he'd had a woman laid out beneath him like this, the circumstances had been much different. Though looking down at her with her face flushed and lips wet, he needed to remind himself of that fact. Heat crawled up his neck and he couldn't draw his eyes away from where her lips stretched over bared teeth.

Unaware of his dilemma, Sofia continued to twist and fight beneath him, her hips shifting against him in rhythm.

"Stop moving!" he seethed, even as she went rigid beneath him. His body was thrumming, with anger and something more, and he knew she now felt his reaction to her. It was pressed against her hip and impossible to ignore. She went limp beneath him and he immediately let her go, pushing himself up.

He turned, straightening his clothes and adjusting himself, trying his best to suppress the red creeping up his neck. She brushed the dirt off herself and combed the leaves from her tangled curls before turning back to him.

"Don't touch me again," she said, sneering as she looked down at his crotch.

"That didn't mean anything. It was a natural reaction."

"I know how cocks work."

"Why are you so crass?"

She gave a sharp laugh. "You don't like me saying cock?"

The heat rose in his face and her smirk deepened.

"C..o..c..k..." she said, slowly enunciating each sound.

"Bitch," he said, copying her tone with a smile. He ignored the snarl that rose from her throat, stepping closer to her. "Don't hit me again."

"Fine." She didn't meet his eyes.

He opened his mouth, not sure what he was even going to say, but she didn't give him the chance. She turned and stormed away, not bothering to wait for him to follow. He was tempted not to. He wouldn't have to deal with her constant verbal sparring or what his body's reaction meant. He wouldn't have to remember the feel of her body writhing underneath him. But it would be a pointless act of suicide to allow himself to be left out here alone—at least until they found water and he could get his brain working again. He had a weapon now and knew a vague direction he needed to go. If he could figure out his water situation, he could easily survive a few days alone in the rainforest as he made his way back to the city. He wouldn't have her, but he'd have the information for the chief commander.

He was still trying to weigh his options, when he saw Sofia, who was walking a few yards ahead of him, vanish without warning. He stopped, staring at where she had just been, as if she might reappear at any moment, her disappearance another nasty trick of the rainforest. Was this some new faery magic he'd never heard of? But in the same moment he thought that, he heard the splash of water echoing from somewhere beneath him.

With more care than he thought possible given his dehydrated and exhausted state, he inched forward, checking his weight on the ground with each step. If Sofia had missed the hole in the earth, he'd likely not fare any better. Once he made it to where she'd disappeared, he saw a small tear in the vines and bushes that crowded across the forest floor and hid the small cenote opening from view.

The ground beneath his feet was unsteady and he carefully moved onto his stomach to yell down into the opening.

"Are you okay?"

There was a splash before he heard an answering splutter.

"I think so, yes."

He leaned back, content to know she was at least breathing. As much as he wanted to simply walk away, the splashing of water beneath him made his jaw ache with need. But he also didn't want to take the same way down.

"Is the water fresh?" he said as he ripped the vines away, careful to keep his feet on solid ground.

"Gods, yes!" she said after a delay that only made his thirst louder. He could almost imagine the cold, fresh water rushing down her throat which each swallow.

Once he'd ripped more of the vines away, he was able to see that the opening she'd fallen into was only a few feet across at its widest and there was no option for getting down without jumping. The hole itself was at the top of a large cavernous ceiling stretching above an emerald lake.

Even as he mentally prepared himself to jump down, he realized that the lake was sparkling with sunlight—too much sunlight given the small hole. He stood up, looking farther in the distance and trying to see the ground ahead, but the thick underbrush was impossible to read.

"I'm going to find the other opening," he called down, trying to see where she was splashing below.

"Farther up. You won't miss it."

He kept his footsteps careful, all too aware that another crevice could appear and it was only luck that would send him into the lake below and not the ground beside it.

A few minutes of searching later, he saw the telltale sign of the trees dipping down, and the ground gave way to a much larger cenote opening. Here, the walls of the cavern below butted up against the opening, allowing for a precarious path down to the lake.

He moved around the cenote from above, tracing the best path down with his eyes. He wasn't keen on climbing down, but it was a safer option than jumping. The closer he looked, the more he realized this wasn't just a simple cliff. Somewhere beneath the yellowing vines and the damp earth, he could make out the occasional stone step carved into the side of the cenote, moving down in a large spiral.

"Can you hear me?" he asked, no longer able to see where she was in the cavern.

"Yes," she said, sounding farther away.

"I'm going to try and climb down."

"Just jump!"

"No, thank you."

"I didn't realize king's men were such babies." The words were muttered, yet he heard them clearly, as if the echo had wanted to ensure he caught her snark.

He gave a small growl, looking over the edge of the wall once more. *Fine.*

He jumped.

The water was surprisingly warm when he hit it, a gasp escaping his lips at the sudden impact. He choked on water, pulled between wanting to drink it immediately and knowing he needed to breathe. In the confusion and desperation, he did both, breathing in a lungful of water before coughing it back up.

Then Sofia was there beside him in the water, dragging him to shore.

"Gods help us, are you trying to kill yourself? Do you not know how to swim?"

He doubled over, coughing up another mouthful of water as he tried to reply.

"I know—how—to swim." He managed to press out the words between hacking coughs. Sofia smacked him along his back a few times and he almost thanked her, but she was probably only happy to have an excuse to hit him.

"I'm good. I'm okay," he said as the air started moving through his lungs again.

"Thank the gods," Sofia said with a tone of sarcasm, as if she hadn't been the one to help drag him out. She was standing before he could respond, taking in their surroundings, and his own eyes followed.

The afternoon sun was slanted, lighting the cavern in contrasted stripes of shadow and light. He had been impressed with the cenote that the resistance had thrown him into, with its cavernous ceiling and twisting tunnels. He now saw that their base was nothing but a haphazard campsite.

The cavern stretched out much farther than the opening above, to the left and right, large and intricately carved columns holding up the ceiling above. They were brown and gray, but he saw the occasional remnants of paint along the grooves. The floors themselves, while dirt and stone along the edge of the lake, transitioned into painted tiles farther on, and lanterns hung from chains on the ceiling, their painted glass rivaling the rainforest's most colorful flowers. They hung dark and limp, but waiting to be lit once more.

This wasn't just a hole in the ground or a hovel to hide in. It was an entire building carved and cherished, stretched out in secret beneath the forest.

It was also a dying thing, the earth around it slowly laying claim to what humans had created. Although Fox saw the intricate lines of the flowers and patterns painted along the floors, roots and vines broke between the tiles, leaving many of them cracked or obscured. A few of the lanterns had fallen, glass shattering onto the ground below and leaving a mosaic of color behind. Most disturbingly, one or two of the columns were beginning to crumble. He wondered if this was why the hole that Sofia had fallen through was beginning to open up in the ground above.

"Did you know this place existed? Is this another resistance base?" he asked, even though a part of him already knew the answer. Everything looked too old yet too beautiful.

"I often fall into holes I know are there," she said, rolling her eyes. "This must be an abandoned settlement, from before the tribal war."

He saw her out of the corner of his eye. She was looking around with just as much awe as he was, her eyes turning bright with unshed tears. He looked away, knowing she wouldn't want him to see, and stood instead. His fingers brushed the dirt and leaves away from one of the tiles along the floor, the color of the paint still shining in the sunlight from above.

Despite the occasional Dragonborn book he'd snuck out of his father's study and read, he'd never expected their homes to look like *this.* The Dereyan history books talked about the king bringing farming, saltwater purification, and commerce to the land. The first kings tamed the monsters that sent the Dragonborn underground and taught them how to make a city and build lives together. The books only talked of Wueco before the kings as a wild and lawless place where the people worshipped and feared the monsters in turn.

He felt half in a trance as he made his way along the edge of the lake and toward the main portion of the cavern where the columns stood and the lanterns swayed in the breeze.

"Is your flint dry?" he asked, looking up and seeing the dirty remnants of a candle sitting inside the closest lantern.

She didn't answer immediately but instead dug through her bag. It was oiled leather, but she'd fallen directly into the lake. Still, when she pulled the small stone out from her pack, he saw the look of satisfaction on her face. He held out his hand, but she simply walked past him to stand under the lantern herself. To his satisfaction, she was a few inches too short to reach the candle.

"Do you need help?" he asked, amusement tinging his tone.

She didn't reply for a moment, as if she were contemplating a heretofore unknown ability to fly.

"Can you hand me the candle?"

"I can light it."

"Do you know how the use a flint?"

"You hit it and it lights," he said.

She held out her hand to him and stared in silence. After a moment, he gave in and reached up to hand her the candle inside. It was caked with dirt and dust, but not as much as one might assume. He imagined it was mostly protected in its small glass cage.

She lit it and handed it back before he slipped it into place. They did this to the next three lanterns they found with candles in good enough shape to light, wiping away the dirt that caked the glass as best as possible. With each one, the cavern brightened, shadows melting away to show the spaces that had been hidden. The walls of the cavern were painted with murals of blue, black, and white dragons, scales and feathers almost gleaming wet with the details of the paint. And beyond those walls stretched hallways in nearly every direction, dropping off into shadow. The large room, with its emerald lake and intricate artwork, was only the beginning of the ancient complex, and for a moment, Fox glimpsed the glory of the Dragonborn before the first king had been born. With all their myths and stories of magic, the reality of *this* couldn't be denied.

And for the first time in many cycles, a seed of doubt bloomed in his chest. If their histories had neglected the architectural beauty of the Dragonborn's cenotes, what else might be lost in the records they were taught?

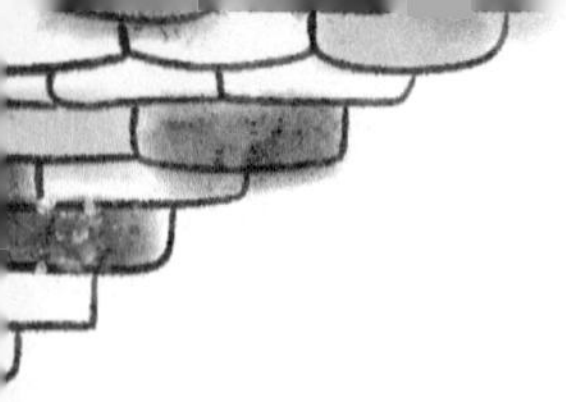

FOX

AGE 13

Prior to the first king's revelation, the tribes of Wueco built their cities underground in the many cenotes that cover the land. While they were happy with their existence, it was the first king that suggested the humans fight the dark creatures of the forest rather than hiding away from them. He saw the forest as belonging to their people as much as the dragons and faeries. It was through him that his tribe laid claim to the first above-ground city east of what is now Suvi.

-The Legacy of the Kings: A History of Wueco's Creation by Francis Knoll

The silence wasn't new to their family. There had been many silent meals and silent evenings before, but it had never been so heavy or so loud. Fox heard the rush of his blood in his ears and the pounding of his heart. He almost imagined his father could hear them both from his place at the head of the table a few feet away. But if he did, he didn't say anything, choosing to keep his eyes on his bowl as he ate another spoonful of the bean stew the cook had made.

A stifled sob from his mother broke the silence. It was a choked-off thing that she almost immediately swallowed. Father's eyes shot up and narrowed as if her cry had somehow interrupted a perfectly good evening. Is that what he thought? That if none of them addressed the empty seat across the table from Fox that they might forget that Leon was gone? Dead? They could simply pretend he was in the barracks and would return for his next leave.

Seven others had died in the explosion. They'd been lucky, the chief commander said. Half the main unit had been sent out on a reconnaissance mission and another handful were taking care of the breach along the wall. The same breach that Leon was supposed to be at before he'd returned to collect Fox.

His father hadn't cried. Not that Fox had seen. And Fox had followed his lead, keeping his jaw tight and his eyes dry. If he focused on his anger and his hate, then the grief didn't feel as overwhelming. He could scream at the Dragonborn maid when she broke the mug his brother had given him two cycles ago. He could kick the dirty Dragonborn garden boy when he looked at him the wrong way. But he couldn't curse his brother for daring to die. He couldn't scream at himself loud enough to make his own guilt and pain go away.

He was starting to hate the sound of silence. It only made the voice in his head louder.

Another broken sob crawled up from Mother's throat and he saw her clench her fist to her chest out of the corner of his eye, as if she was trying to hold herself together.

"Paoletta, if you insist on causing a scene, you can go to your room," his father said, still not looking up from his food.

Mother didn't point out that she wasn't a child to be sent away. She simply stood up and walked out, the sobs left as an echo in the dining room.

"Eat," his father snapped, and Fox quickly returned his gaze to his bowl, the spoon rising to his mouth and his throat swallowing automatically.

That was the last word spoken for the rest of dinner until his father had scraped his bowl clean. Fox had barely made a dent in his food, but the moment his father stood from the table, he knew it was the sign that dinner was done. He stood, giving his father a silent bow as he walked out, following the same path Mother had taken just minutes before.

He went back to his room. At least the silence in there was his and his alone. But when he opened the door, the light from the gas lamps in the hallway fell perfectly across his small desk where the leather-bound book was laid. The cover was cracked now, the gold title gone beneath the dirt and stains, but Fox could still picture exactly what it looked like when he'd plucked it off the shelf. He also remembered how the book felt pressed against his chest in the hours he laid beneath the rubble as the blood trickled down, soaking into the leather. His brother's blood.

Fox's fist crashed against his bedroom wall before he knew what he was doing. He stomped across the room in half a daze, something bigger than anger boiling in his chest. The leather was warm beneath his hands as he grabbed it, twisting it as if he might break it. But the binding was tight, the pages thick. He glanced at the fire in his hearth; he couldn't do that, not with his brother's blood still staining the cover. Instead, he marched to his closet, wrenching the loose panel away. There was a small stash of books hidden from his father tucked in the dark space between the walls. He didn't look at them, shoving the book deeper into the crevice before shutting it away.

It was only when the panel was back on the wall that he felt like he could breathe again, though he still couldn't stay in his room.

He walked down the hall, not sure where he was going until he was standing, looking at the carved door with its detailed ferns and the prowling jaguar looking out through the underbrush. It was Drag-onborn made—a gift from the chief commander when Leon had been born. Fox had his own door, a similar scene with a serpent twisting around a tree branch, ready to strike. When they were younger, his brother had convinced him that the snake would move when Fox wasn't looking.

He rested a hand on the door, feeling the lacquered wood under his fingertips. It was cold against his skin. When he heard the shuffle of movement beyond, his instinct was to step away, muscles tense. His father had always told him ghosts were myths, but sometimes in the night when everyone else was sleeping, Fox thought he could feel something moving in the halls, something watching him.

But then he heard Mother's muffled voice beyond and his shoulders slumped. Of course, it wasn't a ghost. He should have walked away and left his mother to her grief. He didn't need to sit in it. Crying wouldn't bring his brother back, and it wouldn't stop the resistance from murdering anyone else. But his hand was on the knob, turning it and pushing the door open without his permission.

He hadn't spent time alone with Mother in cycles and a stupid, childish part of him simply missed her. She was sitting on his brother's old bed, holding his pillow to her chest. Fox stepped forward without thinking and let her wrap him in a hug. Her arms were tight around his back and the pillow was warm where it pressed between them.

"I miss him," Fox said, finally feeling safe enough to express the words in the muffled folds of the pillow and her knit sweater. He wasn't sure how she understood him, but she did and she held him tighter.

"I do, too, Little Fox." The words were a whisper in his hair.

"The Dragonborn believe the dead don't always go to the afterworld. That sometimes their spirits get stuck." His voice was still muffled and quiet, as if his father might hear him from across the house. "Do you think Leon is a ghost now?"

She was quiet for a while and he wondered if she would answer.

"Leon is with all of the other loyal king's men now in the afterworld, where every king of the past looks over us all after we die."

He wanted to point out that perhaps there was no afterworld and nowhere for the spirits to go after they died, but he was too fearful of breaking Mother's heart over his own doubts. He stayed silent. It was what their family was good at. They stayed like that until his father's voice rang through the hall, calling for Mother. She gave Fox a soft kiss on the forehead before she left, closing the door behind her so his father wouldn't see him in there.

He should have gone back to his room. He should have wiped the hot tears from his eyes and straightened his clothes. Instead, he curled up on his brother's bed, the pillow now clutched in his arms, and he closed his eyes, comfortable with the familiar scent. He woke up the next morning to his father's shouts in the doorway, and that evening his brother's bedroom was empty, every trace of him swept away.

CHAPTER TWENTY-TWO
SOFIA

Sofia didn't even bother to look back at Ocon as the entire cavern came to life under the colorful light of the lanterns. The stained glass cast rainbows across the floor and walls, highlighting the intricately painted designs that had faded away with time. Even the ceiling was painted the color of the sky in the heart of the cold season.

She'd been impressed with the resistance's base the first time she'd seen it, with its dirt floors and torches. But now she realized that the cenotes they'd moved between were decaying things, long dead and nearly forgotten. This one though, no matter how forgotten it appeared, wasn't dead. The light that the lanterns cast danced across the walls and they *breathed.* She felt the ghosts of her ancestors even now taking up space.

She ducked her head into the first hall she came across and saw that the lanterns continued at regular intervals. The light from the main room lit just enough to see a line of intricately carved doors disappearing into the shadowed darkness.

"Ocon!" she called. "I need your monkey arms."

She waited, trying not to be annoyed when he didn't even answer her.

"Ocon," she said, not bothering to hide her frustration as she came back into the main room. He was standing a few yards away now, along the edge of the cavern, newly lit with the candle he was holding.

When he turned, his expression sent ice down her spine and she walked forward with rigid steps. Only once she was closer and able to look past him where the candlelight chased away the shadows on the ground did she see what had caught his attention.

Human remains, clothes turned nearly to dust and bones picked clean by centuries of decay, were scattered across the back wall.

"Oh," she said, a hand covering her mouth. The longer she looked, the more her stomach turned, but she couldn't turn away. There were so many bones—so many people had died here—and some of the skulls she saw were so small. These weren't the bodies of warriors scattered from a battle. These were families, lined up and slaughtered.

Her eyes burned and she felt the tears welling hot. She turned away before Ocon could notice. Bile was sharp on her tongue, the water she had overindulged in earlier crawling up her throat. She had found the ghosts.

"Can you light me a candle so I can look through the halls," she said once she knew her voice wouldn't crack.

"Yeah—yes," he said, turning away from the bones after another moment. She couldn't quite tell in the dim light, but his face was a shade too pale and his eyes a fraction too wide. He turned and walked away before she could try to read his expression, grabbing a candle from an unlit lantern. He handed her the candle, lit with his own.

Although the arched doorways down the closet hallway drew her attention, she walked back to the previous hall, wanting to follow some type of pattern with her exploring. She also wanted some space from Ocon to pull herself back together. He didn't deserve to see her grief and pain over the horrors done to her people.

The first room she entered was small, a sitting mat nearly decayed into nothing lying along the back wall. A doorway to the right led into what had once been a bedroom. The wood and clay base of the bed was obvious, although the pad and blankets that had once sat on it were long gone, eaten away by age and exposure. The next three doors held the same remnants of a family's life, one bed in one, three beds in another. Proof of the people that had once lived and loved here.

Most anything of use—blankets, clothes, or food—had long ago rotted away, although she found a few clay bowls still in one piece. They would make drinking water easier, at least.

She almost turned away, knowing that the other doors likely held similar remnants of living quarters behind them, each patterned the same. But she noticed some of the doors farther down the hall were broken away, the thresholds gaping like lost teeth and her feet moved of their own accord. At the first doorway, she saw that even the frame had been broken away, dirt falling from the ceiling for lack of support. She didn't even need to step over the collapsed doorway to see what waited inside. Another pile of bones, these ones intertwined together in the corner of the room, the fear of their ghosts heavy in the air. She wondered if it was the raw pain that had happened here or her own connection to her ancestors that had her almost hearing the cries of the family as they had died.

Still nauseated with hunger, she turned away quickly and left the living quarters behind. She didn't need to see the other rooms that had been broken into to know what was on the other side.

She found the hall with the arched doorways and saw the rotted remnants of large kitchens and a bathhouse. The water left behind in the baths had allowed the twisting roots and fallen seeds from the earth above to flourish, turning the bathhouse into a small rainforest, the plants somehow thriving here with the barest hint of light from the cracked ceiling above.

An echoing sound from a few rooms away drew her attention, and she followed the flickering light of Ocon's candle through another arch. He stood across a large room, the shadows and light dancing with every shiver of the flame in his hands. He was silent, looking up at the mural that stretched across the wall. Even in the dim light, Sofia saw that the mural wrapped around the entire room, a never-ending landscape of Wueco, from the sea to the mountains. But it wasn't the land that had drawn Ocon's eye. He was staring in wonder up at the large cenote dragon that wrapped around itself, the painting so detailed she thought she saw its wings moving and a sparkle in its blue eyes.

She turned and saw she was standing next to the long tail of another dragon, spiraling up toward the ceiling. She stepped to the left, moving her own candle along the mural to study it closer. Her dragon stood proudly along the wall, the sharp claw-like talons clutching the snow-capped mountain beneath it, each one the length of her hand. Even faded and covered in dust and dirt, the black and silver scales of the dragon were a stark contrast to the white snow. The feathers at the dragon's neck almost gleamed in the candlelight, as if painted with real silver.

Beneath where its claws dug into the mountain peak, a low altar was just visible beneath the detritus of time. She ran a hand along the stone ledge, sweeping away some of the leaves and dirt, uncovering the small candles and gold basin still waiting for their prayer.

A few feet from where her dragon ended, she saw the tail of Ocon's dragon wrapping around a tree, its blue feathers contrasting against brown and green. Its scales gleamed a pale silver that she realized with a small jolt matched Ocon's own eyes. He was still standing below the dragon's head, his hand running along the wall where its mouth was opened in a scream, water pouring forth from it in frothy waves. Looking past him at the other wall, she could just see the white-and-blue-painted sea dragon, twisting through the air above a roiling ocean.

"Is this what they thought dragons looked like?" Ocon said, acknowledging Sofia's presence for the first time.

"The people that painted these didn't *think*," she said, the words softer than she expected, but it felt wrong to curse and yell in a room like this. "They knew."

She lowered her candle and placed it on the small altar that stretched across the front wall in front of the cenote dragon. It was as dirty as the other one, but she began to brush leaves and debris aside, uncovering the stone below.

At one point, there would have been food and trinkets of gold and silver left, but these likely had been stolen by the tribe—the king's men

—that had invaded this cenote. Still, there were remnants of weavings, carvings, and small children's toys left to honor the cenote dragons.

A bright flash of blue beneath a thick layer of soil caught her eye. She pushed Ocon aside without a word and began cleaning away the dirt there. Her fingers brushed against something hot and she carefully pulled out an iridescent blue feather. It was soft as clouds and hot to the touch, as if it had been sitting in the sun, and as she set it back against the altar, it stretched up to nearly her head.

Her mind was spinning. She was touching something that proved the dragons were real—something that had belonged to the gods.

"What is that?" Ocon asked, looking over her shoulder with something between awe and fear.

"A dragon feather," she said, continuing to clean the altar until only the few offerings that had withstood the test of time remained—two small, but intricately carved stone figurines, a tiny wooden doll, and a stained bowl.

She placed her candle at the center and kneeled, eyes gazing up at the painting. Her ancestors had kneeled in this very spot hundreds of cycles ago, praying to the gods, not as childish myths, but known truths. She remembered her thoughts back in the city when Sari was being executed.

It would take the gods to take down the false god that the king believed himself to be. If she could bring them back, prove that they hadn't been killed off by the great king, perhaps her people stood a chance against the Dereyans.

"What are you doing?"

"Praying."

"Even if you think they existed at some point, the dragons are long gone," he said with the slightest bit of sneer to his tone.

"The dragons were murdered by the *great* king," she said, not looking over her shoulder at him. "But plenty of historical accounts note that not all the dragons died and plenty escaped, chased out of Wueco to protect themselves. There are books—"

She stopped. She'd almost told him the truth. There were books in his chief commander's own office that debated if the dragons were truly gone—books that discussed the possibility that they survived some-where far from Wueco and Suvi. Things he didn't need to know.

He let out a snort, telling her exactly what he thought of these historical accounts and a few moments later, she heard his footfalls fading behind her. A sigh escaped her lips at finally being alone.

Yet now that she was, she felt frozen, looking up into the bright knowing eyes of the mural, as if it knew she didn't belong here. She'd said prayers to the dragons before, from the first night she read about them and kneeled at her window, praying to the sky as if they might return then and there because she asked. But now she was here, in front of a true altar to the gods with a dragon feather gleaming in the candle-light, and she felt so insignificant.

Brushing off her insecurities, if only for the moment, Sofia took her dagger and dug the tip into the pad of her finger until she drew blood. She wasn't squeamish about such things, but getting an infection while lost in the rainforest wasn't going to be a good move, so she was careful as she dripped her blood into the small wooden bowl in the center of the altar. And then she spoke words she'd never actually heard out loud, in a tongue she barely knew, reciting the traditional invocation she'd seen in a book when she was eleven and had memorized that same day.

She held her breath, as if something might shift, as if the dragon in front of her might pull itself from the wall and fly away, answering her call for help. But all that followed was silence and she felt the hope she didn't know she was holding on to drift away with her next breath.

WHEN SHE WALKED out a few minutes later, she tried not to let the hopelessness overwhelm her. If she could get Ocon to help her break into the military quarter and into the chief commander's house once more, she could get the books she needed. There was a way to bring back the dragons and she would find it.

She was still thinking about how to convince Ocon to help her as she turned the corner to the sight of him standing in the shallows of the lake, wet and completely naked. He hadn't noticed her, his back on full display. He was dabbing at the three long gashes along his side where the wolfshifter had managed to catch him with his claws and she grimaced in empathy, knowing all too well the pain of cleaning one's own wounds out. He was just deep enough to cover his lower half, but the water lapping at his waist showed a hint of the curve of his ass disappearing beneath the lake surface and she bit her lip. He had the body of a soldier, chiseled from cycles of training.

Against her better judgment, she let her eyes wander over the rest of his back. It truly wasn't fair for such a vile man to possess such a perfect body, and she hated that she noticed. She'd barely glanced at another boy or man since Gabriel.

She bit her mind off, focusing instead on the ink that painted his body. She'd seen the dagger on his forearm and gotten glimpses of the viper that twisted around his neck and shoulder. Now she saw that a large tattoo of a feline-like beast stretched across nearly his entire back, a thick halo of hair wrapped around his head as it roared. The creature rippled with the movement of Ocon's muscles, as if it might jump from his skin and attack at the first provocation.

Beneath the ink were remnants of scars, ridges of lighter skin that she was plenty familiar with on her own back. She couldn't stop the hiss of something feral escaping her throat at the thought of her scars and Ocon jerked, turning to notice her at last.

She wasn't sure what he saw in her expression, but his initial smirk dropped quickly from his face.

"You can wash off, too," he said, face serious. "I can go somewhere else while you—"

She didn't let him finish, knowing she wouldn't feel comfortable bathing with him here, in a separate room or not. "I'm fine."

"I promise, I won't—"

"I said, I'm fine. We should prepare for staying here tonight. I'll go hunt."

She turned before he could say anything otherwise, grabbed her bow and arrows, and marched toward the crumbling staircase that would lead her out. She needed a break from the ghosts that haunted this place so loudly she could almost hear them. Food might do her some good.

SOFIA

AGE 14

Gods grant me the resilience of the dragon scale,
the strength of the fangs,
the patience of the feather,
the reliability of the wings.

May your storms light our spirits,
your rain feed the seeds we've sown,
your wind fill our lungs,
and your waves always carry us home.

-In Praise of Dragons and Monsters by Maria Nunes

Sofia snuck up behind Gabriel while he was focused on his task. If she'd been working with the horses, she'd have taken more care, but he was sitting in an empty portion of the stables, a leather saddle laid across his lap as he rubbed oil into it.

She crept silently up before wrapping her arms around him.

"Hello!"

He jumped, giving a small yelp that had the horse in the nearest stall letting out a snort of air.

"Sof!" he said as he twisted to look at her, eyes wide for only a moment before his smile stretched wide. She'd learned over the past cycle that when his smile was at its widest, he had two dimples. She enjoyed the challenge of bringing that second dimple out.

He stood, wrapping her in a warm embrace, planting a soft kiss on her forehead and then her lips.

"What are you doing here? Aren't you working?"

She gave a sheepish shrug. She was in fact working, but like most days over the past few blinks, she'd finished the transcribing early, and with Mina out sick, she'd been left in the office alone. It was the peak of the hot season and even the breeze through the wide windows was blistering and stale.

"I won't be missed for another hour."

"Jorge might be back before then."

"He won't." Jorge—the head of the stables—was currently in a meeting with the chief commander and general, something she only knew because she'd transcribed the schedule for the chief commander last week.

Gabriel only gave a small smirk and rolled his eyes. She'd never quite confessed what she did in the chief commander's office for him, but he wasn't stupid and had picked up over their time together that she wasn't just dusting shelves.

"Are you ever going to tell me how you know everything?"

"Are you ever going to kiss me without having to give a speech first?" she asked, pressing herself closer to him.

He grinned in the way she knew he would and pulled her in for another kiss, his tongue tentatively touching her lips before he pulled away.

"I do still have work to do, unfortunately. The leathers need to be oiled by the end of the day and at this rate, I'm going to be here until dawn."

She gave a dramatic sigh, but grabbed an extra rag from the workbench and sat across from where he'd been in front of the saddle. He followed suit, although she saw the glint of disappointment in his eyes that made her heart swell and the butterflies in her stomach dance. He'd have been happier to keep kissing.

Their relationship had started as stolen kisses in the evening after their shifts, but over the past few blinks, they'd spent more and more time together after work. Gabriel had even walked her home a few times, despite living in the complete opposite direction. Her parents had invited him for dinner for the coming week, despite knowing it would cut their rations for a few days following.

They worked in companionable silence for a while, Sofia relishing in the work that gave her fingers a break from the constant writing.

"So did the chief commander teach you how to read?"

"Gods no, I taught myself," she said, before snapping her jaw shut, almost biting her tongue in the process.

Gabriel looked at her with such glee that she might almost forget she'd just admitted treason to him.

"I knew it!" he said, voice a sharp whisper. "But Chief Commander Harlow knows. He has to know. It's what you've been doing for him in his office this entire time? Reading?"

"Quiet," she said, voice shrill and heart pounding hard. Her eyes darted around the stables as if a horse might jump out with an *aha* at having heard their conversation.

"No one's around, you said so yourself."

"Yes, I read and write for him, but no one knows. No one. Not even my parents."

"Shit," he said. "That's seriously incredible. I don't know what's more impressive, the chief commander breaking the law or you teaching yourself how to read."

Her cheeks heated and she forced herself to focus on the task at hand. Hot tears burned at the backs of her eyes and she hated herself for it. The tears weren't for sadness, but the realization that beyond the chief commander catching her all those cycles ago, she'd never been able to share this part of her. And she'd never had someone looking at her like this, with such admiration and *love.*

The word popped into her mind and Sofia had to push it away. Love wasn't something Dragonborn experienced.

"Your finger, then?"

He said the words carefully. She knew he'd seen the missing digit back when they'd first started spending time together. He'd likely felt it the first time he'd grabbed her hand as they walked to the inner gates together. But he'd been smart enough to never ask.

"The chief commander caught me. He deemed the finger a worthy punishment if I promised to work for him."

She was still avoiding his eyes, so when his fingers grazed across her cheek, she flinched before finally sinking into the warmth of his skin.

"You are truly amazing."

She looked up and saw his eyes, staring at her with such earnestness. "Most people wouldn't dare call treason amazing," she said, placing her own hand over his, forcing his hand to stay there, cradled against her cheek.

He looked thoughtful for a moment.

"I knew my old boss was skimming stocks back when I worked on the docks." Sofia had to strain to hear the words that he mumbled out.

She blinked for a moment. "What?"

"I knew long before he got caught. He was feeding some of the families in the drowned quarter that didn't have sanctioned jobs for rations." He paused, looking at her. "The point is it's not like I haven't done my fair share of treason. I might have even helped deliver the fish occasionally—not that I would have claimed to know it wasn't sanctioned by the king's food assessor."

Sofia felt something swell in her chest. Even Mina, who loved listening to her stories of dragons and faeries, had never spoken a word against the king or crown. Her parents, for all the anger she knew they held against the crown, had never spoken a single word out loud to threaten their position in Suvi as loyalists.

"I still read sometimes," she said softly, watching his face. "When the chief commander isn't in the office."

"Let's take a break from this. If you help me with a few more saddles, I'll be on track even if we do—other things."

She bit her lip and they stood, and when he pressed her against the wall of the closet stall and sealed his lips onto her own, she almost forgot about their troubles and the sins they had confessed to each other. Almost.

CHAPTER TWENTY-THREE
FOX

Fox was left staring after her, trying to understand what had just happened. He could have sworn when he first heard her standing behind him, silent as he washed his cuts, that she had been ogling him. Not that it mattered to him despite what *certain parts* of him had decided, but he enjoyed when another person appreciated his body. He'd spent the last few sun cycles of his teens and the time since honing his body to be what it was now; he was no longer the scrawny boy his brother knew him as.

But when he'd turned and noticed her, the look in her eyes had been one of fear and then hatred. He should have been getting used to such emotions from her, but she wiped them both away so quickly, he was still unsure they'd been real.

She'd disappeared over the lip of the cenote, and once he knew she wasn't going to fall back into the lake, he moved to get dressed. She wasn't wrong about wanting to stay in the cenote for the night. It was safer away from the creatures that prowled in the forest and close to water, but with the various holes in the ceiling of the cavern, it wasn't as warm as he wanted. A cursory search of the rooms beyond the main chamber told him he didn't want to stay back there. There was something haunting about the bedrooms and kitchens—remnants of lives lost and forgotten.

Then again, as he re-examined the pile of bones against the wall, he knew they couldn't sleep out here with them, either. So he turned to his self-imposed task with a heavy chest, mind unsettled. He wasn't usually squeamish about death, but these weren't enemy soldiers or terrorists that had been killed. He was looking down at the bones of children and families, and it didn't take much to recognize it was likely his ancestors —the Dereyans—who had taken their lives.

Even his people learned this part of their history—when, after decades of warfare going nowhere, their ancestors had been forced to kill the last few tribes of Dragonborn that refused to bow to the king. It had been a last resort to finally bring peace to the area and save people from the constant threat of attack and death. But the killings had been brutal. Anyone not willing to submit was killed. Fox wasn't sure he agreed with the measures taken, even if it meant he had the home he had now. He would have never admitted this out loud.

He removed his cloak, ignoring the shiver that ran up his spine at the cold air against his bare arms, still damp from the lake. It would be faster to move the bones in the cloth than try to carry them in his arms. He moved them slowly, gathering them into the center of the cloak gently. They were fragile in his hands and he didn't want to break them any more than they already were. He was happy that at least time had done its job, leaving truly nothing but bones. Though the bite marks he noticed on some were slightly disturbing.

More disturbing were the small bones he picked up. Not the jaw bones or the fingers, but the small femurs and thin ulnas that he knew couldn't have belonged to adults. The more bones he carried back to the dragon hall, the more it became clear that the majority belonged to children. He imagined the adults had died off fighting the war, leaving the children behind only to be slaughtered.

Did these children pose such a threat to the king that they warranted a massacre?

"Do you ever wonder why your king doesn't do just that? Let us go free into the rainforest?"

But Fox knew all too well, peace came from unity. Without unity there would always be war. Even now, the differences between their people continued to lead to suffering and death. The Dragonborn and Dereyans could never live side-by-side in peace. They needed to unify under a single belief.

Didn't they?

Even these thoughts couldn't stop the guilt from clawing at his chest as he moved the bones and laid them out at the altar for their gods. And underneath the watch of the dragons, he couldn't stop himself from counting the number of skulls. Each life taken was a blade in his heart.

When he was done, the bones stretched along the entire room. He took a minute to clear the two altars Sofia hadn't and light the candles there. Something about leaving the bones alone in the dark felt wrong, superstitious beliefs or not.

Sofia hadn't returned by the time he was done clearing away the remains, but he managed to find a functional broom in the kitchens and used it to sweep a large swath of ground clean. He found the best leaves he could and made two small beds. They wouldn't be comfortable sleeping, but at least the leaves would protect them from the cold tiles below.

He laid down in one. It was the most uncomfortable he'd ever been, but if it meant not waking up to a faery demon or wolfshifter attempting to kill him, he'd deal with it.

He was lying on the ground, staring at the painted ceiling and wondering if there was a position to make it more comfortable when he heard Sofia's call.

She carefully, yet quickly, walked down the stone steps back into the cenote, two dead rabbits hanging from her neck, tied with a vine.

She helped him prep the rabbits. They'd put together the fire, with Sofia quite vehemently pointing out each mistake as he placed the twigs, as if it mattered how the wood looked before they burned it. But he didn't argue, already thinking about the smoky taste of the meat to come. He'd even managed to find them a sealed jar of salt in the kitchens area—one of the only things that hadn't rotted with age. It didn't fix the chewy texture of the wild meat, unfamiliar to Fox, but it helped with the taste at least.

He could have even called himself content by the time they'd eaten their fill. He buried the rest of the rabbit on the other side of the cavern while Sofia took the hearts to the altars as offerings. Why dead gods needed offerings, he wasn't sure, but he chose to keep quiet and not start a fight.

She was quiet when she returned, stoking the fire and checking his burial work without comment.

"These are terrible," Sofia said sometime later as she laid down on the small pile of leaves he'd put together for them. Her tone wasn't as harsh as he expected.

"They are," he agreed. "It was that or dirt."

"At least the fire's warm."

"And there are no faeries down here, just ghosts." He meant it as a joke, but even saying the words sent a shiver through him and he wondered if he'd just imagined the air around him growing colder.

"I saw what you did for the bones." Sofia's voice was soft.

"They were people. They deserved the dignity."

"Thank you."

They were silent for a while, the only sounds the whistling of the wind above and the crackle of the wood burning between them.

"Did your parents teach you about the dragons and the old ways?" he asked.

The question was born of pure curiosity, but she stiffened at his words.

"Sorry, I didn't mean to pry. I—I have to wonder how you know so much when..." He trailed off, uncomfortable.

"When my people aren't allowed to know such things?" she said after too long.

He didn't answer. He didn't need to.

"My parents didn't teach me. They have always been loyal to the king." She went silent again and he thought she might stop there, but then he heard the small intake of breath before she spoke again. "When

I read the stories of my ancestors and the dragons, it was the first time I felt like something more."

"More than what?"

She wasn't looking at him and it allowed him to watch her carefully without fear of judgment. Her eyes were focused on the small sliver of sky they could see from their spot in the cenote, where the two moons rose above the tree line. They were full and bright, blocking out the stars.

"More than an animal. More than nothing." She turned toward him and he quickly looked away. "Do you know any of our beliefs?"

"Some," he admitted, "but I couldn't tell you the legends from the histories."

"The reason we call ourselves Dragonborn is because that's what we are. Quelia, the mother of all things, created the world and when she was done, she shed her feathers, each one falling to the earth, imbued with magic to become all the creatures of the forest. We were born of her own body. Her scales remained in the sky, turning into the stars and her eyes became the moons, watching over what she had made with reverence. She sacrificed herself to give us life. I wonder what she thinks of her people now."

"So if you were created from feathers, where did my people come from?" He risked a glance her way and saw the furrow of her eyebrows as she stared back.

"You say it like we're different species."

He shifted, uncomfortable with the look she was giving him.

"You were born of feathers, too. All of us are Dragonborn. Even those who turned on the gods and murdered their own kind."

"So, we're all the same?" he asked.

"A frightening thought, isn't it?"

"If you believe in ghosts, then the Dereyans can turn into ghosts, too."

She gave another shrug.

"Do you worry about the hundreds of Dereyans you've killed haunting you?" he said, not expecting an answer. He was thinking of his brother. He shouldn't have been. It never led anywhere productive, only to tears or anger.

"Only if you're worried about the thousands of Dragonborn your people have killed."

"So it's okay for you to kill, but not us?"

"We are killing out of necessity because it's the only language your chief commander speaks." She spit the words out.

"Why do you hate the chief commander so much?"

"How is that a serious question?"

He watched her face from across the fire, knowing full well he was right. There was something in her face when she spoke of the chief commander, something more than when she spoke of the king or the Dereyans. It was the same look she gave him sometimes, too. *Hatred. Rage.*

"What did he do to you?"

She didn't answer for a while and he wondered if she even would.

"The chief commander took someone from me. He killed them because he couldn't kill me. I was...too useful."

"I...I'm sorry." He was surprised that he meant the words. He knew what grief felt like. It laid on his own shoulders like a chain. "Is that when you lost your finger?"

She gave a sharp, bitter laugh. "No. My punishment was much worse."

He opened his mouth, unsure of how to ask the question, but she cut him off.

"For that answer, you'll have to ask your father."

With that, she turned over, her back to the fire. To him.

He didn't move for a while, watching her, trying to understand yet trying to not think about what she had said. *Ask your father.* Something akin to anger thrummed through him. He knew exactly the types of punishments his father meted out. Even after he'd been promoted to general, his father had chosen to keep his role as head interrogator. Because he loved the role—took joy in it. He took joy in pain. The thought made Fox's stomach sour and he couldn't explain why. She was rebel filth—a traitor to the king—and it shouldn't matter to him what punishments she'd endured for her treason. It couldn't matter.

Fox was still staring into the fire when he heard her, words whispered so long, he wondered if she meant for him to hear.

"Everyone in the resistance has a story like mine. If you weren't so busy murdering us, maybe we'd share them."

The words didn't ask for an answer and he bit his tongue. When he finally fell asleep, those words still sat heavy on his chest.

CHAPTER TWENTY-FOUR
SOFIA

Sofia woke sometime in the night, her body wracked with shivers. The fire had died out, the last of their wood gone, leaving her with nothing but her shawl and the thin, cool leaves beneath her. The moons were glowing bright in the sky and the light reflected down through the ceiling and across the lake. It gave a magical luminescence to the cavern, but the lake and wind whistling across it softly did nothing to warm her.

"I can literally hear your teeth chattering." Ocon's grumbled voice sounded from a couple feet away.

"Sorry to wake you," she said, pushing all the vitriol into her voice she could manage, but he wasn't exaggerating and it was difficult to talk through the shudders.

"Why don't you have a cloak, anyway?" he said, as if the thought had just occurred to him.

"I was too busy chasing after my escaped prisoner to take time getting dressed. These are the leggings I sleep in. They aren't even double layered." She wondered after that admission if it was awkward to acknowledge she'd been running through the rainforest the last two days in her sleepwear.

"Kings help me," he said and she thought he might be thinking the same thing, but then she heard a shuffling. "Get over here."

"Excuse me?"

"We can share my cloak," he said, sounding as if the idea were absolutely vile to him despite offering. "I need to sleep and I don't need you freezing to death or keeping me awake with your chattering."

"No." She rolled over, hugging herself tightly and trying to still her shaking.

"Have you always been this stubborn?"

"I'm not stubborn. I just don't feel like cozying up with a murderer."

"Why do you assume I'm a murderer?"

"I'm not assuming, I know," she said. "I was in the crowd when you executed Pedro."

She didn't expect him to speak and she definitely didn't expect the vaguest crack in his voice when he did.

"Do you know how many people a single bomb can kill? The damage black powder can do?"

"Do you know how many Dragonborn die daily—not from bombs but hunger? Or how many die every blink on those scales' damned death farms?"

"Criminals," he said, voice low. "The *labor* farms are worked by criminals, and it's a fairer sentence than most of them deserve."

"People who stole food to survive or used forbidden magic to heal a child who was dying. Dragonborn who dared read. Those are the criminals you speak of."

Ocon's eyes sparkled in the dark, drilling into her. "And the ones that do murder? The ones that set off bombs that kill dozens?"

"We are trying to free our people."

"Innocents are getting caught up in the fighting, whether or not you admit it."

"Do you know how many innocent Dragonborn are killed every cycle in the city?" she asked.

"I don't want innocents on either side to die. I joined the king's men to stop the death."

"Do you want me to praise you for your benevolence?" Her voice echoed in the cavern and she heard the shrill pitch of it—the emotion and the weakness behind the words.

"I don't need praise. I thought it might help you to know I'm not pure evil."

"I didn't say you were."

"You didn't need to say it."

She wanted to argue, but perhaps he was right. It was easier to fight against those she hated.

"Fine," she said as she stood up, movements stiff with cold and pain. "This doesn't mean anything."

He was polite enough not to open his mouth, instead simply moving the cloak and letting her slip in beside him. The warmth was immediate, sinking through her bones as his arm wrapped the cloak around her shoulders.

She grabbed it quickly, letting him pull his arm back. They both did their best under the cloak to not touch, bodies close enough she felt the heat of his chest. Every breath he took had his chest brushing against her back, but she couldn't move farther without leaving the warmth of the cloak. She closed her eyes and tried to ignore the nearness of his presence. For a few minutes, she wondered if the cloak was worth it. She was so aware of his body, her own muscles aching with the tension. The idea of relaxing enough to fall asleep seemed laughable.

Yet, not too long after, the warmth and the darkness took their toll and her thoughts drifted until there was nothing.

THE NEXT THING she was aware of was the body pressed tightly to hers, the heat of it suffusing her skin. She was facing him, her face pressed into his chest and his arm draped over her. Her awareness of their position came slowly, the sleep and warmth muddling her thoughts as she let herself sink into the heat.

Her entire body stiffened as she realized exactly who was pressed so closely against her. She was very aware of every point of contact and the steady rising and falling of his chest beneath her ear. If she closed her eyes and concentrated she could almost hear his heartbeat. A good confirmation that he did indeed possess a heart, if not a soul. She was also extremely aware of the hardness pressed against her hip for the second time in so many days. She ignored the zip of heat and electricity the thought sent through her body.

It had been too long since she'd taken her energy out in that way. She didn't mess with love and commitment, but a woman still had needs. There were a few men and women at the inn that she trusted enough to seek out pleasure from without having to worry about emotions, but it had now been blinks since such nights, and Sofia was clearly pent up.

Ocon wasn't moving either and she could only assume he was still asleep. Even her sudden discomfort and tension hadn't woken him. She thought briefly of closing her eyes and pretending she was asleep until he woke and rectified the situation himself. He deserved to wake up to his arms wrapped around her. *She was the victim here.* The other option was to slip out as quietly as possible and save them both the embarrassment of the situation. But then again, she didn't feel like saving him anything.

So she didn't.

Not bothering with his comfort, she simply pushed him off of her, pulling herself out from under his arm. She also *may* have grabbed the cloak tightly in the same moment, ensuring when he went rolling off the small bed of leaves that she was left wearing it.

He let out an—in her opinion—embarrassing squeal and cursed as he woke, jumping up and brandishing his blade blindly. It took a second of blinking before his eyes focused on her. She raised an eyebrow and gave a smirk from where she sat, wrapped in his cloak.

"You couldn't have found a better way to wake me?" he said after a moment. He seemed to recognize his *other* situation in the same moment and quickly adjusted himself, face flushing.

She shrugged. "I could have, but I just wanted you to get off me as fast as possible."

"If I remember correctly, you cuddled into me last night as you were falling asleep."

"And I forced you to wrap your arms around me? How frightening for you."

He shuddered in the cool morning air and he growled at the sight of her wrapping the cloak tighter.

"Give that to me."

"I quite like it," she said. It wasn't a lie. The fabric was soft and did a much better job of insulating her from the chill than her shawl.

"I'm rather fond of it, too," he said, holding out his left hand as his right pointed the dagger in warning. "Now if you don't hand it back, I'm going to have to fight you for it, and although I don't doubt you have the skill to face me, I am taller, stronger, and have a dagger. If I win, you're not getting the cloak tonight. If I lose, you're going to have to stab me, and we know that will be a pain for both of us."

She thought about it for a moment. The chances of her winning were probably slightly below fifty percent considering her weapon was a few feet away and she was still crouched on the ground. And the idea of sleeping out in the open that night without the cloak—especially if they didn't find shelter again—made her chest tight.

Standing with as much dignity as she could manage, she slipped the cloak from her shoulders and threw it on the ground at her feet.

"We should head out soon. I'll be back in a few minutes."

She didn't explain herself as she walked away, leaving him to pick up the cloak from where she'd dropped it. Her footsteps echoed on the tiles as she made her way down the widest tunnel and to the dragons' shrine. She wanted to say one more prayer over the bones of her ancestors before they left. This might be her last chance to do so, given the cenotes closest to the city had been raided and destroyed over the past few generations leaving little evidence of the original habitants of their land. As if they might be able to pretend they had never existed to begin with.

The rabbit hearts she set out the night before after dinner were still sitting along each altar, an appeasement to the ghosts that lingered there. They were untouched by even the insects. Giving a bit more blood to the offering bowl, she kneeled and whispered the words beneath her breath. She asked for them to watch over their journey even as the small voice of her parents and Ocon both sounded in her head, reminding her that the dragons were dead. But she'd believed in many things over her life that she hadn't seen and many of those things had turned out to be real. The resistance had been a faerytale before she'd met Javi.

And there was something about the air in the room that she couldn't quite get past. She could almost feel the dragons here, listening and waiting. Or perhaps she was exhausted and underfed.

Ocon was drinking his fill of water by the lake when she returned. He didn't say anything about her disappearing into the shrine again and she didn't bother to explain.

She slipped the small cups they'd found into her pack and they silently walked together back toward the steps along the wall. She went first, more sure on the steps after coming in and out of the cavern last night. Even still, her foot slipped twice trying to balance on the thin remnants of the staircase that once was. She didn't fall and even Ocon managed to make his way out of the cenote shaking, but whole.

The forest was brightly lit by the time they made it out and the morning birds had already finished their sunrise songs, the sounds of the forest fading into the dull hum of day. Sofia was unsure if things truly looked brighter or if she was simply better rested than she'd been in the last couple of days. They hadn't had any containers to take the water away with them, but they had drunk their fill and then some before leaving.

Still, every step she took away from the cavern and the ruins of her ancestors felt like a weight in her gut. From a young age, her people were taught of the primitive nature of her ancestors before the kings had come to save them all. How they lived in holes in the ground out of fear of the dragons and only knew how to gather food from the forest. But what they had built back there had been art.

She'd been tempted to take the dragon feather—proof of what she'd found. But she also knew that walking toward Suvi with proof of the dragons was the easiest way to get killed on sight if they were caught before she made it back to the base. She felt its absence and the distance with each step.

"What are the chances we'll make it back to familiar territory today?" Ocon asked. His tone was rough and his face was set in a deep frown. She almost laughed because the damn man seemed grumpy.

She thought about prodding his poor mood, but shrugged instead. "Well, if the shapeshifters ran perfectly north with us and we have managed to walk perfectly south this entire time, then we might make it back to the tunnel entrance. Or the general area. Probably."

"You could have just said you don't know," he said. "And I assume your plan is to find the tunnel and to take it back to the base."

"It would be a safer bet than braving the wilds for an extra day."

"Safer for you."

She raised an eyebrow in his direction. "Yes."

They fell into a silence that Sofia took comfort in. She didn't want to talk to him and pretend they had anything in common. She didn't want to know anything about the people she had been fighting against. All it would do is make the guilt heavier when the time came to do what the resistance needed.

She had heard the passion in his voice the night before as he had talked of those who had died in the ongoing fight between their people. Could she truly trust such flowery words without the proof to back them up? The king and his people always talked of peace and saving lives, but they'd order the murder of a Dragonborn without regret in their next breath.

And even if she trusted Ocon's own goodwill, it didn't change what the others were doing—what his father and Chief Commander Harlow had done in the name of justice. The king's men needed to pay for the blood they had spilled.

She didn't need to hear Ocon's excuses, true or not. Perhaps she could get away with walking the rest of the distance in silence. The sounds of the forest were calming with the sun brushing warm against her skin.

Ocon, of course, had to ruin it.

"So what happened to your parents?"

She turned, eyes sharp as blades, a scream rising up in her chest. She was disappointed when he didn't flinch. "How is that any of your business?"

"You know my father. It only seems fair."

Her fists clenched at her sides, but she didn't punch him. "No one said that life is fair, little prince."

"Remember that when I have you chained up in my personal dungeons when we get home."

She spun around, back straight and jaw clenched.

"Over my dead body."

"I can arrange that."

CHAPTER TWENTY-FIVE

FOX

Fox wondered how hard it would be to knock the woman out and simply carry her back to Suvi gagged and tied, because at this point, the chief commander would be lucky if they made it back before Fox killed her.

He was in a particularly grouchy mood after Sofia woke him by flinging him off their makeshift bed, cock harder than it had been in blinks. She wasn't an ugly woman; even he had to admit that. Her hair was always a tangled mess and her eyes were too big for her face, but her body was curved and muscled and he spent too much time staring at her lips, soft and pink. She looked the most beautiful when she was angry and ranting. When her cheeks flushed red, it brought out the sprinkle of her freckles across the bridge of her nose, and her green eyes practically glowed with passion.

But none of that made her ranting and raving any more *true*. The Dragonborn weren't innocent. The resistance wasn't innocent, and their movement deserved to be torn down, each and every rebel punished for the lives they'd taken.

He wasn't lying to her when he said she'd been the one to move closer to him in the night. He would have argued, but the warmth of her body pressed against his chest had lulled him to sleep almost immediately. Somehow, despite spending days in the rainforest and refusing to wash off in the lake, her thick curls smelled of coconut. Based on the few whiffs he'd gotten of himself—he did not.

And as a thanks for preventing her from freezing to death due to her own stubbornness the night before, he'd gotten thrown on his ass.

He wanted to be home as much as she did, and he wasn't the reason they were stuck out here dodging shapeshifters and faeries and discussing the merits of praying to dragons. The first thing he was going to do once they got back—after he threw her in the darkest cell in the prison—was take a hot bath and eat his body weight in anything other than rabbit.

At least they appeared to have finally made it to an area of the rainforest that actually had water. By midday, they had already stumbled on half a dozen other cenotes. Although none of them had been inhabited previously, two had been easy enough to climb down. Each time, they drank their fill of the water and rested in the coolness of the caverns.

The sun was low in the sky, sending long shadows through the trees when they came across another cenote, barely more than a thin crack in the earth. The only reason they found it was thanks to the echoing rush of water traveling up through the opening.

"We should go down," Sofia said, leaning over the crack, a wind from somewhere below, making her curls sway.

"Are you kidding?" he said, legs straddling the thin opening. "We'll find more water later."

"The sun won't be up for much longer and there is no guarantee we'll be able to find water before then."

"So you want to what? Cave dive and hope this widens at the bottom?"

"If anything, climbing down and back up is going to be easier than a wider cenote."

"If we don't get stuck."

"I'm sure your muscles will fit," she said, looking him up and down.

He smirked. "I knew you were ogling me."

She only rolled her eyes. "I'm more worried about your big head getting stuck. "

His lips pinched, holding back a smile. But then he looked back at the opening she was suggesting they crawl into.

"I'm not going down there," he said more firmly this time.

"Fine, have fun dying up here. I'll pray to the dragon gods a jaguar gets you before you die of thirst or exposure."

Her smile was predatory. Before he could find a retort, she was lowering herself down and disappearing between the open earth.

Her wild curls disappeared last, swallowed by the darkness, and his heart spiked. As if calling on the fear thrumming through his blood, the vines behind him shifted and moved under the footsteps of *something*.

He couldn't stay up here alone. He couldn't go down there. He couldn't breathe.

"Stop it," he snapped at himself, taking a deep breath. *Stupid. Weak. Useless. Child.*

He let the voice in his head wash over him, pulling on it for motivation, even as it made his hands tremble.

"This is how I'm going to die," he said as he slipped into the crack, ignoring how close the walls were on every side of him.

The journey down was longer than any other one they'd had, the earth pressed on either side of his body. He kept his face turned toward the widest part of the opening. But even still, he felt the earth against his back as he crawled down. It was convenient that at every minor slip, he had only to throw himself back to catch himself against the wall. The only sounds he heard were his shallow breaths and the steady rhythm of a stream growing louder and louder beneath him until it wrapped around him completely. His senses narrowed to only the feel of the wet, cool dirt and stone beneath his fingers, aware of every change in texture of the wall as he descended.

The earth never widened and then suddenly his feet were touching ground and the earth was still solid, wrapped around him.

The air caught in his lungs. The light from the sky above was gone, darkness surrounding him, choking him. The earth seemed to shift around him, tightening against his chest. His toes and his fingers were numb as he scrambled against the stone, trying to dig himself out. It was too dark. Too tight.

Ocon! Ocon!

His body was shaking and he pushed against the stone holding him down, trying his best to move it but he was too weak and the stone too heavy.

"Fox!"

He felt a hand on his shoulder, shaking him, and it was Sofia's voice only a few inches from his ear.

"Take two steps to your left and duck down about a foot, the cave widens over here."

Her voice was soft and slow, as if she were talking to a child. But he didn't have the breath to berate her or argue. He listened, moving slowly, feet brushing against the ground as if to remind himself he was still standing. His shoulder hit stone and he flinched.

"Okay, duck." Her voice was farther away now, but he listened, moving down until suddenly the air around him opened up and he could see again.

No longer worried about being buried by the earth, his knees gave out and he slumped against the nearby wall. Sofia was standing above him and he could just make out her features in the soft blue glow that seemed to emanate from the earth itself. There was a knowing look in her gaze that he didn't want to examine too closely.

"Slow your breathing," she said, crouching down and looking into his face as if he weren't trying to avoid her eyes. She reach forward and he flinched away.

"Don't touch me!"

Her face tightened, but she didn't snap back. "Breathe. Tell me what you can hear."

He tried to focus his eyes on her, confused at her command, but after a moment he complied. "The water. Your voice. There's a wind from somewhere. My voice."

"Good." Her voice was gentler than he'd ever heard it. "And what can you feel? Beneath your hands?"

"The ground is wet—cold. It's almost as hard as our beds last night."

She cracked a smile and he felt pride at being the cause.

His breathing began to slow. The tingling in his fingers stopped and he was able to refocus his gaze, looking around the cave they were in. It took another minute to realize it wasn't the earth itself glowing blue, but the pinpricks of thousands of creatures, crawling along the walls.

"They're starworms," Sofia said, noticing his gaze. "Are you okay?"

"I'm fine," he said, voice harsher than he intended.

Her lips pursed at his tone, but she only nodded and held out her hand. Not making eye contact, he accepted her help and stood on shaky legs.

"Where are we?" He was as stiff as his words, brushing the dirt from his clothes as if it might matter. He was so covered in mud and filth, he was starting to forget what color his tunic had been originally.

"I'm assuming you don't want to talk about it?" Sofia said, still not looking away from him, as if she cared. As if she weren't asking to use it against him. The last thing he needed was for the resistance to learn all they had to do was lock him in a small space and he'd cry like a baby.

Instead of answering, he looked around, taking in the flowing river that rushed against the farthest wall and the small dry spot of land they were standing on. There was nothing else here. They weren't even in a real cenote, simply a crack in the earth above one of the underground rivers that snaked through the peninsula.

"We can't sleep here."

Sofia looked around, lips pressed tight. "No, I don't think we can."

Fox's gut twisted. "We need to climb back up."

She walked the two steps to the river and looked at where it flowed through the glowing tunnel.

"There'll be more openings down the river," she said. "Wider ones."

"And we have no idea how far away those might be."

"No, but at least down here there is fresh water and shelter from the night faeries and predators. If the starworms are living down here safely, then we'll be okay."

He looked back at the small gap in the wall behind him that led back to the surface—through the narrow crack that had already tried to kill him once. The river, on the other hand, flowed through a high arched tunnel with starworms lighting the stone above like a night sky. There was no dry path of land, but the water looked shallow enough along the edges.

"Fine."

Shoulders straightening, he marched forward, passing her and stepping directly in the river's edge. The water was icy against his boots. He gave a sharp intake of breath, but kept moving, refusing to show weakness again. She was wearing sandals. He wouldn't be the pathetic one here, if she could handle the water.

He heard her own sharp intake behind him and the splash of water as she followed. When he glanced back over his shoulder he saw her picking at her fingers, biting her lips hard, but she didn't complain.

As they walked, Fox's eyes traced the starworms that lined the walls and ceiling. While many of them were scattered across the stone, creating the illusion of the night sky, others were hanging on invisible threads stretched down from the ceiling, as if the night sky were crying stars. All of it reflected back by the river. He had never seen anything so beautiful. He'd seen the waterfalls of Falais across the north sea where his father's father had been from, but the blue glow patterned across these caves outshone even those.

They kept their steady pace, even as the water deepened and the tunnel narrowed slightly. The water was now up to his calves and every time he looked back, he saw the way Sofia trembled even as her face remained impassive.

He hated how much he seemed to care, but he rationalized that any human would be pained to see another suffering. And she had been kind enough to not comment on his panic attack earlier.

"Take my cloak," he snapped after another ten minutes of trying to ignore her clear distress.

"I'm fine," she said, not looking at him.

"My boots are better protected and my pants are thicker than yours. Take the damn cloak and stop shivering so loudly."

She didn't even look at him as she gave in, throwing her arm out to take the cloak. Too afraid her shaking fingers would drop it into the river, he ignored her outstretched arm, pressing close to her and carefully draping it over her shoulders. He hooked it around her throat, ignoring her gaze, even as he let his fingers hesitate there, pressing against the soft skin of her neck. It was ice cold and she shivered against him even as he forced himself to pull away. He crouched briefly and tied the bottom so it wouldn't drag in the water. He made the mistake of looking up at her between his lashes. Her face was flushed despite the cold, lips parted. He pushed back up to his feet before he did something stupid.

"Thanks," she said, mumbling the word, shoulders slumped in the same shame he felt every time she had helped him. Something like empathy shuddered through him.

"You called me Fox earlier."

"You weren't answering to Ocon," she said.

"I liked it."

She didn't respond to this and his face flushed. He was happy it was too dark for her to see. They were walking side by side now and the silence grew heavy between them.

"I don't do well in small spaces," he said, the words slipping from him.

"I noticed."

"I was trapped once..." he meant to say more, but his voice cracked and his mouth snapped closed. "Thank you for helping earlier."

She shrugged off the gratitude, but he could have sworn her lip ticked up in a smile for the briefest moment.

"I think this river might feed directly into my home cenote," she said. The words were sudden, but it was clear in her tone she'd been thinking about it for a while as they walked.

They were walking directly back to her base, if she was correct.

"How do you know?"

"The starworms," she said. "They aren't incredibly rare, but colonies this large are. I haven't been upriver from our base, but others have and they've talked about the colonies that line the river."

He was silent for a few minutes, mind caught between freezing and spinning. "I guess congratulations are in order. You've managed to get me back to your allies."

"They aren't going to kill you."

"They weren't perhaps, but I doubt after this little adventure they'll be so forgiving. And as you said, the prisoners I was a bargaining chip for are likely all dead now. What use am I?"

"All we want is our freedom."

"And you're willing to kill hundreds to get it."

"If that's the only language your people speak," she said, voice raw in the darkness. "Do you know we tried negotiating? A hundred cycles ago, the resistance started as a political group wanting to negotiate our rights. In response, your king's grandfather murdered them at his dinner table."

"That's donkey shit. I've read our history books cover to cover. The resistance pretended peace and then tried to assassinate the king."

"And who wrote those history books?"

He opened his mouth, ready to retaliate when a shudder ran through the ground around them, sending Fox stumbling to the side. He heard the splash of water and looked over to see Sofia, on her knees and drenched in water. The cloak was lying heavy on her shoulders and dripping.

"Shit!" she said as he pulled her up. He could already feel her shaking beneath the sodden clothes.

"Are you good to keep walking?"

"Yes." She took a shaky step and he saw the wince as she placed her weight down, but she kept moving. He didn't say anything and let her continue forward, holding her pride together with the barest of threads.

"We should stop at the first part of dry land we find," he said. "Even if we can't get out of the tunnel tonight, we need to rest."

She nodded silently as she gave another violent shiver. There would be no fire tonight, and she wouldn't be able to sleep in her wet clothes. The thought heated his cheeks, and he bit his tongue to stop his mind from wandering further in that direction.

The second time the earth shook beneath their feet it lasted no longer—only a second at most—and Sofia caught herself before falling again. A shiver traveled up Fox's spine. Earthquakes weren't incredibly rare on the peninsula, but it had been some time since he'd felt two so close together. And he definitely didn't like being underground when they happened.

"Let's move faster," Sofia said, as if reading his mind.

He didn't verbalize his agreement, but he picked up his pace, using a hand to steady her elbow as her own shorter legs struggled through the water.

"Take off the cloak," he said.

"No!"

"It's only making you colder and slower. I can carry it."

She didn't argue and slipped the material off her shoulders even as they continued walking. It was heavy as he scooped it into his arms.

The water seemed to deepen here, even along the edge of the river, pressed up as they were against the wall. It only made it more difficult to walk. He was happy the starworms continued to light their way.

It was because of their light that he realized that the river wasn't just getting deeper but that the water was actively rising around their legs, the current getting faster with every step they took. In the same moment his mind was able to understand this, the water roared behind them, growling like an ancient beast awoken.

"Fox?"

"Run!"

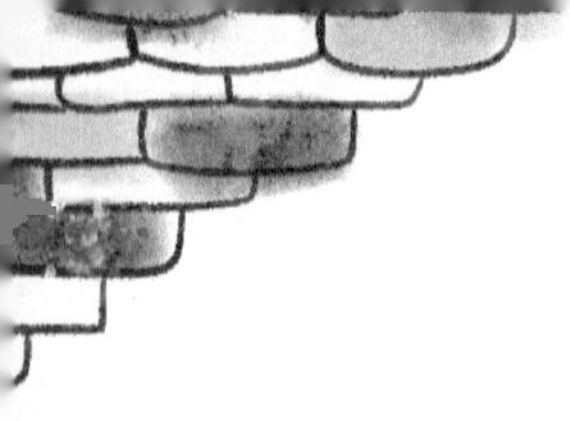

FOX

AGE 13

The old crone eyed the boy as he kneeled before her, begging for his life. She took pity on the creature because although his mother, the queen, was so cruel in her rule, he had never had a chance to know better. So instead of killing him, she laid a curse on him. She turned him into a black raven, the most feared of the creatures of the sky. And when the servants came into his room to find him, they chased him out with brooms and sticks. He slept alone in the trees outside his home that night and the next night.

-The Raven Prince by Emilio Laurn

Fox had relished the last two days, staying with his brother in the military barracks and eating the grueling rations. Anything was better than being home. The visit wouldn't last forever, but his brother had finally convinced his high major to allow him an on-campus leave and a visitor. Their father had seen Leon plenty of times during his training and then even after he had been promoted to scout, but his brother had only visited home twice, briefly. Each time left Fox in awe at the changes that had overcome his brother's body over the last cycle and a half. He could still see their mother's fine bone structure in the curve of his jaw, but his tunics fit tightly against his shoulders and arms and the blond hair dusting his jaw made him look distinctly more like their father.

"Keep up," Leon said, looking back at where Fox trailed behind him, distracted by the unending fields that were laid out to their left, waves of green and yellow. His brother had been assigned to the eastern barracks on the edge of the labor farms. Fox could just make out the bent backs of the prisoners that worked the farms in the distance, weeding and pruning to feed the country they had betrayed. The strongest of the prisoners went into the mines to dig for the gold that kept Suvi prosperous even as the droughts swept in and killed the crops, yet it seemed that there were hundreds of people scattered through the fields.

"It's best not to watch them," Leon said, suddenly close beside him.

"There are so many. So many people willing to betray their own king and people."

His brother didn't answer immediately and he looked up to see his lips pinched tightly. Leon's eyes flickered down, noticing Fox's stare and he shrugged.

"The king's justice can be swift and decisive. There may be some that didn't mean to betray Suvi. They may have gotten caught in the wrong place. But many Dragonborn, and even some Dereyans, are not happy with where the kingdom is going. Where it's gone."

"Where do they want it to go?" Fox said, not hiding the small sneer. "If they think they know so much better than the king?"

Leon paused again, not speaking again for too long, his own eyes now tracing the horizon and the prisoners there. He turned around at last, not meeting Fox's eyes as he shrugged again. "I don't know, but I don't think everyone believes the king is all powerful and all knowing. Now come on, I want to show you the wall. It's twice as high as near the city and the trees here stretch up to meet the height. You'll see nothing like it in the west."

THE NEXT MORNING, his brother left him in the dorms with strict instructions to not wander out. He promised either he or Ian would be back before lunch to take him to the mess hall. He was going east to look at a possible breach in the wall. Fox proudly lasted until midmorning before he gave up sitting on his brother's bunk, flipping through books on military strategy and farming. There was a very narrow range of topics in the barracks' library, but he also knew there was a small library in the fort along the western wall, where they had more books on the rainforest and the indigenous life beyond the wall, for the scouts to reference.

He knew that if he left now, he'd have just enough time to sneak a few books out of the fort library and be back when Leon returned. He slipped his brother's thin coat over his shoulders. It was warm enough outside to not need the protection, but the green and gold would allow him to blend in better around the campus. Knowing his brother, he'd told the other soldiers stationed here that Fox wasn't supposed to be wandering out alone.

The sun was higher in the sky than he expected by the time he finally made it to the large stone building that protruded from the city wall. His brother hadn't been exaggerating. The fort was three floors tall, and yet the wall towered over it. A narrow set of steps led up from the roof of the fort to the top of the wall. They had gone up the stairs the day before and Fox had looked out over the wall to the forest beyond. Even at the top of the wall, there were trees just beyond that towered over them and the vertigo of looking down toward the forest floor, barely visible through the thick foliage, made his stomach swoop.

As Fox approached the fort, someone moved above him on the wall, pausing in their rounds to look down at where he stood. The trees threw shadows along the top, making it impossible to differentiate any details beyond the silhouette. He looked back for a moment, wondering if he was being paranoid, but whoever it was began walking toward the stairs.

Without waiting to see if they were coming for him, he ducked through the side door of the fort. Keeping his head down and walking fast, he quickly found his way toward the library. The hallways were wide to accommodate soldiers moving around with weapons and supplies, the rooms well-marked for new recruits. Less than two minutes later, Fox was standing at the entrance of the library, smile stretched wide. Even the shelves were marked, books organized into categories: edible plants, wildlife, Dragonborn mythologies, survival skills.

The room was empty and he took a moment to simply wander through the aisles, scanning the titles printed along the spines. Many of the books were cheap parchment and linen, but others were leather-bound, their titles written in gold. He plucked one book off the shelf, its title gold and shining against brown leather: *In Praise of Dragons and Monsters.* It was filed under Dragonborn mythology and he flipped through the thick pages. His eyes widened at the rough illustrations along the edges, demented-looking creatures and warped animals.

"Fox!" The yell he recognized all too well had him snapping the book closed. He turned, eyes ready to look sorry as his brother stepped into the room. He expected annoyance, but there was something more in his brother's stare.

"I told you to stay in the dorms!"

"I needed more books." He gave a shrug, as if he hadn't realized he'd ignored his brother's instructions.

"There is a library in the dorms," he snapped, moving forward. Fox wasn't sure why, but he instinctually pulled back, tucking the book he was holding behind his back. He didn't want to give it up.

"Fox," his brother snapped, anger turning to something else— almost fear. "We need to go. You shouldn't be here."

"How did you find me?" His eyes narrowed.

"Ian saw you come in here. Now put the book down and come with me." Fox ignored his brother's outstretched hand.

"No."

"King's balls, you stubborn ass!" his brother cursed.

Fox's eyes went a little wide at his brother's language. He'd never heard those words from his brother's lips. "I'm keeping the book."

Leon looked at Fox for a moment like he wanted to argue. But then Leon grabbed him, pulling him forward and out of the library.

"Tuck the book under the jacket at least," he said, not stopping to berate him as he kept walking, pulling him more than ever now.

"You're hurting me!" Fox whined, his shoulder giving a sharp ache as his brother tugged him around a corner.

"I'll do more when we get back to the dorms if you don't shut up."

They burst out of the front doors of the fort, the sun blinding Fox for a second as he balanced trying to keep up with his brother and gripping the book to his chest under the jacket. He knew he shouldn't have taken it. His brother could get into serious trouble letting him read text about Dragonborn mythology. While it wasn't technically illegal, these books were meant for king's men who needed to know their enemy. Their family library had a few texts on Dragonborn tucked in the corners, but they were mostly children's stories that Fox had practically memorized at this point. This was the exact type of book his father would beat him for reading.

Fox opened his mouth to apologize to his brother. He hadn't meant to get him into trouble or threaten his place among the king's men, but then the world behind them seemed to crack, the sound vibrating through Fox's bones even as his vision went gray at the edges. His brother's body went rigid as he turned, looking at something over Fox's shoulder with a raw terror that had Fox stumbling. His brother moved, throwing himself at Fox before he could turn.

The world shattered into nothing and everything.

Fox was aware of a ringing in his ears and the taste of his blood on his lips. There was only darkness around him, but it wasn't an empty darkness. Stone and dirt and weight pressed in all around him. He tried to squint to see, but his head hurt too much.

"Little Fox," his brother's voice was a rasp, but it was so close. It was directly in front of him and as his eyes adjusted, he saw his brother, lying just above him, chest pressed to Fox's own, the only thing between them the thin leather book. Something wet fell against his cheek and he tasted blood. Fox swallowed, throat moving.

"Everything hurts." The words felt like gravel in his mouth.

"You're going to be okay." His brother's words came out in gasps, but he felt Leon's hand moving in the rubble, rough against his arm.

He tried to sit up. He wanted to find his brother's hand and hold it in his own, but the world was too heavy. He couldn't move. He could barely breathe. And all that he heard in the darkness was the sound of Leon's shallow breaths. Eventually even that went silent.

Fox had no idea how long he was under the rubble. It was long enough that his brother's hand grew cold against his skin.

When the stone that had lain on top of them was finally lifted, the light of dusk was blinding.

CHAPTER TWENTY-SIX

SOFIA

Sofia knew better than to question Fox in that moment. She ran, legs pumping through the rising water as best they could, even as it fought against her body. She lost her footing, propelled forward with the current of the river. Fox grabbed her arm, holding on to her tightly, but even he was struggling through the torrent, barely keeping control of his own legs.

And then the water hit them. A wall as hard as stone came from behind with a roar as it snatched their bodies up and threw them forward. Fox's grip slipped from hers and her head went under. The air collapsed from her lungs as the icy water took her.

She slammed into the cavern wall or perhaps it was the ceiling— hard rock biting into her back for only a second before she was tossed forward again. She was flying through the night sky, glowing spots all around her, the starworms caught up in the water with them. A shadow floated a few feet away and she reached, hands just brushing against Fox before he was pulled away again.

Her throat burned, lungs aching with every passing second. She was going to die. They were both going to die, drowned in this tunnel and no one would know. If they were lucky, her body might wash up in the cenote base so they might know how she ended. She felt her muscles loosen, the lack of air choking out the remaining strength of her body.

Please gods. No.

She could just make out Fox spinning a few feet away, a shadow among the starworms and she reached out with the last of her strength. Her fingers brushed against his arm and then his hand was snagging on hers. They came together in the water and she saw the same fear and resignation she was feeling reflected in his face.

Something hot brushed against her side and she jerked in the water, trying to see through the churning darkness. As flash of something in her mind, a voice not her own. Fox's face went pale—a translucent shade of white she didn't think possible. Before she could get her bearings and understand what had passed by her, there was dry air on her face and she choked in a breath, expecting icy water to flood in. She blinked, breathing in another gasp of stale air as she tried to understand what she was seeing. They were holding each other, heads engulfed in an air bubble as the water continued to churn violently around them.

Across from her, Fox coughed before letting out a long string of expletives.

"How? What? King's balls!"

His hands were still clasped around her arms, but his eyes were focused beyond her and beyond their protective bubble.

Just ahead of them, as if guiding their way through the dark tunnel, she saw a long lithe body undulating through the water, iridescent scales and feathers gleaming as if the serpentine figure itself was glowing. The water around them hummed and warmed with *something*. She could feel it in her mind.

She opened her mouth, but nothing came out, her brain too busy chanting the word she couldn't say.

Dragon. Dragon. Dragon.

Fox didn't need a response, though. His own eyes, filled with something between terror and awe, told her he knew exactly what they were looking at.

The light around them shifted and Fox's stricken face came fully into view, the shadows of the tunnel receding. In the same moment, the edge of their water bubble trembled, unsteady.

"Not good," she said, yelling over the churning water that was echoing around them.

"A genius observation," Fox said, looking around with wild eyes.

"Not the time for sarcasm, you self-righteous—"

"Not the time to argue." With that, he let go of her left arm, linking his right more tightly around her and then jerked backward.

Sofia's shoulder wrenched painfully as the icy water hit her once more. She sucked in water as she attempted to breathe, the pain radiating through her body, but a moment later, her head was above water. Fox was braced against the wall of the thin canyon, arm wrapped tightly around a root as he pulled Sofia closer. The roots were wide and strong and she wrapped her own arm through one, pressing her body against the wall.

The water still rushed, waves hitting against her chest and face. It was more water than she'd ever seen. And it was that thought that had her suddenly pulling away from the wall.

"What are you doing?" he questioned, as she tried to disentangle herself from the root and his grasp.

"If this is the river that connects to our cenote, then the flash flood could kill everyone! I need to stop it."

"You can't just stop a flood! You're going to get yourself killed!" They were both shouting, yet she could barely hear anything over the crashing rapids.

"I need to try!" She let go of the root she'd grabbed and felt her body begin to pull away. Fox's hand wrapped around her wrist, tightly. She didn't fight him, but ducked her head under the water. It was difficult to see anything so close to the surface where the waters churned white.

But it didn't matter. Sight would do nothing for her right now. She closed her eyes and reached out with her mind, trying to touch the presence she'd felt earlier. She had no idea what she was doing, but something about it felt right.

Please, stop the flood. You're going to kill someone. Please.

She didn't know if she was pleading with it or the water or the universe. But nothing spoke back.

It may have been one minute or a hundred, but suddenly Fox was pulling her back, dragging her from the water and back onto the cliff. Just as she was moving to grab back onto the wall, a tree came crashing down the river directly toward them. Fox pulled her into him, twisting to press her against the wall as the tree's branches crashed into them, breaking apart on the wall. She felt more than heard his groan of pain vibrate against her back.

"We need to climb! We can't stay down here," he said over the churning water.

"But—"

She stuttered out the word, not even sure what her argument was. She couldn't feel her face or much of her body. Before she could pull her thoughts together, the earth itself seemed to groan and she saw Fox scrambling to keep his hold on the cliffside.

The river behind them exploded.

The dragon's head, ringed with deep blue feathers appeared first but her eyes were almost immediately drawn to the wings that burst from the water, already spread. The skin along them was thin enough that the moonlight shone through and the scales nearly sparkled in the dimness as water cascaded down its back.

The paintings in the cavern had been so beautiful and intricate, and yet they were nothing compared to seeing the real thing arching into the sky above them. Mist trailed its tail and Sofia realized after a moment that it wasn't just the river water dripping from the dragon, but rain pouring from a newly formed cloud.

Neither of them moved for a moment, eyes focused on the sky and the disappearing dragon. Water was streaming down her face and Sofia realized she was crying, her own tears mixing with the icy river water.

"We should move," Fox said eventually. His voice was soft and she felt the warm breath ghosting against her ear.

She nodded instead of answering, throat too tight for words. It took a few moments to pull her eyes away from the sky where the dragon had disappeared somewhere to the west. And then she felt the icy air around her and realized they were no longer caught in the river's current. Looking down, she saw the water, far beneath them and still receding. The gap between where they clung to the cliff and where the river flowed grew with every second.

Fox shifted behind her and she saw him reaching up, grasping onto the ledge above them. Her fingers were numb with cold as she tried to follow after him, struggling to grip the wet stone. She nearly fell, letting out a curse as her elbow caught on a ledge and she managed to stop herself before she plunged back into the river below.

She looked back up to see Fox, climbing down carefully, his own fingers shaking against the wall. He brought himself level to her and then started climbing again, half-pushing her along with him. For every move he made, he waited until she had a handhold. They climbed slowly, but she only focused on the lip of the canyon above, getting closer.

Fox reached the edge first, pulling himself up before turning to help her. They both flopped onto the ground a few feet from the canyon, breaths heavy in the misty air. Sofia wasn't even sure if she was shaking from cold, exhaustion, or adrenaline.

"What just..." he trailed off.

"That was..." Sofia tried to add, but she was still half-mesmerized looking up at the sky where the two moons glowed brightly, just beginning their blink close.

"A dragon," Fox said, turning onto his side, hovering over where she was lying. "That was a dragon."

She nodded, eyes flickering up to take in the bright look of awe frozen on his face. Fox's blond hair was dripping, small drops of icy water splashing against her skin as he hovered over her. His lips were nearly blue, but his cheeks were flushed and his eyes were wide and shone silver.

"It was real. They're alive." Her face ached with cold and the grin she couldn't stop. It was matched only by the one that Fox was wearing, perhaps the first true smile she'd seen from him since they'd met. He almost looked beautiful when he smiled like this.

"It *was* real," he said. "That was a dragon."

The wet grass seeped into her clothes and she looked up at Fox, his arm braced along her side. Their faces were close enough that she felt the warmth of his breath.

Sofia's cheeks heated up as she looked into his blue-flecked eyes. He stared back at her with the same intensity, as if seeing her for the first time. His body radiated a warmth that she wanted to sink into. She wanted him to press against her as she breathed in the smell of the forest on his skin.

His eyes flickered down to her lips for only a second, but she caught it and saw the flush of his cheeks as he met her eyes again. Would he close the last two inches? Did she want him to? She had to remind herself that she hated him, yet she couldn't remember why as his eyes burned a trail along her skin.

She thought she saw him twitch forward, but an instant later he was pulling back, a groan hissing through his clenched teeth.

Sofia pulled herself up as Fox leaned back, his hands groping at his side. For a moment, she thought the claw marks from the shifters might have been torn open by their adventure in the river, but then the moonlight caught the edge of the branch that was embedded in his side.

"Shit," she said, leaning forward even as he flinched back. "You're injured."

"I noticed."

"Why didn't you say anything?" she practically yelled.

"I was a little distracted!"

Her hands fluttered forward of their own accord, as if she might be able to do something. Do anything. She had a rudimentary understanding of first aid, but this was so far beyond her skills.

"Don't pull it out," she said.

"I know that," he snapped.

"Shit," she said again, looking around the forest like the shadows might hold answers. "We need to make a fire. We need bandages and thread and a needle."

"I don't even have the cloak anymore," he said, face grim. Sofia was glad to realize her bag was still hooked around her arm, though her bow was long gone, along with her arrows. She tore through her bag, searching it as if she could will to life any supplies of use. She didn't have bandages, thread, a needle—even the flint would need to dry out.

"We have to move," she said at last, biting her lip as Fox struggled to stand. "Can you walk?"

"I'm going to have to," he said, hissing out a long breath as he took one step and then another, unsteady on his feet.

She moved forward, pulling his arm over her shoulder on his uninjured side, feeling his weight as he leaned into her.

They hadn't made it more than a dozen steps when the crack of a branch and a sudden rush of footsteps brought them both up short. Fox jerked away from Sofia, moving into a fighting stance even as he swayed on his feet. And they turned to face the dark forest, as a half-dozen figures melted out of the shadows.

CHAPTER TWENTY-SEVEN

FOX

One of the figures stepped forward, the apparent leader of the group. His black hair was long and hung in braids. He wore a dress-like tunic in a style that Fox had never seen before, wide trousers visible underneath. It was a surprisingly clean shade of cream that contrasted with his dark skin.

When he spoke, it took a moment for Fox to realize he wasn't speaking the king's tongue. The words were more guttural and clipped, and he thought he vaguely recognized them from some of the poorest sides of the city.

Sofia stepped forward, hands raised. She responded in kind, her own words hesitant and awkward, but Fox saw the faces of the others soften. They understood her enough, apparently.

The group turned to him, speaking once more. Their words were just as indecipherable as before. Fox looked at Sofia with wide eyes, entreating her.

She spoke again, this time waving at him as she did so. He could understand enough from the body language that some of their group weren't thrilled to see either of them here.

It was an uncomfortable feeling not being able to understand what was being said, but knowing it was about you. Dragon-tongue, while relatively common in the worst of the slums wasn't something you heard wandering around the military or royal quarters. No one outside of the poorest Dragonborn spoke the dying language, too afraid of being seen as disloyal to the king.

"What are they saying?" he said, uneasy with how long he'd let the conversation go on without him.

"They're asking about what we're doing out here. I think."

"Do you speak dragon-tongue?"

"I learned it from books and alley brawls, so I can't say it's perfect."

He wanted to comment on the strange combination of her education, but before he could, a woman stepped forward from the back of the group. The moons' light caught in her hair, and Fox saw the silver strands that marked her age better than her smooth skin.

"Your dragon-tongue is admirable," she said in perfectly articulate king's tongue. Fox felt unsettled as her piercing black eyes focused on him. "My name is Clarita. You say you're lost. How did you come this far?"

Sofia answered first. "We were kidnapped by wolfshifters and weren't able to escape immediately. We've been trying to make it back to m—our base the last few days."

"You are with the resistance?" Clarita said, eyeing Fox carefully.

"Yes," Sofia said.

"We do not align ourselves with the people of Suvi."

"I know," Sofia said, voice softening in a way she never had with him. This is what it sounded like when she cared what someone thought of her. "We're just passing through trying to get back to our people. We've run into...obstacles."

The woman's eyes narrowed at this, eyes sweeping over them both and then the gleam of freshly fallen rain in the undergrowth.

"What did you see? The earthquake—was it just an earthquake?"

Sofia and Fox exchanged a look, neither of them knowing what the woman wanted to hear. The rules in Suvi were easy enough to remember: don't talk of dragons or faeries. But out here?

Sofia made the decision for them. "We saw a dragon."

She didn't elaborate, waiting for their reactions.

"You are mistaken."

Sofia's face hardened into something more familiar to Fox. "No, we're not. I gave a prayer last night, and this evening, a dragon came through the river down there. I know what I saw."

Clarita seemingly repeated Sofia's words in dragon-tongue and murmuring broke out among the others. A few spit out words sharp enough that Fox didn't want Clarita's translation. She gave it nonetheless.

"They are calling for me to kill you."

"For what?" Fox said, tired of biting his tongue, but even as he stepped forward the pain in his side and the wave of nausea reminded him why they needed to end this conversation quickly. He saw Clarita's face resolve into something akin to pity as she took in the branch protruding from his side and the blood dripping from it.

"Perhaps I won't need to kill you myself. I can just leave you out here."

Sofia had gone pale, seemingly uncomfortable at the thought of her own life being threatened.

"Please," she said. "We aren't on the same side, but we both worship the dragons. Let that mean something." She turned to the rest of the group and spoke in dragon-tongue. Fox could only assume she'd repeated her plea.

"What would you have to offer us, other than trouble?" Clarita asked. Her voice warbled, as if through water, and Fox realized he'd lost more blood than he'd realized. His legs trembled and gave out, knees cracking hard against the earth as he fell.

Sofia's voice felt distant.

"We'll give you anything. Please?"

"How did you pray?" Clarita asked.

"What do you mean? We found a cenote and a shrine." Sofia's eyes lit up, as if realizing something. "I can take you—show you! There was a dragon feather. But only if you heal him."

He didn't know how they responded, his mind no longer following the flow of conversation. The next thing he knew, he was being pulled up roughly by his arms. He bit his tongue, swallowing back a scream. It came out as a guttural moan. Sofia was somewhere beside him. She was talking still, but he didn't listen. He focused only on putting one foot in front of the other as the two men on either side of him moved.

The trek back to their camp wasn't far, but it felt like the longest walk of Fox's life. With every step he pushed back the nausea and pain that had him wanting to vomit one moment and keel over the next. Oblivion felt tempting, even as the glow of the fires came into view and the sound of civilization—or the closest thing to it out here—filtered through the trees. Perhaps it was this knowledge that they had reached their destination that finally did it. Blackness swept over him like a wave and he embraced it.

AN INDISCRIMINATE TIME LATER, Fox opened his eyes to warm light dancing across his vision. He was lying on his back, a few feet from a large bonfire; the bedroll beneath him was the softest thing he'd felt in days. If it weren't for Sofia's face hovering over his own, he might have thought he'd died and was with the kings. Then again, the look of worry in her eyes suggested he was dreaming. The pain from his side had receded, but what's more, the dull ache that had been radiating through his body for the last few days was gone, as well. He was hungry and his eyes burned from exhaustion and the river water, but he felt better than he had in days.

"You're awake," Sofia said, voice soft as if not to startle him.

He nodded stiffly, not quite able to find his voice. She immediately moved, bringing a cup to his lips. He assumed it was water, but the liquid smelled of flowers and was subtly sweet on his lips. He finished the first cup and she left to get more.

Whether it was the drink or simply time, his head was beginning to clear when she returned, and he took the cup from her as he looked around. The cenote they were camped out in wasn't nearly as big as the one they'd found the night before, but it was wide, with plenty of dried land stretched between the sparkling lake and the river that rushed along the southern side. Multiple fires were burning and people milled about the main area. So many more people than Fox had expected.

Clarita was in front of another fire, speaking to a few others, but he saw her take notice of his stare and she stood to come over.

"Lia is sleeping," Clarita said, not sitting down, "but she wishes for you to rest for the next two days at least. The wound was clean and you were lucky with how the branch went through, but we have mended your stomach and back."

He lifted his tunic and noticed the set of small, neat stitches along his abdomen. A smear of yellow-green paste covered the wound, any trace of blood cleaned away. Even the ragged edges of the skin along the wound weren't inflamed. It looked like a three-day old wound more than a freshly made one, but he didn't question it. The witchcraft of the Dragonborn was long-banned in Suvi, but their healing skills were well-known still. He'd arrested a few for practicing the old ways before—a fact that sat heavily on his chest as he guiltily looked at the healer's work. That magic had likely saved him.

"We reheated stew from yesterday's supper, if you'd like some. Your friend already ate, so she can attest it isn't poisoned."

He agreed and the woman walked away, leaving him and Sofia alone again. He noted that they had the bonfire to themselves, no one else seemingly brave enough to sit near them.

"Did they give me opium milk for the pain?" He didn't have any moral objections to the drug, but he didn't like to think of his senses being addled while in enemy territory. Then again, his head didn't feel stuffed with cotton like it had the times he'd taken it.

"No," she said, a hand resting on his shoulder. He wondered if she was even aware that her thumb was rubbing against the skin of his neck as she spoke. "They gave you a tincture. The healer, Lia, said it should take away the pain without making you woozy."

"A tincture?" he said, voice wary.

"Mushrooms and herbs, nothing dangerous. I asked."

He nodded. He had more questions, but Clarita had returned, a bowl of something steaming in her hands.

Sofia helped him sit up and a minute later, he was scooping the warm spiced meat into his mouth, trying his best to eat slowly even as the rich smell made his mouth water. It tasted better than even the food he'd had at the castle when he'd visited. The meat was soft despite being the same type of game they'd been chewing on the last few days and the sauce tasted strongly of cumin, salt, and lime.

He felt no shame as he finished the stew, scraping the spoon across the bowl to finish every last remnant. The sound of the wood scratching against the clay made him smile. He thought about how many times his father had berated him for scraping his plates at dinner when he was growing up. He said it was best to leave a bit of food behind. Only those in poverty finished their dishes.

Around him, the few others eating were doing the same, scraping the last bits of the spiced sauce out of the bowl and licking their spoons clean. But they didn't look starving or poor. They simply looked content.

He glanced back at Sofia. She was staring into the fire, the shadows dancing across her face. Her skin had regained its color, no longer gray from the icy water that had brought them here. And her lips were a soft pink. Even as he watched, she sucked in her bottom lip, chewing at it gently with her teeth.

He realized he was staring at her mouth and quickly looked away, face going hot. Her hair was still wet from the water, but it was beginning to dry, frizz and curls haloing around her head, glowing a rich honey against the firelight.

His father had introduced him to many beautiful women over the past few cycles, most from families across the sea. The women had varied in hair color and stature, but their skin was always pale, their voices always soft, and their fathers always rich and powerful. One had owned a vineyard in Falais, another the shipping yards in Terdun. If his father couldn't depend on him bringing glory to the family through his fighting, Fox would bring him influence through his marriage. It was only with Mother's help he'd managed to delay any betrothals.

Sofia was nothing like those women. Her hair was tangled with curls that desperately needed a comb and her freckled skin had seen too much sun to be considered proper. But the way her mossy eyes lit up when she was excited and the tilt of her lips when she laughed—loud and unabashed—made her look something more than just beautiful.

He thought back to the moment after they pulled themselves out of the canyon and the way her eyes had darted down to his own lips, a heat in her eyes he hadn't seen before. He'd wanted to kiss her. He'd thought she might have wanted the same thing. But then the numbness from the icy river had dissipated and the sharp burning pain in his side had broken through his thoughts. Thinking about it now, about what could have happened, made his body heat and his chest ache with something unacknowledged.

"So, what did you agree to for all of this?" he said, trying to remember back to the conversation before he'd collapsed.

"I'm taking them back to the cenote to see the altars. They are giving me a day to ensure you're okay before I leave."

Despite being alone at the fire, it seemed that almost every pair of eyes bore into them as they sat there. There were a handful of fires burning, nearly a dozen Dragonborn sitting around each, ranging from older folks to children. And he doubted this was all of them. It was still the middle of the night, and the only people up were those woken by the chaos the earthquake and their subsequent arrival had created.

The crown knew there were likely some rebels and runaways hiding out in the rainforest, but this didn't look like a makeshift camp for refugees. This was a thriving community of families.

"And we're trusting them not to kill us?" he asked.

"Yes, we are."

"We shouldn't be here. You shouldn't have agreed to anything."

"In case it escaped your notice, you were about to bleed out."

Fox bit back any further retort. He knew she was right. She had made the decision to keep him alive—for whatever reason. But he still hated it.

"They're excited about the dragon sighting," she continued. "They appear more interested in the dragon than us. It's a good sign."

"Perhaps," he said, wanting to trust her, if only because of how tired he was.

"It's why they were out there tonight. Their ancestors always spoke of the quakes that heralded the dragons."

Fox thought perhaps he should be thankful they'd come searching and found them. But distrust sat heavy in his gut.

"How do you think Clarita knows the king's tongue?" he asked, looking back to where she was speaking, leaning close to her confidantes.

Sofia didn't answer for a while. "You should ask her. I don't know."

The answer was vague and he knew her tone well enough to know she wasn't saying everything on her mind. But he let it pass. Now that there was food in his stomach and he was warmer than he'd been in days, his body was screaming its exhaustion at him.

"Do you still think the dragons are myths or long dead?" Sofia's voice was soft and not nearly as biting as it could have been. She was poking him, even mocking him, but not out of malice.

"The history books always claimed they were real. I can't be blamed for assuming a creature that hasn't been seen by the people of Suvi in over three hundred cycles is extinct. They should be extinct."

"You still believe that?"

"You saw what that dragon did back there—what it almost did. Those were your people it might have killed. It almost killed us. Is that something you truly want to worship?"

"It didn't know there were people at the end of the river, and it stopped when I asked."

"Is that what happened?" he asked, shaking his head, trying to understand how her brain worked. "All I saw was a woman insisting on almost killing herself before I was able to drag her up and out."

"She listened to me."

"Who?"

"The dragon," she said simply.

"How do you know it was female?"

She went silent and he glanced up, watching as her lips pressed together and her eyes went unfocused for a moment. He wasn't sure what he expected, but she suddenly shrugged. "I don't know. I just do."

Fox opened his mouth to retort when a voice startled him.

"Talk to us about the dragon, please," a small boy said, sitting down beside Fox with wide eyes. His king's tongue was thick and clunky, but still surprising. Someone Fox assumed to be his parent stood behind him with more than a little trepidation. He smiled at the boy, and the parent's shoulders relaxed incrementally.

He looked around and saw Clarita standing a few feet away, her own conversation paused as if she had heard the boy's question. She whispered something to her companion before moving toward Fox and Sofia.

"I can translate, if you want to tell them," she said, sitting down beside Sofia.

Fox wasn't even sure where to start, but Sofia solved that for him, diving into the story of finding the ruined cenote and the dragon murals. He chimed in occasionally to embellish her words, happy to see her smile every time he did. The others listened, enraptured as Clarita translated, her own tone and motions adding to the magic.

It felt like telling a faerytale from the books he'd had as a child. Except the evil monster was drawing out only awe and wonder from those around him. Perhaps because they hadn't seen the flood waters or nearly been drowned in the black tunnel. They didn't see how dangerous the dragon was. Sofia had prayed to it and it had almost killed her. Yet even she didn't look scared or subdued. Her eyes hadn't dimmed since they'd left the canyon, as if something inside her had awoken.

He didn't know what to think or what to feel. What did one do when their entire life had just been upended? He was surrounded by enemies, yet he was safe and warm for the first time in days. The monsters of his childhood were real, but no one else was scared of them. And the rainforest was more alive than he'd ever imagined, and it had tried to kill him multiple times over the past few days.

He laid back down next to the fire, not moving from where he was, listening to Sofia's voice and Clarita's translation. The dragon-tongue lulled him and he fell asleep enveloped by Sofia's and Clarita's voices and the warmth of the fire. He would have to worry about monsters and magic tomorrow.

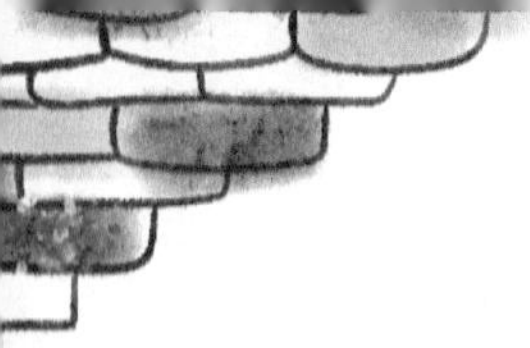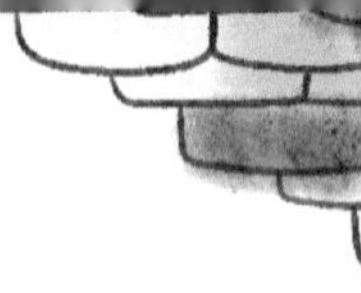

FOX

AGE 12

On the third day of his curse, the prince was too hungry to hide any longer. He flew into the village to look for food. But every stand he stopped at was as unfriendly as the servants, yelling and threatening him until he left. When the village girl with eyes like the sky saw him and took pity on him, he couldn't see the kindness in her expression. He flew away even as she offered him bread and hid in the trees, hungry and alone once more.

-The Raven Prince by Emilio Laurn

Fox had been up since sunrise, huddled in his room, hiding from the cold as well as his parents. The shift in the season sent icy gusts down the halls despite the perpetually burning fires in every room, as if the walls couldn't fight the cold. His stomach was beginning to growl and he knew he'd have to venture down to the kitchens, if only to ask for food to be sent to his room. And still, he sat, not doing much of anything except watching the flames in his hearth dance with the winds whistling down from the chimney.

This had become his new normal since his brother had left for basic training three blinks prior. His father had at least given up on pretending to train him, but the constant picking at every single thing Fox did continued. He was slumping; his writing was too feminine; he was looking thin; he was putting on too much weight—as if any of that mattered when Fox was probably going to end up locked in a back room crunching numbers where his father could pretend he didn't exist. At least his father had been busy with the military recently. He and his mother still had dinner most days, but his father rarely joined them, locked away in his office.

Despite promises made, Leon hadn't written to him at all and Fox was left wondering what his life was like in the barracks with the other junior trainees. His brother wouldn't be allowed leave until the end of the cold season, two blinks from now. Two more blinks of Fox avoiding his father's attention and hoping his brother was safe wherever he was training. At least the resistance had been quiet these past few blinks and the only outbreak of violence had been in the drowned quarter when some fishermen were caught stealing the king's stores. It had ended in three buildings burning down—a feat that Fox had thought impossible in that constantly sodden corner of the city—but only a small regiment had been sent out to quell the rage and none of the king's men had been injured.

He also knew the peace couldn't last forever. He knew his brother would always win against the dragon-filth rebels in a fair fight. Fox had grown up watching him train and fight, and he knew his brother outmatched half the king's scouts and specialists as it was. But the Dragonborn rarely fought fair.

When the ache of his stomach turned to nausea, he finally moved, wrapping himself in his cloak before he left. He went toward the back of the house, hoping to avoid the main staircase where his mother tended to pace, looking worried about one thing or another. It also meant he avoided passing by his father's office. If he was home, he'd likely be locked in there.

"Fox."

The sound of his name on his father's lips made his blood run cold.

He schooled his features before he turned, giving his father a blank, slightly disinterested look.

"Yes, Father," he said, voice cool.

"I was going to give your mother the good news first, but since you're here..."

Fox waited, face unmoving despite wanting to snap that perhaps his father shouldn't act so surprised to find him directly outside his own rooms.

"Leon has been promoted to high trainee three blinks early. He'll be visiting at the next dark moons."

The muscle in his jaw twitched and he could have sworn his father's eyes flickered to the movement with satisfaction.

"Did the chief commander write to tell you? I'm amazed he has time to communicate such small accomplishments."

His father's smile went feral.

"Chief Commander Harlow did send a congratulatory message, but it was Leon who wrote me himself."

His stomach dropped and he knew his father had read the disappointment and hurt in his face, no matter how hard he tried to keep his expression neutral.

"Has your brother told you yet? He expressed in his letter last week that he knew the promotion was likely coming."

"Leon hasn't written me."

"I'm sure he's busy," his father said with such warmth that Fox might have mistaken it for genuine concern had it come from anyone else.

The triumph in his father's eyes made his face flush.

"I assume you haven't seen any letters from him addressed to me?" Fox asked. "They'd come to your office first, of course."

"Son, I'd send any letter relevant to you to your rooms immediately."

It wasn't the first time that Fox had had the passing thought his father might be intercepting the letters from Leon. But he'd thought he was being paranoid. This would be a new type of cruelty.

"Every letter from Leon is relevant to me, particularly if they have my name on them. Unless you're having trouble reading."

His father stepped forward, voice taking on a sharp edge as he leaned over Fox. "I don't know what you're implying, but I'd suggest you show some respect to your father."

"I show respect to those who earn it," he snapped, before he could think better of the words. It had been too long since he had been faced with his father's wrath and forced to bite his tongue.

The hit wasn't unexpected and Fox only stumbled back a step as the knuckles on his father's hand snapped against his cheekbone. Fox didn't make a sound. Before he could savor the surprise in his father's eyes, his father's cane snapped up and cracked against his ribs. He doubled over, the next intake of air sending a wave of pain through his side, but his father's hand grabbed his hair before he could crumple, pulling him upright.

"Don't you ever talk to me that way again or I'll lock you in the king's prison myself and see how you fare. I don't need to earn your respect. I am your father and the king's general. And you are nothing."

He let go and Fox fell to his knees, his scalp burning. By the time he caught his breath, the ache in his side subsiding to a dull throb, his father was gone and the hall was empty.

Hunger forgotten, Fox flew down the back stairs and out the servants' door leading to the back yards and stables. For the first time in his life, he understood what stories meant when they said someone's vision had gone red. The blood roaring through his veins seemed to be coloring the world, a red haze making it difficult to see and think.

He might later try to convince himself he bumped into the stableboy on accident, too distracted with his rage. But in that moment, he knew he'd seen him and he'd chosen not to veer away or stop. His shoulder hit the other boy's, sending the bucket he was holding falling to the ground with a soft thud and a splatter. The donkey shit nearly covered the boy, but Fox's shoes were covered, too.

"Are you blind or stupid?"

He sneered down at the boy. He was around his own age and he'd seen him around the yards before often getting into fights with the other workers.

"You ran into me," the boy said, practically growling as he stood up, brushing the manure off his clothes, but doing little more than smearing it into the fabric. Fox smiled.

"Stupid then, to dare talk to your superiors like that."

"You ain't my superior."

The boy moved first, bringing back his fist. Fox dodged it easily and moved to parry. His own blow went wide, scraping against the boy's ear. A kick to Fox's shin sent him stumbling back and the boy used the moment to his advantage, grabbing Fox around the waist and bringing him to the ground with a scream.

Fox forgot the small amount of training he had, his fists flailing with little strategy beyond making contact. The stableboy's style was no less refined and they made barely any damage before they were being pulled up by the collars of their tunics.

Fox's face was bloody and he licked at his lip as he looked at the man who'd pulled them apart. He saw the man's mouth open, as if to berate them both at the same moment he seemed to recognize who Fox was. He dropped the neck of his tunic where he'd been holding him and quickly gave a short bow.

"Young Master Ocon, my deepest apologies. I'll have young Will here whipped and fired immediately for his insolence."

The boy across from him went pale and he opened his mouth, likely to argue.

"That won't be necessary. The boy was too weak to do much more than pinch me."

"Surely he must be punished, sir."

Fox only shrugged, straightening his tunic and assessing the blood and mud smeared across it. He'd have plenty of bruises tomorrow— mostly from the boy. "Get him back to work and stop wasting my time."

With one last sneer toward the man, he turned and marched back toward the manor. He wasn't hungry anymore, but he'd need to change his shirt before his mother saw the mess.

CHAPTER TWENTY-EIGHT
SOFIA

For the second time in so many days, Sofia woke up curled against Fox. This time, she couldn't claim it was his fault, though. He'd fallen asleep while they'd been talking around the fire. Clarita had offered her a bedroll and a room, but she hadn't wanted to leave the fire, and a part of her hadn't wanted to leave Fox. Not that she thought he'd get very far if he ran in the night, but she didn't like taking her eyes off him.

So, she'd taken the bedroll and laid it out a few feet from him, and in the middle of the night, when he'd woken up after the fire had gone cold, she'd moved to the edge and let him join her. At least they had separate blankets this time around.

Instead of throwing him off the pad, as a biting voice in the back of her mind suggested, she pushed herself up and moved away from where he was still softly snoring. She only stopped for a moment to notice the softness of his face like this, asleep and vulnerable.

The sun had just crested the horizon, a pink glow in the east painting the cenote and rainforest in soft pastels. It was relatively quiet, but people were moving around, relighting fires and setting about various tasks. Sofia wrapped her blanket around her shoulders as she went in search of the washroom she'd used the night before to change and dry off.

After she was done relieving herself, she went to the edge of the cenote's lake and splashed cold water across her face. The sensation made her heart skip, but it restarted her brain. She hadn't slept as much as she should have, but the day before had made it difficult for her mind to shut off, and she didn't want to miss anything this morning. There were some smaller non-citizened tribes around the southern rainforest that the rebels had run across before. But usually it was one or two families who were scrounging their way through life. Here, she felt like she was given a small glimpse of what life would be without the first king or the wars that had followed.

She heard whispering behind her and looked up to see a small group, staring at her. Never one for subtlety, she stared back. There were four of them, and she saw they were all wearing weapons. Three looked her own age, while the other looked barely older than ten. She recognized the trapping ropes hanging off one's belt and the darts on another's. It was a small hunting party.

Keeping her footsteps unhurried, she approached them.

"Good morning." The dragon-tongue came a bit smoother this morning after hours of hearing it spoken last night. Their accents were different than the Dragonborn of Suvi, but she'd been around the language most her life in one way or another, even if her family never spoke it.

One of them stepped forward.

"Lumi," they said, holding out their hand. Deep brown hair hung in waves around their face, one side brushing against their shoulder and the other cropped tightly. "This is Nino, Verano and Paz. I heard you knew some dragon-tongue."

"Not perfect, but okay," she said, knowing her accent probably sounded as strange as theirs did. "Are you going hunting?"

The youngest, Paz, nodded, her tight curls bouncing as she did. At the same time, Verano and Nino said, "No."

Lumi gave a snort of laughter but turned to Sofia. "Do you know how to hunt?"

"I do," Sofia said. "I'd love to join. I taught myself, but I'm sure you know better than me."

Verano and Nino exchanged a look, and Lumi smiled. "Perhaps."

They pulled the dart gun from their belt and handed it to Sofia. "Do you know how to use this?"

"Yes," she said, excited that Lumi was willing to give her a weapon. She felt safer with the weight of it in her hands. Their few remaining supplies had been confiscated the night before. The group took the narrow staircase up the side of the cenote and into the rainforest above.

The sun was a little higher now and the forest seemed to have woken from its slumber. The small group moved quieter than she expected, Verano and Nino moving with such fluidity that their feet didn't even break the dry leaves beneath them. Sofia watched with keen eyes as Lumi jumped over a particularly large root.

She kept quiet, despite the questions forming in her mind. They were officially on the hunt and Sofia wasn't going to be the reason the prey was scared away, but her suspicions were answered a few minutes later when Lumi gave another jump, twisting their body as they did so. In the blink of an eye, a hawk shot off between the trees. The other three stared at Sofia, waiting for her reaction as Lumi flew back with a rabbit between their beak before sweeping off once more.

Sofia wasn't sure what her reaction was, but it seemed to satisfy whatever they were worried about. A moment later, Verano and Nino slipped out of their human forms, leaving their clothes behind, and bounded as one into the forest, black fox tails poised and ready for whatever they smelled.

And then it was just Paz and Sofia left. The girl collected the rabbit off the ground, slicing its throat before hanging it on her belt.

"They hunt," she said, words a soft whisper, "I collect."

"Are you also—?" Sofia started, unsure of how to finish the question in dragon-tongue.

"A *cambiato*?"

"Cambiato," Sofia repeated, slowly. Unsure of what the word meant.

Paz gave a smile before jumping into a crouch and pretending to howl silently. She jumped back up. "Cambiato."

Sofia nodded. "Yes."

"I'm not."

"But they all are?"

She hummed her agreement as Lumi returned with yet another rabbit in their beak.

"She's a hawk? And the other two are foxes?"

"They are a hawk," Paz said as she tied the second rabbit, dead, to her belt.

"They?" she repeated, slowly once more. For a moment, she questioned whether she knew as much dragon-tongue as she thought.

Paz was squinting now at her, as if baffled by her confusion.

"Lumi is neither woman nor man. Or both, perhaps? Like the moss frogs in the eastern springs. They are they, not she."

Perhaps Sofia should have felt insulted by the simplicity with which Paz explained Lumi's gender to her, but then again she had only heard of people that fell between woman and man in the books the chief commander had kept hidden in his office. The king had banned such *practices* as he called them when the first king had first taken power of Wueco.

"But why?" Sofia asked.

Paz laughed. "Why are you a woman?"

"I just am."

The smaller girl shrugged and Sofia had to acknowledge she had no argument against the logic. She picked up the rabbits and mice that Verano and Nino returned with a few minutes later and tried not to jump out of her skin when Lumi came soaring through the trees and with a twist, landed on the ground in their human form. They were naked, and Sofia took only a brief moment to appreciate their well-toned body before her cheeks went pink and she averted her eyes. She heard Paz's soft huff of laughter at the reaction.

"There is a herd of deer about a quarter of a mile north of here. I can lead you there if you're quiet."

Sofia pulled out her dart gun as Paz nodded. It wouldn't take any of the adult deer down, but it could slow them down and help quicken the kill from Paz's arrows. Lumi smiled and then flickered back into their hawk form, darting off the way they'd come.

Sofia took turns with Lumi and Verano carrying the deer back to the cenote. Paz and Nino had a dozen rabbits and smaller animals tied along their belts. They had picked up their clothing on the way back. Sofia felt an ache of pride at coming back with the others, even if she'd only helped a bit.

She knew what belonging felt like. She knew it from the cycles she'd spent by Javi's and Flor's sides, but it was different to feel that sense out here—with strangers. The belonging she felt in that moment didn't come from cycles of fighting together and trust built, it came from the simple existence of sameness and a shared distant history.

Even as they walked she vowed not to tell Fox what she'd learned of the tribe and the shifters they were staying with. She'd have to tell him eventually, but he'd react poorly and she'd need to explain to him that not all of the non-human creatures in the forest were evil. He was still insisting the dragon had been evil for accidentally hurting them. The Dereyans weren't apparently taught nuance.

The hunting party made their way down into the shallow cenote, and it took only a moment to find Fox among the others. His borrowed clothing may have blended in, but he couldn't hide his white-blond hair glinting in the sun, brighter than anyone around him, calling him out as different—the hair of a Falais not a Wuecan. He sat beside a small cook fire, staring in concentration as the old woman next to him spoke in slow deliberate words, using her hands to emphasize what she was saying. As Sofia got closer and heard her words, she wasn't surprised that it was dragon-tongue. What did surprise her was that Fox was nodding along, as if he understood her.

Not wanting to interrupt the lesson, she stopped a few steps away, out of his eyesight and simply watched. The woman pressed the heel of her hands together, flattening the corn dough between them. She pressed and turned the dough in one motion, over and over again until it made a disk she showed to Fox. He followed her lead, picking up a ball and pressing it between his palms, but before he'd even flattened it, the woman was clucking her tongue and picking up another, showing him carefully how she used the heels of her hands instead of her palms.

"*Quidade, lentenente,*" she said and Fox nodded as if he understood the carefully articulated dragon-tongue.

"*Bon?*" he said, holding up his newly flattened dough. The woman's face broke into a wide smile, showing crooked teeth. Fox's own face seemed to brighten at the unspoken praise and Sofia looked away. He so rarely smiled like that—genuine and without hesitation. It reminded her of how young he really was. How young they both were. And how very human.

"Come sit with us," the woman said, noticing Sofia over his shoulder. Before she could refuse, the woman was standing, spry for her age and pulling Sofia over with a warm hand on her elbow. Given little choice, she sat down beside Fox, their arms brushing as the woman handed them each a ball of dough.

As they worked, the woman chattered endlessly, excited to have Sofia there to translate now for her. Her hands moved through the air like wings, the small chain along her wrist slipping up and down with every flourish. She was able to give them more detailed instructions until Fox's tortillas were nearly indistinguishable from her own.

The air around them filled with the rich scent of woodsmoke and corn as they cooked, people from all over the cenote coming to snag the tortillas as they finished. She couldn't help but watch Fox as he smiled —genuine and open—happy with the nods of approval from the others as they ate.

"I didn't take you for someone who liked cooking for others," she said, satisfied to see the smallest flinch as if he'd forgotten she was beside him.

He shrugged. "I think everyone enjoys when their work is appreciated."

"Even by feral Dragonborn?"

He had the decency to blush, but his chin tilted up as he turned to her. "I'm sorry I implied all Dragonborn are feral. I meant only to imply that you were."

Her eyes narrowed, but she bit back the smile that threatened to slip out.

"One of these days, it'll work," he said.

"What?" she asked, frowning.

"Making you smile."

She leaned forward until their faces were a mere inch apart and she smelled the subtle salt on his skin.

"Give the Dragonborn back their land and I'll smile all you want."

The blush was a violent shade of red as it crept from his neck to his cheeks.

"You know I can't do that. You should have kidnapped the king if you wanted that kind of power."

"I'll take that under advisement."

He frowned and she let her satisfaction show.

"Tía Muela is one of the best teachers we have," Clarita said, sitting down beside Fox, a half-eaten tortilla in her hand. "She adds magic to her food, I swear."

"How do you have corn meal out here?" Fox asked. Clarita froze and Sofia choked on the bit of tortilla she'd been chewing. He must have realized the implications of the question because he blanched and shrugged. "Sorry, I didn't mean to question..."

Clarita was looking at him carefully. "We have connections with the city still. There are some things we can't grow in this part of the rainforest."

"That's how you learned king's tongue," Sofia said. "Your accent is near flawless."

The woman smiled, eyes sparkling with mischief. "I would hope so. It was my first language."

Fox's eyes went wide

"I was born in Suvi. I lived there until I was a teenager."

"You ran away?" Fox asked, as if the idea baffled him.

"My mother smuggled us out after my father was sent to the farms on false charges."

"We don't send people to the farms over false claims."

He understood what he'd said in the same moment Clarita did, her eyes narrowing and swinging to Sofia.

"Who is your companion, exactly?"

Sofia bit her lip, wondering how far honesty would take her.

"He's new to the resistance," she said, at last, happy Fox was smart enough not to double down on his slip up.

The woman gave a stiff nod at this before getting up and moving away, cutting any further conversation short. The cenote itself seemed to be emptying out as the others finished their morning meals and left to do whatever they did with their time. They were still far enough from Suvi that they had no fears of being caught.

Muela had gone, too, somewhere during their conversation, and Sofia and Fox were left alone next to the now smoldering cook fire. The tortillas were gone except for the ones they had in their own hands.

They sat in silence for a while longer, finishing the last bites and, at least for Sofia's part, savoring the sense of being full and warm.

"When do we leave?" Fox broke the silence first.

"Is that my decision?"

"It is, oh captor of mine," he said, smirking.

She rolled her eyes. "The day after tomorrow? I still need to take them to the cenote to show them the altars, but we can leave after I return."

"You're going to the cenote without me?" he said, voice doing little to hide his anxiety.

"Lia said you can't travel yet. It will be better to give yourself another day of rest before you move too much."

Fox couldn't argue with the logic although his furrowed eyebrows told her that he wanted to. They fell back into silence, and Sofia allowed the dancing flames to draw her attention.

His question had made her think about tomorrow and the next day, and such thoughts came with too many questions.

No.

There were no questions. She needed to bring Fox back to the base so Micael and others could finish their negotiations. If Dia was still alive. And then—well, they couldn't let him go immediately. He knew too much. But they wouldn't kill him. Micael had always avoided such things as best he could. Unless his hand was forced.

Though, he had killed before to protect the resistance.

She'd always appreciated that about Micael, but for some reason, now the thought made her stomach twist and something unpleasant settled in the pit of her stomach.

But there was no room for doubt or second guesses. She needed to get back to the cenote and prove to Micael she was still useful to the resistance. If her time in the forest had taught her anything it was that she belonged out here—not in the city. She couldn't go back to begging on the streets. And bringing Fox back to them was the only thing that would ensure she wouldn't.

SOFIA

AGE 15

The next day, the prince woke and saw the village girl sitting beneath his tree. He attacked her, sweeping down and snapping at her fingers. Even as he drew blood, she didn't move, voice calm as she told him to take the bread she had brought. She told him that she saw that he was hungry. It was her voice, full of compassion, that finally made the prince surrender.

-The Raven Prince by Emilio Laurn

Sofia was in a horrible mood and she hated herself for it. But she hadn't seen Gabriel in three days and had heard nothing from him either. She'd eventually given in and asked Jorge about him that morning. The stables head had only grunted at her to get out and leave him be.

Even without answers, she was a few minutes late to work and the chief commander was all too happy to point this out as he threw a stack of papers down for her to work on. He left a few minutes later, stating

he had business at the prison, and left her alone to wallow in her misery.

She worked quickly, her handwriting probably messier than it should have been, and a small voice in the back of her mind told her that the chief commander might end up forcing her to rewrite the tables and letters, but she didn't care. She was too distracted to focus.

She finished the pages shortly after lunch and was all too happy to stack her work on the chief commander's desk and sidle over to the bookshelf along the wall. As usual, she was careful when she plucked out a book to read. She never touched the books with a clean layer of dust on them, too aware her fingerprints might give her away. The room was only ever open long enough for her to slip in and out as she picked a book. And she only ever grabbed one when she knew the chief commander's schedule had him out of the manor for the entire day.

Mina didn't even know about the shelf behind the wall. The stories she told the girl had expanded over time as she learned more, but she never dared tell her where she was getting her ideas from. Not even Gabriel knew the books she was reading came from behind the secret shelf, too afraid of letting him in on a secret even the chief commander was keeping—knowledge that could be a death sentence. The thoughts passed through her mind every day she opened up the small room and stepped inside, but they never stopped her.

She sidestepped the stack of books that was in the middle of floor as she crept into the hidden room, always a mouse waiting for the trap to fall.

"Sofia?"

The book she'd been holding fell from her hands with a resounding thump that had her choking on the air in her throat. She whipped around to see Mina standing at the threshold of the secret room, eyes wide as she peeked past the bookshelf to where Sofia stood, pale and shaking.

"What?" Sofia's mouth was dry, her voice a soft rasp. She grabbed the book she had dropped and shoved Mina out of the room, eyes flitting around, as if the chief commander might pop out at any moment with a cry of triumph. But the office door was closed and they were alone.

"What is that?" Mina said, ducking around her to look back at the small room.

In turn, Sofia ignored her question and grabbed her arm, pulling her back. She'd grown over the last cycle, but she was still a few inches shorter than Sofia, frame like a bird. Despite her petite size, the girl put up a fight, not quite allowing herself to be removed from the room.

"You're early!" Sofia hissed.

"I saw the Master leaving with the general earlier. I knew he wasn't here."

"That doesn't matter, I told you to never come before two." It was cruel to yell at the girl, but it felt better to distract from Sofia's own blame in being caught. "What are you doing here?"

She pulled at the girl's thin arm again, and this time Mina turned. Her eyes were still wide and her lip was folded between her teeth. That wasn't what drew Sofia's attention, though. It was the cut across her cheek and the swelling already beginning along her eye. Her nearly translucent skin was a deep red along her temple. It would be a nasty bruise by tomorrow.

"What happened?" She felt like Mina's mother as she tipped the girl's head forward, inspecting the damage in the light of the office lanterns.

"I got a few hits in." She said it with such pride Sofia had to bite back her smile.

"Why are you getting into fights?"

"I was defending you."

Sofia's stomach twisted, unsure if she was angry at Mina for getting hurt or whoever had taken a fist to her face. "I don't need you defending me."

"You didn't hear what they were saying about you!"

"Exactly," Sofia said, leading Mina over to the desk to sit. She kneeled in front of the girl. "I don't care what they say when I'm not around. Gossiping about something doesn't make it true. But what are real are these cuts."

She pressed a finger close to the cut on Mina's cheek. It had stopped bleeding, but the skin was still jagged and red around the edges.

"You should clean this with some water and soap. And you're going to tell me who did this to you, so I can make sure you got enough hits in to make them regret it."

Mina gave her a look that said she was very much not planning on giving up names. Sofia poked at the cut on her cheek with narrowed eyes, but didn't argue. For now.

"There's a washbasin two rooms down. I'm going to go get a wet towel and you are not going to move." Sofia pushed the bookshelf to the secret room back against the wall until it clicked closed. She paused at the office door, listening for anyone on the other side before she rushed out and down the hall.

While the latrines were all on the same side of the manor, washrooms with basins of water were scattered throughout. The maids brought fresh water twice a day, providing the chief commander and his guests with a place to wash or get a drink. There was a full pitcher of water by the basin and clean towels folded neatly on the shelf. Thinking back on the books she'd read on inflammation and first aid, she wet the tip of the towel and rubbed some soap on it. She also snuck a glass of cold, fresh water, drying the cup and placing it back directly where it had been.

She slipped back into the office a minute later, Mina sitting obediently in Sofia's chair next to the chief commander's desk. She kneeled on the soft rug and brought the cloth to Mina's cheek, ignoring the small girl's flinch. Sofia could tell she was in pain, but she gritted her teeth and bore it as Sofia scrubbed the cut.

They both heard the commotion outside the office too late, Sofia having just enough time to stand at attention as the door burst open and Chief Commander Harlow and General Ocon came stalking into the office. Fear twisted deep in Sofia's gut as she took in the splatters of blood across the general's face and the cold rage painted across the chief commander's.

His eyes flickered between the two girls and the office around them, looking for something. Whatever he saw seemed to light something in his eyes and he almost smiled.

"You've been reading," the chief commander said, the words sending ice through Sofia's veins. The cloth dropped from her hand and she began to tremble, the fear coursing through her body in a wave. A soldier stood behind the two officers, hand on his swords as if she posed any threat to these men.

"That's the one," the chief commander said, motioning for the soldiers to move. Sofia went cold. He wasn't pointing as her. He was pointing at Mina. "That's the office maid who's been reading."

General Ocon's lips turned down in a small frown at the chief commander's words, but he didn't question it as the soldier moved between them and into the room.

Sofia tried to step in front of Mina, blocking the small girl from their views, but the soldier only shoved past her with a sneer. Mina let out a cry of pain as the man none-too-gently picked her up from the chair and twisted her arms behind her. She was cuffed a moment later, as if unbound she could have done anything against the towering solider.

She couldn't stop herself as she moved to grab the soldier to try and free Mina. The general was quick to intercept, seizing her and twisting her arms behind her. She was useless when faced with the king's men.

"Should I arrest this one for co-conspiracy?" he asked the chief commander, looking down at Sofia with abject disgust.

"I'll deal with her personally."

A cold numbness washed over Sofia's body as Mina was dragged away, General Ocon not letting go of her until Mina had disappeared around the corner and the chief commander had motioned for him to leave. And then she and Chief Commander Harlow were left alone.

"She isn't...she wasn't..." Sofia said, the words barely coherent.

The chief commander strode forward like a wolf stalking his prey.

"You stupid, thieving, little bitch," he hissed, spit flying from his mouth as he emphasized each word. "I didn't want to believe the damned stableboy, but I should have known. You know how many soldiers heard him accuse my very own maid of treason?"

Sofia felt her lunch rising up and she folded, trying to breathe. *No.*

She wasn't even sure the words came out or if they were strangled and caught in her own brain.

Gabriel had betrayed her.

The chief commander grabbed her hair, yanking her neck back and forcing her to look up at him.

"You're lucky you're useful, dragon-filth. I'll save you this one last time. You better make it worth it."

He didn't bother with requests or commands, but stood, dragging her along by her hair. They shuffled out of the office and down the back stairs until they were underground, Sofia stumbling beneath his grip. She knew the basement existed, but not even the servants were assigned to the floor, cobwebs and dust left to fester here unattended. It was a twisting maze of rooms and halls and Sofia wondered how the house could be so large. The chief commander threw her through a door and into a small room with a fire burning in the small hearth. The room was hot, nearly unbearable and she felt herself choking on the air.

"Give me your arm."

The blood drained from her face as she saw the poker he pulled from the hearth. Not a poker, but a branding iron.

Her body didn't feel her own and he didn't wait for her to follow his command, grabbing her wrist and wrenching it forward.

"No one else will hire you. No one else will work with a branded traitor. You will have nowhere else to go. So hear me when I say this. You won't disobey me again. You won't embarrass me like that again. The next time, I will kill you personally. You and every family member you have left."

You're lucky you're useful, dragon-filth.

Her nails bit into her free palm as she tried to block out the chief commander's words. The searing agony that followed did the work for her and in that moment, her brain only knew pain. Any thoughts of Mina or Gabriel or her future washed away as her skin sizzled.

CHAPTER TWENTY-NINE

FOX

The next morning, Fox stayed behind when Clarita picked Sofia up to show them the way back to the ruins. He didn't know what to make of the small bubble of dread that settled in his stomach as she disappeared between the trees. They left in a group of seven, Sofia with a new bow and arrow set. He shouldn't have worried —why worry about the Dragonborn that had captured him and gotten him into this disaster? But he was still uneasy with their separation, well aware they weren't in friendly territory. They may have only been tolerating them to get back to the dragon altars.

But Sofia was right when she said he needed to rest. Every time he stood and moved around, he felt the stitching tugging at his skin. He continued to take the tincture the healer—Lia—gave him, but he was looking forward to the day he wouldn't need it. More importantly, he was looking forward to leaving once Sofia was back.

It was nearly noon by the time he convinced himself to stand and stretch. As much as he preferred to stay lying on his bedroll all day, he still had hiking to do tomorrow, if not the next day, and it would do him no good to be stiff and sore.

If anything, the last week stuck out here in the rainforest had simply reassured him that his people were right. It was a dangerous and wild place where only a few could survive. He had to give credit to the Dragonborn who had made a living out here, and he would be all too happy to get home.

He wasn't sure if Clarita had told the others to keep an eye on him, but no one appeared to care as he started walking around the cenote. It wasn't nearly as large as the ruins he and Sofia had found, but there were elements of the same artistic flair of the Dragonborn. The main cavern was tiled, although the tiles were as old and cracked as the ruins had been. He imagined they had been here before the tribe had even found the cenote. The walls were freshly painted, however—one vibrant teal, another an orange the color of sunset. Flowers were painted at random intervals, brightening the space with even more color. It made the cave-like space feel alive even in the shadows.

He stumbled upon a dragons' shrine, two doors down from the bathing room. It was nowhere near as big as the previous one, with three small altars and crude paintings of the dragons along the walls. He might have found the murals beautiful had he not seen the ones in the ruins a couple days ago. These were paintings built off stories, not memories. They were the type of reproductions that Fox could have done from the books he'd read growing up, rough illustrations that were missing *something*.

There was nothing of the true terror and power that the dragon he'd seen held. The very air around the dragon had seemed to breathe with danger.

He stood in front of the altar that sat under the cenote dragon, staring up at the blue-eyed beast, and wondered what it had been like for the great king when he decided to turn on these *gods*. He'd read the accounts of the sea dragons destroying an entire fleet of ships in a single hour, hundreds drowned on a whim.

The dragons held a power of the land that no human or faery could come close to replicating. How many had been saved from drownings and storms because the great king had exterminated the dragons. And how many would die if they returned?

He hated himself for thinking it. If he said the words out loud, Sofia would hate him more than she already did. But even if the dragon they had seen had been beautiful—and it had been—it had also almost killed them. She was blinded by her own stubborn faith.

"Do you want to make an offering?" A small voice spoke behind him and he saw a young girl standing in the doorway, arms cradling a bundle of purple flowers. She had thick black hair, nearly as curly as Sofia's and somehow so much more tangled. Her freckled cheeks had deep dimples as she smiled.

"Oh, I was just—"

"Here," she said moving forward, carefully plucking one of the flowers from the bouquet to hand to him. The stem was soft against his fingers. Up close, he noticed that the purple petals weren't a single color, but a blend of blue and purple with streaks that looked nearly silver through them.

"I don't know..." he started, but before he could finish, she pressed a finger to her lips as she motioned for him to kneel beside her. She set the flowers along the cenote dragon's altar and he followed suit when she looked at him, eyebrow raised expectantly. She said a prayer slowly, likely for Fox's benefit. As each guttural word slipped from her lips, a sense of knowing and familiarity grew in his chest, expanding and cutting off his breath. He didn't know what the words meant, the dragon-tongue not magically forming into understanding. But he *knew* the words. He'd read them only one time before, but they were burned into his brain, branded there with his grief. He pictured them now, written gracefully on the first page of a book long hidden in the darkest corner of his bedroom.

The girl pulled the small dagger from the altar and drew the sharp blade across the inside of her wrist. It wasn't a large or even deep cut and it took a second before the blood beaded and she let a droplet fall into the golden basin on the altar.

Fox's stomach turned as she passed the blade to him and stared, waiting. He wasn't sure he remembered this part in the book. The small dagger was warm beneath his fingers from where her hand had been. He realized it was also the first weapon he had held since the Dragonborn tribe had found Sofia and him outside the canyon. He could take it. He could run. He could stab this small child and make his way back home to tell them everything he'd seen.

Instead, he lifted the blade and hesitantly ran it across his wrist, wincing at the sharp sting of it breaking skin. He didn't acknowledge the chuckle that the little girl let out as his blood dropped into the bowl. He quickly pulled his arm back, wiping his wrist and pulling his sleeve down to hide the evidence. What would his father say if he could see Fox kneeling at the altar of the dragon gods?

He started to stand, sure they were done, but the little girl stopped him, a small hand on his sleeve. He noticed she was holding one last bloom, pinched between her fingers and as she pulled him down, tugging on his shirt, he leaned over and she slipped the small flower behind his ear.

Before he could thank her, she turned a bright red and ran from the room, her high giggles echoing in the passage beyond. Fox followed a moment later, holding back his smile. The scent of the flowers had been cloying in the small worship room, but as he left, he smelled the small whiffs from the bloom behind his ear, delicate and sweet.

He didn't bother exploring farther down the hall, heading back toward the main cavern. He was hungry and hoped he'd find someone willing to part with food.

As the tunnel ended, Fox stumbled a few steps, blinking into the sunlight and letting his eyes adjust to the sudden brightness. No number of torches could push away all of the shadows of the caves. But the day outside was cloudless and the sun relentless.

It might have been better to have remained blind, because the moment he stepped into the sunlight and looked around the cenote, he saw the two small black canines running down the sides of the steep cliff. He opened his mouth to scream and warn the few people milling about, but a moment later, two small boys stood in their place. Fox recognized them from that morning at breakfast.

The people around the children didn't flinch, noting the transformation with the casualness that one takes in the dying of a flower in the cold season. The little girl he'd just seen inside the worship hall ran up, laughing and chattering at the two boys before slipping into the form of a rabbit. His eyes flashed to the others that milled about the cenote, a new understanding in his gaze. He saw the way their muscles shuffled beneath their clothes, the gait of their walks. The gracefulness of their movement not quite *human*.

They hadn't stumbled upon a hidden oasis of Dragonborn living peacefully in the rainforest. They'd wandered into a viper's nest of shapeshifters.

Fox didn't let his thoughts wander further. He needed to leave. Now.

Fox allowed himself a small moment of rationality, grabbing the cloak he'd been using that night and stealing a small cooking knife left out beside the fire. Even as he rushed up the stairs of the cenote, he kept his shoulders relaxed. He didn't want to draw suspicion. He had seen the shapeshifters who had first kidnapped him run, and he'd have no chance if these ones tried to chase after him. So, with his heart fluttering in his throat and his thoughts screaming at him, he walked, one foot in front of the other until the sound of the cenote and its people had faded behind him.

Only then did he let himself run, allowing the adrenaline coursing through his body to take him farther. He only stopped once his lungs ached and his breaths came in short bursts. Even the reprieve granted by the tribe hadn't been enough to make up for the days of near starvation and constant walking.

Before he had a chance to think through his actions, he'd collapsed on the ground, shoulder resting on the tree behind him and body cradled between two roots. He lifted his shirt briefly, just long enough to see one of his stitches had snapped. The cut was an angry red, but it wasn't bleeding.

He let out a string of curses, his voice echoing in the trees surrounding him. He was in the forest once more, holding a single knife, and so very much alone. Not even Sofia was here now to act as a buffer between him and the wilds.

Breathing carefully through his nose, he stood and took stock of the situation. At least the sun was out, the dappled light dancing across the forest floor, pointing his way home. If he headed south from here, he'd hit the city eventually. He could make it home.

His feet didn't move.

Sofia was north. She was in the exact opposite direction as home. And she was also alone and unknowingly surrounded by shapeshifters. Had Clarita planned this? Purposefully separating them as a means of making them vulnerable?

Home was south, but Fox turned north—toward Sofia.

He could find them—find her and warn her who these *people* truly were. And then he'd go home. His body ached with every step, but he used his pain to his advantage, focusing his mind when it wandered too far. He didn't think about why he'd turned away from home. He didn't think about why he felt compelled to warn Sofia. He simply walked, knowing that if the shapeshifters harmed Sofia before he got there, he would kill them all.

THE SUN SANK AS he moved, tracing the hours as it crossed the sky. The Dragonborn had once believed the great dragon's spurned lover was the sun, constantly chasing her through the sky, trying to get her back. For thousands of cycles they had danced like that, the sun never quite able to lasso the moons, even when he overlapped with them.

When his brother had died and he was left chasing after a dream of destroying the resistance and avenging Leon's death, Fox thought he had begun to understand why someone might run after the impossible in the smallest hope it was only improbable.

Here he was, chasing after the resistance spy who had kidnapped him and threatened to kill him. And he was beginning to acknowledge, in a dark corner of his mind, that he didn't just want her back so he could arrest her or use her to bring down the resistance.

What do you expect to happen when you find her? When you save her?

His father's voice was a sneer in his mind.

You're as useless as you've always been. A dreamer too stuck in the clouds to see your own feet. As useless as a dead dragon god or the sun chasing the moons.

Dusk came before he saw any sign of the others. The only sounds around him were the soft rustles and far off screeches of animals that he'd gotten so familiar with over the past few days. He picked his way more carefully once night fell. Both moons had already risen and were shining bright, but beneath the trees, their light didn't always reach the forest floor. The night blooms and the glowing mushrooms gave enough away of the outline of the ground for him to make his way over roots and brush. He didn't stop for the night until the moons were sinking low into the sky, and he was starting to stumble out of pure exhaustion. He had to be near the ruins by now, but it would be dangerous to search, when even the moons weren't lighting the sky. He'd just as soon fall into the cenote as find it.

For all he knew, he'd passed its entrance miles ago, off by the smallest angle, he could have veered away from the path without even noticing. He fell against a tree, letting the last few days sink in as the cold seeped through his clothes. He was alone in the rainforest, with only a cloak and a half-dull cooking knife. In the last week, he'd been captured by the resistance, nearly eaten by shapeshifters and a fanged faery, almost drowned by a dragon, and accidentally made allies with another group of shapeshifters. And instead of running back to Suvi when he was given the chance, he was chasing after the woman who created all of his problems in the first place. Who probably would hand him over to the shapeshifters to gain her own freedom.

He was smart enough to bite off the scream that threatened to spill from his lips. The night was quiet, but the last few days had taught him that plenty lurked silently in the shadows. He closed his eyes, trying to forget where he was for a fraction of a second. Tonight, he wouldn't move. Tonight, he'd rest and dream of hot baths and roasted pigs.

Tomorrow, he would decide what to do—save Sofia or turn back to Suvi like the good soldier he had always been.

CHAPTER THIRTY
SOFIA

Sofia wasn't sure what she was expecting as she brought Clarita and the others into the shrine. It was just as she'd left it except the small hearts she'd placed on the altars as offerings were gone. The dragon feather stood sentinel at the front of the room and Sofia could almost imagine it now in its place along the spine of the dragon she'd seen, nestled with its companions.

A hush fell over their group as they paused at the entrance. Clarita was the first to move, striding toward the feather and falling to her knees before it. A sob cracked through the room and Sofia almost backed away—uncomfortable with the show of emotion. But the woman was motioning for her to come and she obeyed, stepping past where Lumi and the others stood in silent reverence.

As she came to stand beside Clarita, the older woman rose and cupped Sofia's face in her hands, kissing her on the forehead before wrapping her into a hug.

"Thank you," she said, over and over. Sofia was rigid in the embrace, unsure of what to do. She heard a shuffling and looked to see Lumi hustling the others outside, leaving Sofia and Clarita alone.

"I didn't..." Sofia said. "I'm glad someone will be here to take care of this place again," Her voice choked as if Clarita's own emotions had crawled into her, making her chest tight.

Clarita looked at Sofia, a softness that hadn't been there before now warming her face. "You have no idea what you had, did you?" she asked, a hand running along the length of the feather, not quite touching it.

"It's a dragon feather," Sofia said, unsure of what else Clarita wanted.

The woman only smiled and motioned for her to kneel. They faced the feather together. Clarita set her candle on the stone altar and prepared for the prayer, just as Sofia had done a few days prior.

"Do you know why our people revered the dragon feathers? Why their barbs were woven into the prayer belts?" Clarita's eyes never left the feather as she spoke.

"The books say the feathers connected us to our gods—to the dragons."

"You assumed it was a metaphor." Clarita smiled, dragging her dagger across her wrist before letting her blood drip into the prayer bowl. "Our blood is the offering, but the feather—the feather is what connects us to the dragon. Not metaphorically, but truly. It's the conduit to the dragon hearing us and our prayers. Without the feather, our prayers are lost on the wind."

Sofia stared at the feather.

"When the blood king massacred the dragons, we didn't just lose our gods. He and his men burned the feathers, too. Destroying them, either intentionally or not, broke our contact with any dragons that might have remained. Our tribe had a feather for a time, when Tía Muela was only a child. It was lost in a wildfire. I've never..."

Clarita's voice cracked again and Sofia laid a hand across her arm.

"You've brought us back a small piece of the gods," she continued. "We owe you a debt."

Sofia left Clarita to finish her prayer. Her mind was spinning with the new information, and she didn't want to disturb the woman's time with the gods. Not while Sofia was formulating plans for war. Perhaps it was the feather that was the key to finding the gods of old. She'd prayed to a feather and a dragon had returned, if only briefly. She could do it again.

She could bring back the gods.

Sofia woke up before the others, slivers of sunlight seeping through the vines above in an almost familiar way. Despite tossing and turning half the night, her mind on dragons and feathers, she was too anxious to stay asleep any longer. She was quiet as she moved around, draping herself in her borrowed cloak and going about getting ready for today's hike back.

She hadn't meant to leave Fox alone overnight, but the trek to the cenote had taken longer than she'd expected. It had been too late to return the night before. She wondered for a moment if he'd be gone when she returned. Perhaps he was headed back to Suvi, ready to tell his commanding officers everything he'd seen and learned. And yet, she didn't think he was.

Instead of leaving the moment she was packed, she headed back into the dark hallway and into the dragons' shrine. She'd give one more prayer to the gods. If she was a better person, she wouldn't have thought about grabbing the feather and running.

"Your accent already sounds better." Lumi's voice was soft, but it echoed in the silent room and Sofia gave a small start, mind still on the feather. She turned and saw the shifter leaning against the doorway, eyes bright in the shadows. She could only hope Lumi didn't see the guilt in her eyes.

"You don't need to lie," Sofia said. "I know I still sound like a five-cycle-old child."

"Oh, no," Lumi said, stepping forward, careful around the bones. "Little Julio sounds way better than you."

Sofia allowed herself to laugh, even if the air felt too heavy for such levity.

"We can't thank you enough for bringing us back here." They kneeled beside Sofia, reaching a hand out, fingers passing just over the feather. "I've never seen a dragon feather before. I was never sure if I believed Tía Muela when she said the tribe used to have one."

"I only did what I said I would," Sofia shrugged.

"It's more than that. These people will finally rest in peace." Lumi motioned at the bones laid out across the room.

"I wanted to bury them, but I couldn't—"

"No one blames you. It seems you've done the best you could. The world isn't kind to our people anymore." Lumi placed a warm hand on Sofia's shoulder and she felt herself sinking into the shifter. It had been cycles since she had trusted someone she only just met, and that thought had her pushing away. They might have had a common enemy in the king and his people, but they weren't on the same side of this war. These people had chosen to stay hidden here instead of fighting, leaving the Dragonborn of Suvi to suffer and die.

"I'm glad you and your people will be here for them," Sofia said after a moment, standing. "I should head back to check on Fox, but thank you for everything."

"Let Clarita know you're leaving, she's in the kitchens going through the supplies."

Sofia nodded and left, suddenly anxious to get back to Fox. Even if they weren't on the same side, at least she knew where his sympathies lay and what he was fighting for.

Clarita was covered in dirt and dust when she popped in and told her she was headed back to the camp. The woman only waved her off, too busy looking through a series of jars and clay pots that she and Fox hadn't seen.

She didn't bother with goodbyes as she left. The others had woken while she'd been in the shrine and disappeared off somewhere. It seemed now that she had kept her word and brought them to the cenote and the feather, they trusted her enough to not care where she was.

By the time she was above ground again, the sun had warmed the air and the morning chill was gone. It was one of those days when the weather might convince her that the cold season was ending early, before the snow had even fallen. But she knew tomorrow or the next day, the icy winds would be back, bringing the frost layer down from the northern mountains.

She appreciated the warmth while she could, face turned up to the sky for a moment before she began searching the ground for their trail. It had taken longer than it should have to make it to the cenote the day before, the trail she and Fox had taken through the underground river impossible to track. But she knew if she tried to simply walk straight back to the camp, she'd have just as much of a chance of getting lost once more. So she stuck to their haphazard trail, even as it wove and looped back on itself.

One moment she was tracing the path, careful not to lose their prints and the next someone was calling her name from only a few feet away. She bit back a scream as she stumbled over a root and toppled into the tree next to her, looking around wildly for the culprit.

Fox was there a moment later, standing above her, hand reaching out to help her up. She hesitated a moment, eyes focusing on his face as if it might shift at any moment. The tales always spoke of faeries coming out at night, but there was nothing to say they couldn't haunt the forest in the day. Fox seemed to read something of her thoughts on her face because his lips twitched and he took a step back.

"It's me, captor oh my captor, bane of your existence, most horrible one."

She waved her hand as she pushed herself up. "I got it. I believe you. Please shut up now."

"Ah," he said, smile stretching wider, "I missed you, too."

"What are you doing out here?" She looked around, suddenly realizing she was nowhere near the camp and Fox was very much alone. "Where in the dragons' names were you heading?"

Fox's eyes shifted, face going slightly pink—or pinker given the tinge of sunburn ever present on his skin now. Sofia narrowed her eyes, unsure of why he looked bashful at the question.

"I...well yesterday I—" He started and stopped, eyes looking everywhere but at her. "They're shapeshifters!"

He spit the last words out with such cold venom that Sofia's own stomach dropped. *Oh.*

"I know," she said slowly. She should have told him. She had known that from the moment she'd talked to Paz and the others, but she hadn't wanted to. It was all too obvious how Fox would respond and she hadn't been ready to face his vitriol for all things he didn't know.

"Of course you do." His voice was flat.

"I'm sorry I didn't tell you. You deserved to know."

His lips pinched tight at her words. He stepped closer to her and she winced as his stare darkened.

"I found out yesterday, and I might have freaked out a bit. I ran off."

"You ran the wrong way," she said, looking up at the sun's position in the sky. He'd run north instead of south. And here she was thinking he was getting a bit better at tracking in the forest.

She looked back at him and saw that the pink blush had deepened and he was looking at her with an intensity that made her chest tighten.

"No, I didn't," he said, voice low and rough. Her body heated and she was suddenly more aware of how close their bodies were. And then something shifted in his shoulders and he moved back. "I thought to warn you before I went back to Suvi. I now realize how ridiculous that was, thinking you weren't fully aware we were staying with the same type of creatures that initially kidnapped us. Well, after you kidnapped *me*."

His voice was cold and the blush faded from his cheeks as if his indignation had cleared away any lingering embarrassment.

"They aren't the same *creatures* that kidnapped us. Those wolf-shifters were a different tribe. Not all shifters—"

"Are evil," he finished, rolling his eyes. "I figured you'd say something like that. I planned to head back to Suvi this morning. I don't know why..." His voiced faded away and he turned away from her. So much for feeling like she understood him. He was confusing her as much as Lumi had with their words of encouragement.

"Right," she said, trying to shrug off her confusion. "Well, I'm heading back to the camp to gather some supplies before I go running off into the rainforest. You can join if you want."

She brushed past him, not waiting for his answer. She didn't need to. He would follow because, despite his rambling excuses, she knew he was smart enough to know he wouldn't make it back to Suvi without food or help. And she recognized—even if he wanted to pretend otherwise—he'd run north to save her, instead of returning to Suvi. Something like lightning went through her chest at the thought.

"I'm impressed you found your way here so well," she said, after an awkward amount of time walking in silence.

"I tried to stick to walking north, and I managed to find pieces of your trail."

"You're actually getting good at this. You can teach your scouts a thing or two when you get back."

"Perhaps," he said, voice soft. "If I still have a place in the military after getting kidnapped by the enemy."

"They can't blame you for that, can they?" she said. She wasn't feeling guilt exactly, but she knew whose fault all of this was.

"Maybe not, but I imagine they will blame me for saving a rebel's life more than once and breaking bread with a camp full of unassociated shapeshifters. My father would—"

He cut himself off. Sofia waited a beat, wondering if he'd continue, but he didn't.

"No, I suppose your people wouldn't like that," she said, slowly. "Do you need to tell them?"

She looked over at him, seeing the shrug even as his eyes spoke of racing thoughts. Would he make it back to Suvi? Did she want him to? Somewhere along the way, she realized she didn't want him dead. But maybe it was just the version of him out here that she didn't hate. Once he was back within the stone walls of Suvi, safe with his bastard of a father, would he remember that he cared enough to save her? Would he remember what it was like seeing the dragon bursting through the canyon? Or would he go back to plotting how to wipe out the resistance?

"What would your fellow rebels think of you saving my life?"

"Did you forget? Getting you back in one piece was always the goal," she said. His lips turned down into a frown. "But to be honest, I don't think they're going to be very happy with me no matter what. They often aren't happy with me."

"Do you often threaten the lives of prisoners without cause? I can see that bothering your superiors."

"I had reasons."

"Does it have to do with you hating my father?" He was silent, waiting for her to confirm, but she only stared straight ahead. "I don't blame you. He's easy to hate."

Her eyes flicked toward his. He was focused on his feet as he walked, but a shadow had crossed his face.

"He isn't a nice person," she said, words careful.

"No, he is not." He turned to her, lips suddenly pulled back in a biting smile. "But you're absolutely awful to spend time with. I haven't forgotten whose fault it is that we're out here."

Whatever tentative vulnerability Fox had shown was gone. The sneering mask he always wore was fitted back into place.

THE REST of the day passed quickly, with only a few occasional jabs sent back and forth between them. By the time the sun had set, they were still a few miles from the camp, and the moons, waning in the dragon's blink, were tucked behind the thick clouds rolling in.

"We can probably make it back tonight," Sofia said as they sat, resting and eating the avocados she'd managed to find before the shadows had taken over the forest.

"I don't know if I'm ready to face them," Fox said, staring at his half-eaten avocado, as though it might show him the answers to life's greatest questions. He'd been his normal snarky self since their conversation that morning, but something seemed to be weighing on him, even now.

Though she had her own troubles ahead. She wasn't looking forward to getting back to base and explaining Fox's absence, either.

"We can make a fire and stay out here tonight. At least we're properly dressed for once."

Fox jumped at the suggestion, standing to gather wood for the fire. Sofia waited a bit longer, sucking the last remnants of the avocado's meat from the pit before she finally stood and prepped a small area for the fire.

They worked in silence, but it was a comfortable quiet, born from days of working together and falling into some version of a routine. Sofia didn't have the energy to hunt for food in the dark and Fox seemed to understand this. So once the fire was lit, they sat together in silence, both lost in their own thoughts and anxieties of the future.

Sofia enjoyed the heat of the flames soaking into her skin, but she couldn't keep her eyes from flicking over to where Fox sat, hunched over his legs. She couldn't get his words from earlier out of her mind. No love was lost between him and his dad, it seemed, despite what she'd heard of General Ocon's constant doting on his son.

"You seem to hate your father as much as me," she said, wincing when she saw Fox blanch at the sudden comment. After a second, his shoulders loosened and he shrugged.

"As I said, he's easy to hate."

"I always heard he loved his son. Doted on the golden child and gave him everything he wanted."

Fox gave a sharp laugh, turning to her with dark amusement dancing in his eyes. "I see the confusion. You're speaking of my brother."

It was Sofia's turn to startle. She should have known that. She'd seen the general many times and heard him talking about his son—never his sons. She'd seen glimpses of Fox from a distance when she was younger.

"You have a brother?"

"Had." He stiffened at the word, even as he spoke it, shoulders going rigid. "Leon was the golden child. He was the one my father doted on. The one who was supposed to take up the role as general when my father finally retired. I was supposed to be locked away in some library, where my father could forget I existed."

She didn't want to ask the question, but she needed to know. "What happened to him?"

"He was killed in a black powder explosion set off by the resistance in their attempt to *save lives and free people*."

She bit back the words she wanted to say. *I'm sorry.* He wouldn't want her apologies or sympathy.

"Were you close?"

"He was my best friend."

She picked at her nail beds. "I'm still going to fight for the resistance. I'm going to fight for my people, no matter what. But I can understand why you hate us."

He was suddenly closer, a hand coming down to cover hers, stopping her from picking.

"It was my fault, too," he said, words low and gravelly. She might not have heard them, had he not moved closer.

"What?" she said, her own tone as soft as his.

"I was somewhere I shouldn't have been and he came to grab me. If I hadn't gone...if I had left when he first told me to, we wouldn't have been there when the explosion went off."

Her stomach twisted with acid. "You were—"

"It's the reason I hate small spaces. I was stuck under the rubble for five hours before they found me. But he protected me. Had he not jumped on me when the explosion happened..."

He didn't need to finish the words.

"I—" she started, before stopping herself. He squeezed her hand before letting go and standing up.

"You should sleep, I can keep watch," he said. His mask slipped back into place, seamlessly. Even as he made the offer, she could see the exhausted slump of his shoulders deepen, as if preparing himself for battle.

"You need to sleep, too. We're probably fine to both sleep." Her lips quirked into a small smile to see the relief clear on his face.

"If we're both going to sleep, we should put the fire out."

She was surprised by his words and she didn't pretend otherwise. "I'm not an idiot," he said, reading her expression. "I did go through basic training."

"I'm impressed your training was adequate in any way." She smiled, letting her own guilt slip from her shoulders and tuck somewhere deep in her chest.

He met her smile with one of his own as he stood and began scooping dirt and sand onto the fire. They had made it small, and it went out easily after a few minutes.

"Before you wake me up shivering, perhaps we can simply agree to sleep together?"

Sofia froze for a moment before slowly turning to look at him, eyebrows raised.

He seemed to realize what he had said in the same moment his eyes met hers, and his lips pursed slightly. "Your thoughts are too dirty for your own good."

"You're the one who said it. Your mind's the one having dirty thoughts."

His eyes darkened, trailing up and down her body for a moment before he answered, sending heat suffusing through her body.

"As if you'd be so lucky."

She moved forward, blood rushing thorough her body. She ignored the pulse of her core as she pressed her palm against his chest. His face blushed pink, and she savored his discomfort, perhaps a bit too much. She brought her other hand to cup him below the waist. He was half-hard.

"I don't think your body's gotten the memo that you don't want me."

Indecision flickered through his eyes before he leaned down. He brought his face forward until his lips were only an inch from hers. The wet heat of his breath tickled against her skin as he breathed and her mouth opened involuntarily, eyes unable to look away from his.

"Trust me. You'll know when I want to fuck you, oh captor of mine."

With that, he pulled away, and Sofia was left trembling ever so slightly. She snapped her mouth shut and shook off the electricity vibrating through her body. The first thing she needed to do when she got back to the resistance was get laid.

She was tempted to curl up on the ground alone after his little comment, but knew he was right. She'd only wake up freezing in the middle of the night. Besides, she didn't want him to think he'd intimidated her. She wasn't a fragile flower. So when he had made himself comfortable and lifted his cloak, she slipped in beside him. He wrapped an arm around her, scooping her closer.

She stiffened slightly as their bodies met, hard against soft.

"It's warmer this way," Fox said, the words murmured in her ear. She only gave a small nod, not trusting her voice. She couldn't disagree and after a few more minutes, she let her body relax, sinking into his and focusing on the warmth. It was all she could do to ignore the hard planes of his body against hers. Despite the flings she'd had over the cycles, she'd never spent the night with anyone except for Flor and Javi. And neither of them felt like *this*.

Sleep eluded her for a while, even after she felt the rhythm of Fox's breathing steady behind her, the warm breath brushing against her hair with every exhale. It wasn't until the moons were high, barely peeking out from the clouds, that sleep finally came for her and she let herself slip beneath its wings.

She dreamed of explosions and darkness.

Sofia woke to the sounds of screams and the acrid smell of smoke. For an instant, she thought her dream might have come to life, but the clearing around them was still. Fox sat groggily up beside her, his eyes slowly sharpening as the sounds continued.

"What?" she asked, but then she knew. She saw the angle of the sunrise and registered where the sound was coming from. Her body made the connections before her brain.

"The camp," Fox said, voice rough with sleep and something more.

Another shriek echoed in the distance and then something Sofia had only heard once before.

The flapping of dragon wings.

SOFIA

AGE 15

Despite no evidence beyond the occasional unreliable account of jungle-crazed scouts, some among the Dragonborn insist the dragons didn't go extinct under the great king's rule. Rather, they insist the dragons went into hiding as a means to protect themselves from the king. Many scholars have placed the blame for continued Dragonborn resistance on this belief, noting the false hope continues to fan the flames of resistance within the community.

-Tales of the So-Called Dragonborn by Jules Vond

Sofia shouldn't have gone to the main square. The executions happened when the moons went dark every blink. Even if she hadn't seen the list of names and sketches posted in the streets, she would have known when Mina was scheduled to be killed—to be murdered. But seeing the name inked on parchment broke something inside of her. There wasn't sadness or grief left, only a burning hot rage.

Gabriel was on the list, too. Apparently even attempting to give

Sofia up hadn't saved his traitorous ass. It had only taken her two cycles and listening in the halls to find out what had happened. He'd been caught stealing leather cuttings from the stables to sell. What he was selling them for, no one knew, although their guesses ranged from funding the resistance army to buying his girlfriend an abortion. Sofia had stopped listening to the gossip after that. All she knew is that Gabriel had betrayed her and in doing so, sentenced Mina to death.

"You're lucky you're useful, dragon-filth."

So that afternoon, she'd left the chief commander's manor early. He was already gone, off to prepare for the executions. No one in the household questioned her exit, and she knew they'd all follow soon enough. To not watch an execution, even the non-mandatory ones that occurred every blink, was a form of treason in and of itself. Only a traitor to the crown wouldn't want to see its enemies brought to justice.

Still, no one would have noticed if Sofia hadn't gone. She could have hidden away in the alleys of the slums, but she couldn't bring herself to not watch. She needed to look into the chief commander's eyes as he sentenced the girl he *knew* was innocent and sent her to her death.

The square was already teeming with people when she arrived. Her small body pushed easily through the crowd, barely even noticed. She weaved through bodies until she was at the front of the mob, looking up at the wooden structure, which stood sentinel over the square.

She couldn't take her eyes off the dark rust-colored stains against the wood and on the stones below. She didn't even know she was picking at her cuticles until she felt a warm smear of blood. Her eyes flickered down, mind in a daze, as she saw the red staining her fingers.

It didn't take long before the roar of the crowd changed pitch and the chief commander, general, and executioner walked onto the platform, a small procession of convicts behind them. Mina was at the front of the line, her body dwarfed by the iron cuffs that weighed down her hands and ankles. She didn't bother to look for Gabriel in the line.

Mina's hair was loose, unwashed and hanging in front of her face. But from where she stood, Sofia could still see the way Mina chewed on her lip and the sickly tint of her skin.

Sofia didn't hear the chief commander's speech. She didn't feel the prick of pain along her fingertips as she continue to rip the skin there. All of her focus was on the slight tremor in Mina's shoulders.

There were no thoughts in her mind of what she might do. Could do.

But as Mina was unchained from the others and brought forward, Sofia felt her body lurching forward, blood burning through her body like a fire. She slipped through the line of guards that stood between the platform and the audience, a thin waif of a girl not even noticed until she was through. She ran, small legs taking her up the steps of the platform, her eyes focused only on Mina's own wide ones.

The girl's mouth gaped and her eyes filled with terror, an emotion Sofia only understood when she felt the cold iron fingers wrapping around her arms and lifting her up.

"No! Stop! She didn't do anything. I—" before she could finish, a gloved hand struck her across the face, the hands gripping her the only thing keeping her from falling over. The chief commander's cold eyes flashed in front of her and she heard his voice, icy but soft.

"Take her to my personal interrogation cell, immediately. I will deal with her after this."

The grip around her didn't falter, lifting her like she weighed nothing and carrying her down the stairs. She thrashed and kicked, teeth gnashing at the invisible man behind her. They weren't quite out of the square when her foot made contact with something soft and the man grunted, fingers loosening. She turned as she tumbled, scrambling back as she looked into the cold blue eyes of General Ocon. He sneered down at her as he reached for her again, taking little care as he pulled her forward.

"I don't know why the chief commander seems to have a soft spot for such a wretched creature. I didn't know his inclinations ran so young." He leaned forward, cheek brushing against her own. "You must be good."

"Fuck you," she spit out, nearly biting his cheek before he pulled away.

She growled as he attempted to pull her up once more. She felt like a feral dog and she didn't care. It's what they saw her as anyway. She clawed at his face, a thrill of excitement fizzling through her as she drew blood and he cursed, slapping her across the face.

"I'm going to make you regret that," he said, his voice a hiss like a viper moving in for the kill. Before she could respond, there was a whistle of air and the whack and thud of an axe on wood in the distance. Her blood went cold.

She heard the sharp intake of breath from the audience. There was no cheering or claps, a silence rarely known at these events permeated the air, and General Ocon's sneer turned into a cruel and cold smile.

It was over. Mina was dead.

Sofia's body gave out, muscles going loose under General Ocon's grip. He lifted her easily and this time she didn't fight, any energy drained from her.

He dragged her through the main hall of the prison, a pair of guards following behind as he brought her into a large room lined with torches. A single wood pillar stood in the middle of the room and the blood drained from her face.

As she was tied to the post, her mind pushed away from her body. By the time the sixth lash fell against her back, it was gone.

"I told you to throw her in a cell," the chief commander's voice was rough and cold.

"The bitch attacked me. She deserved every lash."

"You lost control and killed her before we could execute her."

"We can send announcements of death out, to ensure those that saw the outburst understand—"

She was being dragged by her leg, skin scraping against cold stone floor. She couldn't move. She could barely breathe.

When they stopped moving and her leg was dropped, she became aware of something cold and soft pressed against her skin. She opened her eyes to see the gray skin and glassy eyes of death staring back. She was next to a small pile of dead bodies—she was a part of the pile.

Sofia wondered if perhaps she was dead. Perhaps this was what being a ghost meant? Seeing through the eyes of your body after you were gone.

"Slit the throats before you bury them to make sure they're dead."

The footfalls drew distant and she tried to move again. She wanted to call out that she wasn't dead, but the small part of her brain still working told her she couldn't. So instead, she spent ten minutes slowly relearning how to move her toes again. And then her fingers.

She tried to crawl away, but her body wouldn't cooperate. Her vision went black.

Soil filled her mouth and she tasted rot and wet. Her body rolled down a small hill, stopping suddenly as she hit something spongy and hot. Another body followed behind, trapping her.

"You didn't slit the throats."

"It's fine. They're dead."

"The general said—"

"You can crawl in there and do it yourself if you care that much."

"King's balls, just throw the last two in. I need a drink."

It was dark by the time Sofia remembered how to move her body enough to push her way out from under the corpse on top of her. On her other side, a man half-rotten gave way beneath her hands as she tried to crawl away. She didn't gag. She barely reacted. She kept moving until she saw the stars above her. The smell of rot was replaced with incense, and Sofia wondered once more if she might have died.

"Manny! Someone's alive in there."

Hands grasped at her and she shifted, trying to move away.

"No," she muttered.

"Shhh, I've got you." The voice was soft and gentle, and even as she felt her body being picked up, her mind broke once more as she slipped back into blackness.

CHAPTER THIRTY-ONE
FOX

Another scream echoed through the trees.

Sofia was moving before Fox had even stood, not bothering to grab her bag. He scrambled up, his long strides catching up to her easily. He pulled her back.

"Take your bag and get your bow and arrows ready," he said, roughly shoving her supplies in her hands. She nodded, half listening, but her eyes were set on the horizon toward the cenote where the screams were coming from.

"Sofia," he said, voice firmer, "look at me. We don't know what's happening; we need to be careful."

This time, she made eye contact with him and nodded. Her eyes were wide with fear, but the furrow of her brows and the pinch of her lips spoke of determination. A second later, a cold metal was pressed into his hand and he looked down to see her handing him a large dagger.

"This will do more good than that rusty cooking blade," she said.

He took it without question and then they set off at a run. He bounded over roots, doing his best to not roll his ankles on the soft soil in between. Yet, he moved smoother than he had even a few days before. It was nothing compared to Sofia, who despite her shorter legs sprang through the trees like a deer, drawing ahead of him in small increments as they moved.

The sounds didn't seem to grow any louder as they approached, the echoes bouncing through the trees and disorienting him as they ran. If Sofia wasn't moving so assuredly, he might doubt they were going in the right direction. The time also gave his mind the space to process the fact that he was running through the rainforest toward what sounded like a battle. Not only that, but he was running to save a group of Dragonborn and shapeshifters. Who had he become?

They hadn't gone far, when the screams started to wane before going silent. He expected Sofia to run faster, but something in the silence had her stumbling to a stop. A sound ripped from her throat that made Fox's blood run cold and he lurched forward as she fell to her knees.

He came to rest in the dirt beside her, wrapping his arms around her body and pulling her tightly against him. Her skin was cold against his own. He didn't know where the instinct had come from. The only person who'd ever held him was his mother and he'd made sure she'd stopped that cycles ago.

"Breathe," he said. He felt the wheeze deep in her chest—lungs pushed too far, too fast.

Before he could say more, the earth underneath them shuddered and a sharp wind blew through the trees, sending leaves and branches tumbling. He ducked, covering Sofia with his body as the sounds of flapping wings thundered above. He looked up in time to see the glint of white scales through the trees, set against the cerulean sky. If he hadn't seen a dragon a few nights before, he might have thought it a strange cloud.

"How?" Her voice cracked.

Sofia stared up at the same small patch of sky, now blue and clear.

"We should keep moving," he said, helping her stand. "They might need help." Even he knew the words were likely meaningless.

She trembled beneath his hand. He was tempted to take back his words, pull her back into him and hold her until the tremors stopped and her skin was warm again. But she pulled away, her shoulders going stiff. Her face went from wracked with anguish to blank in the blink of an eye, lips set in a grim line.

"Come on," she said, moving before he could register the change that had come over her.

He followed, their progress slower now that the silence ahead of them seemed to swallow up any sense of urgency. They made it to the camp fifteen minutes later, the time feeling like both an instant and an indescribable length of time.

It was clear what they would find before they came to the edge of the cenote, black smoke rising like ribbons from below and a silence louder than Fox felt possible. Despite the knowing that settled between them, Sofia ran into the indentation of the earth, calling out as she weaved through the rubble. He followed behind her, his own steps careful as he scanned the ground. There were small fires burning across the entire cenote, and he gagged when he saw the limb peeking out from one.

Once he'd seen the first hand, it was easy to see the others. Some small and some larger, the fire eating away the families that had only just lived here.

He heard Sofia's yells echoing through the halls and caves farther in the cenote. Silence the only answer.

"No one's here," Sofia said, coming toward him eyes wild. "Maybe they ran."

His jaw tightened and he shook his head slowly. "I don't think they escaped." He let his eyes settle on the fire closest to them, a dark arm visible between the flames, a delicate iron chain along its wrist.

"Tía Muela," Sofia said. He waited for her to collapse again, ready to catch her if her knees went weak.

"Who did this?" Her question was cold fury.

Fox resisted the urge to step away. "You saw the dragon, same as me."

She shook her head. "Dragons don't start fires. They don't burn bodies."

"An enemy tribe? The wolfshifters?"

Her eyes met his, and he realized that at some point over the past few days, she had stopped looking at him with utter hatred. The look had now returned, burning raw and bright in her eyes.

"It's the king's men who kill innocents and burn bodies."

"We saw the dragon! Dereyans don't even believe in dragons." She wasn't wrong. The king's men had made a name for themselves raiding and burning. But it didn't make sense. "Why now? After how many decades of them living out here, the army has never bothered them, so why now?"

Sofia looked at him, distrust in her eyes. "You…"

This time he did step back, raising his hands in supplication. "I couldn't have—I didn't—"

Her eyes closed and she took a deep breath before she answered. "I know."

She moved, slowly making her way toward the small river that ran through the cenote. "We should put out the fires. Give the others as much to bury as they can."

They worked in silence, using some broken dishes among the rubble to bring the water from the lake and put the fires out. It took longer than he expected and with every splash of water, the flames shrank away, leaving the evidence of what they had been burning behind. He threw up once, too sick to his stomach to bother with shame.

Sofia made no comment. After that, he tied a scrap of fabric over his face to help with the smell; it didn't do much. When they were finally done, the cenote was filled with the acrid scent of smoke and burned flesh.

They'd found bronze-tipped arrows amongst the bodies and a steel blade, stamped with the king's seal. Fox didn't want to admit out loud what the weapons meant, but they both knew. The king's guard *had* been here. His fellow soldiers *had* done this. How any of that was related to the dragon they'd seen, he didn't know. Perhaps it had come to defend the shapeshifters, but if so, it had failed. So much for all-powerful gods.

He couldn't help but wonder if the army had been looking for him.

"We can't bury them all ourselves," he said, looking over the ruins of the camp, feeling the sickness in his stomach churning once more.

"Those you left at the ruins," he said, the realization hitting him, "they need to know. We should tell them."

Sofia looked up from where she was slumped, a hollowness to her gaze. "I don't think we should be around when they get back."

"What do you mean? We need to..." His words faded off as he came to the same conclusion she likely already had.

They hadn't trusted him; Sofia barely trusted him. What was to stop them from blaming him for what had happened? For blaming them both?

"We need to leave before they return."

"It's just me that needs to leave," he said, trying to not sound as bitter as he felt.

She shook her head. "I'm the one that brought you here and vouched for you. I don't know why your people attacked now, but even I admit it looks like we're to blame." Her voice cracked.

This is my fault. I'm to blame. He didn't know how, but he knew.

Had they been looking for him? He doubted his father would bother to rally a search party, but the chief commander perhaps?

"I don't know when the others plan to return." She was looking around, eyes analyzing. "We should gather supplies and leave as soon as possible."

Fox didn't have the energy to argue, all too happy to get away from the sharp smell of death. But it felt wrong to rummage through the remnants of the dead for supplies to steal. Sofia's face was set in a stony mask of determination, so he simply followed her lead.

"I'll get some dried food from the kitchens and a second canteen for myself." He wanted a chance to get away from the bodies. The soldiers who'd attacked had been kind enough to drag all the dead out of the back rooms. There were blood stains across the tiles he had to ignore, but it was better than out in the main cavern where Sofia was digging through rubble and bodies in equal order.

He grabbed a canteen and all the dry food he could carry. They theoretically only had a day or two back to civilization, but after constant near starvation, he wasn't taking a chance again. He collected a small pile of smoked rabbit, mangoes, avocados, and even some stale tortillas, scooping them into an empty sack that smelled of corn and had the king's stamp across the coarse weave.

When he had collected what he could, he found Sofia, sitting cross-legged in the rubble. He stepped around her, uncertain before he saw what she was staring at—a long and battered feather, pale blue, nearly white and gleaming beneath mud and ash. It was a feather from the dragon they'd seen, caught among the detritus of the battleground.

"The dragon was here." Her voice was hoarse, with emotions or smoke he didn't know. "They worshipped the old gods. They paid sacrifice to them. I don't understand."

"Perhaps it came to defend them from the king's men." Fox felt the lump in his throat on the last words.

"No," she said, "it didn't."

He waited and she motioned to the body of an older man he didn't quite recognize. The clothes were burned away, but the body was mostly intact. Mostly.

"The claw marks are too big for anything else. No human or shapeshifter did that."

Fox didn't know what to say. He heard the heartbreak in her voice and knew there were no words that would make it better. She'd spent cycles worshipping the dragons and within a few days, one had almost killed her and another had attacked an innocent village.

They were dangerous creatures, not gods to be prayed to. But she wasn't ready to hear that.

And it did nothing to explain how an army of men who believed the dragons were extinct had received aid from one.

Another thought kept crossing his mind, just a little louder and more desperate. Had he not run away from the shapeshifters two days ago, he might have been here. He might be headed back to Suvi with the others at this very moment. Or perhaps he'd have ended up dead under the claws of a dragon.

Instead of saying anything, he filled their canteens and separated the food between the two leather packs she'd found. They were dirty, but in one piece. She'd already packed them with weapons.

Before he could tie both bags up, Sofia grabbed hers and carefully tucked the tattered feather into it. It didn't quite fit, but she bent it gently until the entire thing was hidden within. The sun hadn't even reached its zenith when they headed out, leaving behind the wreckage that had been their home for only two days. Fox couldn't explain the sadness he felt in walking away. Another question to examine *later*.

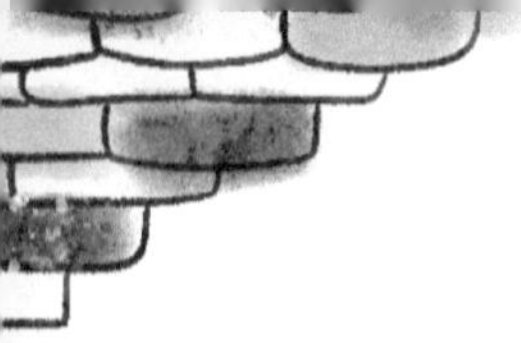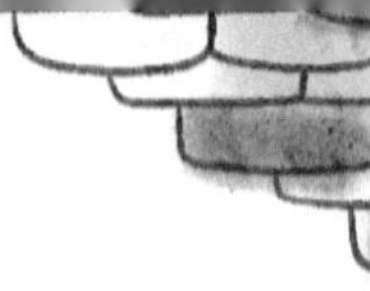

FOX

AGE 11

Over six hundred cycles after the first king was born, the Dragonborn had their last uprising. It was the final choked attempt of a dying race to push back the king's progress. But within two decades the uprising was defeated and what remained of the resistance scuttled back into their holes. It was only after this time that the laws governing Dragonborn behaviors were put into place; the hand of the king forced.

-The Legacy of the Kings: A History of Wueco's Creation by Francis Knoll

The sword was pressed into Fox's neck, wood against skin.

"Take the kill," his father said, voice hard and cruel.

"I defeated him," Leon said, stepping back from where Fox was lying on the ground, shaking and sweating.

Between one blink and the next, their father moved, snatching the practice sword from Leon and cracking it across Fox's face.

"Never hesitate!" he screamed, throwing the weapon at Leon's feet.

Fox's teeth shuddered and he tasted blood in his mouth.

"Father, he doesn't need to train."

"You need someone to fight against. You're clearly not learning otherwise."

"Ian and I train plenty together," Leon said, trying again.

"I didn't ask your opinion, Leon. Now, again!"

Fox stood on shaky legs, knowing it would only be worse if he refused. Their father had never been interested in Leon's training before, but today, he'd dragged Fox from his chair in the library and sent Arik away with a barked order.

He and his brother had been sparring for two hours already and their father had no plans of them stopping.

"You fight him, or I do," his father said when Leon still hesitated.

His brother picked up the practice blade again and they returned to their positions, Fox's arms shaking. Leon swung and Fox parried, but even he could tell his brother's swings were slower than normal. He was pulling his swings.

"Perhaps you both need some better motivation."

Their father strode across the yard to the rack of weapons along the wall. A minute later, two long swords landed between him and Leon.

"Pick them up," he said, voice cold.

"Father."

Leon's protests had turned weak and Fox knew he wouldn't win. Neither of them could win against their father, even the golden child.

Fox struck first. Leon wouldn't and Fox knew their father would only punish Leon for his trying to protect him.

"Scared, Brother?" Fox asked, smirk hiding any shake or hesitancy in his voice.

His brother's bright eyes narrowed, but he bent and picked up the blade. The silver of its steel caught the light, a stark contrast to his brother's golden locks. Fox had always been wan compared to Leon, his skin sallow, hair and eyes drained of the color that made Leon glow. It was as if their parents had put all they had into their firstborn and Fox had been left with only the remnants of beauty and power.

His father treated him as such.

Fox moved first, ignoring the scream of his muscles and the ache in his forearms. He'd thought the wooden training sword was heavy, but the steel blade made his muscles protest every move. It was long and unwieldy, meant for an adult already trained in the basics. Even at sixteen, Leon strained under the weight of it; Fox could see it in the crease of his eyebrows and the pinch of his lips.

His brother parried his swing easily, the hit reverberating through Fox's arms. But he didn't drop the blade; a scream built in his throat, coming out in only a broken groan. His father was silent as he watched, not content yet with the show. Fox knew what he wanted. His brother did, too, but he wouldn't give it to their father, not until he had no other choice.

Fox didn't have the energy to wait. The next time he stepped forward to swing, he purposefully went wide, body tilting forward as Leon's blade came down to block it. The blades brushed against each other, not quite hitting. Leon's steel sliced forward and into Fox's arm with a sickening twist.

He didn't bother to bite back the scream of pain, the blade dropping from his hand as his muscles went slack against his will.

"Fox!" his brother stepped forward, face pale at the sight of blood running down Fox's arm.

"Get away from me," he snarled. "Don't you dare touch me."

He saw Leon's lips go tight as he looked between Fox and the blade, knowing then what he had done. Fox didn't regret it. His father wasn't going to let them stop until Leon drew blood. At least this way, it was on Fox's terms.

Leon didn't move to comfort Fox where he kneeled. He tilted his chin to meet their father's gaze.

"I win," he said and then he dropped the blade and walked away, leaving Fox still bleeding in the dirt. His father followed, no longer entertained by his youngest son's pain.

"You're an idiot," Leon said, pushing Fox into the chair in front of the desk. He glanced away from his brother only to meet his eyes in the small mirror on the wall. They were heated and angry as they glared down at him. His brother had already been in his room by the time Fox had managed to push himself up from the training field and go inside.

"I was ending the torment," he said. "Do you know what set him off, anyway?"

"There was another resistance attack in the royal quarter. Three wagons of supplies were destroyed with black powder."

Fox clenched his jaw. He didn't understand what the Dragonborn were after. They claimed to want peace, but their attacks only angered the crown and the military. They were mosquitos biting at the ankles of jaguars, and somehow Fox was the one paying the price.

Leon read his thoughts plainly on his face. He hadn't quite learned to hide his emotions the way Leon had, another reason for his father to always come after him. "I'm sure the instigators will be caught soon and his mood will switch right back to his normal grumpiness. Now, take off your shirt."

Fox rolled his eyes as he did as his brother commanded. He groaned at the movement, but managed to get it over his head without help. When his chest and wound were bared, he met his brother's eyes in challenge.

Leon's lips pulled down in a frown, but he went to work, fingers poking at the cut.

"I should stitch it. The edge is a bit deep."

"Just do it," Fox said, teeth already clenched and ready. Leon shook his head before he stood. "I said do it!"

"I'm going down to Ms. Bela. You should have some opium milk before I begin. It's going to take a handful of stitches."

"I am fine. I'll be fine."

"I already hurt you enough today," Leon said, eyes earnest in a way that had Fox shutting his mouth, unable to argue. He went quickly and Fox was left, slumped at his desk, hand wrapped back over the cut as blood continued to seep from it.

He knew Leon would try to get back as fast as possible, but he'd also have to be careful. His father would never forgive him if he found Leon caring for Fox. He'd spent the last few cycles trying his best to tear them apart.

But no matter how many times he tried to show Leon how far he stood above Fox and his weaknesses, Leon refused to take the lesson.

Fox wasn't sure what would happen after his brother joined the military next cycle. When Leon was no longer there to act as the executioner of his father's lessons, would he take over or would Fox finally be able to disappear into the stonework of the manor, forgotten by the man he disappointed with his every breath?

Either way, he'd be alone and that thought made his eyes swim. He ducked his head, too afraid to be caught crying, and waited for his brother to return.

CHAPTER THIRTY-TWO

SOFIA

For the first time in a week, Sofia knew where she was going. Not a vague sense of direction or following the sun, but a true understanding of the path back home. Clarita had drawn out a map of where the shapeshifters' camp was and Sofia had been able to figure out where her own base was from there. They'd missed the entrance back into the tunnels by a mile or two, veering too far west. The flood down the river and trip to the camp had brought them farther off course, but they hadn't backtracked too far. If her estimates were correct, they'd be back at the base by tonight or tomorrow. That thought made her stomach churn with an unease that she didn't have the energy to examine. Instead, she focused on the man trudging behind her.

Fox was as quiet as she was as they walked, not questioning the confidence of Sofia's stride as she blazed the trail toward home. He was following her still, without coercion, and she wondered if he knew he was being led back to the resistance. He'd wake up from whatever stupor he was in eventually and realize where they were going. He'd fight her then, she was sure of it. And then what would she do?

A few days ago things seemed black and white. Fox was on the side of the king and deserved his fate, whatever it would be. But now? Could she convince him to come to their side? Would the others even trust him if he did? Would she?

Time trickled by, as sluggish as their steps through the underbrush. It was in sharp contrast to the thoughts racing through her mind with every passing moment. Fox seemed lost in his own thoughts, communicating with only the occasional grunt as they passed dried meat and fruits between them during a break and then headed out once more.

Despite her hunger, she only managed a few bites of food before her stomach turned and she had to stop. Her mind wouldn't let her forget the hands that had prepared this food, all of the bodies they'd left behind, unburied and unhonored. She had only known them for a couple of days, but the grief and guilt burned through her. They were just more people she'd failed to protect from the king and his men—more lives laid at her feet.

It was as if the pain of seeing the tribe massacred had opened up the dam she'd built around her grief for Mina. The anguish crashed over her like a wave and all she could do was breathe and hope she didn't drown in it. She'd learned over the cycles while in the resistance that grief wasn't a simple emotion to be felt and forgotten. It was a tide, ebbing and flowing in its own rhythm between sadness, hate, and something more. And it was more than missing a person. Grief was the pain of the utter destruction of every moment that could have and should have been—every life that might have been lived, extinguished in a flash.

She should go back. She should tell Clarita and the others. She could only imagine the look on their faces when they returned home to find nothing and no one. And Sofia and Fox would be gone, run off like the ones that massacred them. How would they not blame them?

"It wasn't your fault." Fox's voice startled her and she flushed to see the look of knowing on his face as she met his eyes.

"I wasn't...I don't—" she started.

"Your face speaks for itself," he said, his voice soft. "I'm actually quite surprised you've managed to spy as long as you have. You're way too easy to read."

"Not all of us can look like we just smelled a dead skunk constantly."

"You didn't kill them. If anything, they were looking for me."

"All that death for a single person? You think you're that important?"

He didn't speak for a moment and she wondered if he had taken the small jab as a true insult. But he didn't look annoyed, just thoughtful.

"I don't suppose I am. But why else were the king's men out this far?"

"Maybe they don't need rational reasons to murder. Not when they don't even see us as people. Sometimes it feels like we're screaming at the top of our lungs, trying to remind the crown that we're human just like the Dereyans. Our children feel the same hunger and bleed the same red."

"It shouldn't be your responsibility to convince your government of your humanity." The words were uncharacteristic and brought Sofia up short, but Fox wasn't looking at her. His eyes were focused in the distance as if his mind wasn't quite there.

"I wish the rest of the country saw it that way. It seems the louder I scream, the less people listen."

They fell back into silence once more, though perhaps not as hostile as Sofia had expected. It was a comfortable silence, albeit still heavy with sadness and grief.

The sun was low, but still visible through the trees to the west, when Sofia recognized her surroundings—a familiar rocky outcrop. The knot in her chest released. Almost as soon as she noted the sensation, a new tension fell across her shoulders and she stopped, looking around.

"We should make camp here for the night."

"Are you sure? There's enough light to keep going for a bit longer."

"No, this is a good spot to camp. We should take advantage of it."

The space they were in could barely even be considered a clearing, with only a small patch of ground visible between the underbrush of ferns and vines that knotted the ground. At least there were no large roots and the ground wasn't sloped. It was *good enough* at best.

He didn't argue with her, though the small crease between his brows was not quite wiped away by her flimsy explanation. She wasn't even sure she could have been honest with him in that moment. It would have meant having to understand her own motivations, swirling in her gut in waves of anxiety, sadness, and anger.

She was finally only a couple hours from home after a week of chaos. She had Fox, ready to return to Micael as her peace offering. And she had a dragon feather tucked safely away in her bag, proof that she'd been right all these cycles with her ramblings about the dragon gods. Yet all she could think about was the softness in Fox's voice when he'd talked about his brother and the broken bodies they'd left behind. She wasn't ready to face her people. She was barely ready to face herself.

Fox sensed her mood and didn't speak as he began to gather wood for the fire, setting it in the cleared out space she'd made with perfect precision. She bit the inside of her cheek to stop from smiling. She knew he'd become defensive if she pointed out that he'd been learning over the past week.

They ate their dinner in front of the fire, the warmth suffusing them, even as the temperature dropped. It was well into the cold season and Sofia could almost catch glimpses of her breath in the air when she stepped too far from the fire.

"Do you think the Dereyans are working with the dragons?" Fox's voice held a tone of uncertainty that she hadn't ever heard before.

"I can't imagine why or how," she said, hands opened wide in her lap, as if trying to grasp an explanation. "Your people don't even believe the dragons are alive. They're the reason most of them are dead and the rest are in hiding. What could convince the dragons to follow any Dereyan orders?"

Fox's eyebrows furrowed and his eyes darkened as if the shadows had been pulled across his face. "I don't know, but we both saw what we saw back there."

"The dragons were above human politics. They didn't take orders from humans, only responding to prayers and the blood offerings when they wanted. Even then, the history books talk about the dragon gods turning their back to the wrong types of prayer or selfish requests from their most devoted followers. It doesn't make any sense. These aren't the gods that I've read about—that I spent cycles studying. No dragon would..."

Sofia stopped short when she saw the small tick of Fox's smile barely curling his lips. He was laughing at her. She snapped her mouth shut.

"I didn't mean to make you stop," he said, his voice more genuine than she expected.

"I was rambling. I get too much sometimes, I know."

"You're not too much," he said, face serious. "You're passionate. It's...nice. You shouldn't have to dim your light for others."

Her cheeks heated, unsure of the compliment.

"My brother used to go off on rants, too. It was the one trait my father hated in him." His smile dropped as if remembering something. "But it's a good thing to be passionate about things."

"Tell that to the rest of the resistance," she said, letting the bitterness slip between her teeth.

"I'm not sure they'd care about my opinions."

"We'll be at the base by tomorrow mid-morning." His expression didn't change at her words; he blinked.

"I assumed."

"If you want to run...you should do so now."

"I thought I was your prisoner. Aren't you going to knock me out in my sleep and tie me up?"

"With how thick your skull is, I don't think I have the strength to knock you unconscious."

He smiled. "I'll take that as a compliment." And then he frowned. "What will your people do if you show back up after a week without me?"

She shrugged, stomach sick with all of the things she could think of. "I don't think it much matters, at this point. They were about to kick me out for insubordination anyway. I have no job, no home, and no place in the resistance. Maybe I'll walk off into the rainforest and start my own tribe."

"Your friends won't defend you?"

"They'll be glad to see I'm not dead." Sofia said. "Even Micael will have to admit that, but it won't change his choice. My impulsivity got in the way one too many times. I'm not always great at following orders or asking for help."

Fox snorted and she saw his silent agreement plain on his face.

"What happened to you wanting me to be passionate and not dim my light?" she asked.

"Oh, that's not a passion problem. You can care about something and still know how to ask for help."

She grumbled to herself, even knowing she couldn't argue with his logic.

"If I go back with you, will they still kill me?" he asked, voice just above a whisper. "Even if I try to bargain with this Micael guy?"

She picked at the skin on her fingers and didn't answer immediately. She was trying to justify an answer she knew she couldn't give him. She wouldn't lie.

"Probably," she said eventually. "If the chief commander followed through with his threats, the rest of the prisoners will be dead by now. You're too much of a risk with your connections to your father and Chief Commander Harlow. They'll get any information they can out of you and then they'll silence you."

He nodded. He'd known the answer before he'd even asked it.

"I'll stay tonight. I'd break my ankle trying to get back to the city in the dark. But tomorrow morning, I should leave."

A fine line of blood welled up along her thumbnail where she was picking, dark red in the firelight.

"That's only fair."

"I can't give up on my people and I need answers," he said, as if defending his decision. "If someone is using the dragons, I have the opportunity to learn more."

"The resistance will change bases, if they haven't already, so don't bother bringing your friends to visit."

"I didn't doubt it," he said with a twist of his lips that didn't quite look amused. "They'll ask me about my time in captivity."

"I didn't doubt that."

They put out the fire and set to work clearing the minimal space left for their blankets and bedrolls. It was the most luxury they'd had camping since Fox's scheme to run away had dragged them both out here.

By the time she was tucking herself into the bedroll, her cloak draped over the other blankets, the air around her was icy, her breath showing in small puffs in the moonlit darkness. Fox's bedroll rested against her own, no space in the clearing to move it farther.

She found herself turning toward him and a moment later, he did the same. He was buried in his bedroll and cloak, his pale face and hair showing starkly against the dark surroundings.

"I might not be able to remember everything." His voice was loud in the darkness.

"What?"

"My superiors are going to want to know everything that happened out here—everything I saw and heard. But I might not be able to remember everything. Maybe I won't even remember your name or face. It's all been very traumatic."

Sofia didn't even know where she'd begin with telling Flor, Javi, and the others what had happened while she'd been gone—if Micael even gave her a chance before kicking her out of the cenote the moment she tried to enter.

After everything she'd been through, after discovering she'd been right about the dragons being alive, she was still in the same position she'd been in before she'd left. She had no job, no home, and no idea what to do.

"I'm still going to kill your father someday," she said, "and the chief commander." He didn't respond immediately and she might have wondered if he'd fallen asleep if it weren't for the glow of his silver eyes.

"And I'm going to find out who was responsible for the bombing that killed my brother, even if it's one of your friends."

"I know."

A small voice in her mind told her that she could ask Micael when she got back. It was the least the old man could do before throwing her out of the resistance. But even if she did, what would she do with that information? Would she tell Fox, knowing he'd want to kill them? But didn't he deserve to know? At least she had someone to blame.

She stayed silent, unable to make a promise she wasn't sure she could follow through with. Fox turned over in his bedroll and she quickly followed suit, not wanting to be left staring at him as he slept.

Despite being more comfortable and warm than she had been in weeks, she couldn't get her mind to shut off. Tomorrow and all of its unknowns loomed nearer and nearer with every beat of her heart and the night seemed to stretch out in front of her.

"Can you please stop fidgeting and fall asleep." She had no idea how long it was before she heard Fox's voice, rough with exhaustion from behind her.

"I'm trying," she hissed back over her shoulder. "It's cold."

It was a stupid excuse. It was colder than it had been, but they'd slept in much more uncomfortable situations. The cold had nothing to do with the dread settling in her stomach.

Fox's large hand wrapped around her waist and he pulled her back into him, the few inches of space between them disappearing in a second. His chest was warm and hard.

As she tried to focus on the rise and fall of his chest, she felt her mind spinning, thinking of Clarita, of the dragons, of Micael.

His breath was warm against her ear. "Stop thinking."

"Easier said than done," she said, voice just as soft, as if they were both afraid of shattering whatever they'd built in the darkness.

His hand ran softly along her arm, goosebumps rippling in its wake. He didn't say anything even as she shifted farther into him. She was all too aware of the heat and hardness of his body at every point of contact between them, yet in that moment, it didn't feel close enough.

Fox seemed to be thinking the same thing because a moment later, his hand shifted, running across the hem of her tunic and then under it, calluses brushing against soft skin as he pressed her closer.

His hand was a hot brand against her stomach and she bit her lip, trying to ignore her body's reaction to him. His heat was a shocking contrast to the icy air around them, and she shifted, as if she might burrow into the warmth of him. The soft groan that slipped from his lips was so quiet, she wondered if she'd even heard it, but when she shifted again, she felt the rumble this time through his chest.

Her hips were notched perfectly with his, and she felt him growing harder behind her with every shift of her body. She should pull away. She didn't want to.

"Sofia?" His voice was ragged as he continued to stroke the skin of her stomach, fingers brushing the underside of her breast.

"Yes?" she asked, trying to keep her voice neutral.

"You should probably stop moving." Even as he said it, his hand moved higher and his finger brushed across her nipple. It tightened painfully.

She swallowed hard before she answered, not wanting her own voice to quaver. "Probably."

But, against every thought screaming through her brain, she rocked her hips back, pressing her ass against the hardness she felt there, savoring the groan that slipped from his lips once more. His hand cupped her breast, holding it roughly as he ground his hips back into hers, breath hitching in her hair. His nose traced along the sensitive skin behind her ear.

Her body was thrumming and for the first time in blinks, Sofia wasn't thinking about consequences. She wasn't focused on the rage and grief that had been nestled in her chest since the moment Mina had been dragged from the chief commander's office.

She pushed her hips back into him, rotating them slowly when his breath hitched.

"If you don't stop moving," he said, voice a rough growl against her, "I'm going to have trouble controlling myself."

She should pull away. The last thing they needed was to get physical entanglements involved. But then again, if all went to plan, they'd never see each other again after tomorrow. They'd go back to their separate worlds of trying to kill each other's friends and be done with everything out here.

And gods, did she need to stop thinking? She didn't want to worry about tomorrow. Or Micael. Or Clarita. Or who Fox's father was. She wanted to feel.

"Then don't control yourself."

Like a flood released from a dam, Fox moved with surprising speed, flipping them with a single arm so Sofia was lying on her back, looking up at him. Even with the moons closing into their blink, they were still bright through the trees, caressing his face with their light. He leaned forward, eyes focused on her own and for a moment, she was afraid he would kiss her, but then his head ducked lower. His teeth scraped the skin of her neck as he licked his way down, pulling her shirt down to taste her skin.

When he reached the limit of how far the collar would go, he gave a grunt of frustration before grabbing the bottom hem and pulling it up, exposing her breasts to the cold air of the night. Before she could protest, his lips closed over her nipple, his hand coming up to cup her other. The heat of it had her forgetting about the icy night that surrounded them and most everything else. A groan slipped from her lips and he hummed against her skin, even as his tongue flicked across her nipple.

Of course, the Dereyan soldier with a body like his would also be skilled with his tongue. Life wasn't fair.

"You're still thinking," he said, the words hot against her skin.

"Then stop talking," she said, raking her nails down his back until she reached the hem of his shirt, pulling it off. She wanted to touch every inch of his skin. He didn't protest, even as she ran her hands over his body, tracing the ink that wrapped across his chest.

His hands shifted, fingertips brushing across her back. Against one of her ridged scars. He stiffened, mouth opening.

"Don't," Sofia said, before he'd even drawn breath. She hated the way his gaze was shifting, cooling into something akin to pity. She reached between them, cupping his hardness and squeezing. "We're not thinking, remember?" she said.

He stared at her for another moment, indecision in his eyes, but then she gripped him again, stroking him through his pants. The groan that escaped his throat made the decision for him, and he returned to running his tongue over the skin like he was trying to memorize the flavor of her. "If you don't stop that," he said, "this will be over too soon."

Her core throbbed, heat radiating through her, but she released him, moving her hands to his hips and trying to pull him down to her. She wanted friction. She needed his body on hers. But he didn't give it to her. He kept his arms and hips rigid, hovering just over her so their bodies didn't touch. He switched his assault to her other breast, teeth nipping in a way that made Sofia's breath stutter.

"Fox," she said, hating herself for how his name tasted on her lips.

"Yes, my captor?" he said, the words hot against her skin.

"Move," she said, attempting to pull him down once more so their hips would meet.

"I am moving," he said, punctuating his words with a soft pinch to her breast.

"Not what I mean and you know it," she half-growled.

"Patience." The words were a murmur, but he finally released her nipple, lips and tongue tracing a path down her stomach and toward the band of her pants.

As his fingers came up to untie her pants, she let out a groan and placed a hand on his shoulder to stop him.

"I usually take a tonic, but with our...trip."

She didn't need to finish the sentence. He hadn't moved his face from where it hovered over her stomach, silver eyes looking up through impossibly long lashes.

"There is plenty more fun to be had. Now stop talking."

And she did, mouth snapping shut as he untied her pants with one hand and yanked them down along with her undergarments.

"Good girl," he said, grinning up at her, his face between her exposed thighs. He ran a finger through her folds not breaking eye contact. "And already wet for a Dereyan bastard like me."

"Shut up," she ground out between clenched teeth, even as her core went molten.

He only smiled in his infuriatingly knowing way that had her tempted to clench her legs closed. But before she could dare, he was dipping down, his mouth moving over her core, and any thought was gone from her mind. Her awareness zeroed in on the sensation of his tongue and lips against her, every single hum and groan vibrating through her body. She grabbed at his hair, fingers running through the silky strands, unabashedly pressing him closer and he continued to devour her.

He didn't complain, sending a long lick through her lips before she felt his fingers at her entrance, brushing gently. He looked up again as if asking for permission, but all she could do was let out a soft whine, shifting her hips forward. It was all he needed as a finger plunged into her.

"Gods," she said, gasping as his finger went deeper, pumping and seeking. When he found what he was looking for, she let out a series of curses in dragon-tongue, his laugh vibrating through her.

He added a second finger, and she lost control of her body then, rocking and shuddering against him as he worked. When his lips found her clit and sucked, she shattered. She was only aware of his hand holding her legs open as her hips bucked, the flood of pleasure over-whelming every sense.

When she finally came down, he was holding her, soft lips pressed to her inner thigh. He looked up at her, his lips shining with her plea-sure and eyes sparkling in the moonlight.

"This means nothing," she said, practically panting the words out.

"Less than nothing," he agreed with a kiss to her inner thigh, moving up to hover back over her once more. She hated how her eyes lingered on his lips, wanting to pull him forward and taste herself. Before she could wander farther down that path, she hooked a bare leg over his hips, using the skill she'd gained from fighting to flip them until she was straddling him. His eyes only widened for a single moment of surprise as he looked up at her.

"Can't say I've been with a woman who could do that."

She didn't respond, shifting down his body as she loosened his pants, pulling them down only a few inches. She left his legs trapped there as his cock sprang free, and her jaw clenched at the sight. She had felt him enough times to know he wasn't small, but seeing it was differ-ent. His legs shifted and he let out a groan of frustration at his inability to move. It made her smile and she finally broke her gaze away from his rigid length to see him looking up at her, eyes black as night. She wrapped a hand around the base of him, not breaking eye contact as she leaned down and ran her tongue up his cock. He smelled of wood and soil and tasted of salt and musk.

"Fuck," he said, his words a hoarse groan. She smiled, happy to have switched the tides of power. She could have left him like this. Grabbed her pants and walked away now. But a part of her wanted this, too. She wanted the weight of him on her tongue. There was no tomorrow for them and she'd never been one to turn away good sex. So instead, she leaned down and wrapped her lips around his cock before taking him down completely.

His body jerked and his groan reverberated through his chest where her hand rested, but she didn't stop. She licked and sucked, moving up and down his length, savoring his soft flavor. And if a sense of power thrummed through her with every twitch of his body, then so be it. When his hand came up to wrap in her hair, she stopped moving, teeth just grazing against the delicate skin of his cock until he released her.

"Fuck you," he hissed out.

She didn't respond, only increasing her pace. His hands clenched the blankets, his knuckles white. She hummed in satisfaction and swallowed around him as he cursed her with every swipe of her tongue.

When his hips stuttered beneath her and his hand flew back into her hair, she didn't stop him. His touch was gentle, fingers flexing against her skull as if he were trying to stop himself from grabbing her. And then he came, his seed filling her mouth, salty on her tongue. She swallowed the best she could, but when some dribbled out, he pulled her up before she could wipe it away. His pupils were blown wide as he watched her tongue dart out to lick away the spilled seed.

His fingers were soft on the back of her neck and he didn't remove them immediately, watching her—for what she didn't know. He let go suddenly, as if realizing that he was still holding her.

She unhooked her legs from his, using the moonlight to find her pants and shuffle them back over her hips. The cold of the night was sinking back into her skin, the fine sheen of sweat there making it worse.

She didn't know what she expected, but when she laid back down into her bedroll and pulled the blankets over her, Fox reached out and drew her back into him. They were back in the position that had started it all, his nose in her hair, warm breath moving her curls.

"Are you done thinking?" he said, his voice a whisper in the night.

"Yes," she admitted.

He gave a small hum, as if proud of himself.

"That meant nothing."

"I know, my captor. Now go to sleep," Fox said, the words tickling her hair.

She closed her eyes and followed his advice. She pushed all thoughts of her friends and tomorrow from her mind and focused instead on her breathing, letting it fall into beat with Fox's.

It worked, and she drifted into sleep a few minutes later.

CHAPTER THIRTY-THREE

FOX

Fox felt when Sofia finally drifted off to sleep, her muscles giving out between one breath and the next. He didn't know what he had been thinking when he reached over and pulled her to him. And he'd thought perhaps if they just gave in, he could shake her from his bones and rid himself of the ache he felt every time he looked at her. But it didn't feel like that now. He could still taste her on his tongue and he wasn't sure he'd ever forget the feel of her core clenching around his fingers as her body writhed with the pleasure he had given her.

Fox wanted to scream. The feeling that curled itself through his body and lodged itself into his chest was more than lust and that was too dangerous a game to play right now. He needed to stop. But it felt like driving a blade into his own chest.

Her tangled curls moved with his every exhale, a mere inch from his face. He could just barely make out the scent of her hair, coconut and florals from the oils she'd put in it a few days prior before the military and a dragon had torn apart their small oasis in the rainforest.

Their time at the camp with the others couldn't have lasted, even if he hadn't thrown a fit when he'd realized they were shifters. He was always going to go back to Suvi and she was always going to go back to the resistance. Yet somehow, he felt like he might miss his time out here.

He'd grown to appreciate the beauty of the rainforest. The colors were more vibrant out here, the sun softer, and the scents better than anything the breeze brought into the manor.

And he knew even the sewers on his side of town smelled better than the slums of Suvi or the drowned quarter. You'd think if the streets were constantly being washed, it would sweep away the scent, but the stench of low tide only tangled with the human waste and garbage, embedding itself into the stone.

He'd been to the slums only a handful of times on various orders, but he'd never stayed long. He knew that some of his colleagues spent time at the Wall's Inn when they were off duty, but he could never feel comfortable even on the edge of the slums. He found his pleasures elsewhere with women his father would approve of. He'd spent his entire life doing what his father would approve of, begging for scraps at his feet like a dog, as if he might finally recognize Fox as a son rather than a disappointment.

He could never be his brother. His brother couldn't even live up to the pedestal his father had placed him on. His father never knew that his brother talked of peace and compromise with the Dragonborn, that when his back was turned, his words spit on the king and his spoiled son. When Fox was at his worst, after his brother died and his father had none-too-subtly stated he was disappointed that Leon had sacrificed himself to save Fox, he'd wanted to shout out the things his brother had told him in confidence in the dark of night. But he couldn't bring himself to do it. Not for his father's sake, but for Leon's. He would never betray that trust.

And the longer he lay against the ground, the scent of Sofia's hair drifting through the space between them, the more he wondered, not for the first time, if his brother might have been right. The kingdom's treatment of the Dragonborn had only worsened over the last few decades in reaction to the resistance. But the violence against them wasn't shutting their movement down, it was only fanning the flames. What would it take for the tension between them to finally snap, and how many would die in that explosion?

He'd joined the army to avenge his brother and prove he was worth something to his father. And yet, all he had done was grow more bitter and lose sight of what his brother had believed in.

He was brought back to the present as Sofia shifted against him, and he became aware once more of how perfectly her body fit with his. He tried not to shift; he didn't want to wake her.

He closed his eyes and focused on the sounds of the forest at night. The soft chorus of crickets, cicadas, and moon wasps lulled him in a way the silence of the royal quarter never would. He drifted into sleep slowly and painfully, never quite losing awareness of the movement of Sofia's breathing or the warmth that crowded the small sliver of space between them. And in his last moment of wakefulness, he admitted with a raw ache that he'd miss Sofia when he returned to Suvi.

Fox woke to Sofia stirring against him, hips and shoulders shifting as she let out a soft groan. They were fitted together, their breaths moving as one, even as he felt her waking. Last night had been a fluke—a stolen moment to be forgotten immediately. They both knew that, yet neither of them moved, as if they could both convince the sun to sink back down beneath the horizon and extend the night.

At last, she pulled away, the cold morning air rushing to fill the space between them. Fox shivered.

Neither spoke as they stood, and he realized that Sofia was avoiding his eyes just as much as he was hers. They weren't going to talk about yesterday and he was perfectly content to play along.

They packed and split their bedrolls and supplies in silence, agreements made with stiff nods and nudges rather than eye contact. Fox, for his part, simply was unsure of what to say. Ignoring the awkwardness of the morning, he was still saying goodbye to the woman who had kidnapped him—to a known and proud member of the Dragonborn resistance. And he wasn't even considering arresting her or double crossing her.

The thought of this made his gut twist in unease and distrust. She said she wasn't planning on capturing him to return him to the others, but who was to say she was a woman of her word? They'd known each other for just over a week, and pretty lips made the sweetest lies.

When at last they were packed and ready, they stared at each other. She was likely as wary of his word as he was of hers, and the tension in the air didn't release. If anything, it grew thicker and heavier with every breath.

"Do you know where you're going?" Sofia asked after a moment.

Fox pointed at the sun, low on the eastern horizon. "South. I should hit the scouting regions before nightfall easily."

She nodded. She wouldn't have asked if she planned on attacking and capturing him. He tried to tell the muscles in his back to relax, but they ignored his plea.

"Right," he said, when neither of them moved. He didn't want to turn his back first, despite what he was trying to tell himself.

Suddenly her hand shot out and he gave the smallest flinch before realizing what she was doing. She was offering him her hand to shake. He took it, wondering if she could feel the sweat on his palm or the nervous flutter of his pulse.

And then she turned, marching away with a false confidence he saw in the rigid set of her shoulders and the tilt of her chin. She was listening to see if he'd try to follow. If he was going to attack her. He didn't move, watching her until she disappeared into the thick foliage ahead of him, toward the southwest. Even then, when he turned to move south, he did so carefully, veering to the southeast for the first few minutes to make sure she wouldn't be able to find him immediately if she turned back.

But after thirty minutes of walking, the sun's heat beginning to warm the forest air, he knew she wasn't following. The forest was anything but quiet, the birds singing their morning trills and a family of monkeys seemingly fighting over their breakfast somewhere to the west, but the sounds of humanity were absent through it all. He had learned what her footfalls sounded like, even when she was moving with stealth, and he didn't pick up anything as he walked. He kept his own steps soft, a skill he had been gaining over the past few days. It wasn't something they were trained for in the army, which made him laugh now. Of course Sofia had been able to capture him easily before. He'd been stomping around, a beacon in the forest. Stealth in the trees was going to be one of the first changes he implemented when he returned. He'd have to bring it up with the chief commander.

His father never listened to him or cared for his opinions, as useless as he saw them. But the chief commander was different. Even when his brother was alive and the glowing star of the army, the chief commander still asked for Fox's opinions and listened to him as if he cared. It was one of the reasons he felt confident enough to join the military after his brother's death. His father thought it was a suicide mission, but Chief Commander Harlow had faith that he could become a strategist one day.

He was the one who would listen if Fox had ideas—or questions. Like who had gotten hold of a live dragon and trained it to attack its own worshippers and if the chief commander knew what was going on. That would probably have to be a question he approached gradually.

Fox went over the arguments and approaches in his head over the next two hours, trying to figure out the best way of accusing the chief commander of hiding dragons without immediately getting called out for treason and being beheaded. They rarely publicly executed Dereyans, but he still might be flogged or sentenced to life on the farms —which was as good as a death sentence when the conditions usually left people dead within a few cycles. He'd seen the true wretchedness of the farms during his time at the base with his brother, before the bomb.

Now he wondered if any of the people he saw that day had known Sofia.

But that didn't matter now.

It couldn't matter. He needed to focus back on his own goals and his own life. He might have softened on his position against the Dragonborn's plight, but it didn't change the fact that the resistance needed to be taken down and he couldn't do that if he was worried about what one low-level resistance woman thought.

He continued south, tracking his path by the sun which raced past the horizon and into the sky as he walked, and he wasn't sure if time was moving faster or he was moving slower.

And then he heard the distinct sound of a footstep—human, in the forest to his right. Fox froze.

For a brief moment, he wondered if Sofia had finally changed her mind and come for him, ropes and bow ready to take him captive. But no, the next two footfalls were as loud and graceless as the first and Fox knew that only a Dereyan would make such blundering sounds in the forest.

Despite the questions and the hesitation over the past few days, Fox moved without thinking. He kept his footsteps quiet, not wanting to get an arrow to his side from a jumpy scout. So he waited until he saw the scout through the trees to shout out.

"May the king keep you brother!"

He stepped into the open as quickly as he could, wanting the scout to see his face and the golden blond of his hair that would never be mistaken for a Dragonborn. Even still, the man jumped back, hand reaching for his bow. His reactions were slow and if Fox had been the enemy, he could have easily overpowered him.

"What—" the boy—which now that Fox was closer he could see he was—started to speak but then he froze, eyes moving across his hair and face. "Junior Sergeant Ocon. You're the general's son."

Fox felt a wave of relief at the recognition—the familiarity of hearing his name and rank once more.

"We've been looking for you."

Fox had to hide his surprise. His father definitely hadn't sent out a search party, but perhaps the chief commander.

"You're a hero."

It was those words that made his heart stop and his face pale—his mouth open.

"What?"

"The resistance base you marked. They found it two nights ago during a search and confirmed the intelligence this morning. Your...the general is leading a raiding party there now."

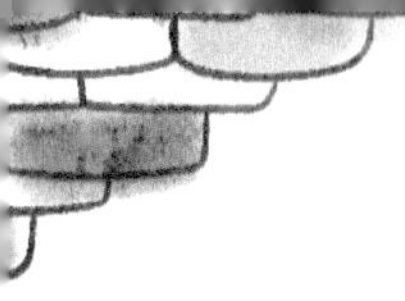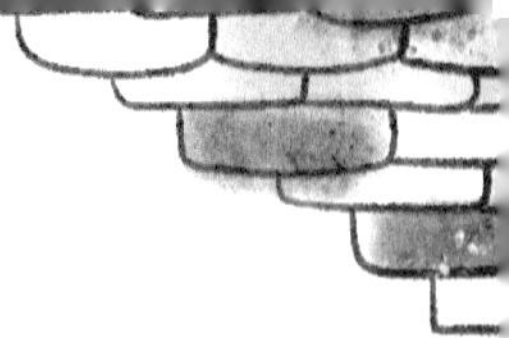

FOX

AGE 8

As the prince finally came to sit next to the village girl, she passed him the bread she had brought. He ate until he was full and when he saw the blood on the girl's hands, he realized what he had done and he wept. He cried for the pain he had caused and as the tears fell, the girl's eyes widened and the prince glanced down at his own hands—human once more. He looked back at the village girl with the mud across her nose, and in her face he saw the beauty he'd been blind to before.

-The Raven Prince by Emilio Laurn

Fox sat with his back to the window, the thin glass warm through his tunic. It was the rainy season, but the sky had been cloudless the last few days and the sun had dried out the earth. He preferred it when it wasn't raining. The air was drier and it usually meant his father was outside of the house all day. He'd been promoted to general this past cycle and it seemed more days than not now, he was

gone either at the chief commander's house, at the barracks, or with the king.

They'd even been invited to dinner at the castle a few nights already, his family dining alongside the king and his son, as well as a few other favorite military leaders. Leon loved listening to their conversations over the extravagant courses, going on about the Dragonborn, farmlands, gold mines, and strategic trades with other kingdoms across the sea. Fox hated the list of places and names he'd never heard of and preferred to try and get the prince's attention. He appeared to be about his age, though Fox wasn't sure. The boy didn't talk at meals and rarely even glanced up to look at anyone. This left Fox staring at his plate and wishing dinner was over so he could retreat back into his room.

It's where he was now, tucked against the large window that overlooked the courtyard below. If he squinted, on a clear day, he could just make out the thin line of azure on the horizon that marked the sea. Right now, his eyes were facing inward, looking at the book splayed across his lap. He'd snuck it out of the library last week and it had been hiding under his pillow ever since. He knew his father wouldn't approve. It had been cycles since he'd let him or his brother indulge in reading faerytales, but it hadn't stopped Fox's love for the stories.

This one was illustrated with colorful paintings of dragons and rolling hills of gold and silver where the land was ruled by a cruel and cold prince who didn't care for his people.

Fox was at the part where the young peasant girl had stumbled upon the raven once more and was trying to convince him she wasn't an enemy. Fox already knew what happened. He'd read the story three times since he'd found it, but he felt his heart pounding, nonetheless, anxious to see when the prince finally relented and learned to trust her.

He was so focused on the words on the page and the small picture of the raven, swooping down from the corner of the page, that he didn't hear the door of his bedroom open or the heavy footsteps that must have followed. His father had never been a silent man and wasn't one to tiptoe around in his own home.

Yet Fox didn't notice him until the book was being ripped from his hand. His father's face was a mask of disinterest as his eyes flickered across the page. He turned a few more before looking up at Fox with an icy expression.

Before he could understand what that meant, his father was walking away, silent as he crossed the room, book still clutched in his hands. Fox jumped up to follow, as if he might save the precious book from whatever his father had planned.

He couldn't, of course. He barely managed to keep up with his father as he swept down the main staircase and circled back to the servants' quarters. The back staircase would have been a more direct route, but his father never deigned to use it. It gave plenty of time for Fox to realize what his father's plan was, though not enough to do anything but watch.

His father didn't acknowledge the staff as he burst into the kitchens and flung the book into the giant hearth that sat at the center of the room, dinner already stewing away over the fire. Despite the hopelessness of the situation, Fox couldn't stop the small squeak that burst from him and he didn't stop his body from lurching forward, hand reaching out as if he might snatch the engulfed book from the flames.

But it was too late. It was too late from the moment he hadn't noticed his father walking into his room. It was too late from the moment his father had opened his door.

He hated himself when he felt the hot sting of tears along his eyelids, pressing out of him against his will. And he wasn't surprised when his father turned, noticing the tears, even unshed, and slapped him hard across the face. He fell, knees hitting the ground as he attempted to catch himself. A few tears leaked out then, impossible to hold back and Fox clenched his fists in anger. At his father. At himself.

His father strode from the room, calm and quiet, as if he hadn't just slapped his youngest son or burned his book. He seemed at peace once more. Fox stood, shaking, trying to pull himself back together.

When the older cook, with her soft eyes and creased face, came over to him and set a gentle hand on his shoulder, he turned on her, snarling and wild.

"Don't touch me!"
"Young Master Ocon—"
"I don't need your pity."
And then he left, eyes dry and face blank.

CHAPTER THIRTY-FOUR
SOFIA

Sofia listened for the sound of Fox running after her for longer than she should have. It was clear after the first fifteen minutes that he wasn't following, but she kept an ear out nonetheless, heart jumping at every rustle of leaves behind her.

It was another hour before she relaxed enough to focus on what was ahead. She wasn't sure if she wanted to find the base empty, abandoned after Fox's disappearance, or if she hoped Micael would be standing in the kitchens waiting for her. Both options left her stomach twisting, the taste of acid in the back of her throat.

She'd made a mistake in letting Fox go. She should have betrayed him. But the thought of walking him to his death no longer felt like something she *could* do. This morning, she'd woken before him, the feel of his warm body wrapped against hers left her begging for the sun to stop rising and the night to resume. She was probably just missing Javi and Flor, but she'd felt something akin to safety. She had to remind herself who Fox was. Not just a stranger she met in the forest, but the son of the man responsible for so many deaths. The man responsible for the scars striped across her back.

No temporary truce in the shadows of night could rewrite their history.

Sofia thought again of the drawn and pained look Fox had had when he'd seen the devastation of the shapeshifters' camp. It hadn't been the victorious eyes of the enemy, but the heartbroken sadness of someone who understood loss.

She was tempted to reach into her pack and touch the warm barbs of the dragon feather tucked there. But she didn't want to risk losing the only item that proved the last few days had been real. That she had been right. The dragons were still alive.

And they were working with the king.

She needed to convince the others of what she'd seen and what she knew. This wasn't just about freeing the Dragonborn from their oppressors. This was about the ancient gods and their entire history.

After a couple hours alone in the trees, she'd twisted her thoughts so tightly in her mind she thought she was going to throw up at any second. She decided to go through one of the back tunnels to avoid making too much of a show with her appearance. Or perhaps she was afraid Micael would order her shot on sight for abandonment and betrayal of the cause. As if he might know she'd let Fox walk away.

The entrance she chose was hidden beneath a small pile of boulders. It was a narrow opening, barely big enough for her hips. But the moment she squeezed through, she fell into the tunnel below. The tunnel was partially flooded, icy water splashing against her legs as she landed and seeping quickly into the fabric of her pants.

The path slanted down first, the water rising higher as she passed through the underground river. It was pitch black in the tunnel and she dragged one hand across the cold wet stone wall as she walked, keeping her grounded in the darkness. At last, the water began to recede again, moving from her hips to her thighs to her ankles until the ground beneath her feet finally rose above the water line. The chill of the tunnels left her prickled with goosebumps, but she ignored them, happy to smell the familiarity of wet mud and stone. She was home.

She stayed on the edge of the water for a moment, eyes closed against the blackness and breathed deeply as if she could memorize the scent and hold it for later. Even if she convinced them of what she and

Fox had discovered about the dragons, she had no doubt that this would be her last time in the cenote.

She'd go back to the city. She'd go back to scrounging and stealing and waiting for the day she'd get caught and executed.

It wasn't until she was stepping into the main hall a few minutes later that she realized how quiet it was. The tunnel dropped her off in the back of the cenote only a few dozen yards before the twisting tunnel that she'd followed Fox through just last week. But even back here, the tunnels allowed the echoes from the other parts of the cenote to travel and bring life to the place. The sleeping rooms usually held a few people even during the day.

Her stomach sank when she passed the first few open doors and saw nothing. There was no one walking the halls or tucked away in the rooms. They had abandoned the base and left her—probably presuming her dead. She already was mapping out the other bases in her mind, but then again, if they thought she had been captured, they might have moved to a new cenote. One she didn't know about. There were hundreds spread across this end of the peninsula that her people could hide in and even she'd never find them without spending cycles searching the rainforest.

Just as she was preparing herself to turn around and go back to the city to resume her life prior to meeting Flor, she came across a lit torch. She saw the hint of light first and then the shadows on the walls dancing.

They wouldn't have left the torches lit if they had abandoned the base. And then she saw the splintered wood along the edge of the hall and the chaos of footprints across the dirt floor became clear in the light.

Sofia felt a stone drop in her stomach and every muscle in her body went tight. Any thoughts of Micael and his punishments for her impulsivity left her mind. She was quiet and careful as she set down her pack and pulled out a dagger. She tucked it into her belt before slipping her arrows and bow back over her shoulder along with her bag.

And then she crept like a thief through the tunnels she had considered home. She heard the voices before she could understand the words, but the bright lilt of their voices was clear. It was the king's tongue as spoken only by the men and women raised in the tight circle of the city that surrounded the castle.

There were king's guards in the cenote.

Her hand tightened on the dagger at her side, and she was tempted to run out screaming, praying to get a few stabs in before she was killed. Her eyes burned with anger, and she bit back the rush of emotions that flooded her. Where were her friends? Were they gone, dead, or captured?

And had Fox known? Had he somehow sent them here before her?

She let out a slow breath, pressing herself against the cool stone wall behind her. The voices were still distant, probably a few more turns through the cenote. She judged that they were coming from somewhere between the dorms and the kitchens. Closing her eyes, she let the warm hilt beneath her hand center her. She could attack, but it wouldn't do anyone any good. She needed to retreat. She needed information and she needed time.

So against every bone and muscle in her body, she stepped back, toward where she'd come from. She'd leave the same way she'd come and then head into the city to find out what the resistance's network had to say of what was happening. She had been gone too long. How much had she missed? When had the cenote even been emptied?

"Breathe," she said, the softest whisper of a mantra chanting through her mind with every step away from the voices and her home.

And then before she could register the sound of footsteps louder than her own, a large callused hand wrapped around her arm and then around her shoulder, pulling her back into the body of a man.

SOFIA

AGE 16

The weeping willow which grows throughout the southern and central peninsula and thrives off the nutrients provided by dead animals decaying near its root system is named due to its unique ability to rain. Its branches and leaves are able to produce a poisonous water which falls around the tree, attracting prey, and then poisoning them before they are able to stumble away and thus provide the tree with its food.

-Tales of the So-Called Dragonborn by Jules Vond

The sun was low enough in the sky that the shadows in the streets and alleys had finally stretched wide, giving Sofia her first sense of safety since that morning. It was the dry season and the days were long and hot, leaving her little time to relax. Dragonborn caught not working could be sent to the farms without cause and the ugly scar on her wrist was enough to send her to the execution block if she ran into an angry guard. It meant that most days, when she wasn't actively trying to survive, she had to stay moving around the lower slums, looking busy and keeping her head down.

She was lucky on the days she found an open barn she could sneak into long enough to rest her eyes and escape from the sun. Her skin, once sallow from hours locked away in the chief commander's house was now a dark ochre, freckles she hadn't known she possessed painting the evidence of her cycle on the streets across her face.

"Get out of the way!"

Two guards stormed down the street, a bloodied man struggling between them. Sofia stumbled in her bid to get away, her foot catching on a stone along the edge of the street. The guard pushed her instead of waiting for her to straighten herself. Her knee scraped across the hard road as she fell, but she bit her tongue to stop from crying out. Silence was safer around here.

She stayed crouched on the ground, not moving until she heard the trio disappear around the corner. The moment they were gone, she sprang up, careful not to draw attention to herself even as she shuffled away as fast as she could. Three turns later and she was in the narrow space between two houses, just wide enough for her shoulders. Only then did she pull out the small sack from her pocket and count through the coins. It was a dangerous game stealing from the guards, but they were always distracted in the middle of an arrest and they were some of the few people on this side of the slums who were actually worth stealing from. Lately, she was more likely to pickpocket stones or fake coins from a fellow Dragonborn than anything useful.

There was a gold coin and four coppers, based on the size. It was too dark to inspect them carefully, but she doubted more than one or two were fake. Guards were usually able to keep counterfeit coins out of their purses. Her stomach gave a low growl, but she didn't move from her hiding space. It was safer to spend her earnings tomorrow or the next day and stay hidden tonight. If it meant going to bed hungry, well that wasn't anything new.

So instead, Sofia curled up in the space between two crates tucked in the narrow alley. She fell asleep before the streets had even gone quiet.

SHE'D ONLY BEEN BACK HOME ONCE since *that* day. Her parents hadn't seen her. She stayed tucked in the shadows, watching as her mother passed in front of the window.

She wondered if they'd been given the news directly or if they'd simply seen the papers announcing her private execution after the scene she'd made in the square. Either way, she couldn't quite bring herself to cross the street and knock on the blue-draped door.

She was dirty and unwashed, the scars on her back still ached when she moved too much. And she was supposed to be dead. She had to stay that way. She was grateful the chief commander hadn't taken his anger out on her family. He could have easily had them arrested and sent them to the farms. She wouldn't put them in further danger.

So instead of running to fall into her parents' arms, she sat huddled in the shadows until they lengthened into night and then she walked away without looking back.

She hadn't been back to that side of town since, preferring to stay in the western slums or wandering the drowned quarter. The streets were always dotted with puddles, and if she wanted to sleep through the night, she had to find a roof to perch on to avoid the tide, but the guards avoided that section of Suvi and rarely bothered searching out the homeless there.

And that was what she was now, in part by her own hands. She could have stayed with the couple that had saved her—Talia and Manny. They'd been giving the rites to the dead in secret the night Sofia crawled out of the grave.

She learned their names eventually, when she was healed enough to sit up and talk with them. That took two weeks. She'd almost died twice from the wounds and infection. It was only their adherence to illegal Dragonborn medicine and a compassion that she didn't deserve that saved her.

They would have welcomed her to their home with open arms, but three weeks into healing, when she was able to sleep through the night without the opium milk that made her mind foggy, she'd heard them fighting over her. There had been three raids in the neighborhood in a single week, the army cracking down on illegal dragon worship after a resistance bombing.

They wouldn't have kicked her out. She heard that in the frantic whispers between them, but she was putting them in danger by existing in their house. And they were worried about their daughter—someone Sofia hadn't even met. She decided to not give them a choice. She left the next day while they were sleeping.

THE SUN WOKE her the next morning, a sharp beam between the buildings shining directly into her eyes. Her body was cramped and stiff from the awkward position she'd fallen asleep in, not quite lying down. The positive of the dry season was that despite the sun being high enough to wake her, the streets were still quiet, with only the most motivated workers going about their mornings.

Her empty stomach, however, was awake and already loudly making itself known. She looked down at the coins she'd stolen the night before and wondered if she should buy breakfast. What she'd managed to steal was likely worth a bowl of corn porridge, or even some fresh bread. It would also leave her penniless once more. Either way, she needed to start moving before the streets filled and the guards began patrolling more actively.

The first place she tried to use the coins, they chased her off before she'd even handed them over, the distrust in her appearance clear. Her hair had grown long over the weeks, and it was pulled back into two braids, but her skin was marred with mud. The decision was made for her, and she headed east toward where she knew a few barns and yards sat. It was the best place to sneak in a small bath and fresh water from the troughs left out for the livestock.

She hadn't meant to get distracted, but the smell of the roasted meat was rich and thick in the air as she trudged down the street. Without realizing it, she was drawn to the small stand where a tall, thin woman rotated skewers of meat over the small cook fire beside her. She heard the words exchanged with the customer and her stomach sank.

"Two gold for a skewer."

"That's robbery!"

"It's fresh meat," the woman said, with a shrug. "I killed the deer myself when it wandered by my home."

The last part was a lie. Deer didn't just wander into the city. She'd probably illegally hunted the deer or bought it off a dirty scout, but no one in the slums questioned fresh meat, and the man handed over the coins with a few choice words.

Without opening the purse or moving it from her belt, Sofia fingered her coins again. She didn't have enough between the copper and gold she'd stolen, but her stomach didn't care about logistics and it gave off another obscene growl.

She kept her head down as she strolled by, not wanting to draw attention to herself as she carefully took in the setup of the woman's stand and where she kept her purse. This wasn't like the guard, who she could simply pluck the purse from while he was distracted. She'd have to take a different strategy.

Once she was around the corner, she unbraided her hair, combing the strands until her thick curls tangled around her, obscuring her face from most angles. She waited a few minutes before circling back, not wanting to be remembered immediately as having just passed by. She would cause a commotion near the stand. The woman would reach for her purse—protecting her coins—and leaving the meat unguarded for the briefest of moments.

She was so focused, she barely noticed the other girl coming down the street from the opposite side, a chicken crying out and struggling in her hands.

The first step of the plan went smoothly. With a well-practiced lack of grace, Sofia tripped over one of the men standing in line, swinging sideways and knocking into the small table that held the woman's supplies, including a steaming cup of tea. The woman cried out as the hot tea splashed across her lap. She reached out, protecting her purse, but not her wares, and Sofia struck.

The skewers sizzled hot against her palms as Sofia grabbed a handful, but she didn't care. The moment they were in her hand, she straightened herself and readied to run. But before she could, an iron hand came down on her arm, fingers bruising.

"No, you don't!" a man's voice sneered from above her.

In that moment, Sofia forgot her hunger and her exhaustion. Hot fear exploded within her and she swore she felt the searing pain of the whip against her back once more. But then someone else was yelling behind them pulling the street's attention.

"My chicken! My chicken!"

The man's hold on her didn't loosen, but then a smaller hand was there on Sofia's elbow, helping her wrench herself from his grip.

Sofia was running before he could register what had happened, the girl she'd seen earlier beside her.

"You lost your chicken!" Sofia noted, looking back to see the others chasing after the creature even as the man yelled after them.

"Not my chicken," the girl huffed out. "I can steal another one."

Sofia glanced at her from the corner of her eye. The girl's face was clean, but her braids were haphazardly tied and now that they were closer, she noticed the brown drab color was due to a layer of mud streaked throughout and an unkemptness in the stained and tattered blouse. She was a street kid like her.

They took a few sharp turns before they both started to slow, having come to the agreement that they'd lost any tail or attention.

"Follow me," Sofia said, sliding down a narrow alley to their right. She didn't look back, but the girl followed without question until Sofia found the small stack of boxes that allowed them to both climb to the roof of a barn, out of sight of the ground. Once they'd sat, Sofia handed over two of the five skewers to the other girl.

"Thanks for saving me."

The girl didn't answer, but plucked a third skewer from Sofia's hands.

"Extra payment for losing my chicken."

"You said it wasn't yours."

"But now I have to steal another one, and that's work that I need nutrients for."

Sofia pursed her lips, but didn't argue. The girl had saved her ass back there and was the only reason she wasn't being dragged back to the prison right now. So instead, she stuffed the first skewer into her mouth, barely bothering with chewing as she tasted the charred meat against her tongue. She savored the second skewer more slowly, eyes closed as she appreciated the first taste of seasoned, hot food she'd had in weeks.

"Sofia," she said after she finished. The girl was still eating her own, apparently better at making the food last. The girl looked at her, brown eyes narrowed for a minute, examining her like a target. Whatever she saw, she seemed to approve of.

"It's nice to meet you." She wiped her hand on her blouse, making it clear where the stains had come from, before holding it out for Sofia. "I'm Flor."

CHAPTER THIRTY-FIVE
FOX

Fox wasn't sure why he reacted the way he did. Or at least he wasn't ready to admit it. The moment the words were out of the scout's mouth, he'd turned northwest, toward where he assumed the cenote would be. He kept his head down, eyes focused on the ground to avoid thinking of his destination or what he even planned to do.

It didn't take long to find the path his father and the king's men had made through the trees. There had been no stealth in their operation and there was a trampled path cutting through the forest.

The scout was following him, close on his heels.

"Sir, shouldn't we go back into town? You've been missing for over a week and Chief Commander Harlow—"

"When did you say my father left for the base?"

"It would have been hours ago, now," he said, stumbling over a root as Fox picked his way carefully through the underbrush. "They left before I started my shift, but I've seen a few groups returning with prisoners. The raid was successful it seems."

Prisoners. They'd already had the raid and found the rebels. Would they still be in the base then?

"But the general hasn't returned?"

"Not that I've seen. They may have taken a different route."

"What's your name, Soldier?"

"Junior Scout Smithian, sir," he said, giving his best impression of a salute even as he tripped again. Fox might have felt guilty for moving so fast, but he didn't much care at this point.

"Go back to your post, Junior Scout Smithian. I need to speak with my father, but I will make sure they know you were the first one to spot my return."

The boy's cheeks tinged pink even as he tripped over his feet once more, giving an awkward bow.

"Yes, sir. Thank you, sir."

Fox didn't acknowledge the scout as he turned back to where he'd been walking. He wasn't lying. He'd drop the boy's name and give him some extra points in the military's eyes, but he had more important things to worry about, like what he planned on doing when he got to the cenote.

And if he wanted to see his father's face when he realized Fox was alive. He didn't expect a joyful, tear-filled reunion, but he knew his father would make a show of it if there were others around.

What he truly wanted to do was find Sofia and take her far away instead of having to see his father. But that thought only sent him into another spiral because how was he going to explain to Sofia why he was so bent on saving her when he couldn't even explain it to himself? It was his fault she was now in danger to begin with.

She probably wouldn't even need his help. If anyone was going to find a way to outwit his father, it would be her.

He was so caught up in his own thoughts he was almost surprised when he heard the echoing voices through the trees. It was only another few minutes before the forest opened and he saw the opening of the cenote stretched out before him. It was smaller than he remembered. Nothing compared to the others he and Sofia had stumbled upon during their accidental adventure.

He could hear the voices clearer now, and he recognized one with a lurching certainty.

"They must be storing weapons elsewhere. This couldn't be their entire stash."

A mumbled response followed, too garbled to hear it properly.

Fox swallowed down his uncertainty, moving forward to where he saw the rope ladder stretching downward. It was anchored at the bottom, making the climb in and out easier for the soldiers. He was all too happy to be entering using this more comfortable method.

"I hear you've been looking for me," Fox said, voice strong and unwavering despite the acid churning in his stomach.

Crouched over the opening as he was, he was just able to see where his father stood speaking to a pair of sergeants he didn't recognize. Even from this far, he could see the stiffening of his father's shoulders as the man recognized his voice. Both sergeants' faces found his and their eyes flashed in recognition—if not of him—of the familiar white of his hair.

"Fox." His father's voice rang out hard and cold, perhaps a product of the echo, but then he was smiling and moving toward the ladder. Fox took it as his cue that he could climb down without being shot by an arrow for trespassing and quickly descended.

His father was waiting for him when he reached the bottom. And they embraced, cold hands resting against Fox's back for only a second before he pulled away. His father met his eyes, eyebrows furrowed, as if trying his hardest to understand something. Fox kept his face neutral, not wanting to give his father anything. At least not yet. He needed a proper meal and a few nights' sleep before he was ready to sort through the past two weeks with his father and his people. But he had more important things to worry about before then.

The cenote was quiet and calm. Whatever prisoners they'd taken upon their first raid already gone to Suvi. He heard the footfalls of other soldiers in the back tunnels, likely raiding supplies. It was only when his attention was drawn back by his father's cough that he noticed a few bodies left facedown on the edge of the underground lake. Red blood seeped into the ground, tinging the nearby water pink and Fox looked away before he could recognize the shape of anyone in particular. Not that he cared.

But Sofia would care.

And she wasn't here. Not yet. She wouldn't have arrived at the cenote that much earlier than he did; she wouldn't have been with the earlier group of prisoners. Perhaps he'd been right to trust her instincts. She may have gotten into the tunnels and immediately sensed something was wrong. She was already gone and he was wasting his anxiety on nothing.

"I have too many questions, but now isn't the time to ask them." His father's words drew his attention back to the present. The taller of the sergeants, a thin and wiry male with a shock of black hair against pasty white skin gave Fox a small salute.

"I hear that you're to thank for our operation here."

"Theoretically—" his father cut in, words cold, as if he doubted the entire thing, "it was hypothesized that you left the markings. We also assumed you'd been killed soon after. There were traces of a fight and blood left in the forest."

"That probably was my blood, but as I'm sure you're so very grateful, Father," Fox said, "the scuffle didn't kill me. It just delayed me a bit."

Before his father could respond, the other sergeant spoke, a high sergeant he noticed from the two bronze stars on his breast. "Either way, thanks to your quick thinking, we've taken nearly a dozen resistance spies into custody. General Ocon is sure the leader is among them, though they have refused to speak."

"*Yet*," his father said, a spark of joy in his eyes that made Fox's stomach twist. Such happiness was never a good thing when it came from his father.

He looked back over his shoulder at the darkened tunnels and wondered if he could convince his father to allow him to look around. If he could find Sofia before the others.

A cry from the shadows had Fox paling and the three men he stood with followed his own stare as a guard came stumbling out from the darkness.

He was cursing, a trickle of blood seeping from beneath the torn arm of his tunic. He held Sofia pressed firmly against his body, the iron grip of his forearm along her waist. She was hissing and fighting, but he looked to weigh two times Fox's own weight at the same height, and despite the anger at the bite she'd clearly gotten in, keeping her subdued didn't appear to be a struggle.

When he made it to where the four of them stood, he dropped her unceremoniously at their feet.

"Found this creature sneaking around in the back tunnels. She must have been hiding during the initial raid."

"She looks feral," the high sergeant said with a laugh behind the words.

Fox was too busy trying to keep his breathing even as he took in the sight of her. She didn't look any different from when he'd last seen her, albeit a bit muddier. But her face was a bright scarlet and her eyes shone with a rage and hatred he hadn't seen since their first few days together. She wasn't even looking at him—she was looking directly at his father.

His father sneered down at the woman, as if she might jump up at any moment and bite him, as well. Perhaps he was afraid of rabies. And then Fox saw the shift in his father's face, his eyes widening in something akin to fear.

When his father moved forward, grabbing Sofia by the arm and throwing her facedown into the dirt, Fox almost stopped him. He clenched his fists by his sides and counted his exhales, wiping his face blank of any emotion. He'd had practice. He knew how to do this. How to *not feel*. It would be worse for both of them to react.

But even the sergeants and the specialist blanched as his father grabbed her tunic and tore it, nearly ripping it from her body to reveal her back. And Fox saw what she'd been hiding from him.

There wasn't an inch of smooth skin to be seen. Ridges snaked across her back, painting her skin. Some scars were thin silver stripes, while others were raised and ugly puckers, dark red and purple.

It was a lashing that she would have been lucky to survive—that anyone would be lucky to survive—and his father was looking at it like a prized painting.

Acid crawled up Fox's throat, choking him. He swallowed it down along with the sick twist of disgust and anger tightening his chest. He pulled his gaze away, knowing she wouldn't want him to see this. The specialist that had brought her over stood, his own face blank, and Fox saw the small bag he held over his shoulder. Sofia's bag.

The one with the dragon feather tucked inside.

"You," his father's voice drew his attention and he reluctantly looked back to where Sofia now kneeled, glaring up at his father. Her tunic was ripped at the shoulder, but it was covering her once more. Her cheeks were a bright red, but Fox could tell from the heat in her eyes it wasn't from embarrassment or shame.

And then the look was turned on him and the blood drained from his face. She snarled and spit, a glob of it falling just short of him.

He met her glare with a sneer.

"This is your fault," she said. There was no playacting in the words, and he didn't blame her. This was his fault. No matter their truce or his intentions when they split that morning, he was the reason her friends lay dead behind them and why she was kneeling at his father's feet now. He saw the hint of red along her collar where the other man had grabbed her. It would bruise by tonight.

He flinched as his father's eyes flashed to him, ineffectual rage roaring through his blood.

"She knows you." The look his father was giving him sent a chill up his spine.

"Meet the delay I faced," he said, waving dismissively. "The bitch captured me. She and her resistance trash."

"You let dragon-filth capture you?"

The words were a sneer.

"I was outnumbered, and you can see how well it worked out for her." He shrugged again. He wanted to stop talking about her. He wanted to be home and have this all behind him.

"At least you did us the favor of marking the passage into the cenote. You made your capture useful."

It was the closest his father had ever gotten to complimenting him, but Fox felt nothing.

"Since you're back," his father continued, "you should head into the city to report to the chief commander. He will want an explanation for your delay. I'm sure he'll be happy to congratulate you on finding the resistance's base at last. The kingdom owes you."

"Of course, General," he said, trying to ignore Sofia's eyes burning into him. If he didn't look, he wouldn't have to see whatever emotion would be there. He stared instead at the bag clutched in the meaty fists of the man who'd captured her. If his father found the feather, Fox knew it would disappear before he could understand what it all meant.

"And tell your mother you've returned. I can't go another night with her thinking you're dead. The woman hasn't stopped wailing."

His father turned to the specialist. "You can return with Junior Sergeant Ocon and your platoon to bring this creature to the prison. Keep her separated from the others. I wish to interrogate her myself before the chief commander sees her."

"Yes, sir."

With that, his father turned away, unconcerned once more about his returned son, but not before he threw one last sneer at Sofia.

CHAPTER THIRTY-SIX

SOFIA

Sofia's face was hot with rage and something bordering on shame, though she refused to acknowledge it. Fox wouldn't meet her eyes, but the three other soldiers with him had none of the same qualms. The one that had caught her in the back tunnels was still leering down at her, seemingly excited that her tunic was hanging on by a thread.

She was angry at him. She was angry at General Ocon. She was angry at herself for getting caught. Yet, despite everything, she had no idea what she was feeling toward Fox. He had marked the cenote's entrance during his escape. He was the reason for everything happening now and she saw the truth of that in his face. But the Fox that had let her walk away this morning—the Fox that had touched her gently and called her passion a gift—he was different than the one that had marked the base. Wasn't he?

Or perhaps she was simply lying to herself to stop her heart from breaking and her soul from shattering at the realization she'd trusted the wrong person, again.

She watched the men gathering, dragging sacks of food and weapons they'd raided from the storerooms and kitchens. She knew she had bigger things to worry about, but she still wanted to scream. They were stealing a cycle's worth of dry goods and the meat that she'd helped collect. And where would they take it? To the military quarter where meat was never in short supply, or the royal quarter where food was squandered without care.

"That's not yours." She bit the words out, regretting it even as she said them. But the soldier walking by with the sack of cornmeal only gave her a jeering laugh, and her personal guard, still standing behind her, smacked her hard across the head before she could say more.

"Shut up, dragon bitch. The food is as stolen as the weapons we found."

She wanted to say more, but her gaze rested on Fox. He was looking at her again, for the first time since she'd spit at him, and his face was pale. The sneer he'd been wearing for his father was gone and he looked at her now with something akin to pleading in his eyes. Her stomach twisted, but she closed her mouth.

There was a time for passion and impulse and a time for waiting. She needed to watch and make a plan. She might be able to escape between here and Suvi. Depending on how many walked with her. She knew the forest better than any of them. She could climb a tree and slip into the leaves before they found her.

Her chest expanded with a slow breath, and she closed her eyes for a moment as she released it, slower still. And then she let her eyes take in the soldiers moving around her, calculating. Careful not to draw attention with her surveillance, she counted the soldiers gathering together to move back to Suvi with her. There were so many of them.

She chanced a glance behind her, seeing the movement of a few other soldiers out of the corner of her eye. Any ounce of hope and happiness drained from her. There were bodies on the ground she hadn't noticed. Viola's face was turned away from her, but she recognized the silver and black strands of her braid and the small ceramic flower comb she always wore. The one Javi'd gifted her cycles ago. It was stained now with the blood no longer leaking from the wound in her head. Another two bodies lay just behind, but Sofia couldn't see them from where she knelt. Not without standing.

She moved automatically, too afraid to not see who was lying next to Viola. Javi? His heart-mother, Elena? But before she made it even an inch off the ground, a large hand laced through her hair and yanked her hard. Back arching painfully, she let out a small cry. Her hands scraped against the ground even as she tried not to let the tug throw her off-balance, but the momentary jerk had her tunic falling. The skin of her back was again exposed, her breasts nearly bared. She scrambled once more to cover herself up, but the man kicked her hard in the side.

"If you can't keep your shirt on properly, I should just take it from you."

She hated herself for the flush of shame and fear the threat sent up her spine. Before she could retort, she felt soft fabric slipping over her head. Fox was above her, avoiding her eyes as he arranged the dirty but intact shawl around her shoulders.

"You're giving the creature clothes?" the guard asked.

Fox looked at him with a coldness she'd forgotten he could possess. "I don't take enjoyment in staring at a Dragonborn's bare flesh. It's beneath *me*."

The guard gave an indignant snort, but didn't comment.

She might have been thankful for it, but not even a minute later her guard was back, pulling her up none-too-gently from the ground. He tied her hands behind her, but she was at least covered by the shawl that Fox had found and she sent a small thanks to him in her mind.

Then they were moving—toward the ladder that stretched up and out of the cenote. She watched as the other soldiers climbed out, confused as to why her hands were already tied when she had to make the climb, too. But her question was answered when she was thrown at another guard, like a sack of potatoes.

She nearly let out a snarl as she realized their intentions. She was going to be lifted up by a rope and pulley alongside the other loot. Exactly like a sack of potatoes.

The man yanked her hands up, twisting her shoulders with little care for her comfort and tying the rope to her bound hands. She was hoisted up in the air by her hands, her shoulders flaring hot with pain as they were pulled and twisted by the weight of her own body. She tasted blood as her teeth sank into her cheeks stopping the scream that wanted to crawl from her throat at the sensation. The rope twisted and tugged harder with every flinch of her body and she tensed every muscle in her body, trying to keep herself still.

She was panting, hands gone numb by the time her feet touched the ground above. Her eyes burned and she blinked hard, refusing to let the tears fall. Before sensation had even come back to her fingers, she was being shoved in a new direction, brusque hands moving to tie her feet together, as if they weren't about to walk the miles back to Suvi. The soldier tying the knot slapped her for pointing out as much, but at least he loosened the length between her feet, allowing for a decent stride.

It wasn't until they were walking, her steps stumbling over the undergrowth as the rope tying her legs caught on every root and branch, that she saw Fox again. He was walking a few yards away, just behind the others in the group. She hated the sense of relief she felt in seeing her bag slung over his shoulder. She wanted to assume he was protecting the feather. She wanted to assume he was helping. But his eyes never even flickered to where she was stumbling, his face a cold mask of indifference.

Sofia dragged her eyes from him, focusing on the path ahead. Right now, whatever was going through Fox's head didn't matter. She needed a plan. It was clear from the sheer number of soldiers around her and the ropes binding her wrists and ankles that she wouldn't get away if she tried to run now, which meant she needed a plan to escape the prison and get to her friends—whoever was left.

She nearly laughed at the irony. All this started because Sofia wanted Fox to sneak her in so she could save Dia and the others. Now she was getting her wish. Fox and his fellow king's men were bringing her straight to prison, in chains.

SOFIA

AGE 17

It's said that the day the last dragon died, the clouds that had covered the sun for two blinks finally dissipated. The streets ran with wine and spirits as the people of Suvi celebrated the victory at last against the beasts that had plagued them. Even the Dragonborn tribes resisting the king fell silent for an entire sun cycle, giving a taste of peace to the king's people.

-The Legacy of the Kings: A History of Wueco's Creation by Francis Knoll

The chicken wiggled between Sofia's hands, soft feathers slick beneath her palms. She clenched her hands harder and the chicken let out a squawk of indignation. The street was busy, customers and sellers flocking to the market to buy and sell goods that hadn't been available for over a cycle. It was nearing the end of the dry season, the unusual rains in the wet season having allowed the crops and economy to flourish. At least for some.

There were still plenty of hungry eyes and sunken stomachs in the poor souls crouched on corners and in the darkest-skinned Dragonborn who struggled to find work. But the wealthy had been more generous in their charity.

None of that mattered to Sofia now. The busy street meant distracted vendors. She and Flor had staked out the stands earlier in the morning, looking for who kept their purses visible and who seemed most distracted by the occasional call of others around them. So when Sofia passed by the stall with the sliced fruits sprinkled with dried chilis, she gave a passionate cry and let go of the chicken.

Finding itself free at last, the fowl let out a loud squeal, feathers flying as it flapped its wings in a desperate attempt to escape.

"Help me!" Sofia yelled, "My father's chicken! He'll kill me."

They'd learned over the past few blinks what got people to help the fastest. Apparently, the threat to a man's property and his dismayed daughter's fear of his fist did the trick for most. Sofia enjoyed this part of the trick. The melodrama and the small moment in time when she actually worked to draw the attention of those around her. For just a minute or two, she wasn't a rat slinking in the shadows, invisible.

But then the charade came to an end. A man with a scar across his cheek caught the chicken in his large hands and handed it, squirming, over to Sofia.

"Thank you! May the king bless you!" With that last bit of flourish, she rushed away, stolen chicken clutched in her hands. The most important part was to be gone by the time anyone realized their purses were missing.

FLOR WAS ALREADY BACK at their roof by the time Sofia returned. It was harder to hurry when the chicken wouldn't stop squawking and squirming. She was all too happy when she could pass the chicken off to Flor before making the precarious, but well-learned climb up the side of the building and onto the roof.

They were in the drowned quarter and it was low tide, but the buildings were perpetually wet, moss and algae coating the stones. They kept a path of jagged stones as clean as they could to use on the way up, a secret all their own.

When Sofia made it to the top, she pulled herself up and rushed to see the pile of coins and trinkets Flor was sorting through on the flat cement roof.

"Gods!" Sofia's hand skimmed over the pile, careful not to touch and ruin Flor's system. There were at least a dozen gold coins, a small pile of coppers, and even a few bracelets and a ring.

"The rains have made people stupid," Flor said, blunt as always.

The chicken let out a yelp from its cage, as if in empathy for the man, and Sofia made a rude gesture at it. She would be all too happy the day it stopped laying eggs and they could pluck it and roast it.

Its cage was crammed in the corner of the flat roof, a threadbare blanket tossed over it during the day to keep it *somewhat* quiet. On this side of town, though, no one bothered with screams or yells from humans, let alone animals. The rest of the roof was an assortment of stolen and bought goods collected over the past few blinks. They both had bedrolls now and a blanket apiece. Though at night, they curled up together, too used to the sense of sleeping beside another person to feel comfortable separated. And if their hands wandered at night, they didn't speak about it in the morning. They also had a few pots and pans for cooking, a teapot, and a stash of dishes. It was a risk to collect so much. It meant they had a lot to lose. But so far, they'd managed to keep their small world tucked in the crevice between taller buildings, with only two windowless walls facing their hideaway—the home they'd built together, on the edges of a society that didn't want them.

Flor didn't talk about her family much, but then again, neither did Sofia. What she did know is that while she wasn't Dragonborn, both her parents had been sent to the farms on charges of treason when she was young. Branded the daughter of traitors, none of her relatives bothered to care for her, and she ended up on the same streets as Sofia.

"I also got something else while we were out," Sofia said, fishing through her pockets for the scrap of paper she'd stuffed there. Flor eyed her suspiciously as she slid the paper across the ground over to her.

"What's this?" She squinted at the markings.

"The meeting place I promised. A representative will be there tonight when the moons set."

"No. Absolutely not."

"This is the only chance we have. If we don't show for the meeting tonight, we lose their trust and we won't be given another chance."

"Good," Flor said, picking up the paper, throwing it in the small fire burning beside them. Sofia didn't flinch.

"I already memorized it."

"They're trouble. We don't know if this boy you've been talking to is even a part of the real resistance. For all you know, this is a trap set up by the king."

"He knows dragon-tongue and the old prayers!"

"And where did you learn those?" she asked pointedly.

"We'll be careful. They didn't say we had to come unarmed, and we can stake the area out beforehand. We know the roofs of this town better than anyone."

"I am not putting our lives in danger for a chance to join some cult! Did you hear about the bombings over the last few blinks? They've killed hundreds."

"Of soldiers!"

"And civilians."

"I'm going, with or without you. I'm sick of watching the city fall to ruin while the king and his son hide behind their gilded walls."

"And I'm not going to let you go on a suicide mission," Flor snapped.

"Perfect!" Sofia's smile was wide. "It's settled. We'll leave when the first moon hits the horizon."

Sofia might have been overconfident when she suggested they stake out the meeting place first. As soon as they were a block away, she spotted a shadow on the roof watching them, his tall, lithe silhouette unmistakable. She averted her gaze quickly, but not before Flor noticed. Her face twisted into a scowl and Sofia practically felt her muscles go rigid beside her.

"I am going to kill you if they don't," she muttered.

"I trust him."

It had been almost the blinks since the first time Sofia had made contact with the boy—Pelo—and started the process of convincing him to set a meeting between them and the resistance. The rebels had done more for the Dragonborn over the past few cycles than the king ever had. They'd been sneaking food into the city and passing out supplies to those who needed it most, even when the rains were rare and the Dereyans had turned a blind eye to the impact of the drought. Still, she understood Flor's hesitation. Trust wasn't something built easily on the street. It had taken blinks for Flor and Sofia to trust each other enough to sleep in front of the other, but Sofia had had time to study Pelo with his open face, crooked smile, and always messy hair. She knew how to read people, and she did trust him. At least enough for this.

When they made it to the alleyway, Pelo jumped down, the shadows obscuring everything but his eyes.

"This is Flor?"

In the same moment Sofia nodded, Flor let out a harsh, "No."

"Well, if you aren't Flor," a voice from behind them said, "we'll just need to slice your throat and throw your body over the wall. I don't meet with unexpected strangers."

"Jag," Pelo said. The word was a rebuke, but given the look on the much older man's face as he stepped forward, Pelo had no authority to do so. The younger boy looked down, admonished by the silent glare.

"This is Flor," Sofia said, firmly. "She's a little paranoid. I think you can relate."

The man looked them up and down.

They hadn't come overly armed, but they both had daggers tucked beneath the waistband of their pants, which thanks to their recent influx of stolen coin, were freshly sharpened and cleaned.

With the reflexes of a snake, the man moved, catching Sofia's wrist and pulling it forward to stare at the scar set into her skin—the crooked and red "T".

"What did you do to earn this?" His voice was gravelly and she felt it in her chest as he spoke.

"I read. I also have some scars on my back that I earned for biting the general." She raised her chin and swallowed back any quaver in her voice. Flor's breath hitched beside her. She'd never admitted that part to the other girl in their very brief exchange of horror stories.

"And why do you want to join us?" the man asked, face impassive.

"I'm sick of just surviving and breaking the law. It's the king and his government that need breaking, and the way I see it, you're the only ones trying."

Pelo and Jag exchanged a look and a few hand signals that Sofia couldn't read. The older man's face hadn't changed and she found herself at a loss for what he was thinking, to her great discomfort. But she wasn't going to back down. The chief commander had done his damnedest to beat her into submission, and if her time on the streets had taught her one thing, it was that he'd failed. She would never submit to the king's rule. If she had any say in it, she was never going to feel as helpless as she had when she heard the axe whistle down over Mina's neck. She'd keep fighting until the last Dereyan fell to their knees before her, begging for mercy.

At last, after minutes of silent exchanges, Pelo turned from Jag and held out his hand.

"I'll be your point of contact until you've earned our trust."

"And why should we trust you, Pelo?" Flor asked, arms crossed across her chest in a clear sign that she wasn't going to take his hand yet.

He ran a hand through his hair, leaving a bit sticking up, visible even in the shadow of night. "Er, firstly, in the spirit of trust, I guess I should say my name is Javi. Pelo is a code name."

"And *your* real name?" Flor said, turning on the older man.

"Is none of your business, yet," he said.

"You've got to earn our trust, just the same," Flor said. Her words were harsh and her arms were still crossed, but her shoulders had relaxed incrementally. Sofia read the statement for what it was—a concession.

"We're excited to help the cause," Sofia said, with a genuine smile.

Javi returned the gesture, showing off a set of dimples.

"Welcome to the resistance."

CHAPTER THIRTY-SEVEN

FOX

Fox was all too happy to see Ian among Sergeant Melin's ranks. Speaking to his brother's old friend was a distraction from all the anxiety and the grief. He couldn't quite shake the look Sofia had given him when she'd seen him standing beside his father. The shape of her scars on her back haunted him, along with the look of pride on his father's face.

A scream clawed at his throat, lashing against his clenched teeth.

"I should have visited your mother," Ian said, a gleam of guilt written across his face.

"It wasn't your responsibility to comfort my mother."

"She thought she'd lost both her sons," he said, and his voice cracked, surprising them both. "And you know the general wasn't there to help."

The muscles in Fox's jaw twitched at the thought of his mother alone. "Was my father truly out looking for me?"

"You're surprised?"

"You know it was Leon my father cared for. I'm just surprised he spent the energy."

"The chief commander ordered it. You were the third soldier to go missing while scouting and the highest ranked. He wouldn't let your father write you off."

Fox let his blank mask slip for a moment as he rolled his eyes. "I guess I should be grateful," he said.

Ian clapped a hand on Fox's shoulder. "From what I hear, you rescued yourself from the Dragonborn, and helped us sniff out their hovel. You should be proud."

Fox forced himself to smile. "And all because I didn't listen to you when you told me to let the scouts go out."

Ian smiled back. "I don't know whether to be glad you ignored me, or angry that it got you into all of this."

Fox didn't know what he was feeling either. Perhaps after a good meal and a bath he'd have a better grasp on why—after cycles of working toward this goal—he was left feeling so numb having achieved it.

The resistance was crumbling. The people that had killed his brother would pay in blood.

And Sofia had been caught in the crossfire, as he knew she always would be. She was a rebel, just like the rest. She had Dereyan blood on her hands.

But he couldn't shake the smile she'd given him after they'd seen the dragon, or the moment of grief they'd shared after the tribe was massacred. She'd care for him—saved his life multiple times.

But did it make him throwing away his entire life for her worth it?

Fox broke away from the procession after they passed through the gates of Suvi. No one questioned the bag he possessed, the sergeant too busy in a discussion with his junior to remember the Dragonborn captive had had a bag. Fox would get the feather and anything else he needed from it before bringing it to the prison. After two weeks held captive in the rainforest by heathens, he wouldn't be blamed for forgetting something so mundane.

The unit and their captive took the main road left toward the prison on the edge of the military quarter, but Fox turned right. Technically, the chief commander's home was only a few blocks west of the prison, but he wanted a moment away from the others as he walked. What would he say when he got there? Today wasn't the day he wanted to confront the chief commander about the dragons and he wasn't even sure he wanted to tell him about Sofia. The man definitely didn't need to know that Fox couldn't shake the scent of her from his mind or the taste of her from his tongue.

Fox shook those thoughts off quickly, wondering if the chief commander would notice the smell of liquor on his breath if he stopped by a cantina before making it to the compound. His empty purse made the decision for him and gave him a new sense of guilt at using his badge to obtain free food. He thought of the pounds of dried goods and meat the platoon had dragged away from the rebel's cenote and wondered where it would end up. Likely in the military's store rooms where they already housed more rations than they needed. It wouldn't end up in the slums where it belonged.

He berated himself for the thought and stalked faster through the throngs of people on the narrow street. This wasn't the worst of the slums, mostly thanks to its proximity to the main road, but even here he could see the separation from the military and royal quarters. The road was rough, missing stones creating divots that made the passage of any carts difficult, if not impossible. And when he let his eyes wander too far from the path directly ahead, he noticed the children tucked away in the shadowed alleys, wire-thin and faces streaked with mud.

By the time he'd made it to the front of the chief commander's manor, and the main military compound sprawled beside it, the sun had long disappeared beneath the horizon, leaving the air chilled. But nothing as cold as the forest after dusk. As much as he missed the sweet smell of the night blooms, the scent of stone, dust, and sweat was a familiar bouquet. His shoulders relaxed at last with the familiarity of home.

He didn't enter through the compound gates, instead walking directly up and knocking on the chief commander's door. The unit would have already sent a messenger with the news of his return.

His suspicions were confirmed when Don Hernandez opened the door with a wide smile.

"The chief commander is waiting for you in the study, Junior Sergeant Ocon." The words were formal, but the man wrapped his hand around Fox's arm for a moment longer than necessary as Fox stepped over the threshold and into the home. Don had been working for the chief commander since Fox could remember, and the white haired man still looked at him like he was a child.

"Thank you, Don."

"He suggested you likely would want refreshments. Tea is already waiting for you, and Ms. Garcia will have food delivered shortly."

Fox's stomach gave a sharp growl and he saw Don's eyes glint with joy. He smiled and thanked him again before turning to where he knew the study sat.

The housekeeper hadn't lied. A tray with tea was laid out in the sitting area next to the study's fire, a few snacks already waiting for him. The chief commander was at his desk, writing furiously across his paper, but he stopped when Fox stepped into the room.

"Junior Sergeant Ocon," he said, the relief and warmth one might have excepted in his father present here, at last. "Fox."

It was all the chief commander said before pulling Fox into an embrace he only saved for these moments in private. Both his wives had died before being able to produce the son he'd always wanted, so he treated Fox as his own.

"I'm glad to see you in one piece," he said, pushing Fox away to examine him as a mother might. "You look atrocious."

Fox winced, running his fingers through his blond hair. At least, he attempted to, but his fingers got caught in the knots almost immediately and he was left feeling like an idiot as he tried to pry his hand away.

"It's been a journey."

There was a knock on the door before Chief Commander Harlow could respond, and a maid walked in with a tray weighed down by every delicacy Fox had dreamed of over the past weeks. He could smell the spices of the pork and the fresh-baked bread, already sliced and ready to eat. There was also a pile of dark berries, grown and imported over the sea each blink.

"Let's discuss your journey while you eat. You look half-crazed with hunger."

"Yes, sir," Fox said, jumping at the opportunity. Another soldier might have shown restraint in front of the chief commander, but Fox dove in with fervor. He ate three slices of bread and half the pork before he finally took a breath.

Fox's story of the last two weeks' events didn't take him long. Skipping over the majority of the details, he explained his capture and escape, as well as his travels back to Suvi. He didn't even mention Sofia's part in the adventures past the initial lure and the chief commander asked no questions about her. He seemed much more interested in the general interrogations he went through along with his treatment during captivity.

When he made it back to his run-in with the scout, he dropped the boy's name as promised, and he took the opportunity to ask the chief commander for information on the operation.

"I haven't gone down to see the prisoners personally, but we captured thirteen in total. Five were killed in the raid, but I'm sure the rest will provide plenty of information." He took a sip from his tea cup, an air of quiet contentment about him. "My hope is that this was the last dying breath of the resistance. There will be holdouts, for sure, among the city and Dragonborn, but I believe we've cut off the head, as it were."

Fox hated the stone that settled in his stomach as he wondered about the numbers. Who was captured and who had been killed? He didn't want to care.

Chief Commander Harlow drew him from his thoughts with a hand on his knee. A brief touch, but warm from the tea he'd been sipping.

"Your brother would be proud of all you've accomplished."

Fox's throat bobbed in a sudden attempt to swallow. "Of course, sir."

"I know we never talked about it when you joined, but I also know that this hadn't been your plan originally. I still remember the little boy who spent every waking moment in the library reading and avoiding the training field."

"I was young—"

"Perhaps. But I also know you didn't decide to join until Leon was killed in the attack all those cycles ago. It's been an honor to watch you serve. I always knew you'd do great things. You have a head for strategy."

Fox gave a crooked smile. "I suppose reading was good for some things."

The chief commander gave him a long look before nodding. "Yes. I believe you're right." He stood suddenly, stepping around his desk without a word and pulling a small stack of books from the drawer. "It was with that in mind that I had these compiled from my personal library."

Fox gave a small start when the chief commander placed the small stack into his hands. There were four books in total, bound in leather of varying ages. He could just make out the faded script on the first cover: *War Strategies in Fighting Against Faith.*

"Sir?"

"I feel you may find these helpful for moving forward."

Fox was confused at the direction their conversation had taken.

"They aren't required reading, of course," the chief commander continued.

"Required?" Fox asked, a finger running over the smooth texture of the top book's cover.

"For your promotion."

Fox looked up, startled, face all too open.

The chief commander only smiled.

"The ceremony will be later, once we've had time to deal with the resistance prisoners. But I've already started the paperwork," he waved back toward his desk and what he'd been writing out before, "Junior *Major* Ocon."

Fox left the chief commander's house with the books tucked under his arm and permission for time off to visit his family before returning to his duties. Their manor was just a few doors down; their family being in the military for the past five generations had its perks.

It would have been kind of his father to remind the sergeant to send a messenger to Mother. Fox should have known he wouldn't. When Ms. Salves opened the front door, she let out a scream, face going white at the sight of him. He didn't bother with words of reassurance because a few moments later, he saw Mother come out from the drawing room, a letter opener clutched in her hands like a sword.

"I know I'm a bit late to dinner, but you don't need to stab me."

The snarky words fell from his tongue before he could stop himself, but it didn't matter. He wasn't even sure she heard him. The moment she saw his face, she dropped the letter opener and ran toward him with a speed impressive in the slippers she wore.

Her hands fluttered around his face and shoulders, torn between wanting to pull him into a hug and assuring herself he was real. He made the choice for her, gripping her hands and pulling them to his face.

"I'm okay," he said. "I'm back." He pressed a kiss to her forehead.

She didn't speak and the tears traced down her face even as he felt his own at the corners of his eyes. He couldn't remember the last time he had cried. He should have been embarrassed, but he didn't care, not when she was looking up at him like he'd been raised from the dead.

"Have you eaten? Ms. Salves, put together supper for Fox!"

He smiled, a sense of comfort in her worrying about something so mundane as his hunger.

"I already ate. I had to stop at Chief Commander Harlow's to debrief."

She stepped back, lips pinching down in a frown and he knew the interrogation was about to begin.

"Where have you been this entire time? Are you okay? You look horrible and you smell like the slums. We thought you were dead. Your father *told* me you were dead." She let out a sob, biting on her knuckle for a second as she breathed. "I knew you weren't. I could feel you were still alive. I prayed to the dead kings to protect you."

Fox gripped her shoulders, gentle but firm, as she swayed.

"I'm okay. I can explain what happened tomorrow, but I haven't had a proper bath in weeks and right now all I want to do is sleep."

She nodded, placing a hand on his cheek once more, as if checking to ensure he was still real. His chest tightened and the tears burning in his eyes fell again, hot on his cheeks. He wondered if they were making tracks through the dirt caked there from his days in the forest.

THE BATH TOOK LONGER than he wanted, the energy draining from his body at the same pace as the dirt from his skin. But it took three rounds of filling and emptying the tub before the water finally ran clean. His skin was red and raw by the time he was done, in part from scrubbing and in part from the sun. The tint of his skin was tanner than normal after days out in the forest, darker than even his stint as a scout when he spent most his time napping under the shade of a tree.

Now he was a junior major.

He hadn't even told Mother yet, the idea not quite settled into his mind as reality. Nothing felt real at the moment, even the brush of the soft fabric of his pajamas across his skin. It was the softest thing he'd felt in weeks. Except for...

No.

When he came out of his en suite bathroom, his mother was sitting on the small couch in the corner, mind lost to something else.

"Mother," he said. The words were soft, but she still flinched, head whipping over to him. He realized as her eyes swept over him that she didn't quite believe this was real either. Was she expecting him to disappear into the bathroom and never come out, a figment of her grief?

"I'm sorry, I can...I just—" she moved as if to leave, but her body just jerked, eyes darting around, lost.

"You can stay," Fox said, saving her from her own thoughts. "I want you to stay. I think it will help me sleep."

He wasn't sure how true the words were. A part of him wanted to sit alone and forget the last few weeks. But the words had an immediate effect on his mother and her shoulders slumped with relief as she fell back onto the couch.

In the end, he wasn't necessarily annoyed at her presence in his room. It was almost a comfort to open his eyes and look over at her in the dark and remind himself that this wasn't a dream. He was back. He was home.

And Sofia is here, trapped in a cell because of you.

He fell asleep with this thought spiraling through his mind, her voice an echo he couldn't tune out.

This is your fault.

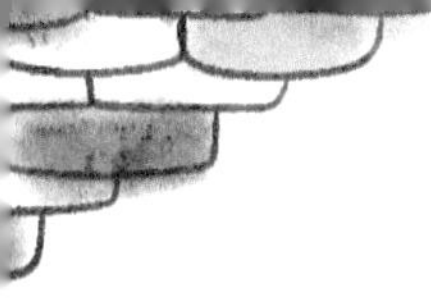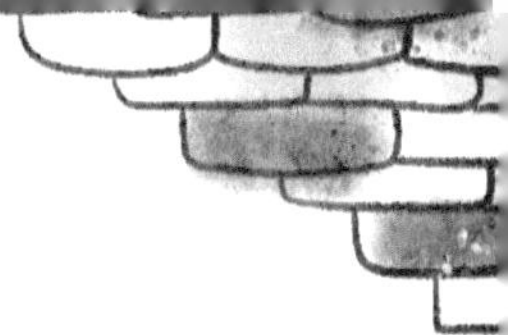

FOX

AGE 7

"Back with you, faery spawn!" Fox cried, pushing forward with his sword née tree branch until his brother was forced to retreat.

"I will eat your blood!" Leon said, spinning and slashing out with his own blade—a true practice sword carved of polished wood that their father had gifted him last week.

"You can't eat blood, you idiot." He followed his words with a jab to Leon's side.

"I'm magical. I can do what I want, *Dumbass!*"

"Language," their mother said from where she was sitting beneath the small pitaya tree. A servant had brought a small wooden chair for her to sit on, the shade of the leaves above her protecting her olive skin from tanning. His father hated it when she looked too dark.

They were outside the manor wall, down by the small man-made canal that carved through the royal and military quarters. It was the peak of the dry season and the sun shone long and hot through the day. Perhaps Fox and Leon should have taken this as a hint to stay inside, at least in the sharp heat of afternoon, but they were far too bored of wandering the manor's halls. So instead, they moved between playing in the field and jumping in the canal to cool their reddening skin.

Fox leaped back as his brother jabbed his sword at him, the wooden blade smacking him on the side. He squealed loudly, falling back into the grass with a dramatic kick.

"You will not defeat me," he said, doing his best impression of imminent death. "My dragon will protect me! He comes now!"

Leon gave an equally dramatic cry, hands raised to protect himself from the threat of the unseen creature.

"What is this?" a cold voice asked.

Fox stopped his thrashing along the ground immediately and pulled himself up. His father was striding across the grass, face pulled into a scowl. He'd been meeting with the king, and it didn't look like it had ended well. His long golden hair was tied back, but countless strays had escaped, giving him a disheveled appearance. It was a look that never boded well. Leon had gone quiet, too, standing at attention as his father stopped beside them.

"Leon?"

"Yes, Father," he said, voice smaller than it was a moment earlier.

"Are you barbarians?"

"No, sir."

"Are you traitors to the king?"

"No, sir."

"Only barbarians and traitors believe in dragons and magic."

"Yes, sir," Leon and Fox said together.

"Men and soldiers fight against the Dragonborn rebels and true threats to the kingdom, not mythical monsters." He paused, as if waiting for an argument, but Leon and Fox both stood, unmoving. "Go inside. The tutor left you extra work to complete, and I need to speak with your mother."

With reluctance, Fox dropped the tree branch he'd been using onto the ground and followed his brother as he headed back up the small hill toward the manor. He looked back only once just as his father's hand cracked across their mother's face, the sound of the clap echoing across the field.

THAT NIGHT, the bruise was already starting to bloom across Mother's cheek, a red darkening to mauve beneath the powder pressed against her skin. She gently took his hand as he automatically reached up to touch it, as if he could wipe it away.

"Do you want me to read you a story?" she asked as she sat on the edge of his bed, the plush mattress dipping beneath her weight.

"It's okay," he said, eyes lingering on the bruise with guilt.

"You always love a story," she said. Her skin was cold as she pressed her hand against his cheek, cupping him and forcing him to meet her eyes. "This wasn't your fault."

Hot tears burned his eyes. It was the most she'd ever acknowledged the marks that Father occasionally left on her.

Her fingers gently tipped his chin up, meeting his eyes once more. She wiped away his tears.

"Never let them see you cry, Little Fox," she said.

He nodded, biting back the tears until his eyes were dry once more.

"How about I read the dragon and the hare, again?" She pulled the book from the small pile of stories tucked hidden beneath his bed.

"Can I listen, too?" Leon was leaning in the doorway, voice a whisper.

Their mother smiled and opened her arms in answer, waiting until Leon was sitting on the bed beside Fox to open the book. Her voice was soft, never rising above a whisper.

His father was somewhere in the manor, probably in his study or in his room, separate from her own rooms. One day, his father would find the small stash of books Mother had hidden. She had tucked them away last cycle when his father had decided Leon—and Fox by extension—was too old for faerytales and books. The stories would be burned and the punishment meted out. But for now, in the dark and quiet of the night as his mother did her best impression of the deep timbre of a dragon's voice, Fox was happy with their little secret.

Someday, their little safe space would crumble, but not today. Not yet.

CHAPTER THIRTY-EIGHT
SOFIA

Sofia hated herself for the thrum of fear that rushed through her veins at the scent of the prison. The familiarity of it sank into her skin even after a decade. She had a hood over her head, but she strained her ears, listening for the sound of anyone else. The prison was quiet except for the echoing of footfalls. When she was pushed into a small, cramped cell, her hood removed, there was no one else around except for the single guard. He didn't even look at her as he locked the door and walked away, taking the only light with him.

Sofia wasn't afraid of the dark. She'd spent the last five cycles living in the dark tunnels of the cenotes. Yet, as the lantern disappeared out of sight, Sofia's chest caved in. She gasped, trying to suck in a breath, but the air had been sucked from the room and she was left scrabbling at her throat, trying to understand where it had gone. Her hands went numb and she slumped against the cold stone wall before she lost the ability to control her muscles.

A scream caught in her throat, unable to work its way out without air. She was going to die here, alone in the dark before General Ocon even had a chance to break her.

No no no no no.

Her mind chanted the word until she finally choked it out, the sound of her own voice startling her in the dark.

"No!"

Her hand pressed against her chest, feeling the rapid patter of her heart. She was having another panic attack. She wouldn't let this kill her. Screwing her eyes tightly closed as if she might forget the darkness around her, she hissed out a breath through her nose, trying her best to slow it. Her hand stayed firm against her chest and her breaths became a mantra.

She was left shivering in the darkness, a film of cold sweat layered upon her body. Pins and needles raced across her skin, but she curled up all the same, pressing herself into a tight ball until she could focus more on the feel of her own skin instead of the rough stone. She breathed in the odor of her body, sweaty and dirty, and pushed away the stale scent of the prison.

Sleep came slowly and she sank into the quiet darkness of oblivion until the nightmares tangled around her. She felt the bite of the whip against her skin and heard her own screams, echoing from every direction. But there was only blackness around her. When the pain stopped and she managed to turn and see the man holding the whip, it wasn't General Ocon's face she saw, but Fox's, her blood sprayed across his brow.

SHE WOKE with a start to the sound of metal on metal. Despite the heaviness in her limbs, she scrambled up before the guard could grab her. She was sick of being dragged about. Even still, by the time he'd snapped the rough cuffs onto her wrists, her shoulders were aching from his rough jerks that were anything but necessary.

She was led up a set of steps out of the basement of the prison onto a level with high windows. The light blinded her for a moment until her eyes adjusted to the bright sunlight filtering in from outside, but then she was shoved once more into darkness.

When her eyes adjusted again, she was greeted with the sight of a small room devoid of any furniture. General Ocon stood against the wall, his eyes following her closely as the guard forced her to kneel in the middle of the room, moving her hands to the cuffs that sprouted from the ground in front of her. She tested the binds, wondering if the general would get close enough for her to claw his eyes out. She doubted it.

Her eyes darted around the rest of the room and she immediately regretted it. Not because of the wall of weapons hanging beside the general, but rather the man standing in the corner, blond hair tied up in a top knot, looking cleaner than she'd seen him in weeks.

Fox's face was a pasty white, even for him, and he didn't meet her eyes when she looked at him. Despite this, just the sight of him broke something in her and her stomach dropped, her heartbeat a staccato in her chest. He *had* truly betrayed her—forgotten everything they had spoken about and seen in the forest. Had he given up so easily? She clenched her fists, nails biting in her skin as hard as she could manage, and she wished she could draw her own blood to distract her thoughts.

She needed to leave here. Now. And if she couldn't do it physically, she'd do it mentally. She found herself seeking out Fox once more and she hated herself for it. But looking at him, as he stared anywhere but at her or his father, she could still smell the night blooms and damp moss growing between the stones in the cenote. The wind whistled through the trees, rustling the leaves of the canopy above, and she could feel the rush of water in the underground rivers just beneath her feet.

And then General Ocon was directly in front of her, voice pushing through over the sound of the forest.

"It's really you. I kept thinking I'd made a mistake."

She snarled as he grabbed her left hand, examining the stub of her ring finger. He didn't even flinch at the empty gesture, but dropped her hand a moment later with a sneer of disgust. As if it were her fault he'd touched her.

He leaned down, his face a few inches from hers.

"How did you survive? You should have died of your wounds. You were supposed to be buried with the rest of the filth."

She smelled the sour odor of his breath.

When she didn't speak, he asked again, spit flicking across her face with every word.

She didn't answer. She didn't look away from him and watched as his pupils constricted with anger.

"Did one of my men save you? Sneak you out? Someone healed you —more than that. Was it a witch?"

The thought was laughable. Witchcraft had died out with the dragons generations before. Even the most skilled healers who knew the old medicines couldn't truly practice magic.

The general didn't seem to like the laugh that bubbled from her throat. He stepped away, blond hair brushing against his shoulders with every step. He'd have been a handsome man were it not for the perpetual twisted sneer. The thought made her shudder. It made her think of his son.

Her eyes flickered to Fox's corner involuntarily, but he wasn't looking at her. He was focused on his father. She followed his gaze and saw the general picking out a whip from the wall.

As he approached her again, she didn't look away, knowing the surprise would hurt more. But she still couldn't keep the low hiss of pain from escaping her lips as the whip lashed across her back. Once. Twice.

The hits radiated through her body, the air choking in her lungs for just a moment. But once she caught her breath, she smiled, looking up at him.

"Planning to add to your previous work?"

"I plan on finishing what I started. But I have some questions first."

This time he used his fist, cracking it across her face. She tasted blood mixing with the bile in her mouth.

"Who leads the resistance. Are they who saved you?"

"Not. Telling. You," she spit out, along with the blood.

He delivered a sharp kick to her side.

"Why did you kidnap Fox? What information were you hoping to get?"

She didn't bother answering this time and the next hit came faster.

The chains pulled at her wrists, chafing the skin as her body jerked against her control. She focused on the sensation, blocking out the pain radiating through her side and back. She felt her tunic being torn away, the bite of the whip against her skin. Her back was wet with blood and she wondered if the new scars would simply blend in with the old.

She closed her eyes and let the scent of her own blood take her back to her time in the ruins, praying at the dragons' altar.

She prayed now. Perhaps the dragons no longer protected her people. Perhaps they worked for the king now, but she wouldn't give up on her faith.

"Father—"

Fox's voice broke her from her thoughts, and she hated him for it. She was happy lost there.

Their voices were slurred or perhaps that was her own head, but she could just hear bits and pieces.

"—not working—not answering."

"—know—do it yourself—"

She looked up, vision blurred to see Fox gripping his father's wrist hard, stopping him from bringing the whip down again. Even as she watched, his father's fist crashed against the side of Fox's face, sending him to the floor.

"Leave."

"Father—"

"Everyone, leave," he said, motioning to his son. "Take him with you. I wish to question the prisoner alone."

She might have heard some argument, but between one blink and the next the room was empty. Almost empty. The general towered over her, leaning on a cane.

It was polished to a shine, unnecessarily she thought, given its purpose.

"You're back," he said, noticing her focus. "Good." He stepped forward and lifted her chin with the tip of the cane. The wood was cold against her skin and she glared up at the man that had haunted her nightmares for so many cycles.

"You were out in the rainforest. What did you see?"

The question was vague and seemingly harmless, but there was a glint of something in the general's eyes that told her he didn't care about the cenotes they found or even the wolfshifters.

"I saw trees and animals. What else would there be?"

The words were slurred, but she kept her eyes sharp, watching the tic of frustration along his jaw.

"I know it was you, somehow," he hissed. "You brought that *thing* back. How did you do it?"

He was talking about the dragon.

"Did my son see?" Something like fear tinged his words.

"The trees?" she said, spitting out more blood. "He's blind and stupid, but I don't imagine he missed them."

"You know exactly what I'm talking about," he hissed, face only few inches from her own and she wondered if she could bite him before he jerked back.

"Say it, then," she said through gritted teeth. "Ask what you really want to ask."

He didn't though, instead bringing the cane down across her already shredded back.

"We massacred an entire tribe of people looking for it. Did you know that?"

Sofia didn't know what face she made—too lost in the pain—but she heard the general's laugh.

"You did know them, didn't you? Did we murder your friends? Even your little resistance base was found because we were out there, looking for your *dragon*. Now tell me how you called it."

Her lips were nearly numb, but she formed the words slowly and deliberately, making sure he heard them. "I don't know what you're talking about."

He brought the cane down again and she let out an involuntary groan. The pain overtook her body and she thought she might choke on it.

Something cracked inside of her. She only realized she'd crumpled to the ground when she felt the cold press of stone against her cheek and she closed her eyes, letting it soak through her skin like a balm.

She embraced the blackness and waited for her mind to give up and drift away. The pain would stop eventually. It always did.

CHAPTER THIRTY-NINE

FOX

Fox shook off the grips of the guards as they attempted to drag him from the interrogation chamber. He kept his shoulders rigid, back straight, as he left, not pausing his stride as the door closed behind him. His father wouldn't listen to him. He wouldn't listen to reason. He wouldn't get any information out of Sofia, but he'd kill her in the process of trying. So Fox would get the one person that his father would have to listen to: the chief commander.

The chief commander didn't question Fox's intentions when he burst into his office and explained that his father was compromised. Fox was protecting the best interests of the military, Sofia had information, and her death wouldn't get them anywhere.

The soldiers that had left the room on his father's command were stationed at the door when Fox returned. They paled under the chief commander's glare.

"Open the door," Chief Commander Harlow barked, not bothering to even slow down, assuming his order would be obeyed. The taller soldier—a high specialist that Fox vaguely recognized—jumped at the command.

Fox kept his eyes down as he followed the chief commander into the room. A small voice in his mind told him his father would *know*—if he looked Fox in the eyes, he would know *why* Fox had stopped the interrogation. But his father only had eyes for the chief commander as the taller man strode into the room with an air of authority rivaled only by the king.

"General Ocon, stand down."

"Chief Commander, sir," his father's voice was rough and low. Fox glanced at him only briefly. His face was splattered with blood, skin tinged pink, and hair disheveled. And as the chief commander kneeled down, Fox couldn't stop his eyes from following, taking in the crumpled form of Sofia. She was covered in blood, and Fox had to swallow back his rage. He kept his face neutral even as he held in his own scream.

He was going to kill his father for this. Fox had never been so sure of anything in his life, and the anticipation of knowing one day he would see the life drain from his father's eyes—that he would be the cause of it—gave him the strength to not lunge at his father now and wrap his hands around his throat.

The chief commander lifted Sofia's head, moving the matted curls from her face. He picked up her left hand and examined the stub of a finger and Fox heard the sharp intake of breath.

"King's balls, it is you." The chief commander stood before Fox could even register the foul curse. "Take her to my personal interrogation room. I wish to speak with her myself."

Fox jumped at the order, along with the two guards. They unchained her and Fox picked her up, feeling only slightly queasy as her blood soaked through his tunic. They took the direct tunnel that led from the prison into the chief commander's house, the two other soldiers leading the way. She only stirred briefly as they walked, but he was happy she didn't wake. He didn't want her to see him like this— covered in her blood and escorting her to her next prison cell.

The moment he'd laid her out in the new cell and one guard had rechained her hands, he snapped at the other to fetch medical supplies.

"If the chief commander wants to speak with her," he snarled when the guard hesitated, "you better ensure she's alive for it."

The room was small, but it was warmer than the last they'd been in, a fire already burning merrily in the hearth. There was an ornate and cushioned chair in the corner, clearly made for the chief commander's own comfort while interrogating his prisoners. There was still a small rack against the wall, lined with various equipment and weapons. This was no less a torture chamber than the one before.

Fox stared at the rack while he waited. He wanted to check over Sofia himself, brush the hair from her face, but he didn't deserve to touch her. Eventually, the guard returned with a healer and a bag of supplies.

The weathered man with his hunched back and wiry hair stripped off Sofia's shirt, not bothering with her modesty. Fox averted his eyes and snapped at the two guards, sending them away on orders to prepare their reports.

And then he watched as the healer dabbed away the blood, stitching up the worst of the wounds and smoothing on a balm to keep infection at bay.

With the man's back turned, Fox made quick work of perusing the man's bag, grabbing out a few supplies for himself. He still hadn't admitted to anyone that he had stitches running across his stomach and back. The wounds were easy to explain, the treatment he'd received from the non-citizen tribe wouldn't be.

He had just slipped a small tin of numbing powder into his pocket when the healer turned back to Fox with the smallest of frowns. "She has a few broken ribs, but they aren't life threatening. The salve will stop the infection from setting in long enough that you'll have time to get your information."

Because that's all that mattered.

"Thank you."

The healer left, muttering something about not needing to heal prisoners if the interrogations weren't so violent, but Fox ignored him, kneeling at Sofia's side with gritted teeth.

She was still unconscious and a part of him recognized he should be thankful for this. The healer hadn't given her anything for pain, so it would return once she opened her eyes again.

He hated himself for caring. Caring hurt. It made his chest ache and his eyes burn. It made him want to grab her and run. To take them both far into the mountains and away from anything that might hurt her again.

"Fox?" His name was a prayer on her lips. She was lying on the ground, arranged on her stomach so the worst of the damaged body was off the ground. She tried to sit up.

"Don't," he said, stepping around her so she could look at him directly without jarring her wounds.

She didn't move again, but her eyes roamed around the part of the room she could see. As her eyes fell on the fire, she jerked back, as if burned.

"Stop!" he snapped as she pushed back and let out a guttural groan. She kept flailing, like a fish on dry land, attempting to escape despite the impossibility of it. "Stop," he said, voice more earnest.

"You're okay. You're okay," he said. It was a desperate lie. *You're okay for now.* "Breathe." The word was as much a mantra to him as it was to her. Her moss green eyes met his, and he realized she was afraid. No, not afraid. Terrified.

He grabbed her hand, the only part of her seemingly uninjured, and squeezed.

"The chief commander wants to talk to you himself. Just give up what he wants. Answer his questions with half-truths. Whatever you need to do to make him happy. *Please.*"

His words seemed to rouse her and she moved, just barely, to turn her face up to meet his.

"Fuck you. I won't give him what he wants. You can tell him that yourself."

She pulled her hand away and closed her eyes. Fox was left sitting beside her, helpless and disgusted at himself for his own inability to act.

F OX HEARD the snap of the chief commander's boots down the hall long before he entered the chamber, giving him time to step away from Sofia and lean himself against the wall as if he'd been waiting for him there the entire time. He was surprised to see the chief commander shut the door behind himself. There were no others with him.

"Sir," Fox said, giving a salute. "I had the healer do enough to make sure she was alive and conscious for your questioning."

The chief commander patted Fox's shoulder and smiled. His eyes were focused only on Sofia. She was sitting up, at least as best as she could with the damage to her back and body. She was sneering, but Fox saw the hitch in her breathing. It was taking everything to keep herself upright.

"Sofia, Sofia," the chief commander spoke at last and she went rigid at the sound of her name. "You thought I'd forget about you? I always regretted how you died—well, then again, I guess your death didn't take, anyway."

"Sir," Fox said, still pressed against the wall. "Should I leave, sir?"

"Stay, Junior Major," he said, turning to him with something akin to pride. "From what I hear, this is the one that kidnapped you, yes?"

Fox bit his tongue, willing his face not to give anything away. "Yes, sir."

"Is she a leader among them?"

"I don't think so, just the bait."

"Pretty bait, at that. I do hope you didn't get distracted."

Fox's stomach churned. "Not by that, sir."

"Tell me, Sofia," he said, leaning over her. "What are the resistance's plans?"

She looked feral, baring her teeth at the man. He reached out as if to touch her and she snapped at him. He didn't react, only dropping his hand.

"Were you responsible for the dragon my men saw out there?" Harlow asked.

Fox was glad the man's back was turned because his mask slipped for the briefest moment.

"Were you controlling it? Did you call it?"

"The gods can't be controlled," she said, the first words she'd spoken since Harlow had come in the room.

"We killed all your friends," he said, voice so soft, Fox barely heard him. "There are no feral beasts left to help you. So tell me, where are you keeping the dragon?"

She only glared back him at.

He stood after a moment and walked around the room, brushing his fingers against the weapons along the wall. When the chief commander stopped next to the last one, a finger running along the metal, Sofia went even grayer. He was caressing the branding iron.

"Is the resistance trying to bring the dragons back?"

"The dragons are dead," Sofia said.

"You and I both know you don't believe that. You never have. Now, tell me, where is the dragon?"

The questions went on for another hour, the chief commander never raising his voice or even his hands. He didn't so much as threaten Sofia. He knew, just as Fox did, that pain wouldn't convince her of anything. His father had tried that tactic.

Eventually, Chief Commander Harlow slipped from the room, motioning for Fox to follow, leaving Sofia slumped on the floor.

They walked halfway down the hallway before the chief commander turned to Fox.

"What are your thoughts?"

"Sir?" Fox felt wrung out and too tired to understand what Harlow was asking of him.

"How might we get her to talk? Put all that strategy reading to use."

Fox had to swallow back a startled laugh. The chief commander was using this as an opportunity to train him, to teach him. He pushed away all thoughts of Sofia. He couldn't think of her.

"Pain won't work. Threatening her own life won't work. And—" he paused, wondering if he should say it, but knowing the chief commander wasn't ignorant. He knew what Fox had seen in the room. "And I don't think she'll give anything up to you specifically, sir. She doesn't appear to *like you*."

"I imagine she hates me and wants me to burn in the dragon hells or whatever those heathens believe in." He smiled and Fox let out a breath. He'd passed the test. "She won't admit anything to anyone with only her life on the line. Take her back to the cells and put her with the rest of her comrades. We'll see how she feels when her friends start their interrogations."

Fox nodded, realizing that in trying to save Sofia, he might have just condemned her friends.

"Fox," the chief commander spoke again even as he turned away. "You've done well. Marking the base, escaping, and returning to immediately help with the interrogations. You've already proved my judgment correct. You're going to make a fine soldier, Junior Major. I'm proud of you."

"Thank you, sir."

He turned, taking his time returning to the cell where they'd left Sofia. Despite the exhaustion and the horrors from the last day, the chief commander's voice rang in his ears and sent a thrill racing through his blood.

I'm proud of you.

CHAPTER FORTY

SOFIA

Sofia was only half-aware when Fox returned without the chief commander, freeing her from her binds and carefully picking her up. Even with his slow and gentle gestures, the movement sent waves of pain through her body and she almost threw up on him. She thought he might have whispered something to her, but she didn't hear it. She didn't hear anything after that.

When she opened her eyes an indeterminate amount of time later, the pain hadn't stopped. But the aches had settled into something bearable in their sharp presence. At least the aftermath was predictable and steady.

She was lying on the ground again, cheek pressed against cold stone. But the darkness was no longer impenetrable, and this time, it came with voices and the sound of movement around her.

"Sofia," a voice whispered.

The voice, sharp with anxiety, roused her before she slipped back into unconsciousness. Someone was crouched in front of her and there was a dim light coming from somewhere above.

"Fox?" she muttered, mouth clumsy around the word.

"Sofia, don't move," the voice said again. "It's Flor. You need to stay still. I don't know if anything is broken, but I can't—"

The words choked off in a small sob and Sofia moved automatically, wanting to comfort, but nausea roiled through her and she ended up dry-heaving instead. A hand patted her shoulder softly and she finally managed to look up into Flor's pale face.

Fox hadn't brought her to her cell in the basement where his father had first thrown her. She was with the others.

Flor leaned against the same bars as Sofia, but on the other side, in her own personal cell. Her hair was matted with blood, red on red, and her face gaunt, as if they'd been captured for weeks instead of days. But she was here. And she was—

"You're alive," Sofia's voice scraped over the words. "I didn't know—"

Flor let out a soft huff of air, almost a laugh. "I should be saying the same of you. Micael practically fainted when he saw the soldier carrying you in."

"Micael," Sofia said, slotting the name on the list of those who had made it out. And then her stomach twisted. "Javi? I saw his mom. Is he—?"

She didn't need to finish the sentence. Flor was already shaking her head. "He wasn't in the cenote when they invaded. He was looking for you, actually."

"Hopefully, he doesn't find me."

"Carmen is okay, too. She broke her wrist in the process of trying to protect Viola, but you should have seen the punch she threw."

Sofia smiled, lips cracking and she tasted fresh blood. "Dia?" She almost didn't ask, not wanting to know if they'd been too late and when Flor shook her head, she regretted the question.

"But there was no record of her execution, either. We're hoping she's being kept elsewhere."

Flor went through the list of the other survivors, and Sofia kept her breathing steady. It hurt too much to do more.

A rough hand brushed against her forearm, one of the few places she wasn't bruised and sore, and she realized she had closed her eyes. She looked back up to where Flor was sitting, pressed against the bars.

"We thought you were dead. We assumed he had found a way to force you to free him and then just killed you."

"Why didn't you all leave? Why stay in the cenote after he escaped?"

"We left, at first. We packed up and moved into a secondary cenote a few miles east and Micael kept an eye on the base. But after a week of nothing, he assumed you were both dead—that he'd never made it back to Suvi."

Sofia almost laughed. He wasn't completely wrong.

"There is a lot to catch up on," she said, even as another sharp ache vibrated up through her back and hip.

"Before that, I should look at your injuries."

Sofia shook her head. "I already had a healer."

"One of *their* healers," she said, clearly not taking Sofia's no as an answer. "Now, shirt off."

"Trying to get me naked? I thought we tried this before. It didn't work."

Flor didn't crack a smile and Sofia eventually complied. The shirt was sticky with blood and hard to separate from her skin in places. Flor poked and prodded where she could through the bars.

In the end, Sofia didn't think she had more than a broken rib or two. Her legs and hips seemed unbroken despite the deep bruises along them. Her injuries were nothing to shrug off, but they wouldn't stop her from running if she needed to.

When she needed to.

"I'm mostly worried about the open cuts on your back," Flor said, apparently content with her assessment at last. Sofia pulled her tunic back on to cover herself. Something fell from the side pocket, pinging against the stone. A small round tin had been tucked into it without her noticing. She picked it up and gently opened the lid, assessing the white powder inside.

"What is that?" Flor asked, straining to look through the bars.

"I'm not sure." She pressed a finger into the powder, bringing it to her nose and then her mouth.

"Dragon scales, you did not just put a mysterious power in your mouth."

"It's numbing powder," she said, practically breathing out the words. She felt the tingling along her gums and let herself take a bit more, already dreaming of the relief the medicine would bring.

"That won't stop infection," Flor said, almost petulant at her previous concerns being ignored.

Sofia could only shrug. "The healer put something on the cuts. We'll be gone before I need more."

Flor gave her a blank look. "You got carried in here looking three-fourths the way to dead and now you have a plan for escape?"

"Not yet," Sofia said, not meeting Flor's eyes. "I need to work on that. But that's not the most important thing."

"Of course not. Escape can wait. Please tell me what is more important."

Sofia almost smiled. She'd missed Flor.

"Listen," she said, pulling herself closer to the bars and dropping her voice. She ignored Flor's attempt to change the subject back to her wounds with a sharp hiss. "We saw dragons."

Flor blinked, expression flickering from confusion to concern. "I should check your head."

She wished she had the energy to grab her friend and shake her.

"My head is fine."

"You have a black eye and blood in your hair."

"I don't feel dizzy."

Flor stared blankly at where she'd been dry heaving just a second before.

"I don't feel *that* dizzy. And that's not why I'm talking about drag-ons." She tried keeping her voice low even as she wanted to scream.

"You saw dragons."

"Yes," she said. "A cenote dragon and what I think was a sea dragon —it was farther away. Scales, Flor, I saw the damn thing up close. I felt its presence. I had a feather. The chief commander and the general both asked about them. They must have seen them, too. Or known about them. Heard about them."

"The dragons." Flor's voice was flat.

Her friend looked at her like she'd truly gone crazy, and she couldn't blame her. Maybe she had gone crazy. Maybe she'd been killed by the shapeshifters and the rest of this had all been a dream. A horrible and strange dream. It would explain why she couldn't stop thinking about Fox.

"I'm not crazy," Sofia said, wondering how many times she could say it before it made her sound more crazy.

"Who is we?"

"What?" she said, looking back at Flor.

"You said 'we saw dragons'," Flor said carefully.

With dread churning in her stomach.

"Fox Ocon."

"The bastard that started all of this? The one that threw you in here, looking like—" she waved a hand at her. "You were gallivanting through the forest with him looking for dragons?"

"It was more complicated than that, but this wasn't his handiwork. The general didn't particularly like finding out I was still alive." She fiddled with the small tin, knowing without proof that Fox had been the one to slip it into her pocket. Did it make up for him watching her tortured and interrogated? Perhaps not. But it meant *something*. It had to. "I have a lot to tell you," Sofia said at last.

And she did. She told Flor everything, even the parts the other woman probably didn't need or want to hear, but it was all she could do. She needed Flor to trust her. She needed Micael and the others to trust her.

Because they were going to get out of this, and she couldn't do it alone. She needed her friends.

CHAPTER FORTY-ONE

FOX

Fox threw up in the alley on his way home from the prison. He couldn't get rid of the metallic smell of Sofia's blood from his skin or shake the cold looks from the other prisoners in the cells. He'd recognized the redheaded woman from the cenote and given Sofia the cell next to hers, but it also meant he had to listen as she hissed out a series of dragon-tongue words that he was pretty sure he recognized from the worst drunks in the slums. He didn't need Sofia awake to translate them for him.

He tried his best to hold on to the look of pride the chief commander had given him, but he also couldn't shake the discomfort and horror of watching him stand over a broken Sofia. For the first time since before his brother had died, Fox had the sense that something was seriously wrong with the system.

People were dying, but what the crown was doing wasn't working. If anything, things were getting worse. Perhaps if the people of Suvi knew the dragons were alive—that they were real—they'd recognize that the Dragonborn weren't stupid or even superstitious.

But he could only imagine the wave of fear that would crash through the city if they knew the monsters of their childhood nightmares were real—and just as destructive as the tales warned.

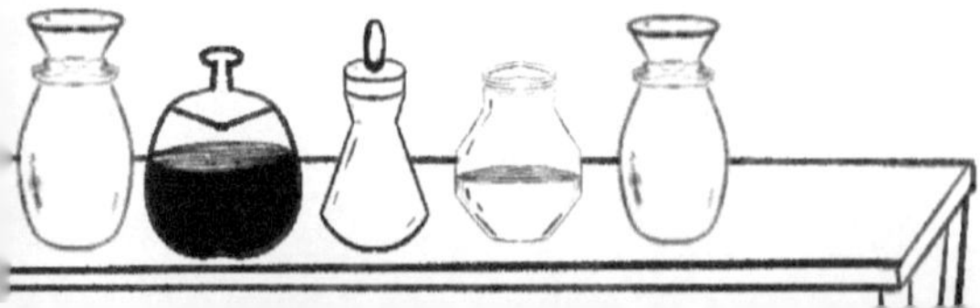

It was nearly nightfall by the time he made it back home, stopping in the kitchens long enough to order food to be sent up. He collapsed in his reading chair the moment he was alone in his room.

He was only a bit surprised when someone knocked on his door a few minutes later, the cooks having apparently worked faster than normal.

"Come in."

But it wasn't a kitchen maid who stepped through the door a second later.

"Ian," he said, straightening up, as if stiff shoulders might hide his bloodshot eyes or the strain along his brow.

"Your mother said you just came home. You look like shit."

"About what I'm feeling," he said, shrugging. "It's been an adjustment."

Ian gave a nod, lips pursed. He didn't look like he believed Fox, but he didn't ask any follow-up questions, either. Instead, he took the chair across from Fox. He hadn't visited Fox since those long blinks after Leon's death. It was turning into a habit for Ian to show up when Fox was at this lowest—first when his brother died and now. Except this time, Fox couldn't explain what he was feeling to Ian. At least not everything.

"It's strange being back," he said, perhaps to break the silence or perhaps because he simply wanted to say it out loud to someone. "There were definitely a few points where I didn't think I'd make it home."

"The rainforest can feel like a world of its own. You were out there alone?" Ian watched him carefully. Fox hated the scrutiny.

"No." The word slipped out before he could question why his brother's old friend was the one person he wanted to trust with the information. "I was out there with one of the Dragonborn that originally kidnapped me."

"Is that why it took so long to return?"

Well, we got kidnapped by shapeshifting wolves that ran so fast it took us two days just to get back.

"We...were captured by some men," he said, knowing just how

ridiculous he was sounding. "They knocked us out and dragged us out the opposite way in the forest. It took a while to figure out where we were and what direction to go after that."

Ian nodded, as if contemplating this. "Perhaps we should add way-finding to the training regimen for all recruits."

"I think there are a few skills we've been missing out on given the assumption we wouldn't be out in the rainforest." He looked at Ian, a finger tapping on his leg slowly. "There were...things out there. Animals I can't explain."

The corners of Ian's mouth tightened and his brow twitched, but it wasn't the look of a man that thought Fox was crazy.

"There's a reason our ancestors built the wall," Ian said. "I imagine there is a lot more than feral humans out there that it's protecting all of us from."

"So you believe the Dragonborn stories about monsters and faeries? About the dragons?" Fox asked.

For as long as he'd known Ian, they'd never talked about their beliefs around these things.

Ian didn't answer immediately and Fox could see the thoughts flickering across his face, even if he couldn't read them. At last, he nodded.

"They may be a superstitious bunch, but I think their ancestors knew this land. There is a lot that our people chose to forget over the centuries. It doesn't take magic for monsters to exist."

Fox might have held the same sentiment if it weren't for the image of the first faery he'd encountered still burned into his brain. The black smoke seeping from its skin and the black hair of the woman he would have sworn he'd been trying to help. There was more he'd seen out in the rainforest than could be explained by monsters born purely of flesh.

He remembered Sofia's words.

The dragon shed her feathers, each one falling to the earth, imbued with magic to become the creatures of the forest.

"Did you bring in the woman you were lost with? Or is she still out there?"

"She's in the prison with the rest," he said, skipping over the part where he wasn't the one to arrest her.

"I assume they're in the basement, readying for execution?" Ian asked, voice thick with bitter vitriol.

Fox shook his head. "Not yet. The chief commander is still hoping for information. There were some interrogations today."

Ian nodded, and Fox had to wonder if perhaps he wasn't the only one seeking revenge for what the resistance had done to his brother after all this time. "I'm sure they'll schedule the executions eventually."

Fox's empty stomach churned at his own words and Ian's eyebrows pinched.

"You should sleep," he said. "You look exhausted."

Ian was right, but the idea of sleeping—of closing his eyes—sent a tremor through Fox. He already knew that the crack of the whip on Sofia's bloody back would haunt his sleep. It was nothing he hadn't seen before. He'd seen his father's form of interrogation, although usually there were more questions interspersed between the blows.

But this was different. He knew Sofia. He knew the feel of her hair between his fingers and the smell of her skin, salty and floral. He knew the taste of her—

"Thanks for coming by," he said after a moment, shaking away the thoughts of Sofia. "But you're right. I'm still catching up on sleep and food. Can you tell my mother I plan to sleep the rest of the evening and not to disturb me?"

Ian took the dismissal with a soft smile and a nod. "Of course." Before he closed the door to Fox's room, he looked over his shoulder one last time. "I'm glad you made it back alive. I'm not sure what I would have done losing you...after Leon."

Fox gave a tight smile as the door clicked shut. He was alone once more, the silence of the home settling over him like a blanket, not comforting, but suffocating and heavy.

He didn't touch the food the kitchen maid finally brought him, falling asleep in his chair by the fire.

Two days later, he slipped from the house before his parents were awake, when the sun was still below the horizon. The day before, he'd made the mistake of coming down for breakfast only to spend the day listening to his mother's muffled sobs as she followed him around the house, refusing to let him out of her sight. He couldn't take another day of it, but he was no more ready to return to the barracks and his job with the king's men.

It was still early for the wealthy in the city, and the streets on this side of the inner gates were quiet. It was easy to make his way north, out of the royal quarter and into the outer city where the Dragonborn were already rushing around for the day.

He kept his cloak hood up and his hair tied back as he walked through the gates that separated the privileged from the poor. At one point, the small stone wall between the two sections hadn't existed. But as the resistance grew more and more bold, it was another measure to ensure the safety of those within the wall from those outside. But this early in the day, there were no questions for walking in and out, especially for a Dereyan.

The ring of storefronts and houses that bordered the royal quarter were clean and freshly painted. The windows had glass panes, unbroken. Gas lamps lined the streets, ensuring they never were truly dark, and the workers kept the streets swept of debris and human waste. But a few blocks farther, the gas lamps dwindled and then disappeared altogether.

He wasn't sure what his plan was as he carefully stepped around the feces that stained the roads here, and walked farther into the slums. He only knew he didn't want to be home. He wanted to be away from the royal quarter. It smelled, even this early in the day, the sun having baked the filth into the stones long ago. A few blocks from the gates, the polish of the buildings was gone and the poverty flourished.

Perhaps for the first time in over a decade, he actually looked at the city he lived in.

He looked through the windows, which had only a sheet of fabric protecting them from the cold and the wind. While the smell of roasted pork and chicken had drifted through the air on the other side of the gate, here there was nothing. No small booths selling treats. No breakfasts wafting from the houses, despite their exposed windows and doors.

"The Dragonborn are the first to starve and the first to die, yet we wonder why they hate us?"

He remembered his brother's words, hearing them now as if whispered in his ear, and it startled him to realize that it wasn't his brother's voice he heard, but Sofia's.

"Excuse me, but where is the nearest healer?" Fox asked a man leaning against the wall of an unmarked building. The man didn't even acknowledge his presence. With a heavy frown, he moved to the following block, asking the next person he saw, a woman with wide hips and a bright face. But the moment he spoke, her eyes clouded and the smile she'd been wearing disappeared.

He could hide his hair and skin beneath the cloak, but he couldn't hide his accent. Switching tactics, he moved on to asking the children that huddled in the shadows, carefully flashing a coin for only them to see as he asked. The first child he asked pointed him down a narrow street that dead-ended a few minutes later and he realized he'd been lied to. The next time he asked, he didn't hand the coin over until the small girl had walked him the two blocks to a small shop, an oil lamp burning in the windows where a woman was chopping away at a cutting board. He placed two coins in the child's grubby hands. He grimaced as she swallowed one before running off, the other tucked in her mouth. That was one way to hide your money.

Ten minutes later, he left the shop with a balm and two tinctures tucked away in his pockets. He'd been overcharged, but he laid down the coins without complaint, handing over two more before asking that she not remember his visit. The small tin of numbing powder he'd slipped from the healer's bag while he'd been treating Sofia would be gone by now. And he knew there were more interrogations to come. He'd ensured that with his advice to the chief commander.

By the time he made it back to the royal quarter, the sun had fully risen and the guards only stood by as people flowed in and out of the gates. Fox kept his hood up and his face down, not wanting to know if he'd become famous over the past few days since his miraculous return and promotion.

The prison was silent as he approached, a single guard stationed outside. The young soldier barely looked at Fox's face as he flashed his golden junior major badge and stepped around him. He could get used to the newfound respect this station held, even if he felt like a fraud having earned it.

Inside, the prison was quiet. Unnaturally so, given the hundred or more prisoners it held at any given time. But there were four floors, and each hallway was locked behind its own door, keeping everything separated and all the more quiet. The upper floors housed the minor criminals who would be released after a day or two, or at most a blink. The main floor was where the prisoners under active investigation were locked away, and the basement floor, where darkness was perpetual, was where the condemned waited for the next new moons.

Guards were stationed at the doorway to the resistance cells, but they didn't even blink as he passed them and opened the doors. He had been here yesterday, after all. The doors closed behind him with a click, the hall quiet except for the hum of the gas lamps that hung high above. They were never turned off, leaving the cells perpetually dimly lit. It was a torture in and of itself to never let the prisoners sleep properly. He knew the guards were ordered to walk along the hall every hour or two, waking up the prisoners who dared to fall asleep.

He moved quickly, ignoring the stares from the other prisoners he recognized. He saw the older man who had saved him from Sofia back in the cenote and the dark-haired woman who had helped capture him.

Sofia was at the end, lying on her stomach, slightly curled as best she could. Her hair was fanned out around her and for only a second, his fingers twitched to touch it.

"You," a voice said from the cell next to hers. "What are you doing back here?"

It was more accusation than question. Her red hair was barely visible under the grime and blood, and he combed through his memories for her name.

"Flor," he said after a beat.

She sneered and looked away.

"Ocon." He was immediately distracted by Sofia's voice.

His name—his *last* name—on her lips burned like acid against his skin. Especially when he could still see the dried blood staining her clothes and the bruise peeking out from the torn collar of her shirt. He knew worse scars lurked beneath and it made his empty stomach churn. But he couldn't throw up here or now.

"You should leave," she said, looking away from him.

"Not until you take these." He slipped a hand into his pocket and pulled out the vials and balm, passing them through the bars.

She didn't move and Flor hissed out another few words in dragon-tongue he refused to acknowledge.

"Take them." His voice was firm.

Sofia moved carefully to sit up and he watched, face blank, to stop himself from screaming. She reached out and carefully took the medicine from him, sniffing the balm first and then the vials before looking up at him once more.

He expected rage, hatred, or maybe some gratefulness, but instead all he saw was exhaustion.

"It won't fix anything, but it should lessen the pain." He spoke the words softly, but he knew Flor heard them from the snort that followed.

"Fixing her up so your father can tear her apart again tomorrow?"

"I'm trying to help."

"You can help by unlocking the doors," Flor growled back.

"Perfect," he said. "You look ready for a fight. I'm sure you'll make it out of the city before they kill all of you."

"Well, then. What's your plan?" she said.

"I don't have one yet!"

"You marked the cenote," Sofia's voice was soft, but both Fox and Flor stopped arguing immediately.

Fox turned back to her, his stomach twisted. He needed to meet her eyes in this moment, even if he hated everything he saw there—raw pain, betrayal, anger, and acceptance.

"When I first escaped—before everything. I..." He stopped. He didn't have an excuse. There was none.

"Do you regret it? I heard you got promoted for your work." Her face was carefully blank now, too.

Fox didn't let his gaze falter. "I regret a lot of who I've been and what I've done these past few cycles."

"Why should we trust you?"

The question was so genuine, he didn't hesitate. "I joined the military to follow in my brother's footsteps and avenge him. He'd hate who I've become."

Sofia nodded, not taking her eyes off of him as she reached for the small tincture he'd brought her and took a sip from it. His shoulders slumped in something akin to relief.

"We have a plan," Sofia said.

"That he doesn't need to know," Flor muttered before snapping her mouth shut again.

"We've spoken—" Sofia started.

"Don't—"

Sofia glared at Flor before continuing. "We've spoken with one of our spies. We got a message out to whatever allies we have left, and Vato thinks they can get us out of the cells, but you're right. We're in no condition to fight our way out even with a handful of allies. We need a distraction."

"Who's Vato?"

Sofia bit her lips and Flor scowled. "I can't tell you."

Fox nodded, taking no offense at the distrust. "What kind of distraction?"

"You want to prove we can trust you?"

"Yes," he said, in half-prayer.

"I was thinking maybe a dragon."

Fox stared at her blankly, unable to do more than open and close his mouth.

"I saw you steal my bag back in the cenote. Do you still have it?"

"Yes—I needed to hide the feather—"

"Exactly."

"Absolutely not," he said, before his brain could even process what she was asking.

"Why not?"

"Because I'm not Dragonborn!"

Sofia closed the distance between them, the bars the only thing separating them as she wrapped a hand around his own as it clung to the cold metal.

"Remember what I said back in the rainforest? There is no difference between us. We all come from this land. They'll listen if you pray."

"I don't know how to pray! I saw the prayer once—in dragon-tongue."

"Fox, please. I can teach you. Just let—"

A sound from the door had Fox reeling, wrenching his hand from Sofia's as his father stormed through the doors. Two soldiers dragged a body behind him, blood painting his father's face and clothes. Fox guessed his interrogation hadn't gone well from the scowl on his face.

"Fox," he snapped, not bothering to watch his soldiers throw the woman they'd been dragging back into her cell. "What are you doing here?"

"The chief commander had some follow-up questions for this one after his interrogation, sir."

It was a dangerous strategy to drop the chief commander's name; his father always hated the relationship between Fox and him—confused as to why the chief commander cared about Fox. Sometimes Fox wondered the same thing. The tick in his father's jaw told him he was holding back his true thoughts on the matter. He eventually nodded, turning to where Flor sat.

"We'll take this one next," he said.

Sofia practically lunged at the bars, but she could do nothing as the soldiers opened the cell next to hers and yanked Flor out, hissing and scratching. Fox walked away before his face gave him away, but not before he sent a silent prayer to the first king—or to the dragons or whoever was listening that Flor gave his father hell.

CHAPTER FORTY-TWO

FOX

He felt half a thief as he snuck back into the house through the back door, not wanting to face Mother. At least he knew his father would be busy with the interrogations—the torture sessions—for the rest of the day.

He threw himself down onto his bed, fully clothed and smelling of slums and the prison, but he didn't have the energy to care. His mind was racing with what Sofia had asked of him—to pray to the dragons. She said she could teach him, but they hadn't gotten that far in their conversation. What if he was unteachable? He didn't know where to start other than some muttered dragon-tongue words and slicing open his skin. He doubted the dragons would even listen to him.

But he did still have the feather. It was tucked away in his closet behind the loose wall panel he'd used to hide his books growing up.

Fox's stomach lurched and he jumped out of the bed, unsteady on his feet from the sudden rush. Once he'd regained his balance, he strode to his closet. He grabbed a small candle off the side table, lighting it before he quietly slipped into the small room and closed the door behind himself. There were no lamps inside and the candle sent shadows stretching and swaying along the walls, demented bodies

created by his clothes. He ignored them, setting down the candle and prying open the wooden panel.

He removed the bag first, the feather tucked inside. He hadn't returned the pack like he had promised himself, unable to part with it, and no one had even bothered to ask after it. He set the bag aside and then reached back into the space behind the wall. Two small paperbacks came out first—romances he'd stolen from his father's office after he'd almost been caught reading them. One still had tea stains splattered across it. They weren't what he was looking for, though.

When he reached in again, he had to twist his arm, hand patting around in the dark blindly before his fingers grazed the cool leather of a spine. He pressed himself harder against the wall, changing the angle just enough that he got a grasp on the book and pulled. A web and a few dead spiders came out with it, but he brushed them aside with only a small grimace.

His hand wiped away the layer of dirt and dust that had settled onto the cover. He could make out the faint splotches of blood staining the cover, but the gold lettering of the title was all but gone. The cover creaked as he opened it to the cover page and he read the words he hadn't thought about in cycles: *In Praise of Dragons and Monsters: A Compendium of Dragonborn Mythology and Worship.*

The book had spent ten cycles tucked away in the wall, waiting for him to remember he'd stuffed it there.

He didn't need Sofia to teach him the Dragonborn prayer. He had it here sitting in his hands.

Fox stared down at the title page of the book, not ready to flip through it, though he knew tucked inside were the words to the traditional dragon's prayer. This little leather-bound book had been the reason for his brother's death—or at least that's what he'd believed for a while. He remembered that sun cycle, sitting with the guilt and the anguish—the reality that his foolishness had gotten his brother killed. It had taken that long for him to recognize that his brother's death had never been his fault or even a stupid book's fault. They should have been safe in the small fortress built into the wall of Suvi. His brother should have been safe working for the king's men in a time of peace.

It was the resistance that had taken that away from them. It was the resistance that had killed his brother. And for what? A freedom they still didn't have? For a revenge that had just circled back around over and over again?

Sofia had lost people. Did it make it fair or right that she, in turn, killed?

Did it make it fair that Fox killed, too?

A muffled knock shook him from his thoughts and he was all too glad for the excuse to tuck the books and pack back behind his closet.

"Give me a second, I'm dressing!" he called, quickly wrapping a robe around his clothes before hurrying out to open his door.

His mother was standing on the other side wringing her hands, looking as if she half-expected Fox not to answer—as if she were still trying to convince herself his return hadn't been a hallucination.

"Mom," he said, reaching out a hand to squeeze her forearm, for reassurance.

"I hadn't seen you yet today. I thought you might have returned to the barracks," she said, eyes drinking him in like someone starved of water.

"I'm on leave for two more days," he said. "Give me a minute to dress properly and we can take tea together downstairs."

She nodded and moved as if to turn before changing her mind. She pulled him in and pressed a kiss to his forehead, her hands clinging to him harder than they needed to before she let go and left.

He slumped against his door as he closed it, hating himself for so easily being swept up in his mother's grief once more. She'd never quite been the same since Leon's death. Most days, her small fits of crying or silence were easy to ignore, but Fox's disappearance had brought all her pain and grief to the surface and it bled from her every pore. The air around her was saturated with it. But Fox couldn't turn away from her.

He took a deep breath, changing into his house clothes before heading downstairs, locking away all the questions of what was to come behind his bedroom door.

Fox spent the rest of the day with Mother. They took their tea and then he watched as she stitched. He could have been doing something useful —going through logs or reading one the strategy books the chief commander had gifted him. Instead, he sat watching her work. There was a brightness in her movements now that he was beside her and he enjoyed the sense of his existence meaning so much to someone.

He didn't even realize night had fallen until he heard the front door slam open and the stumbling, stomping footsteps of his father coming through the main hall to the sitting room where they were enjoying their silence.

"Did either of you think to call for dinner?" he asked before he'd even slipped through the doorway.

It didn't take the slurred words for Fox to realize his father was three drinks past drunk. Whatever foul mood he'd been in earlier in the prison had only soured further and his bloodshot eyes searched over Fox and Mother. He was looking for a fight.

"Father," Fox said, voice a low drawl. "We can call for dinner now. Perhaps you can have some black tea while you wait. I can bring it to your study."

His father's icy blue eyes swiveled to meet his, the sneer crooked and wavering. "You," he spit.

"Mother, why don't you go call for dinner?" Fox said, not taking his eyes from his father.

She stood silently, slipping out the back door into the servants' hall, leaving Fox alone with his father.

"Is there something you'd like to say, Father?" he said, standing. He wasn't sure why he'd never noticed that he was taller than him. When had that happened? He used his size, striding forward with his head held high.

Something akin to surprise flickered through his father's face, unused to being confronted. There was something freeing in the realization that he'd never make his father proud. He didn't need to.

"You think you're so special because the chief commander likes you?" he said, swaying as he stepped forward, meeting Fox's own glare.

"You are nothing. You've always been nothing. A pale imitation of your brother."

"Jealous of me, Father? How childish."

"I'm still your superior even if you've sucked the chief commander's cock enough times to convince him to promote you."

The words were foul and Fox didn't think before he reacted, slapping his father across the face.

The world froze as both of them stared at Fox's hand. His father's cheek went pink. In all their cycles of fighting, he'd never hit back. Never.

His father swung his fist, aiming for Fox's face, but his reactions were sluggish and weak and Fox sidestepped out of the way easily. He wasn't expecting his father's other hand coming up to snatch at his hair where it hung loose around his shoulders. The sharp tug at his roots had him hissing and his father brought his head back, twisting his neck. The stitches along Fox's side pulled tight.

"Don't you dare raise a hand to me again. I don't know what happened to you out there with those dragon-filth traitors whispering in your ear, but you've changed. I will find out the truth, and if you've stepped one toe out of line, I'll send you to the execution block myself."

He let go, storming from the room before Fox could respond, leaving him standing in the sitting room, breathing heavily and trying not to scream. He didn't know if Mother had actually gone to request dinner be served, but he didn't care. Not bothering to change into a different set of clothes, he grabbed his cloak and exited through the front door.

Fox didn't return until many hours later when he'd had enough alcohol of his own to wash out the feeling of his father's fingers in his hair.

CHAPTER FORTY-THREE
SOFIA

Sofia spent the next few days after Fox had delivered the salve forcing it on the others as they each returned from their interrogations. Her entire body ached, the medicines Fox had brought doing just enough to take the edge off the pain. But she'd survived worse, and she'd survive this, if only to kill the general and chief commander slowly and painfully.

Sofia hadn't been taken back in for questioning, but every other Dragonborn had. And General Ocon made sure she saw them as they returned, bloody and broken. Each time, he'd sneer down at her, reminding her that this was her fault for not giving him the information he wanted. She could stop it all.

Fox hadn't appeared again, and she tried her hardest not to think too much of his absence. She couldn't even tell if it was disappointment or relief she felt every day she went without seeing him. If she was being honest, she didn't know if she trusted him. He'd seemed in earnest when he'd come with the medicine, but going against orders to give her the pain tincture was much different from committing treason against the king gods. Either way, he hadn't come back to ask about the prayer, and all she could do was wait. That thought alone was enough to make her mind scream in the middle of the night as she woke from nightmares.

On the worst nights, she dreamed of waking up in the cells, everyone around her dead. Flor's hair would be splayed out, matching the blood trickling from her head. Micael would be crumpled on the ground, an old man instead of the fighter she knew him to be. It was always just her left alive to sit, steeped in blood and death.

She was pulling herself from such a nightmare when she heard the distinct clatter of steps and chains that announced the soldiers were back from their latest interrogation. Sofia didn't understand what the general expected after a week of interrogations. No one had given them anything. Most of the supposed resistance fighters who joined them in the cells were nothing more than families caught with too much meat or an altar in their house. But what did that matter? This was all an excuse to pare down the number of Dragonborn in the slums.

As Micael was haphazardly thrown back into his cell, Sofia noticed the trail of blood he'd left behind in his wake. A deep cut crossed his face, nearly bisecting his eye. He'd be lucky to not lose it.

Bile rose in Sofia's throat and she didn't bother swallowing it back down.

"Fucking king's spawn." She spit the words at the general who was speaking with his men.

She nearly jumped when one of the soldiers turned, his familiar face jarring. He stepped toward her, fist raised as if to hit her through the bars, but his comrade stopped him with a hand to his shoulder. Yet, as the others filtered out, he stayed behind, waiting until he was alone to turn fully to Sofia again.

"Vato," she said, voice soft as a whisper. Happy to see the man again after three days of nothing.

He didn't smile, face tight with contrition. "The messages were sent out. I have a few direct allies in the city and a few connections across the wall, but we'll see who can rally and make it. I gave them until the new moons, but I don't know if it will be enough time."

He spoke the words softly, eyes focused on the door the other soldier had just passed through.

"Any news on your distraction?" he asked.

Sofia answered before anyone else could, "No, but I...I think there is still hope he'll follow through."

The young man's bright green eyes flickered to her briefly and narrowed. "You want to tell me who it is you're trusting?"

She bit her lip. They'd been through this already when Vato had first found them in the cells, but she wasn't ready to give Fox's name up. Whether it was to protect him or protect herself when his loyalty inevitably fell through, she wasn't sure. He definitely didn't know that her planned distraction was a dragon.

"Scales, you're a stubborn one," he said when it was clear she wouldn't answer. "No wonder—" he stopped himself with the shake of his head and looked away.

"What's the plan if we don't get all of our allies rallied in time?" he asked.

"Then I murder as many Dereyans as I can on my way out of here until I'm across the wall or dead."

Vato's eyebrows rose only slightly, ever the good soldier trained to hide his emotions.

Flor gave a small huff from the cell beside her. "Let's hope that doesn't happen," she said. "But either way, if you can smuggle us weapons, we'll have more of a fighting chance of breaking out."

"I can get as many weapons to you as possible," Vato said, addressing Flor. "Inventory is taken weekly, so we'd have a maximum seven days to collect enough for everyone."

"Do it." Micael's voice was strong, despite how he leaned against the wall, still bleeding from his interrogation. "Sofia's right; we either die on our knees or we die fighting. I'd rather die fighting."

"I'd rather escape and live," Flor said, voice falsely bright. "Just as a heads up. So if we could focus on that plan first."

Vato's lips gave the smallest hint of a smile at this. "Very well. I'll start smuggling you weapons after the next inventory count. Until then, stay alive."

After he left, Micael and the others started whispering plans back and forth—paths out of the city, strategies for fighting without armor.

Sofia half-listened, her mind still caught between planning their breakout and praying that Fox followed through.

What did it mean after everything that she was still hoping he could help them? His father was the reason her back was a twisted knot of scars and scabs. *He* was the reason Javi's blood-mother was dead and all of them were thrown in prison. He'd told her himself that he still wanted revenge for the murder of his brother. He'd watched her as she was tortured.

Still, he'd been the one to offer help. He'd been the one to say he was wrong and wanted to make things right. She wanted to trust him, even if only because she still remembered the feeling of his fingers in her hair and his lips on her skin.

Sofia pressed the palm of her hands into her eyes until she saw stars, pushing the thoughts from her mind. And then she turned back to the others, ready to make plans. She'd told herself the chief commander would never make her feel helpless again, and as she looked across the barred cells at the friends and allies she had, she knew she wasn't. Because no matter if Fox came through or not, Sofia wasn't alone.

CHAPTER FORTY-FOUR

FOX

The day after the fight with his father, Fox woke up hungover and exhausted. He didn't pull out the Dragonborn book. Not yet. He told himself he'd say the prayer the next day. Five days later, he still hadn't. He didn't want to believe it had anything to do with his father's accusations of him being a traitor. His father didn't have that influence over him anymore. He'd simply been busy.

Fox knew he was only fooling himself.

He'd moved back into the barracks the day after his hangover, suddenly happy to get back to his job if it meant getting away from his father's looks of disgust. The job itself left him exhausted. Every night after dinner, he flung himself across the bed in his new private room without even changing. He was in charge of two of the dozens of raiding parties that were sweeping through the city, hunting down the last remnants of the resistance.

He knew, deep down, where the information for their raids was coming from. Whether it was from Sofia's bleeding lips or one of her friends, he didn't know, but he knew the information was being paid for in Dragonborn blood. He tried to ignore this fact as they stormed homes and dragged out parents and children, tearing down walls in search of hidden rooms and resistance paraphernalia.

And for small incremental moments, he could pretend that he was the person he was last cycle. Last blink. When things were simple and he didn't see Sofia's face in every Dragonborn he dragged to prison. The mother of three who had her moss green eyes. The single man who had her freckles. The small child born into the wrong family who had her same heart-shaped face and curly hair as he was dragged away with the rest of his family for the hunting bow behind the icebox and the illegal meat inside.

The children still looked too skinny, even with the stolen rations.

Trying not to think too hard, he left his shift that day and went straight to the prison, handing the guards his own dinner rations and asking them to give it to the three children and their parents. The older solider blinked at the request, but didn't question it and Fox walked away before he could second-guess his own command.

He returned to his parents' home, walking in without knocking and gave a brief hug to his mother, telling her he wanted to spend one last night on his good mattress before returning to work full-time. She didn't question him, sending him off with a soft kiss on his forehead.

His father wasn't home, but he still crept through the house as quietly as he could, closing the bedroom door softly behind him. He collected a few items before ducking into the large walk-in closet. The room went black for a second before the spark of the match flared and he lit the candle in his hand.

His mind was blank as he went about making his impromptu altar to the gods he had never believed in. But something in him had broken that afternoon. He didn't have it in him to go to sleep that night without finally following through on his promise to Sofia, even with alcohol buzzing in his blood and softening his thoughts. He had to do this.

He didn't have the ceremonial dish or dagger, but he set a small copper bowl he'd stolen from the kitchens on the ground next to the candle. He pulled the feather out from behind the panel along with the book, only briefly noting he'd put the panel on crooked in his rush to greet his mother before. It had been a stupid move that he couldn't make again.

He should burn the book anyway. After all these cycles, it would go from a souvenir of grief and guilt to proof that he was a traitor. He shook off his thoughts and flipped through the pages until he found what he needed.

The text was faded, old ink on older parchment. But it was clear enough. He couldn't read Dragonborn very well, but the words were familiar from hearing the child in the cenote speak them, and it only took a few times reciting them before he was confident he was saying at least a semblance of the prayer. He didn't understand the words and he hoped that didn't matter.

He set it all up neatly before unsheathing his dagger and placing the blade against his hand. It was only then that he stopped, suddenly conscious of what he was about to do and what it *meant*. And in all the irony possible, he sent up a prayer to the old kings asking for forgiveness.

He hissed as the dagger bit into the soft flesh between his finger and thumb and blood welled immediately. The candle flickered as he rushed to move his hand over the bowl and let the blood drip. And then he prayed. If one could consider chanting the words in a language he didn't know a prayer. The air seemed to press in around him as he tried to infuse the words with all the piety he'd never even felt for the kings.

One moment he had his eyes closed and the next his arm was being wrenched back, the dagger clattering to the floor as his wrist was twisted. His eyes flashed open. The candle had been knocked over, the flame sputtered out, but the closet was lit from the gas lamps of his room.

"It was only a matter of time before you gave yourself away." His father's voice burned with victory as someone pulled Fox from his closet.

He bucked, trying to throw the man off of him, but he only managed to get in a sharp elbow before someone punched him hard across the face. His teeth rattled and a sharp snap ran up his nose as blood streamed down his face. The guard behind him cuffed him quickly as the other went into the closet and pulled out the dragon's feather and book, handing them to his father who stood nearby, smiling.

He hadn't heard them come in, but his bedroom door was wide

open. He was only thankful that the hallway was empty, his mother hopefully oblivious to what was happening.

His father tucked the feather into the book before he stepped up to Fox, his smile wide.

"The possession of this book and feather alone would have been enough to arrest you, but I can't wait to see the chief commander's face when I tell him you were using them for some heathen ritual." He leaned down, breath hot against Fox's face as he whispered for only him to hear. "Congratulations for proving me wrong for once. You're not just worthless. You're treasonous filth."

Fox spit into his father's face, satisfied when he reared back.

"I can't wait to watch the life drain from your eyes when I finally get my chance to kill you, Father," Fox said, venom in every word.

"You're no son of mine. And I'll kill you long before you get the chance to raise a sword against me."

Fox lunged forward, but the man restraining him held tight and he let out a growl of frustration, teeth gnashing.

"An animal just like the rest of your dragon-filth allies," his father said before he turned and motioned for the rest of the soldiers. "Let's go."

They dragged him out through the servants' staircase, as if even his father didn't want to face his wife's reaction.

The night was dark, the blinking moons now crescents and the stars providing little in terms of light, but the gas lamps cast a warm glow across the street as they made their procession. Fox's stomach gave a lurch of shame when he saw Ian coming up the street, his strides toward the manor faltering as they came into view under one of the lights.

"What's going on? General?" he said, eyes sliding over Fox to the general.

"We have a traitor in our midst, it seems."

"Sir?" Ian's eyes flickered back to Fox, wide and unblinking.

"Tell the chief commander his presence is required at the prison. I'm over playing nice with these beasts."

With that, his father continued their procession, leaving Ian blinking back at them for only a moment before he turned and ran for the chief commander's house. Fox didn't bother turning his head as he emptied his stomach onto the boots of the soldiers dragging him.

CHAPTER FORTY-FIVE
SOFIA

When Fox walked through the door to their prison hallway, Sofia thought the moment had come. He returned to ask about the prayer.

But Fox wasn't alone. He was being dragged by two soldiers in full regalia, his face smeared with blood and his wrists in chains. Sofia's stomach dropped, and she heard Flor let out a series of curses beside her as the general filed in behind them looking smug, as if arresting his son was his greatest triumph as a soldier.

They moved down the hall until they were directly in front of Sofia's cell, the general piercing her with his gaze. She returned the glare with all the malice she could muster, refusing to back down despite the hammering of her heart.

"Arresting your son now? That's a new low even for you," she said, barely running her eyes over at Fox. A million things could have gone wrong. Either that or this was a trick. She needed to know.

He ignored her, turning to his men. "Throw him in with his whore."

Sofia didn't think, spitting out the bile that had been rising in her throat at the feet of the men.

One of the soldiers threw open the bars, grabbing her by the hair and tossing her back as the other shoved Fox in. His knees cracked on the stone floor as he fell and Sofia scrambled up, ready to claw at the soldiers even as they retreated behind the closed cell door.

"What are you playing at?" she said, snarling. "I don't want this Dereyan scum in here with me."

A moment later, the general pulled a feather and a book from beneath his jacket, dropping them on the ground in front of her cell. The cover was faded and stained, impossible to read, but the feather said enough.

Sofia had placed her trust in the right person, after all. And yet everything she'd worked for had still imploded.

"I found my son performing some heathen ritual against the king and true god with this *thing*," the general said. "The chief commander is already on his way to decide the next steps." He stepped forward, leaning just far enough away she wouldn't be able to strangle him through the bars. "It's obvious you aren't giving up the information we need. Time to make an example of what happens when you work against the king."

"You can kill each and every one of us and it still won't stop the resistance," Sofia said. "The Dragonborn will keep fighting as long as even just one of us breathes."

"Perhaps we'll need to fix that," he sneered.

Sofia couldn't stop the laugh that slipped out. "If you kill the Dragonborn, who will clean your homes and serve your tea? Who will work the farms to feed you? You would all die without us."

"You're right," he said, smiling in a way that sent ice down her spine. "Your worth is in your servitude. Our mistake has been ever treating your *people* as people. Why confuse the donkey by allowing it to think?"

Sofia lunged at him, knowing there was nothing she could do locked in her cell, but unable to control the urge to wrap her hands around the man's throat. He only stepped back, laughing as she slammed into the bars.

"Face me like a man," she sneered.

"I don't fight livestock," he said.

Sofia was still pressed against the bars, seething but helpless, as the doors of the hallway opened and the sound of footsteps approached. The echoes beat through her body in time with her heart, sticking in her chest as she tried to breathe and ready herself to face *him* again. She needed a plan, but she couldn't think through her rage.

The general turned first and her own gaze followed, a new emotion thrilling through her body as she saw Vato walking down the hall, two soldiers behind him that she didn't recognize.

"Where's the chief commander?" the general barked.

"There's been a change of plans, *sir*." Vato stepped forward, his eyes focused only on the general.

"Excuse me?" The general's jaw twitched, the confusion in his face satisfying to see.

"Ian?" Fox said, pressing up against the bars next to Sofia.

"My friends and I are going to leave now, I think." Vato cracked his fist across the general's face.

CHAPTER FORTY-SIX

FOX

Fox's father was a big man, never relenting on his training even after two decades out of the field. But he also wasn't expecting to be sucker-punched by his inferior. In the same moment the general stumbled back, his hand touching his bleeding lip in surprise, Ian tossed a set of keys from his pocket into Sofia's outstretched hand.

Chaos erupted.

As soon as Sofia opened their cell door, she ran to the others, unlocking them with practiced fingers as she dodged the fists and weapons amid the fighting.

Fox watched for only a minute, trying to understand what he was seeing, but a yell from Ian drew his attention and then the hilt of a sword was being thrust into his hands. He was tired, his nose likely broken, and he had no idea what was happening, but it didn't matter. Taking a deep breath, he shoved his way into the melee, lashing out toward his father.

His sword made contact with his father's own, rattling up through his arms. He was still weak from weeks of near starvation, but his anger seemed to count for something.

"Traitorous scum," his father hissed as their blades met again and again. "Your brother would be disgusted by what you've become."

"You never truly knew Leon," he said, feinting to the side before swinging at his father's leg. He didn't know how true the words were until he'd said them out loud. Yes, his brother was always questioning the treatment of the Dragonborn, but Fox was starting to suspect it was more than that. He cared. He would have been on Fox's side—on Ian's side.

It was this thought of Ian that had him stumbling, his father's blade cutting into his arm before he could dodge to the side. Ian was fighting for the Dragonborn. He'd come to save Fox, but it wasn't just that. He'd looked at Sofia like he knew her. She'd known him. *Vato*.

Fox hissed out a painful breath.

"You never stood a chance against me," he said with a sneer as Fox stumbled back.

"Fuck you, Father," he said, even as his father's sword swung down toward him. He already knew his own parry was going to be too slow. Too late.

His father's sword went flying as a blur of black and brown attacked him from the side. Sofia was latched around his waist, hands flailing as she scratched and raked at him, weaponless though she was. She drew blood, hissing and howling like an animal, and Fox could only watch with wide eyes. It took a minute, but his father threw her off, her body crashing into the bars of the nearest cell.

But even as his father straightened himself and looked around, Fox smiled.

It didn't matter; his father had lost. Every cell was open, half the Dragonborn already holding weapons. The two soldiers who had been with his father were bleeding out on the ground.

His father was outnumbered. With a growl, he swung his blade one more time, nearly taking Sofia out at the knees as Fox pulled her back. And then his father ran. Like the rat he was, scurrying away down the hall and leaving them to their small victory.

A few Dragonborn cheered, but Fox ignored them. This was only the beginning of the fight.

"Are you okay?" he asked Sofia, hands searching her body for wounds. Blood was smeared across her face, but he couldn't find any cuts.

"It's not mine," she said, grin feral.

"We need to go after him," Ian said, coming up behind Fox and looking at where his father had disappeared around the corner. "If he gets back up or tells the chief commander…"

"Got it," Fox said. All too ready to finish this, he grabbed the sword and turned back to Sofia, mouth going dry as he looked at her. "Get the hell out of here. Get them all out of here."

He didn't move for a second, his body fighting with his brain. His hand was held in midair, halfway to reaching for her, fingers twitching. He wanted to grab her. He wanted to kiss her. He needed to go.

Body finally coming under his command, he turned and ran, following the sound of his father's footsteps. He forced himself to not look back.

CHAPTER FORTY-SEVEN
SOFIA

Sofia watched Fox go, her chest tight and her throat dry. When she finally turned, she saw Vato staring at her, a small smirk dancing on his lips. She ignored it.

"We need to get everyone out of here. Do we have any allies coming?"

The man's smirk fell, face growing serious. "I sent out a message before I came here, but I have no idea who's in town to receive it. We were hoping for backup from beyond the wall, but I doubt we can rely on that now."

"Is there a way out of here that doesn't require us waltzing out the front doors?"

"The only other passage out leads directly to the chief commander's house. I don't think we want to go there either."

"So we're out of our cells and trapped in the prison," she said, trying to keep her voice low. It wasn't a secret, but no one needed a reminder of how screwed they still were.

Sofia turned, surveying the crowd. There were over two dozen of them, but half were actively injured and the other half were civilians picked up under false pretenses. There were even a few young children no older than ten clinging to their parents' legs. Ian and his friends had brought weapons, but they had a shortage of people well enough to fight.

Then again—they didn't have a choice. She automatically sought out Micael, assuming he'd want to take control. But he leaned heavily against Luis. He was looking at her though and he gave a small nod of his head.

"Sofia's right; we either die on our knees or we die fighting."

She hadn't been sure she'd heard his words the other day correctly.

Something between pride and horror shuddered through her. But she shut those emotions down. She'd face them tomorrow. She turned back to the group.

"Everyone well enough to fight," she said, "move to the left, everyone else over here. But take a weapon, whether or not you can use it. It's best to appear like a threat even if you can't be one. Vato— you lead the group. We can at least throw off the guards and catch them on their back feet if they aren't expecting an ambush from within."

"No one should be expecting us," Vato said. "As long as Fox catches up with the general and—"

He hesitated and perhaps for the first time, they both realized the implications of what they were depending on. Fox catching up with his father. Fox willing to kill his father or at least incapacitate him. Fox able to win the fight.

She looked back at the way they had run, farther into the prison. "And what's that way?"

"I think there is a tunnel that connects the prison to the chief commander's house," Vato said. "I can only assume the general headed that way."

Before she could respond or even think of what she wanted— needed—to do, the ground shuddered and a crack sounded from some- where not too distant.

"Shit," Flor said as she stumbled. "Is that the king's men?"

Vato didn't answer for a moment, face looking through one of the high windows at the dark night beyond. And then the sky lit up with red and the earth shuddered again.

"I don't think that's the king's men," he said, smiling. "I think that's our backup."

Their allies had come. Sofia didn't know how many or what chance they even had at making a difference. But they were no longer alone.

"Vato—"

He cut her off before she finished, placing a hand on her shoulder. "I can lead them out to the rendezvous. We'll have allies waiting there. Go. He might need your help killing the old man, and at least one of us will have the pleasure of watching that bastard die. We'll be at the inn if you make it back to us."

"If," she said, a small smile on her lips. They both knew the odds of her making it to the rendezvous alive and in time to escape with all of them.

Vato pressed his lips together, clearly regretting the admission.

"Javi's sister, Dia," Sofia said, "she was in the prison before any of us. Can you get her out, too?"

Vato's brows pinched together and he bit his lip. "She disappeared from the records last week while you were gone. I assumed she—I don't think she's still alive."

A part of Sofia had known. Dia would have been thrown in with the rest of them if she'd been alive. But her chest ached with the realization that after everything—she'd been too late to stop the girl's death.

The hot tears that burned her eyes didn't fall, and she covered his hand with her own squeezing it lightly. "Get the rest of them out for me. No matter what."

He nodded and turned, rallying their bedraggled group of prisoners-turned-warriors. Before Sofia ran off, Flor pushed forward, wrapping her in a tight hug.

"If you die, I'll journey to the Depths and kill you again myself."

Sofia tightened their hug, pressing her face into Flor's shoulder for a moment, smelling the musk of her beneath the reek of prison.

"I love you, too," she said when she was sure her voice wouldn't crack.

"May the dragons be with you," Flor said, pushing Sofia away, as if needing to force herself to let go. Sofia clenched her jaw, giving Flor once last glance before she turned and ran.

CHAPTER FORTY-EIGHT
FOX

Fox followed his father's path. He knew where he'd be going—the tunnel that cut directly from the prison to the chief commander's basement. It was narrow and dark, but it was the most direct route to the chief commander's home. So Fox ran, ignoring the looks of the other guards and prisoners as he passed. No one stopped him, word of his betrayal still held secret with his father. But it wouldn't last for long.

Just as he was turning the corner to begin the descent down to the tunnel, the ground shook beneath his feet. He paused, ears straining. There was some yelling and then he heard another explosion, echoing in the night outside the prison. Help had come for the resistance. He smiled.

But it didn't change his mission. His father couldn't get away.

Fox knew when he came to the passage and heard only the faintest whisper of steps ahead of him that his father had slowed down. He hadn't had his cane with him and his old injury was probably flaring up. Fox kept running, thankful for his time trudging through the forest. He was confident in the dark, not worried about his feet stumbling over the uneven stones beneath him. He'd run through worse.

Even in the darkness with the sound of his footsteps echoing in his own ears, he could tell he was catching up. Just another minute. He pulled his sword as he burst through the door at the end of the hall. The light of a line of torches blinded him. He skidded to a halt, blinking against the brightness and trying to understand which way his father had gone.

Before he could regain his sight, the whistle of wind against his right side told him exactly where his father was.

He swallowed back a scream as his body jerked and he fell, something cold and iron cracking against his shoulder. He rolled to the side in time for the iron to crash down onto the stone where he'd just been. He scrambled, pushing against the nearby wall and using it to pull himself up even as his body protested. He held his blade in front of him, despite the quaver in his arms. His father held the branding iron from the chief commander's personal interrogation room, wielding it like a sword.

As his father lunged forward, Fox's arm swung of its own accord, his blade stopping the rod mid-swing. He used the wall behind him, leveraging himself forward to push his father back a few steps.

Fox smiled as his father stumbled back. He was weaker than Fox remembered—his swings slower.

"You won't win, Father," he said, savoring the flash of anger in his father's eyes.

"You've never won a fight against me," his father hissed. "The chief commander can give you as many polished badges as he wants, but you've always been useless."

He lunged forward and Fox parried, but the action sent him sideways and away from the wall. Their feet moved in a familiar dance. It had been cycles since he'd dueled his father, cycles since his father had made him bleed. But the last time they'd fought, Fox hadn't been trained. He hadn't spent the past cycles in the military becoming the best soldier he could be.

"You doubt the chief commander's choices? How brazen can you be, *General*." Fox spit the words out like a curse. "Perhaps that's why the chief commander has always refused to retire or name you as his successor."

"This has nothing to do with that," his father snapped.

"But it does. Doesn't it? It always has. You can't get over the fact that he would rather wait for me to climb the ranks than give you the position." Fox was nearly laughing at the realization, the truth painted across his father's face. "You truly are envious of his attention."

He didn't wait for his father to process his anger. He slashed forward with his sword.

His father brought the branding iron up just in time to stop the blade from lashing across his neck, but the tip still nicked him across the shoulder, drawing blood.

His father sneered. "You'd kill your own father? And for what? Dragon-filth? Did she sleep with you? Perhaps she truly is your whore."

"I just enjoy the idea of killing you." Fox was surprised by the truth behind the words. It was a relief to say them out loud.

His father's mouth curled in a sneer.

Fox's smile stretched as his father and he danced in sync with blows and parries, too many cycles spent training in the same army, trained by the same men, but he could see the sweat along his father's brow and the hair falling from where it was perfectly tied up in a ribbon. This match would be won through endurance.

"You wanted me to be stronger, colder, crueler," he said, emphasizing each word with a strike. "Don't regret what you spent cycles beating into me now."

"I never beat you. I trained you. I did the best I could with what I was given," he said, lashing out with the branding iron hard enough to knock Fox's blade back.

"I learned more from my time in the military than you ever taught me."

His father sneered. "And that's the problem." With a feint and a jab, the iron hit hard into Fox's ribs, the air stuttering out of his lungs. Before he could catch his breath, another hit cracked across his right hand, sending his blade clattering to the floor.

"You never learned anything from me."

His father picked up his blade as Fox held his throbbing hand. He could already feel it swelling and knew at least one bone was broken.

"You should have been the one to die," his father said, blade raised, pointed at Fox. "I will always hate Leon a little bit for saving your pathetic life."

Fox tasted blood, teeth gnashing into his tongue as he stared up at his father. After all of the work he'd done, he was still not strong enough to beat him.

"You disgust me." His father flicked his wrist, the blade slashing lightly across his cheek, drawing out a line of blood. "I should arrest you and let you be killed with the rest of your traitor friends, but I don't think I will. I want to be the one to end your pathetic excuse for a life."

A flash of movement behind his father caught Fox's eyes. Sofia ran toward them a few yards away through the open door to the tunnel. Her eyes were wide as she took in the scene—him crouching weaponless at his father's feet. In that moment, Fox wasn't just angry for himself and everything his father had taken from him. He was angry for everything Sofia had lost by his father's hand. He was angry for every Dragonborn and Dereyan alike that had been left helpless at the hands of a man who cared only for himself and his own pride.

His eyes move back to his father. He'd seen Sofia, too.

"Your bitch has come to watch you die."

But Fox wasn't going to die. Not at the feet of a man as weak as his father.

"No, she didn't." He kicked out, the sole of his boot connecting with his father's bad knee. It was a dirty move—one his father would have berated him for. And one Sofia would be proud of. His father crumpled, lashing out with his blade even as his legs gave out, but Fox had already rolled to the side. Fox used the moment to bring his foot down on his father's arm, grabbing the sword as it fell to the ground. His father rushed to grab the branding iron, bringing it across him as a shield, but Fox only sneered above him.

"You think your cruelty and hate make you strong, but that's never been true strength."

He kicked his father, sending him sprawling on his back with a grunt.

"And there *was* something you taught me. Never hesitate," he said, sneering down at the man he'd tried so many cycles chasing after as if his pride meant anything. And then Fox moved. His sweeps anything but hesitant. There was no regret left. No fear. No guilt.

When his last hit had the branding iron spinning out of his father's hands, he didn't wait. He slid the blade hard and deep into his father's chest, beneath the ribs and up like his superiors had taught him.

When he made the deadly strike, it wasn't pride in his father's eyes. Only disgust. It only would have ever been disgust. He could never be Leon. But it didn't make Fox weak. This pathetic old man on the ground in front of him didn't get to determine what made him strong. Not anymore.

"Goodbye, Father."

CHAPTER FORTY-NINE
SOFIA

Sofia watched as the blade sank into the general's chest. For only a moment, she regretted letting Fox finish the job. She would have enjoyed the feel of his blood between her fingers as she saw the light leave his eyes.

But then Fox's shoulders straightened and lifted as if released of a weight they'd been holding for decades. She watched his face as his father's body fell to the ground; though pale, it remained free of tears. He'd needed this moment just as much as she did. It was okay. She'd have her own retribution in the end. She would be the one to kill the chief commander and she'd make it slow and painful when the time came.

"Are you okay?" she asked when Fox didn't move immediately, still looking down at his father.

"I am," he said, looking up at her at last. "Does that make me a horrible person?"

She didn't know the answer to that. She'd never killed a family member or even a friend. "*He* was a horrible person. Cruel for the sake of cruelty. If it takes a horrible person to rid the world of that, then perhaps it's worth being one."

His lips lifted, just barely before his face turned serious again.

"We need to leave. You're already supposed to be on your way out of the city."

"There is something I need before we go."

His eyes narrowed. "I swear to the dragon gods myself—if you are going to try and kill the chief commander after all of this."

She shook her head, looking around and seeing the staircase up in the distance.

"I'm not going to kill the chief commander. Not today. I know I can't do that on my own. But I need information."

"You need to live through this day." He grasped her arm and forced her to look at him. "Every moment you spend here is dangerous. We should get back to the others."

Her hand reached out, against her own volition, and she rested her fingers against his cheek.

"Trust me, please."

His throat bobbed before he nodded reluctantly. He released her and she saw the blood he'd left behind, his hand imprinted on her.

She ran, talking the steps from the basement two at a time until they crashed through a set of heavy doors and into the main manor.

She didn't explain where they were going, knowing he'd follow. She darted through the all-too-familiar hallways. The chief commander's home was practically dead, but it wasn't empty. She caught the whispered sounds of servants behind doors, but they were too scared to poke their noses out anyway. The chief commander didn't have a family. He hadn't had a family in over three decades, before Sofia had even begun to work for him.

As they came to the third floor, her heart was hammering in her chest, bile rising in her throat. She could mark the exact day she'd last passed these doors—the day Mina died.

The closer she got to the chief commander's office, the louder her heart seemed to beat, and by the time she grasped the handle and turned it, she could barely even hear the click of the latch opening over the roaring in her ears. She didn't bother looking around the office, instead going straight to the bookshelf and pulling the book she knew so well. The shelf slid aside.

Behind her, Fox let out a muffled curse as he stood back and watched.

She paused only long enough to shoot him a told-you-so smirk before she slipped inside.

The closet was just as she remembered, and yet nothing like she remembered. There were more books than there used to be, and she wondered whose collections he had stolen—how many had died to fill this room. But there were also some missing. At least she couldn't find them in the chaos. She doubted he organized the room, likely throwing in books and walking away. Still, there was a clear pile that had been recently shuffled through and read, their covers clean of dust.

A History of Suvi and Wueco Peninsula

Dragons and Demons: Religious Fanaticism of the Wuecan People

Myths, Monsters, and Magical Thinking of the Dragonborn

Fox stepped in close to watch her, not questioning what she was doing, only grabbing a couple books off the shelf and handing them to her.

She smiled when she saw the titles. Works on dragons and the history of the great king's hunt. Fox hadn't needed to ask.

"Keep this one for yourself," she said, pressing a small tome into his chest. "I memorized it when I was younger."

He nodded, fingers wrapping around the leather cover.

"I'll find a bag, you can't walk out balancing all of those without drawing attention."

She nodded, focused on the task of finding the most relevant titles she could. The chief commander would know exactly who had broken into his study and stolen his precious books. This would be the last time she'd see any book she left behind. Whether he hid them, locked them away, or burned them.

She smiled at the thought of him returning to a ransacked office, knowing exactly who was responsible. But even as she smiled, another thought shuddered through her. The chief commander knew she was alive now, which meant her parents were in danger again. Once she'd fled the city, she'd be leaving them behind to be taken and interrogated by the king's men. Were they even still alive? It had always been too painful to seek out information on them when she couldn't do anything with it.

Her teeth cut into the sides of her cheeks until she focused her thoughts once more. One step at a time.

When she had enough books that her arms were shaking under the weight, she finally left the room, trying hard not to regret each and every volume she was leaving behind. Fox was there in an instant, a leather satchel open and ready for her haul. She tucked them inside and he looped the bag over his shoulder.

"Those are mi—"

"Heavy and will be perfectly safe with me. I promise." He gave her a look so earnest she couldn't not believe him. She could see the blood of his father still drying under his nails.

He was wearing a cloak—one he must have found in the main study. His sword still swung from his back, joined now by the bag of books. She met his eyes and he smirked. She realized she'd been staring, a stupid smile on her face. For the briefest moment, she thought of kissing him. Her smile turned into a scowl and she pushed past him.

"Let's go, then."

They ran into no one on their way out of the manor and once they exited the black gates, it was clear why. The city was on fire. However many allies they had started with in the initial attack, it seemed many others had heeded the call. Flames littered the cityscape in every direction and explosions echoed in the distance, toward the prison. Civilians were scattered about, some carrying buckets of water from the canal and others clinging to their possessions.

It was easy to slip through the crowd, just two more people running in the chaos, and Sofia led them down turn after turn, the streets of the military quarter more familiar than she expected. Fox followed close behind, unsure of where they were going. It was when they were deep into the slums, only a few blocks from the inn that Fox grabbed her, forcing her to slow.

"You're wheezing!" he snapped when she tried to pull him, needing to go faster.

"I'm fine," she said, but her words came out in a squeak and a cough that only had him raising his eyebrows. Her breaths were knives in her chest and she cursed her lungs for their unwillingness to function when she needed them.

"I'm going to get you out of the city," he said, as they continued to move, slower now. "Trust me."

She nodded, not wanting to talk. Not wanting him to hear the rattle of her breath if she tried.

They made it to the street the inn sat on at last, the tall, crumbling structure visible in the distance, towering above the smaller buildings around it. But even if she hadn't seen it, she would have known they were in the right place.

A ring of soldiers were converging on the inn as a mob of civilians screamed and waved makeshift weapons—a ring of soldiers standing between them and the inn. Sofia wasn't sure if the mob was purposefully defending the resistance at this point or if the rising tensions between Dragonborn and Dereyans had finally snapped.

"We're going there, aren't we?" Fox said, looking at the crowd.

"They couldn't make it easy, could they?" she said, looking around, trying to make a plan.

Fox had already lifted his hood, throwing his face into shadows, and pulled out his sword by the time Sofia noticed.

"Slow down, Hero," she said, resting her hand on his shoulder. "I have a plan."

Fox only gave a small frown as she directed him into a nearby alley and pointed to the small stack of crates along one wall. He didn't move immediately.

"Go on," she said, impatient.

"Yes, my captor. I missed you ordering me around."

She barely caught the glint of his smile before he was moving, more gracefully than she expected up and over the wall. She followed, pulling herself up without his offered hand.

He only rolled his eyes. "Which way?"

It wasn't a perfect route, and a few times they had to jump across the rooftops to reach the street over, but they were quiet, slipping through the orange-cast night without being seen. The flash of Flor's red hair among the mob made Sofia's stomach swoop, the tension in her shoulders easing.

Sofia dropped down a few feet from where Flor was standing. She nearly stabbed her, but Sofia ducked out of the way, showing her face in the light as she raised her hands in surrender.

"It's me!"

"Scales," Flor practically shouted as she lunged forward, pulling Sofia in so tightly her next breath came out in a wheeze.

Fox landed behind them with a soft thud.

"So, what's the plan?" he said without preamble.

"What in the dragon gods is he doing here?"

Javi's voice sent a shock of lightning through her and she turned, parsing through the shadowy figures until she saw him, dirty and a bit gaunter than before but there—and alive.

Sofia didn't bother with words, throwing herself at him before he even registered she was there. He let out a yelp and pulled back, squinting at her face in the dark before his eyes widened.

"Scales, Flor said, but—" He pulled her back into the hug and she couldn't stop the tears that were burning her eyes. He smelled of the rainforest and of himself and she didn't want to let go. His heart-mother hovered behind him, her eyes still wet with unshed tears.

"The demon-spawn has a point," Flor said from behind them. "We need an escape plan."

Sofia pulled back. "We don't have an escape plan?" she said slowly, looking between them. She saw Vato standing a few feet away, as well, drawn by their conversation.

"The plan was to go out the gates, but the army reacted too quickly. Once the bombs went off, some of the more *zealous* civilians started attacking the king's men forcing the army to put up their defenses." He paused, as if hesitant to say the next thing. "We're surrounded."

"What about the way Sofia and I came?"

"It just leads us deeper into the city," Sofia said. "And there is no way everyone would make it. Especially without being seen."

"So we fight our way out?" Flor said.

Sofia looked at their group. Even with the townspeople screaming and throwing rocks, the soldiers were closing in and behind the front lines children were huddled. Their injured leaned heavily against walls, some looking half-dead.

They had escaped the prison only to be trapped here, in the slums that had already held them, a prison of its own.

And, then like a silent explosion, the air around them crackled and sang. A wind blew through the street, sending the flames dancing violently, and a deafening roar filled Sofia's ears, causing her eardrums to shudder. She gripped the side of her head, teeth clenched, and she wondered if this was what death sounded like.

CHAPTER FIFTY

FOX

Fox's ears popped as the air shuddered around him. In the darkness he could have sworn he felt the press of stone and debris hitting him, throwing him back. But no. His eyes opened, and he watched as the crowd screamed and cowered, some covering their ears but more watching the sky. Their faces filled with terror.

With a sense of knowing, his eyes rose. The sun was a couple hours from rising, but the stars still lit up the sky, and a gray line stretched along the horizon where the sun bided its time. Even if it had been pitch black, the silvery glow from the dragon's scales would have shone against the sky. Its wings stretched wide—blocking out the stars beyond.

Though this was his second time seeing a dragon, the sight of this one stretched across the sky above Suvi stole the breath from his lungs. And the chorus of screams coursing through the city only heightened his awareness.

There'd be no more denying it. The dragons were back and now all of Suvi would know it.

The ground quaked beneath their feet and people scattered as the dragon touched down on the street, creating a barrier between the civilians and the soldiers. Despite its clear wish to protect them, the majority of the townspeople that had been so brave in the face of the king's men dispersed into the alleys, disappearing in the shadows like rats.

But not everyone did. Flor gazed up at the celestial beast with eyes wide and mouth hanging open while a few of the other rebels he recognized stood in similar awe.

It was Sofia who moved first, eyes bright as she stepped forward and stretched her hand out to brush her fingers across the dragon's scales. Its hum sent a shudder through the air, the feathers along its neck and spine vibrating.

"She came for you," Sofia said, soft voice somehow carrying amid the chaos.

"Who?" Fox said. She turned, looking at him with tears shining in her eyes even as her smile stretched wide.

"The dragon answered your prayer."

"How do you know?" he said, coming to stand beside her. He examined the dragon's silver scales as if they held the secret. She was running her hand along its flank like one might pet a donkey, but he was too afraid to get closer.

"Listen."

Fox didn't bother asking her to clarify, he was too busy staring at the dragon's head which was turned to face him. It—she—had eyes so blue he might have believed they'd melt into water at any moment. And suddenly, he did hear.

Eha wanted to come. She could not. So I answered.

Eha?

She is in the dark. But I am not.

Fox shook his head, trying to understand where the thoughts were coming from. There was a pounding in his skull, as if he'd swum too far underwater, and he had to step back and remind himself to breathe.

"Javi, grab some crates. We're climbing on," Sofia was barking orders and it took Fox a moment to realize what she was planning.

"Are you insane?"

"Yes," she said, not quite meeting his eyes.

"You can't ride a dragon."

"Yes, I can. We all can." Her tone brooked no argument.

Fox turned back to the dragon, her eyes sparkling with sharp intelligence. She'd come for him. She'd answered his prayer, not to bring destruction to Suvi, but to save him—to save the resistance. He didn't think, reaching forward to run his hand along the scales of the dragon's side, like a moth to the flame. They were hot to the touch, but not painful—hard, yet soft.

"You can take them?"

"I can hold most. Some. Probably."

He wasn't sure, but he thought the dragon might have been stuttering over her words. Or maybe even she wasn't confident in what she could do.

"You better protect them," he thought, hoping his tone was conveyed.

"Your tone is plenty clear, Pale Scales. I don't need threats. I will protect them. I will protect her."

He stepped back, his head swimming, but he shook it off. He didn't know if he should trust a dragon, but then again, if he couldn't trust a god—who could he trust?

The others who had remained in the street were growing braver, slowly stepping back toward the dragon when they realized she didn't plan on eating them.

Fox helped Flor move a few crates to the side of the dragon to use as steps, her back higher than a donkey's would be. Another rebel was already lining people up. Some were from the prison, but there were others, too. Civilians who hadn't run and were now looking up at the dragon with awe.

"Not everyone will fit," Ian said beside him before Fox could admit even the dragon didn't think so. "It can hold a dozen at best and there are more than two times that many left."

"I know." Sofia bit her lip, doing the calculations herself. "We can take trips."

"That won't work," Ian said, shaking his head.

"Then we prioritize the most injured and the children," Sofia said, voice strained.

Flor stepped closer, keeping her voice low. "We can't send children into the rainforest unprotected and the injured need to be looked after."

"I can take the children and the civilians," Ian said. "I can hide them in the city until we can find another way out. But Sofia, Micael, and those from the cenote, you need to get out now while you can."

"Vato—if you get caught—" Sofia started.

"I've always been one step away from getting caught," he said, and Fox was reminded once more how little he knew about his oldest friend—his only friend. "The king will punish the Dragonborn for tonight, but he can't execute everyone or even most of the people that fought back tonight. He'll be looking for you most of all. As long as you make it out, you can help us from the outside."

Fox watched the exchange with a sinking feeling in his stomach.

"Ian's right," Fox said, stepping forward, resolute. "The soldiers won't know who actually fought against them tonight and they can't kill the entire work force of Suvi. Ian and I will keep the others safe until they're able to escape."

Sofia's face went gray, the only color left the slight tinge of pink along her cheeks. "You're staying." It wasn't a question.

Fox hadn't made the decision until that moment. Or perhaps he had never made the decision at all because it had already been made for him. He couldn't leave his mother behind. He couldn't leave behind everything he'd built until this moment. He had a real chance of making a change—he had power here.

"I...I have to," he said, hating himself as something broke in her eyes.

"After everything, you'd choose them? You'd choose him?"

He didn't need to ask who *him* was. The chief commander. Was he choosing him?

"No," he said, shaking his head and stepping forward even as she tried to pull away. He grasped her hands in his own and forced her to look at him. "I'll serve you better from here. I have the chief commander's ear. I have his trust. I need to understand why they are so interested in the dragons—why that dragon was working with them. I can't do that from afar."

She snarled, her teeth bared even as he leaned closer.

"Don't look at me like that, please."

"How can I trust you won't betray us? Me? What happens when the chief commander hands you everything you've ever wanted on a golden tray? Will you truly betray him?"

Fox pressed his forehead to hers, the cool sweat of their skin mingling. "I don't want to betray anyone. I want the deaths to end. But you can trust that I won't betray you. I can't—"

His voice broke and he almost sneered at himself.

She shook her head. "How do I—"

Before she could finish, he pulled her closer and his lips surged forward to meet hers. The kiss was rough and hard and he bit at her lips even as they opened for him, her tongue meeting his in a duel. His hand wrapped around the small of her back, pulling her flush against him, every muscle rigid with need at the feel of her. His body throbbed with heat and something cracked open within him. He wound his fingers into her curls and groaned. Her answering whimper had his head going light. She clung to him, pressing into the skin along his neck, teasing the hairs that had fallen from his bun. Why had it taken him so long to kiss her? He regretted every moment before he'd spent not knowing the taste of her lips.

Too soon, with the blood singing through his veins, she pulled away.

"Fuck," he said, pressing his forehead against hers. He almost grabbed her again, his body thrumming with want. Instead, he rested his large hand across her chest and pushed her away, even as his fingers twitched to tangle in her tunic. "Go."

She blinked up at him, eyes wide, pupils blown. Fox looked over her shoulder and saw the rest of the rebels were already sitting along the dragon's spine, clinging to her feathers for dear life. He ignored the look of utter horror on some of their faces, eyes finding Ian where he stood helping the last person onto the dragon. Twelve rebels were sitting along its spine, a single space left for Sofia.

She was the only one left.

It was Ian who moved first, grabbing her gently by the shoulders and leading her back to the dragon. She moved as if in a daze, but turned back before she stepped onto the crate.

She looked at him beseechingly. "Find my parents and protect them. If they're still alive. The chief commander will go after them, even if they have nothing to do with me."

Fox could only nod. "Of course."

And then she turned, confidently pulling herself up onto the dragon's back between Flor and a man he vaguely recognized as her friend Javi. He was glaring daggers at Fox as if he hoped he'd die where he was standing.

Only when the dragon's wings lifted, its legs pushing up off the ground, did Sofia finally look back, eyes finding Fox's. With a stifled movement, he lifted a hand in a pathetic attempt at a wave.

She only touched her hand to her lips before she disappeared into the sky.

Sofia had never felt anything like the exhilaration of flying through the sky. The city burned beneath them, but she couldn't feel regret.

The scales were warm beneath her, the feathers along the dragon's spine were soft beneath her fingers. She could just hear Flor letting out a small whoop as the dragon twisted into the air, sweeping toward the wall and the rainforest beyond.

The wall was easy to see in the gray dawn, alight with torches and gas lamps, and lined with more king's men than Sofia had ever seen. The dragon curved upward, even as a volley of arrows arched into the sky toward them. Sofia cursed as two of the arrows embedded themselves in the dragon's side.

The silver scales vibrated under them as the dragon let out a deafening shriek and dove. Sofia's grip on its feathers was the only thing keeping her on its back as it swept low across the wall. It reached out with extended claws, crashing through a line of soldiers and sending them tumbling onto the hard ground below.

Sofia saw him amid the chaos—the chief commander—standing at the top of a tower. He bellowed orders, face red with rage. His eyes found hers, as if drawn there by the thread of fate and vengeance that connected them and his scowl deepened.

A shift pulled Sofia's gaze away from the chief commander; the dragon was lifting into the sky once more, past the wall and into the forest beyond. Sofia looked back, but she could no longer see him, only a flicker and light between the trees that told her where the wall was.

THE SUN WAS JUST BREAKING over the horizon, the world shifting from blue to pink so quickly Sofia almost missed it. It was a new day, but it was much more than that. The world had changed. Suvi had seen a dragon for the first time in centuries. War was inevitable.

And Fox had stayed behind.

Her fingers traced across her lips. She could still taste him.

She shook the thought off. There were more important things to think about now. There was a fight to win.

A humming awareness moved through her mind, and she sensed more than heard the dragon beneath her. They were headed back to the cenote where she and Fox had found the original feather.

"He worries. Protect you. Protect many."

The words were choppy in her mind.

"I haven't spoken to many humans, or any," the dragon thought. She'd heard Sofia's thoughts.

"Yes. You think very loud."

Sofia laughed and Flor glanced over her shoulder, giving her a quizzical look that Sofia ignored.

"We're going back to the cenote where I first prayed. Was that your feath-er?" she asked.

"No."

Sofia waited, feeling the dragon's hesitation.

"My mother's feather. She not come, though. "

"Your mother. There are more dragons."

More silence.

"No."

The lie was so obvious, Sofia didn't know how to respond, but she felt the dragon's ire even as she thought that.

"My name is Chalia," the dragon said, clearly frustrated with being called "the dragon".

"Chalia," Sofia repeated in her mind. *"Thank you for coming for us. We won't hurt you."*

"I know, but others of my kind don't think like me. My father speaks of the before times and warns of the dragon killers."

Sofia's chest swelled with hope. *The others of her kind.* How many more had survived?

"None," Chalia thought again. *"None none none none."*

"Okay, okay," Sofia said feeling the dragon's body twitching beneath her, clearly distressed. Javi let out a series of curses behind her and a few others screamed. *"There are no other dragons."*

Chalia seemed to calm, her wing beats evening out.

This was clearly a conversation that Sofia had to have with Chalia alone and on the ground. She stopped her thoughts from wandering, finding herself focused on Fox once more. She didn't like this any better, but Chalia practically crooned in her mind when she pictured his face. Gods, the man had charmed a damn dragon without even trying.

Her chest tightened and she wiped her thoughts once more, focusing her eyes on the horizon. The forest and the mountains spread out before them, a nature untouched by humans. She was leaving Suvi behind, yet for once that thought wasn't a comfort. It felt like giving up —running away.

But Sofia had to remind herself that they weren't running. They weren't giving up. This was a temporary break to heal their wounds and reassemble their allies. And then they'd be back. This time with an army —of humans, of shifters, of dragons. This time she'd get what she'd been waiting for. She would kill the chief commander and avenge Mina's death.

She wrapped her arms around Flor's waist and pressed a cheek into her warm shoulder, happy to smell her familiar scent—petrichor and moss. Javi shifted behind them, his arms coming to wrap around them both, as best he could. Sofia could feel his heart beat against her back and she closed her eyes, enveloped by the family that the chief commander couldn't take away.

They would finally get what they were waiting for. They'd avenge the death of every Dragonborn crushed under the chief commander's boot. Together. And nothing was going to get in their way.

EPILOGUE
FOX

Fox didn't sit down until late the next night. When he did, his feet collapsed underneath him as the sitting room chair caught him. He was alone—his mother finally sent to bed with enough drugs to kill a small rodent. She hadn't stopped crying since Fox had delivered the news of his father's death. He explained how his body had been found in the basement of the chief commander's home that morning when the civil unrest had finally been quelled. He'd apparently been killed by an escaping Dragonborn.

That was after three hours of moving the few Dragonborn he could manage into safe houses alongside Ian. He'd discovered there were tunnels connecting some of the houses in the slums together where Dragonborn had been hiding weapons and supplies this entire time. He and Ian hadn't had a moment to talk about what the last day meant for each other. Fox had only given himself the briefest of moments to wonder how long Ian had been a traitor to the crown. Had it been before or after his brother's death?

He hadn't found Sofia's parents yet, but if they were that hard to locate, then the chief commander wouldn't get to them immediately either. He'd focus on that tomorrow once he'd eaten or at least slept.

He'd barely even let the healers do more than wrap his wounds and spew some advice he didn't listen to.

Sitting in the chair next to the fire, he wondered if he should even bother going up to bed. The chair was so soft and the room so warm.

A knock on the manor's door had him groaning with pain. He stood, not sure where he was getting the strength. He was alone in the house, the Dragonborn servants locked in the slums until further notice. There was no word from the king on what would happen to them, but until decisions were made, no one was allowed outside their homes and the king's men were patrolling the streets in shifts.

Fox almost jumped when he opened the door and saw the chief commander standing at his threshold.

"Sir," he said, standing up straighter and regretting the sleeping attire. The chief commander only waved his hand.

"No need for formalities, Son," he said. "My condolences to you and your mother."

"Thank you, sir," he said, trying to keep his voice even.

The chief commander stood, gaze distant for a moment before looking back up at Fox. "That's not why I'm here, though. I'd like you to come with me. No need to change."

Fox's stomach twisted, but he only nodded, turned, and grabbed his cloak from the wall. He stepped out into the night, wondering if he was being led to this death. He'd thought they'd killed everyone who had seen him arrested, but he could have missed someone, or perhaps Ian had betrayed him.

His mind spun with all the possibilities as they walked, but they weren't moving toward the prison or even the chief commander's home. They ventured around the back of the royal quarter, south of the palace.

When the chief commander finally stopped in front of a nondescript house, Fox felt no safer. But the chief commander was looking at him with warmth and pride, showing no indication that he knew what Fox had done last night.

"You must not tell anyone what you're about to see. Not your mother. Not your friend Ian or anyone else. Even those who know about this are forbidden from talking about it outside this building, so don't be tricked into breaking that silence."

Fox was too tired to keep his face blank and his confusion must have shown, but the chief commander only waited.

"Yes, sir," he said after a beat.

Chief Commander Harlow nodded and opened the door, leading Fox inside. It was dark, and he moved carefully as he quickly realized the door had opened up directly to a staircase descending into the earth. He could smell damp soil, yet the narrow stairwell wasn't cool as one might expect. If anything, the deeper they moved, the hotter it became, the air thick and damp with every inhale.

Just when he wondered if they'd walk directly into the Dragonborn's underworld, a light trickled through the crack of a door just ahead. The floor evened out and the chief commander opened the door without preamble.

The brightness blinded him for only a moment before his eyes adjusted and he saw the giant cavern—pit, whatever it was—laid out before him. The door opened to a narrow wooden platform that circled the entire cavern, the floor dropping steeply to a wide cavity in the center. Fox's jaw dropped as he realized what he was looking at. A brilliant white dragon was curled in the heart of the pit, a long iron chain around its neck. Even curled up as it was, he could tell it was nearly twice as long as the one Sofia had flown out of Suvi on. He wanted to see it upright, with its wings outstretched. Would it stand as tall as his manor? As tall as the walls of Suvi?

Even as he looked, her head twitched and her eyes opened, silver pools searching out his own.

He could hear the chief commander speaking beside him, voice muffled as if spoken through water. He couldn't understand him.

It was a female voice he heard instead, soft and cool in his mind, and so very clear. He knew exactly who was speaking as the dragon blinked slowly, not breaking eye contact.

"You've come for me."

END OF DRAGON GODS
BOOK ONE OF DRAGON GODS DUOLOGY

PLEASE LEAVE A REVIEW!

Thank you so much for joining me in the journey through Wueco! This is a long-brewing story that, after starting out as an inside joke between me and my husband, turned into a real labor of love. I also finally listened to my sister and sister-in-law and wrote a book about dragons!

If you enjoyed the book, please leave me a review!

Dragon Gods on Amazon:

WANT A FREE BOOK?

Experience a new story set within Kiersten's Mage World universe!

Journey to a world full of magia and conflict. Hundreds of years following a great war between those with magic and those without, an era of discontent arises. The unlikely friendship between an overzealous mage-in-training, Alara, and a wild and free bruya, Quenti, will be the catalyst that ignites a new war within the borders of Sombria.

This action-packed Epic YA Fantasy is perfect for lovers of *The Children of Blood and Bone*, *Shad & Bone*, and *We Hunt the Flame*.

Conjure up your free copy with the QR code!

THANK YOU, PATRONS!

This book was a over a year in the making, and in the deepest midsts of drafting, editing, and everything in between, I had a handful of loyal Patrons at my side. I want to thank each and every one of you for your loyalty and support.

PATRONS

Specter Seeker Tier
J Soderberg

Mage Tier
AJ Nadolsky
Alison Conners

Bruya Tier
Michelle Anderson

Magite Tier
Bernardo Nuno
Steven Beal
Derek Alan Siddoway

Join us on Patreon and get featured in our next book!

ACKNOWLEDGMENTS

As always, a book isn't written in a vacuum and there are so many supportive, wonderful people who kept me sane and made *Dragon Gods* possible, from my husband, my friends, my beta readers, my editor, and my coffee.

Thank you to Scott Moreland, my editor, for accepting my imperfections and my inability to choose between British English and American English. Although I still stand by the fact that GREY looks better. And a huge thank you to Cherie Mathis, my wonderful proofreader, for catching my typos. If she missed any, they're meant to be there now. They are one with the book.

Another toast to my husband and all the read-throughs he did with me, the tears he put up with, and the back and forths around the title (thank you for telling me to go with *Dragon Gods*, you were right. It was the best option.). And thank you to my beautiful and wonderful beta readers, AJ N., Kaci R., and Amerita M., for the time they put with reading a less-than-perfect copy of the book to help me in its progression.

Again, thank you to Acon, Maddie, and Lindsay who taught me graphic design via osmosis over the many years of being your friends. You made the cover possible!

And thank you to my best writing companion, Jobin, for the endless cuddles, even when they made it difficult to work.

ABOUT KIERSTEN MICHELE

KIERSTEN MICHELE is an author and bookworm who spends her mornings, evenings, weekends, and in-between times reading. She grew up on mysteries, fantasies, historical fictions, and any other story that would take her on an adventure. Her love of reading turned into a love of writing, and she took that love to college and...got a PhD in counseling psychology. Plot twist. But when she's not writing *extremely fascinating* academic articles, she's creating stories to take her on more adventures.

Her books so far consist of *The Shadow Weaver's Gambit*, *The Mage War Chronicles*, and *Dragon Gods*.

When not tucked into her reading chair, she's out adventuring in the real world, climbing rocks, hiking rocks, and taking way too many photos of rocks.

instagram.com/authorkiersten

youtube.com/@magiareads

threads.com/authorkiersten